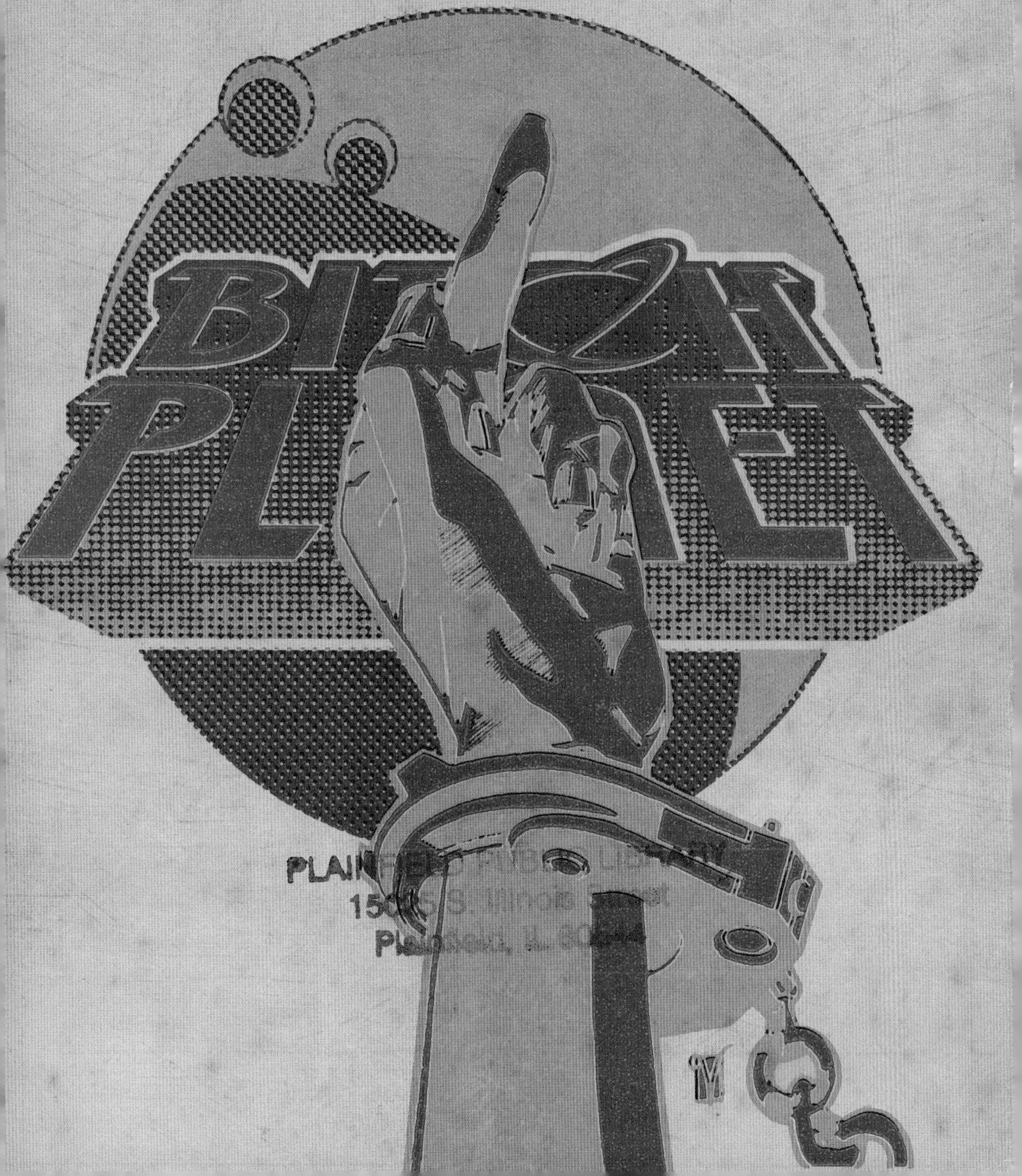

PRESENTS

KELLY SUE DECONNICK
SCRIPT / CO-CREATOR

VALENTINE DE LANDRO
ART & COVERS / CO-CREATOR

SPACEMOTHER

EARTH IS THE FATHER

AND FOR YOUR WICKEDNESS

YOUR FATHER HAS CAST YOU OUT

ROBERT WILSON IV
ART (ISSUE #3)

WITH

CRIS PETER
COLORS

CLAYTON COWLES
LETTERS

RIAN HUGHES
LOGO, ORIGINAL COVERS DESIGN, BOOK DESIGN

LAURENN MCCUBBIN
BACKMATTER DESIGN

MATT HOLLINGSWORTH
#3 COVER COLORS

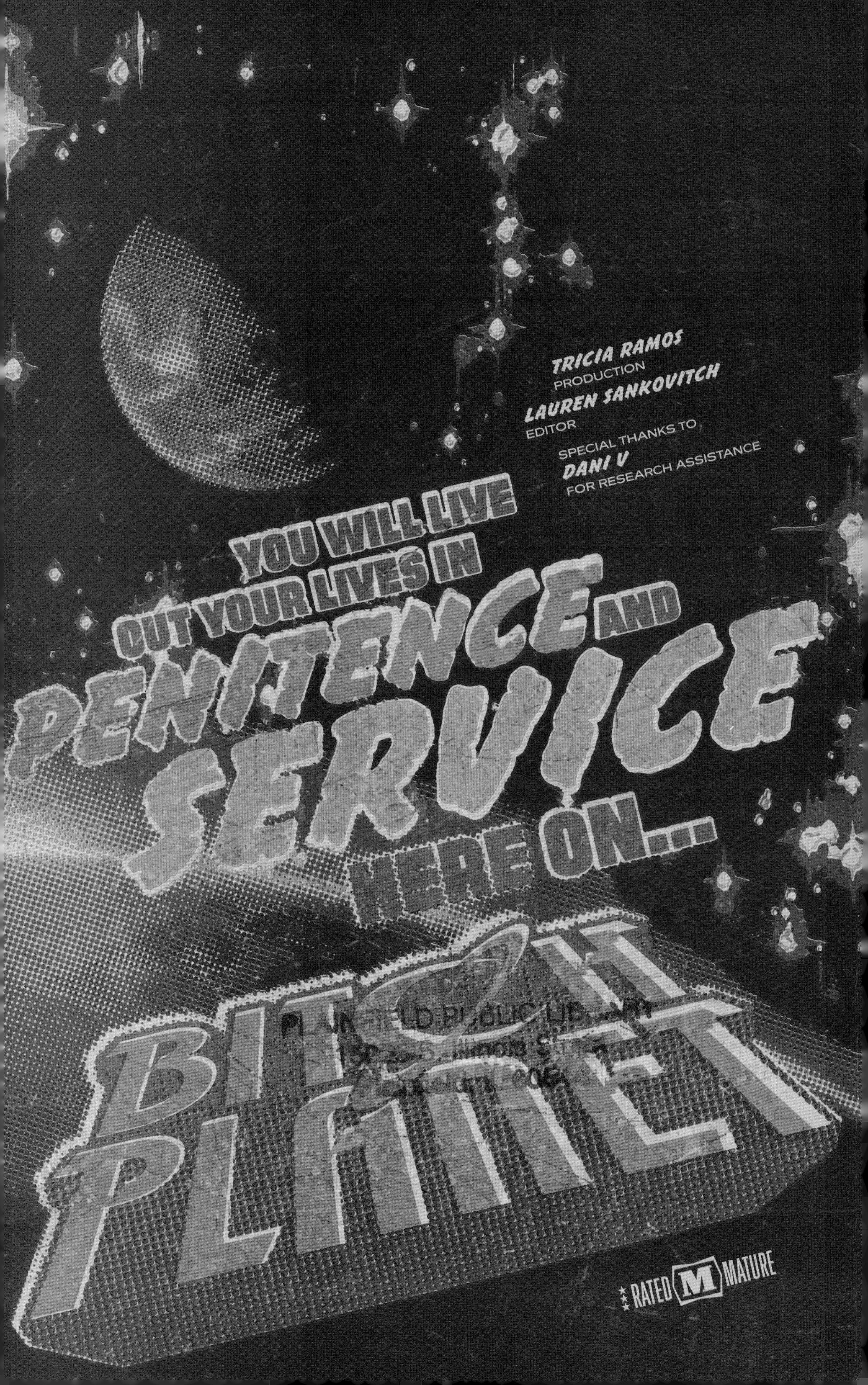
TRICIA RAMOS
PRODUCTION
LAUREN SANKOVITCH
EDITOR
SPECIAL THANKS TO
DANI V
FOR RESEARCH ASSISTANCE
YOU WILL LIVE
OUT YOUR LIVES IN
PENITENCE AND
SERVICE
HERE ON...
BITCH
PLANET
RATED M MATURE

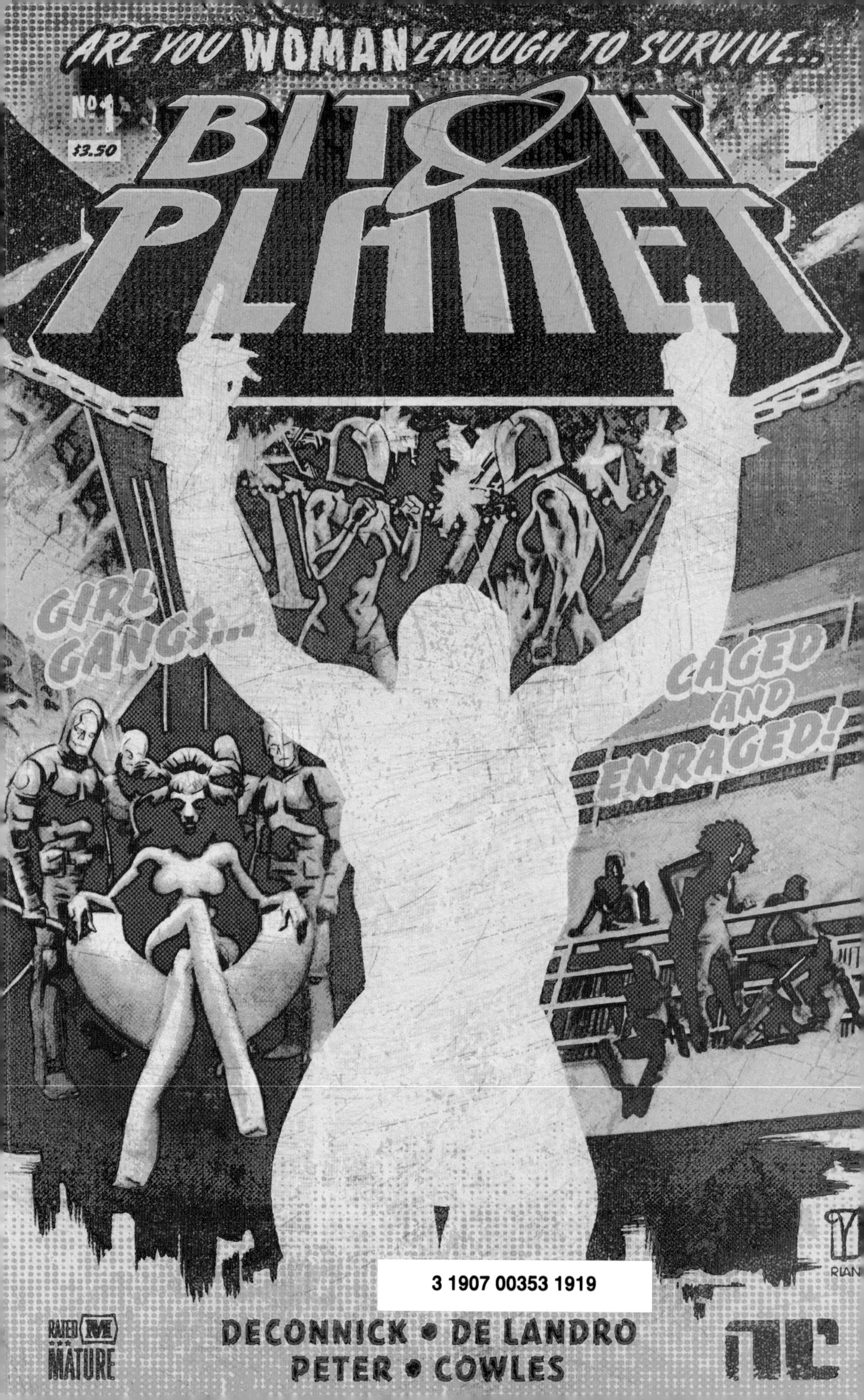
ARE YOU WOMAN ENOUGH TO SURVIVE...
No 1
$3.50
BITCH PLANET
GIRL GANGS...
CAGED AND ENRAGED!
RATED M MATURE
DECONNICK • DE LANDRO
PETER • COWLES

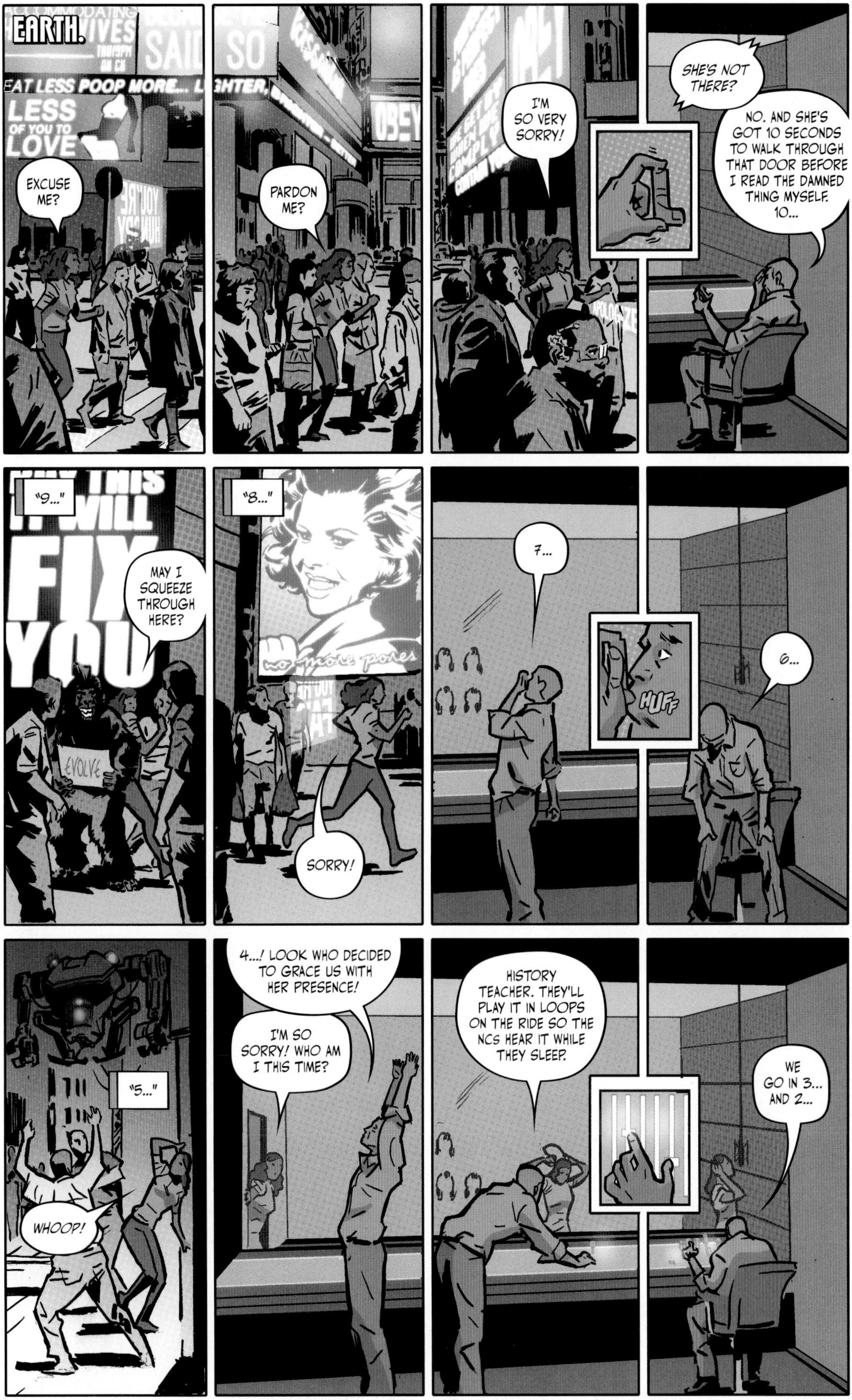
EARTH.
EAT LESS POOP MORE... LIGHTER,
LESS OF YOU TO LOVE
EXCUSE ME?
PARDON ME?
OBEY
I'M SO VERY SORRY!
APOLOGIZE
SHE'S NOT THERE?
NO. AND SHE'S GOT 10 SECONDS TO WALK THROUGH THAT DOOR BEFORE I READ THE DAMNED THING MYSELF. 10...
"9..."
FIX YOU
MAY I SQUEEZE THROUGH HERE?
EVOLVE
"8..."
no more pores
SORRY!
7...
HUFF
6...
"5..."
WHOOP!
4...! LOOK WHO DECIDED TO GRACE US WITH HER PRESENCE!
I'M SO SORRY! WHO AM I THIS TIME?
HISTORY TEACHER. THEY'LL PLAY IT IN LOOPS ON THE RIDE SO THE NCS HEAR IT WHILE THEY SLEEP.
WE GO IN 3... AND 2...

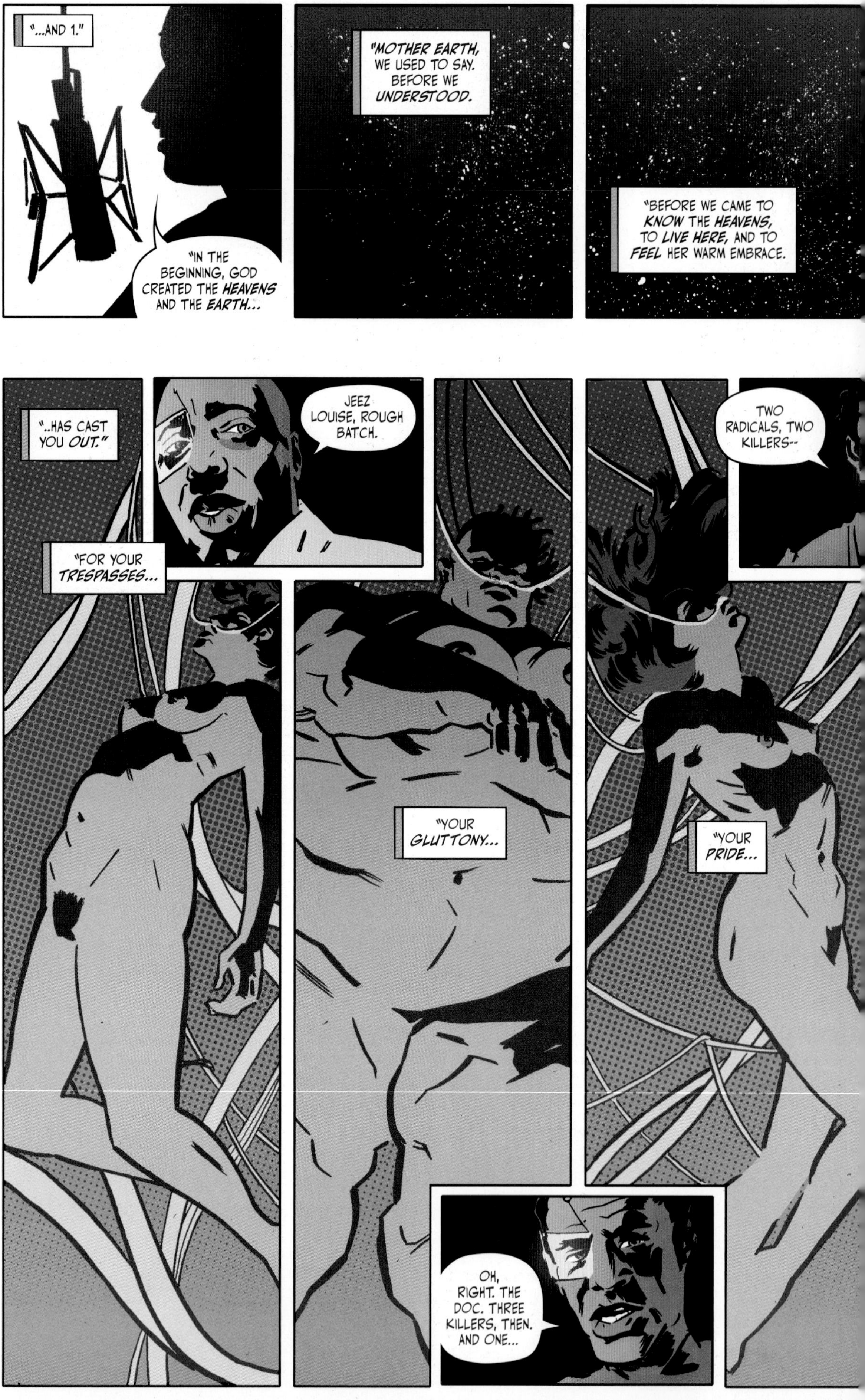
"...AND 1."
"IN THE BEGINNING, GOD CREATED THE *HEAVENS* AND THE *EARTH*...
"*MOTHER EARTH,* WE USED TO SAY. BEFORE WE *UNDERSTOOD.*
"BEFORE WE CAME TO *KNOW* THE *HEAVENS,* TO *LIVE HERE,* AND TO *FEEL* HER WARM EMBRACE.
"..HAS CAST YOU *OUT.*"
JEEZ LOUISE, ROUGH BATCH.
"FOR YOUR *TRESPASSES*...
"YOUR *GLUTTONY*...
TWO RADICALS, TWO KILLERS--
"YOUR *PRIDE*...
OH, RIGHT. THE DOC. THREE KILLERS, THEN. AND ONE...

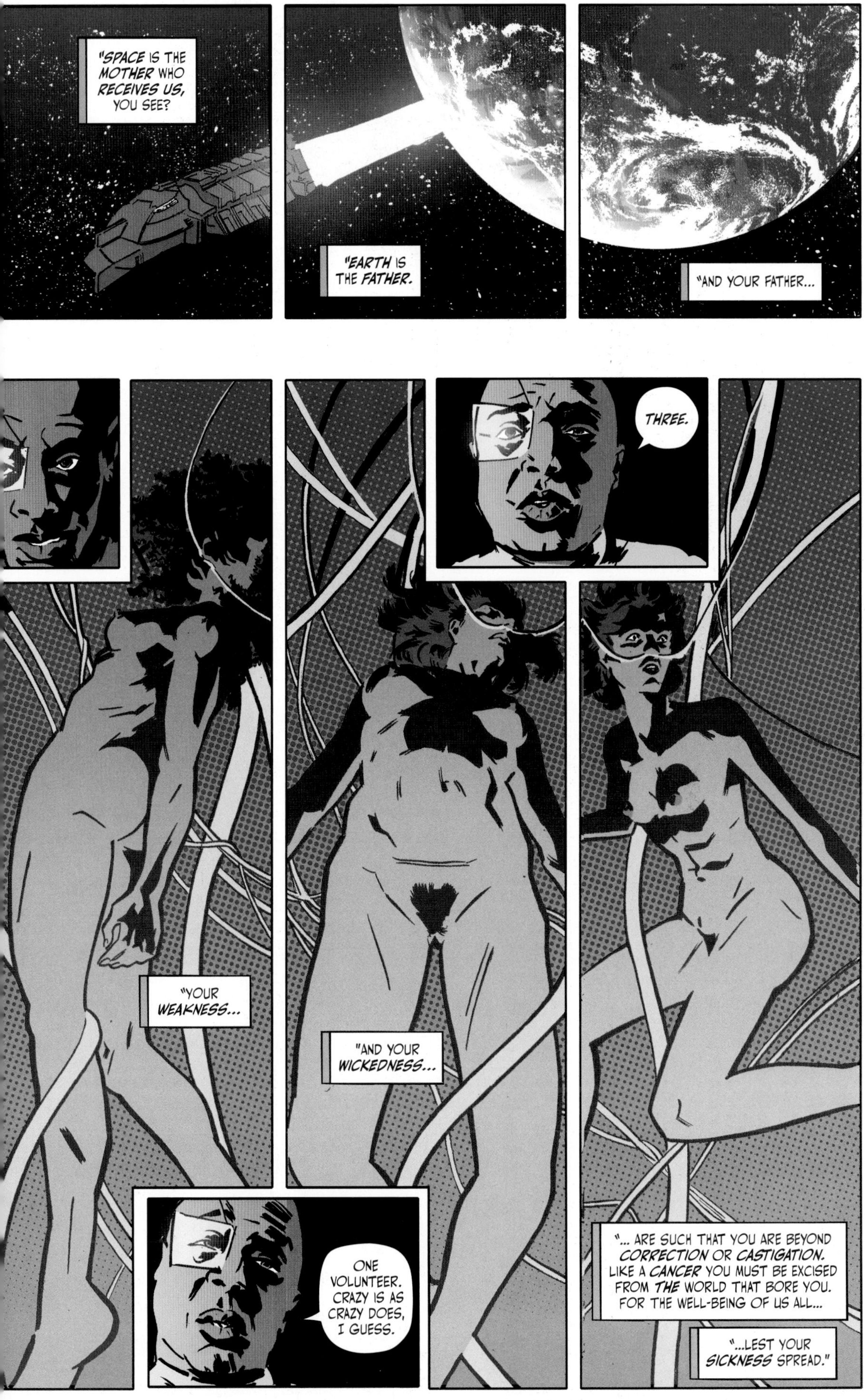
"SPACE IS THE MOTHER WHO RECEIVES US, YOU SEE?
"EARTH IS THE FATHER.
"AND YOUR FATHER...
THREE.
"YOUR WEAKNESS...
"AND YOUR WICKEDNESS...
ONE VOLUNTEER. CRAZY IS AS CRAZY DOES, I GUESS.
"... ARE SUCH THAT YOU ARE BEYOND CORRECTION OR CASTIGATION. LIKE A CANCER YOU MUST BE EXCISED FROM THE WORLD THAT BORE YOU. FOR THE WELL-BEING OF US ALL...
"...LEST YOUR SICKNESS SPREAD."

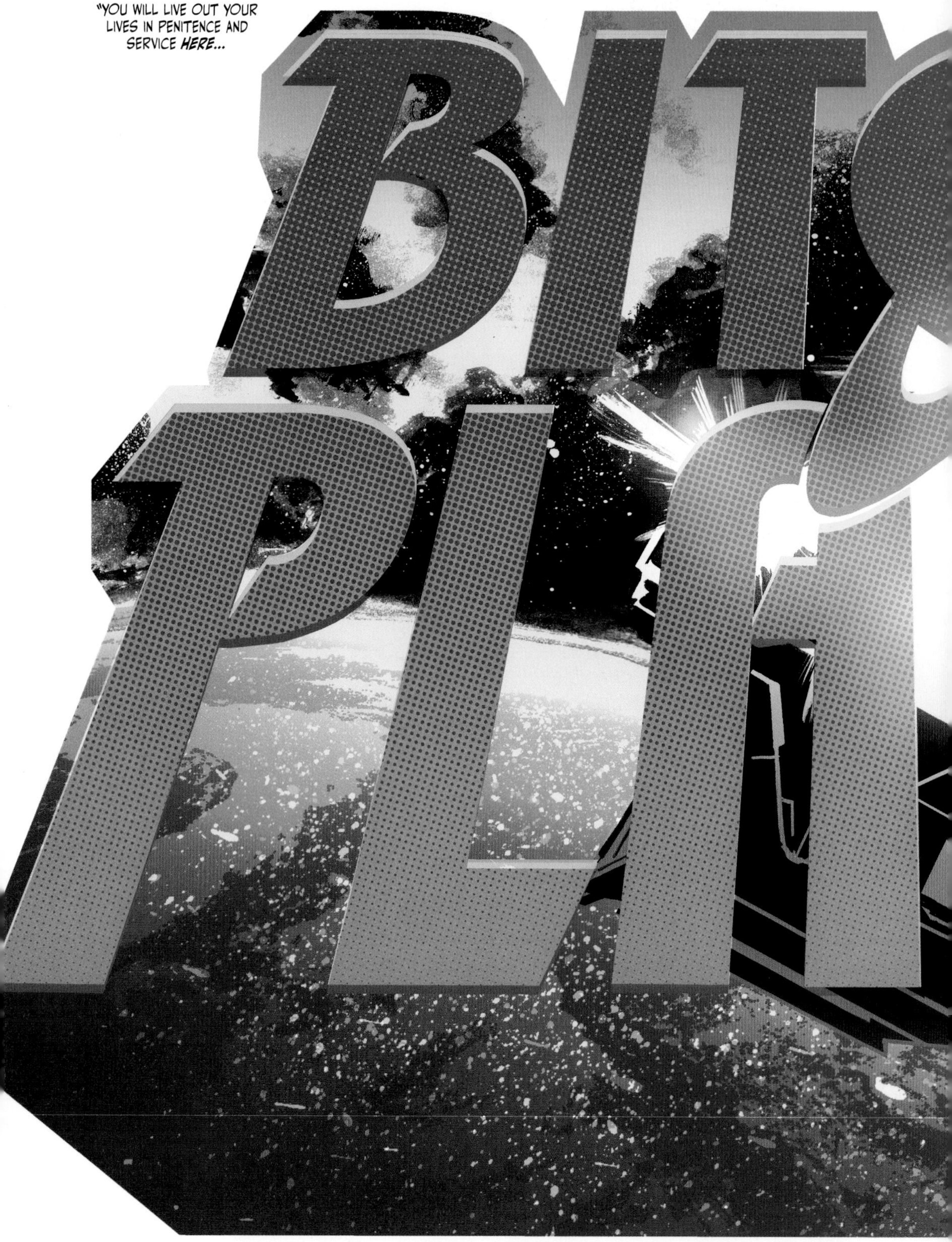
"YOU WILL LIVE OUT YOUR LIVES IN PENITENCE AND SERVICE *HERE*...

KELLY SUE DECONNICK
SCRIPT

CRIS PETER
COLORS

CLAYTON COWLES
LETTERS

RIAN HUGHES
COVER DESIGN & LOGO DESIGN

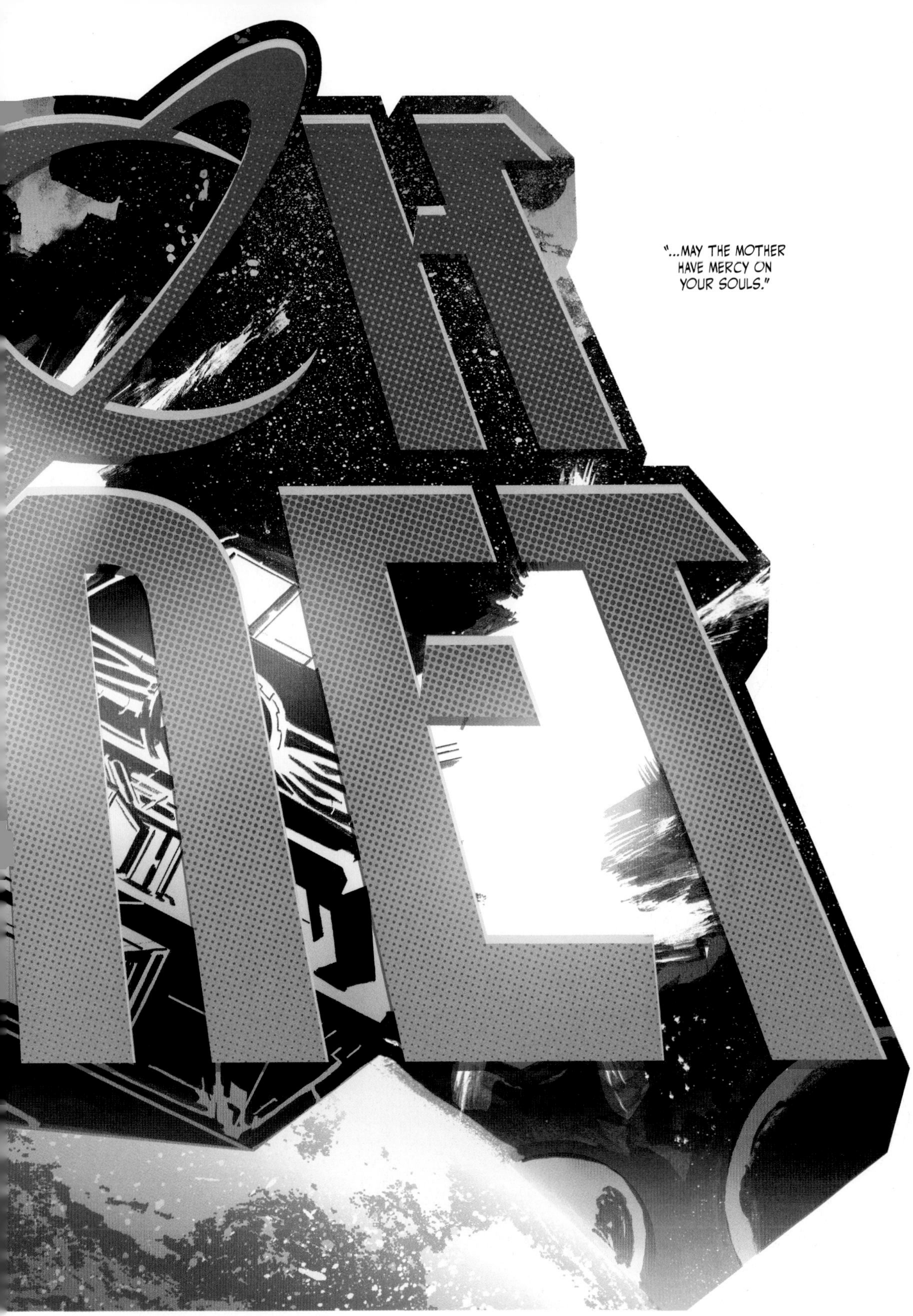
"...MAY THE MOTHER HAVE MERCY ON YOUR SOULS."

VALENTINE DE LANDRO
ART/COVERS

LAURENN McCUBBIN
BACKMATTER DESIGN

LAUREN SANKOVITCH
EDITOR

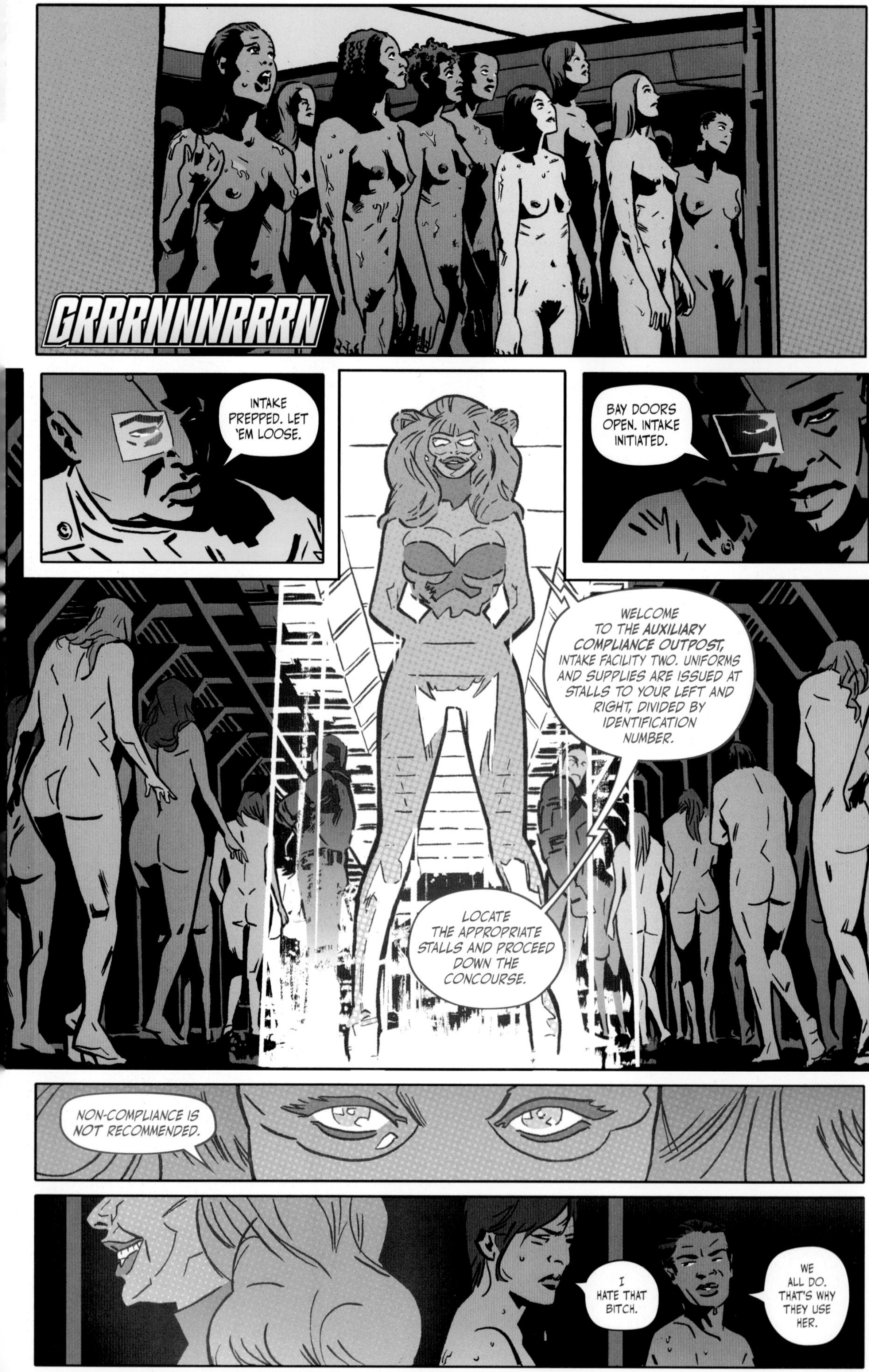

GRRRNNNRRRN
INTAKE PREPPED. LET 'EM LOOSE.
BAY DOORS OPEN. INTAKE INITIATED.
WELCOME TO THE AUXILIARY COMPLIANCE OUTPOST, INTAKE FACILITY TWO. UNIFORMS AND SUPPLIES ARE ISSUED AT STALLS TO YOUR LEFT AND RIGHT, DIVIDED BY IDENTIFICATION NUMBER.
LOCATE THE APPROPRIATE STALLS AND PROCEED DOWN THE CONCOURSE.
NON-COMPLIANCE IS NOT RECOMMENDED.
I HATE THAT BITCH.
WE ALL DO. THAT'S WHY THEY USE HER.

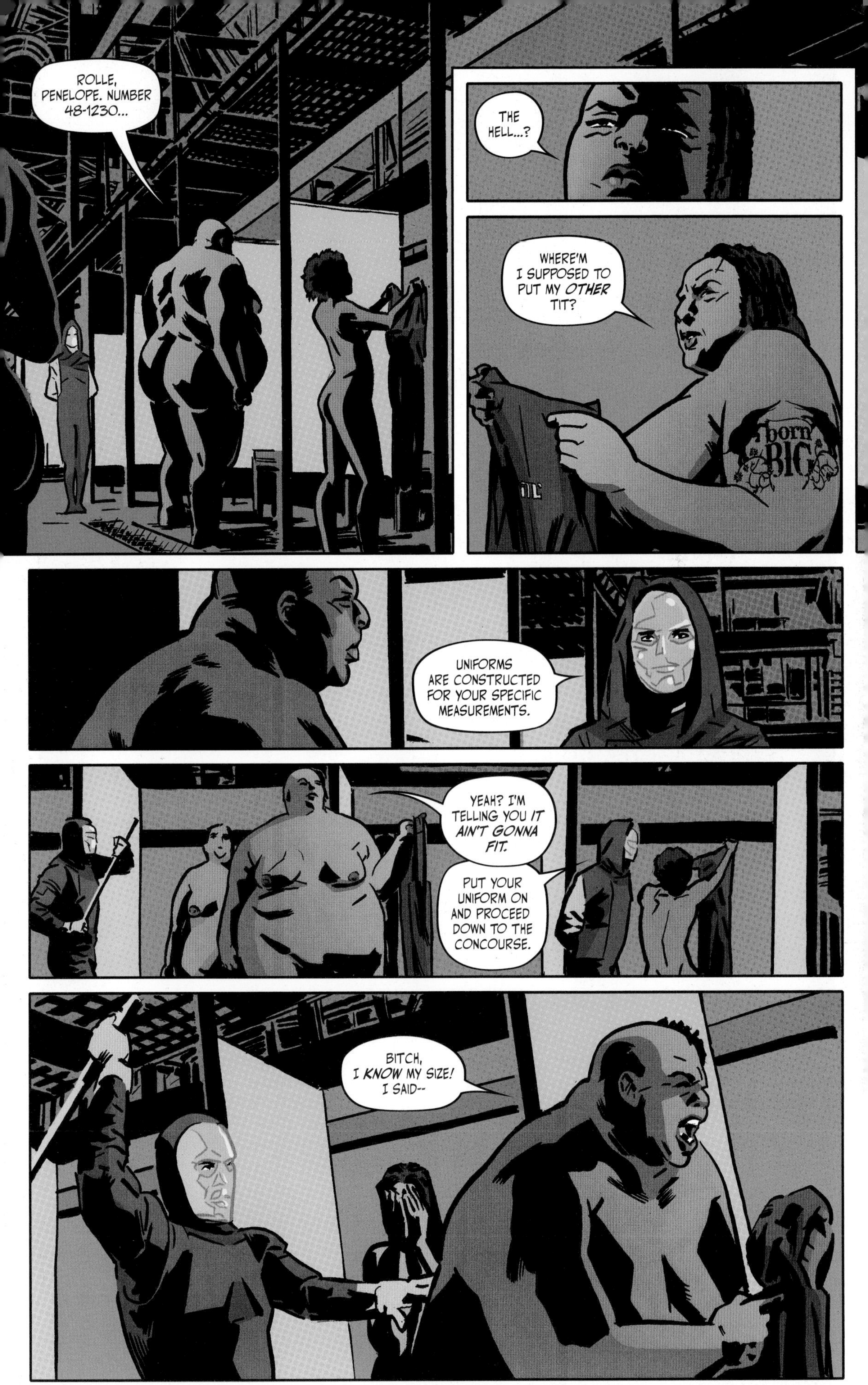
ROLLE, PENELOPE. NUMBER 48-1230...
THE HELL...?
WHERE'M I SUPPOSED TO PUT MY *OTHER* TIT?
born BIG
UNIFORMS ARE CONSTRUCTED FOR YOUR SPECIFIC MEASUREMENTS.
YEAH? I'M TELLING YOU *IT AIN'T GONNA FIT.*
PUT YOUR UNIFORM ON AND PROCEED DOWN TO THE CONCOURSE.
BITCH, I *KNOW* MY SIZE! I SAID--

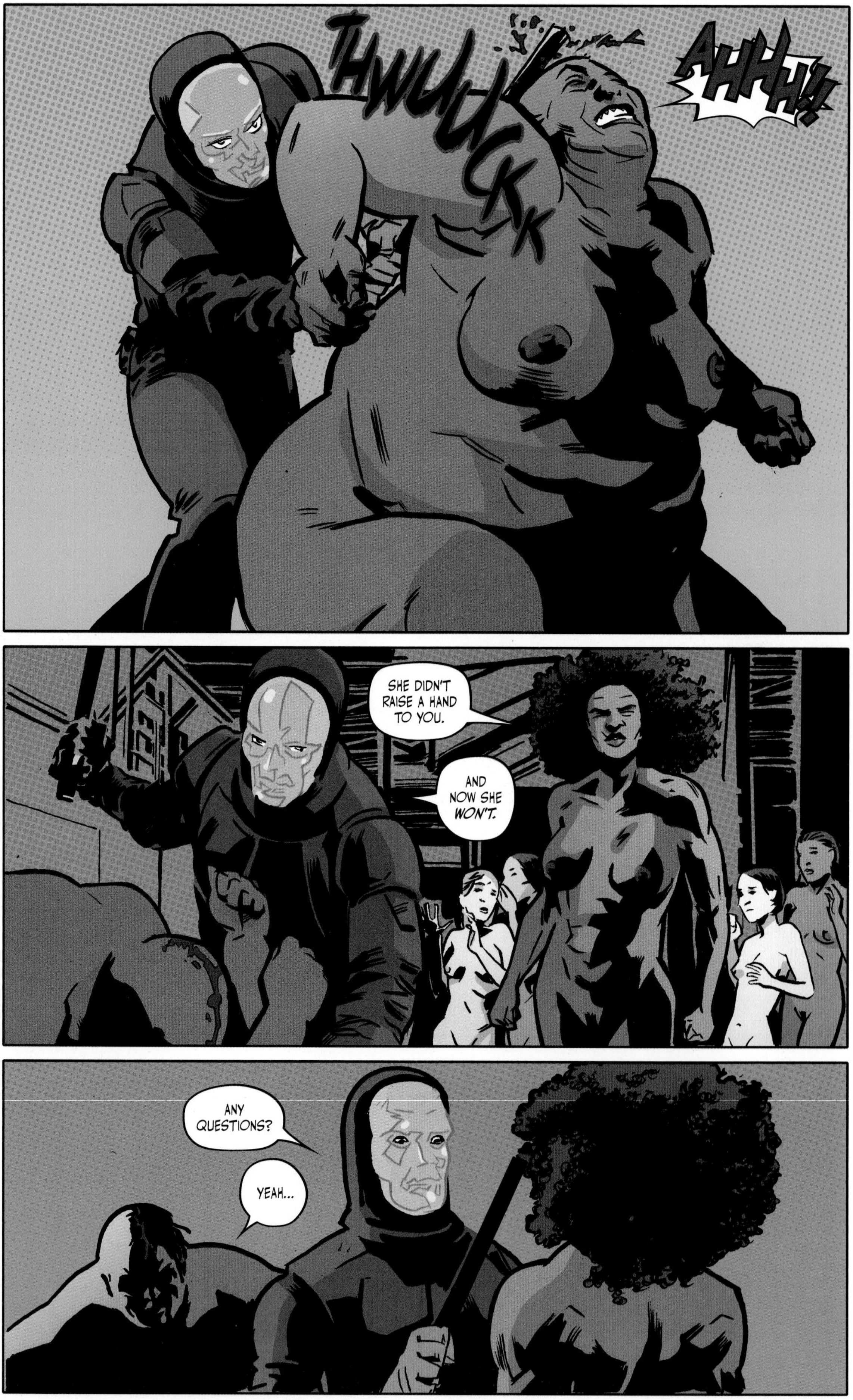
THWUUCKK
AHHH!!
SHE DIDN'T RAISE A HAND TO YOU.
AND NOW SHE *WON'T.*
ANY QUESTIONS?
YEAH...

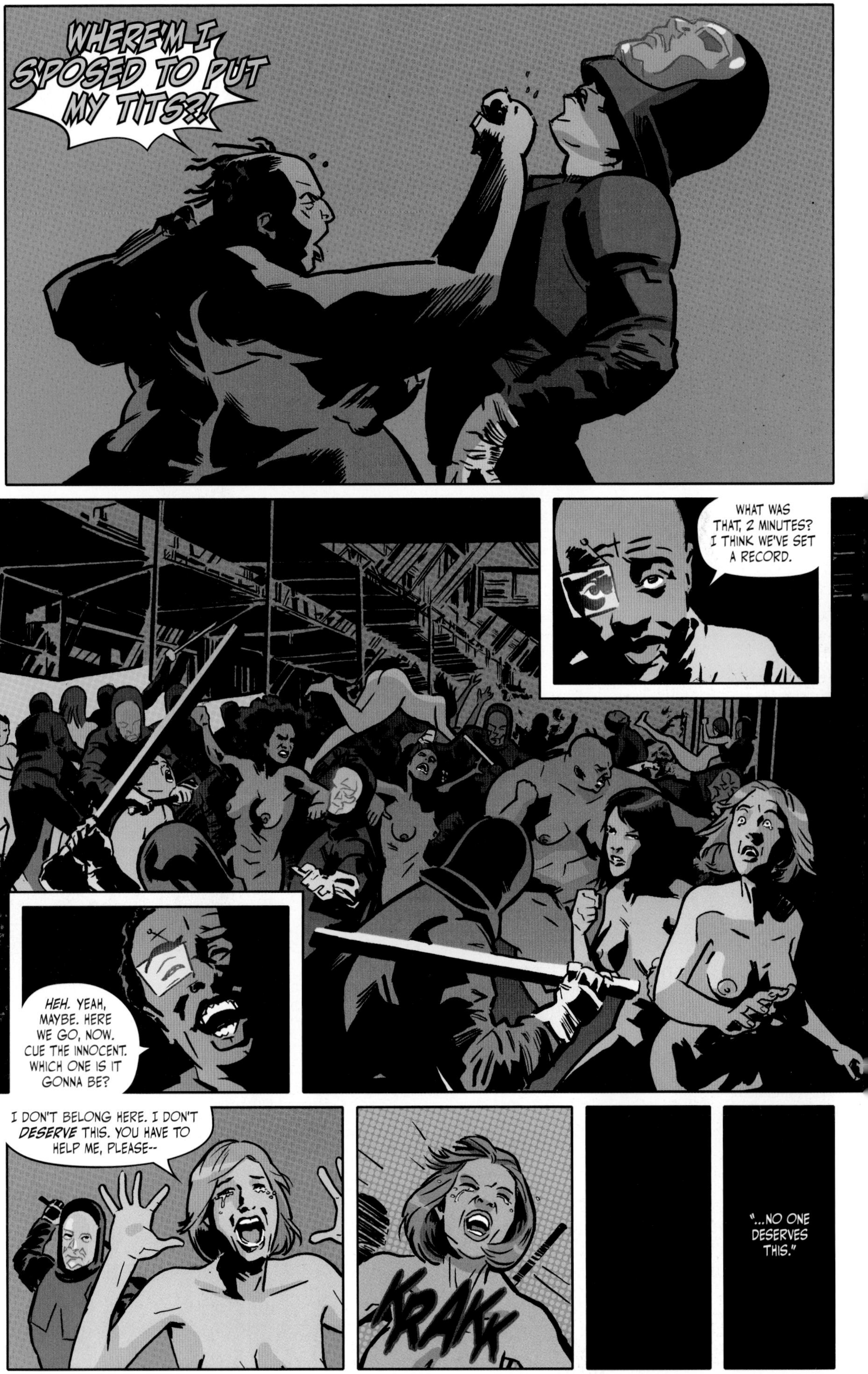
WHERE'M I S'POSED TO PUT MY TITS?!
WHAT WAS THAT, 2 MINUTES? I THINK WE'VE SET A RECORD.
HEH. YEAH, MAYBE. HERE WE GO, NOW. CUE THE INNOCENT. WHICH ONE IS IT GONNA BE?
I DON'T BELONG HERE. I DON'T *DESERVE* THIS. YOU HAVE TO HELP ME, PLEASE--
KRAKK
"...NO ONE DESERVES THIS."

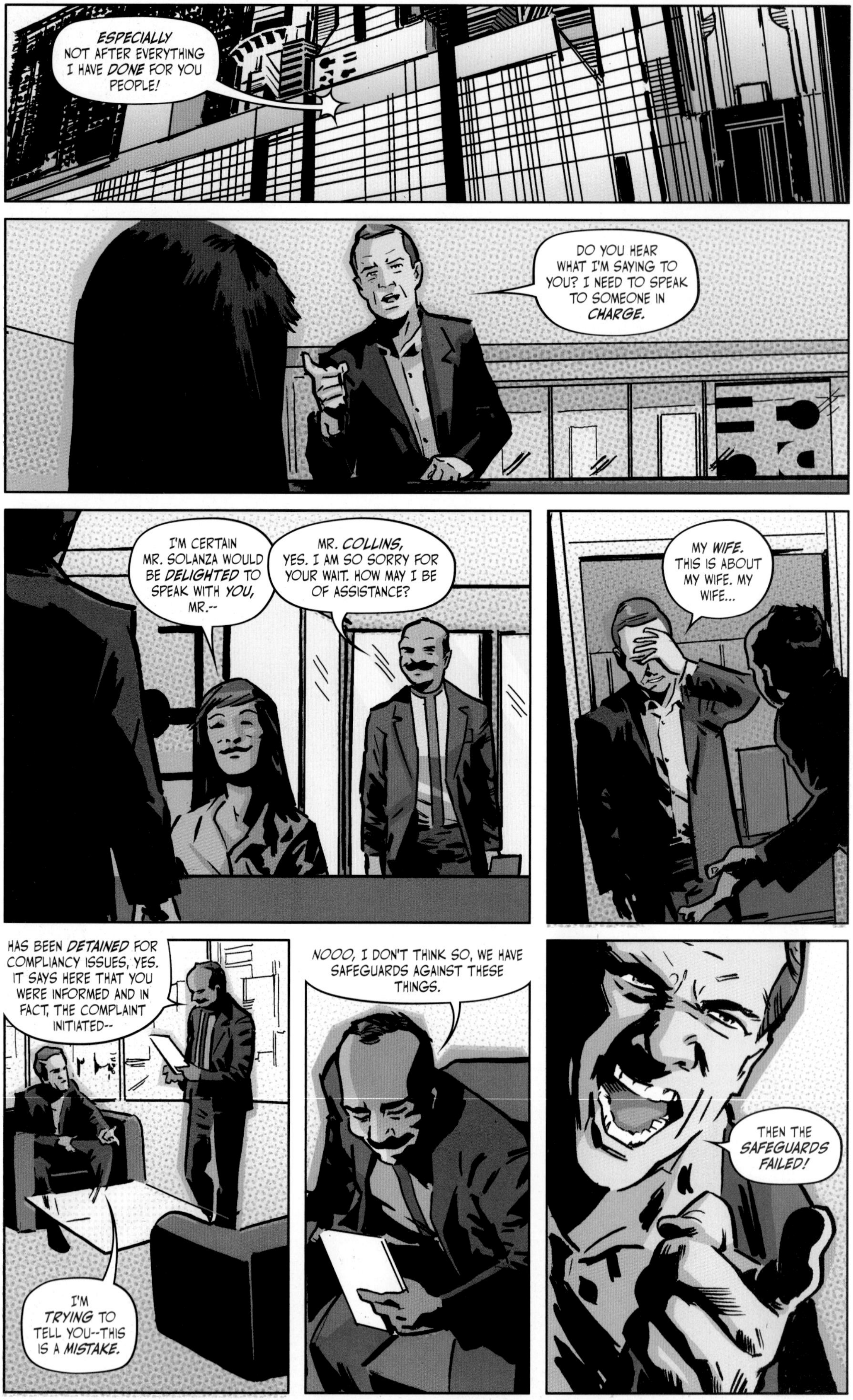
ESPECIALLY NOT AFTER EVERYTHING I HAVE DONE FOR YOU PEOPLE!
DO YOU HEAR WHAT I'M SAYING TO YOU? I NEED TO SPEAK TO SOMEONE IN CHARGE.
I'M CERTAIN MR. SOLANZA WOULD BE DELIGHTED TO SPEAK WITH YOU, MR.--
MR. COLLINS, YES. I AM SO SORRY FOR YOUR WAIT. HOW MAY I BE OF ASSISTANCE?
MY WIFE. THIS IS ABOUT MY WIFE. MY WIFE...
HAS BEEN DETAINED FOR COMPLIANCY ISSUES, YES. IT SAYS HERE THAT YOU WERE INFORMED AND IN FACT, THE COMPLAINT INITIATED--
I'M TRYING TO TELL YOU--THIS IS A MISTAKE.
NOOO, I DON'T THINK SO, WE HAVE SAFEGUARDS AGAINST THESE THINGS.
THEN THE SAFEGUARDS FAILED!

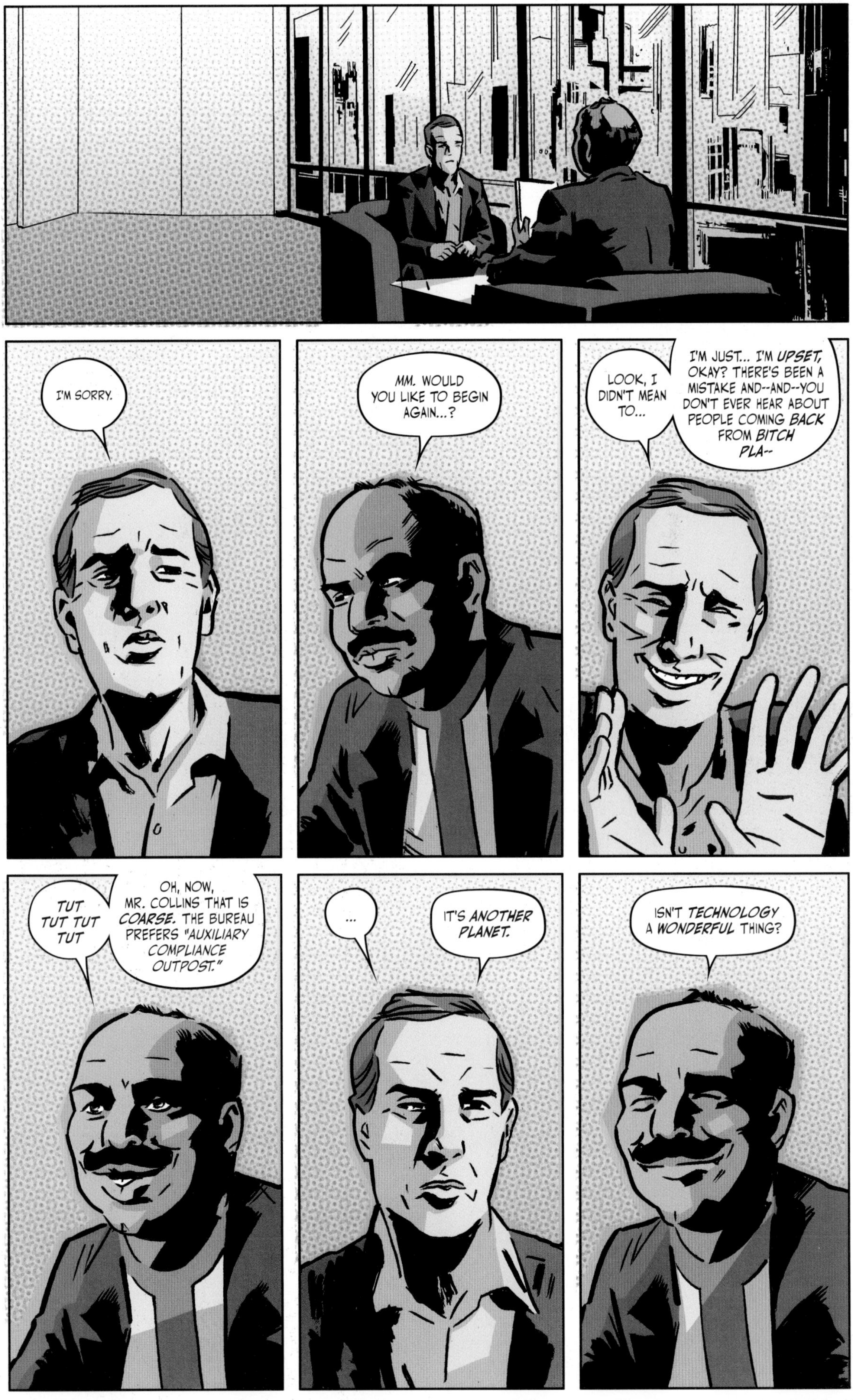
I'M SORRY.
MM. WOULD YOU LIKE TO BEGIN AGAIN...?
LOOK, I DIDN'T MEAN TO...
I'M JUST... I'M *UPSET,* OKAY? THERE'S BEEN A MISTAKE AND--AND--YOU DON'T EVER HEAR ABOUT PEOPLE COMING *BACK* FROM *BITCH PLA--*
TUT TUT TUT TUT
OH, NOW, MR. COLLINS THAT IS *COARSE.* THE BUREAU PREFERS "AUXILIARY COMPLIANCE OUTPOST."
...
IT'S *ANOTHER PLANET.*
ISN'T *TECHNOLOGY* A *WONDERFUL* THING?

IT'S THEIR OWN *FAULT* THEY DON'T SEE IT COMING.

SOME OF THEM *MUST.*

THEY WON'T LET THEMSELVES! RUNS COUNTER TO EVERYTHING THEY BELIEVE.

AS FAR AS SHE'S CONCERNED, SHE'S DONE EVERYTHING RIGHT?

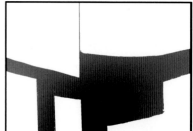

AYEP. IF ANYTHING, YOU'D THINK *WE'D* LEARN TO STOP BEING SURPRISED.

SO WHICH ONE IS IT?

WHITE GIRL.

OF COURSE.

NAME'S *MARIAN COLLINS.*

WELL, MARIAN COLLINS WANTS TO TALK TO *"SOMEONE IN CHARGE."*

LET HER. LOAD THE MODEL. RUN 'THE CATHOLIC.'

I *LOVE* THE CATHOLIC!

I LOOK AFTER YOU, DON'T I?

YOU DO, YOU DO. RUNNING THE CATHOLIC... NOW...

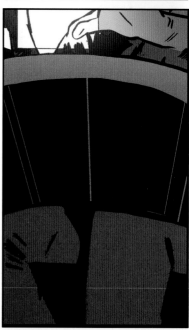

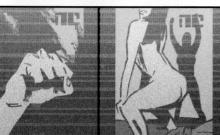

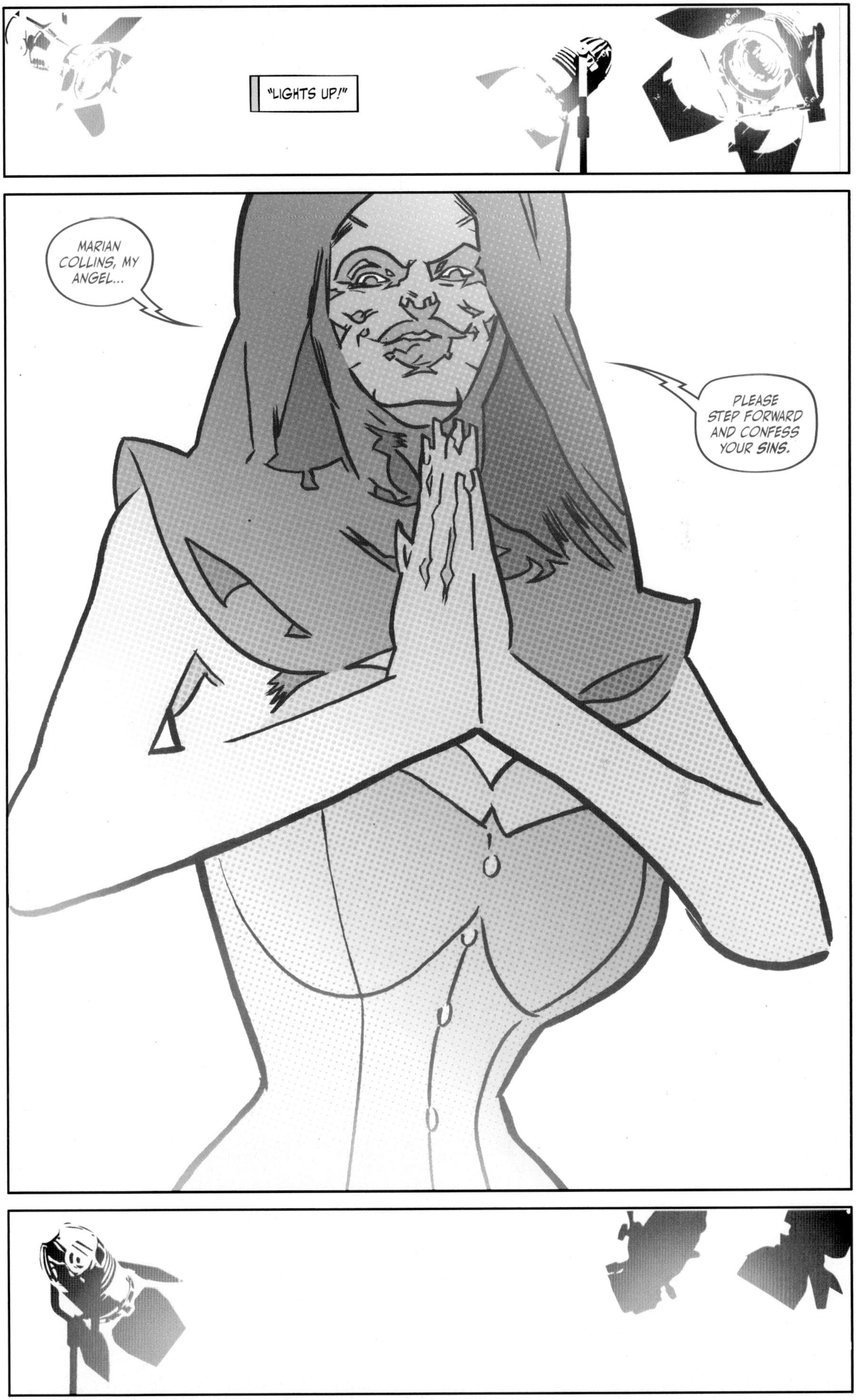
"LIGHTS UP!"
MARIAN COLLINS, MY ANGEL...
PLEASE STEP FORWARD AND CONFESS YOUR SINS.

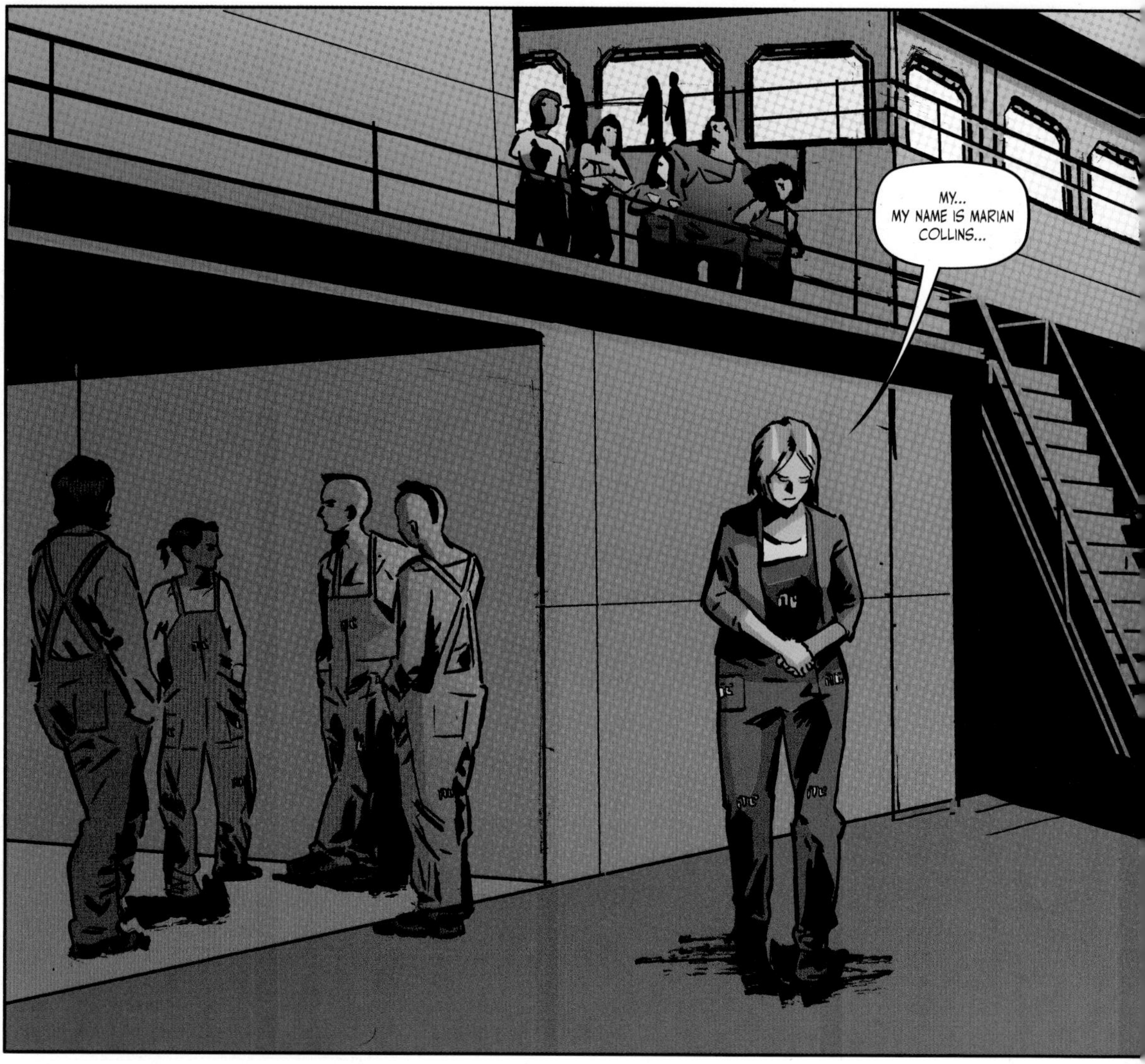
MY...
MY NAME IS MARIAN COLLINS...

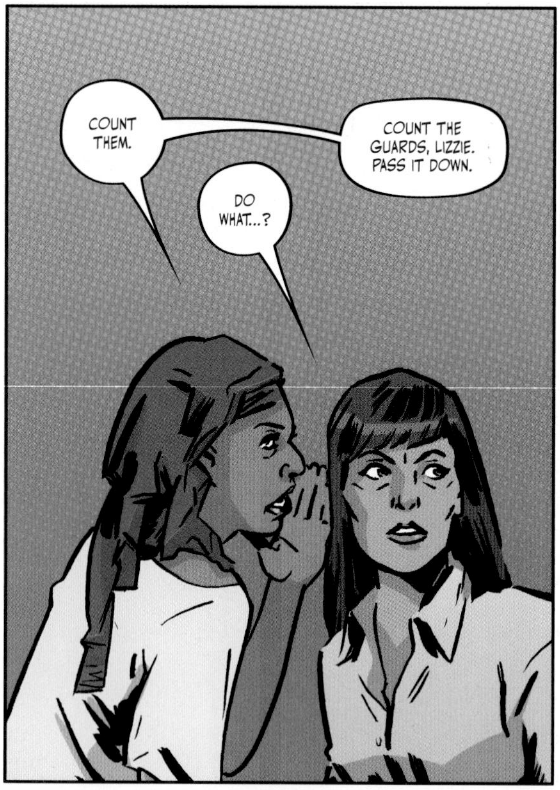
COUNT THEM.
COUNT THE GUARDS, LIZZIE. PASS IT DOWN.
DO WHAT...?

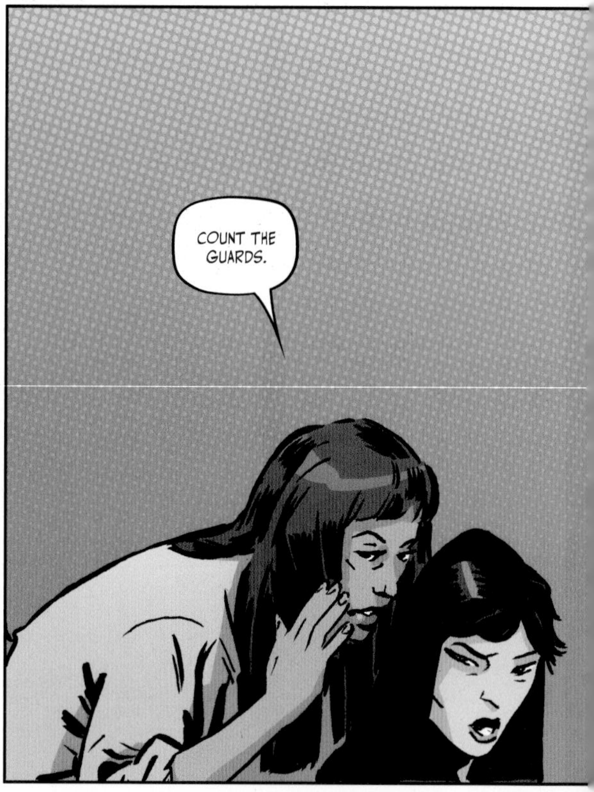
COUNT THE GUARDS.

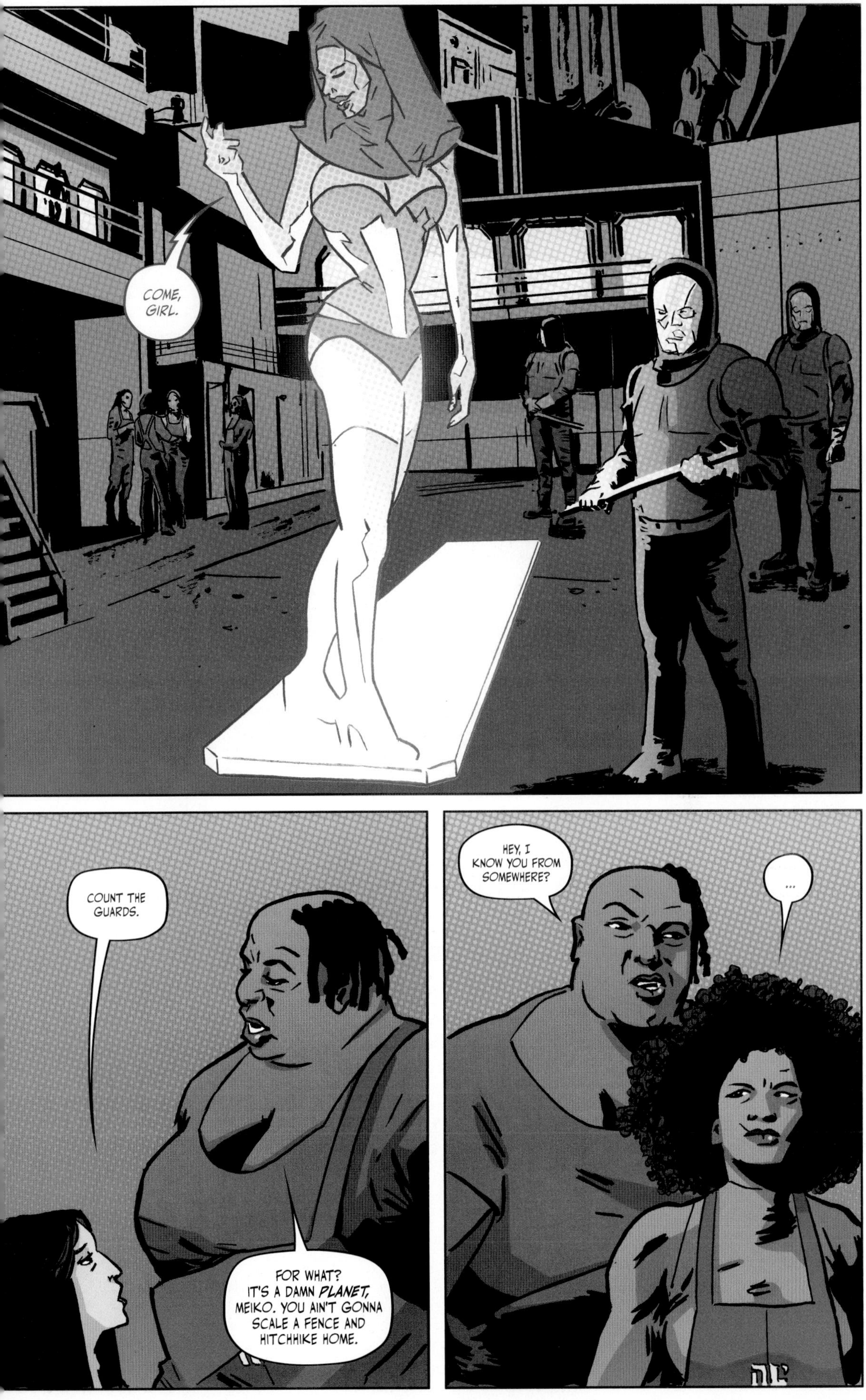
COME, GIRL.
COUNT THE GUARDS.
FOR WHAT? IT'S A DAMN *PLANET,* MEIKO. YOU AIN'T GONNA SCALE A FENCE AND HITCHHIKE HOME.
HEY, I KNOW YOU FROM SOMEWHERE?
...

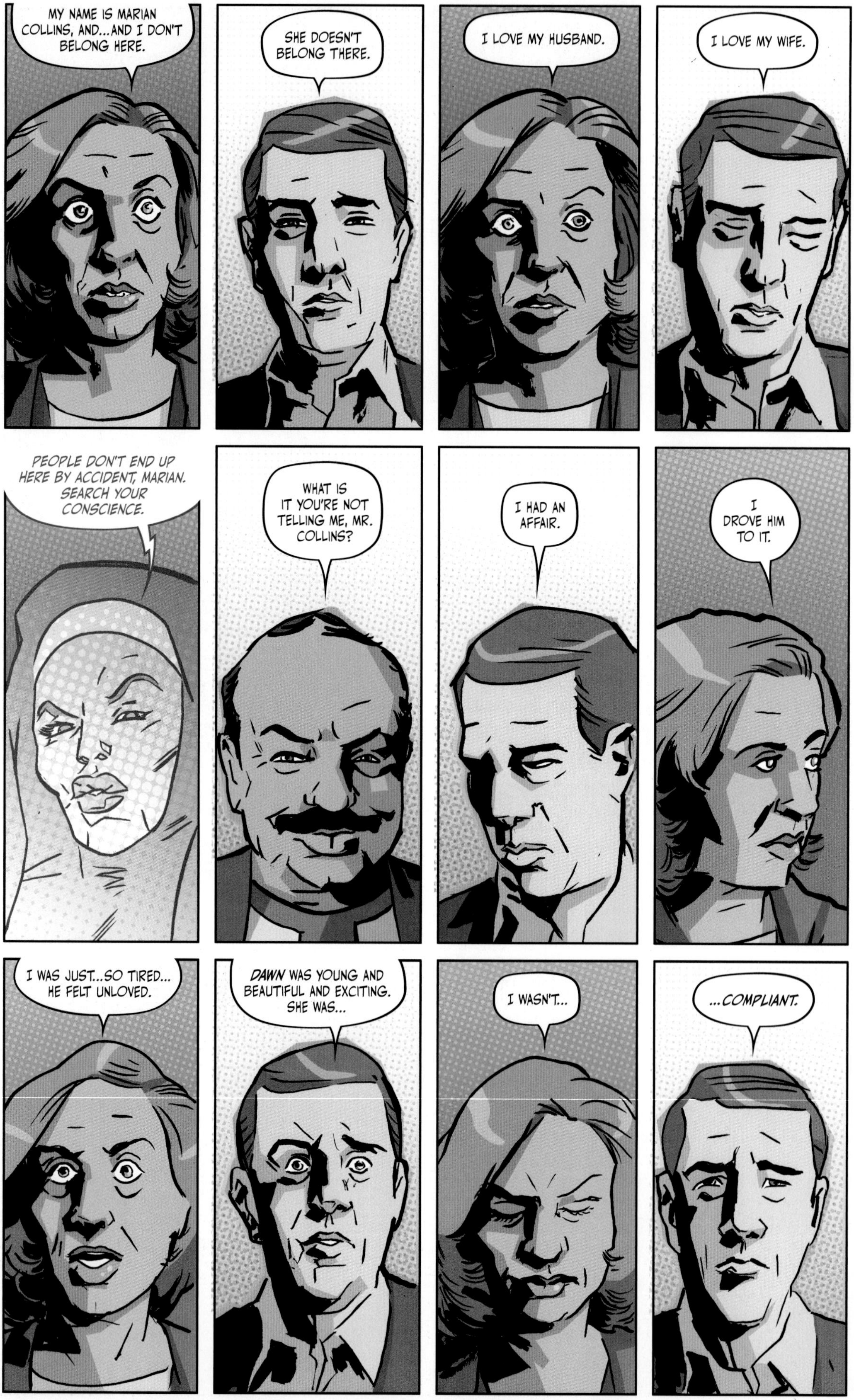
MY NAME IS MARIAN COLLINS, AND...AND I DON'T BELONG HERE.
SHE DOESN'T BELONG THERE.
I LOVE MY HUSBAND.
I LOVE MY WIFE.
PEOPLE DON'T END UP HERE BY ACCIDENT, MARIAN. SEARCH YOUR CONSCIENCE.
WHAT IS IT YOU'RE NOT TELLING ME, MR. COLLINS?
I HAD AN AFFAIR.
I DROVE HIM TO IT.
I WAS JUST...SO TIRED... HE FELT UNLOVED.
DAWN WAS YOUNG AND BEAUTIFUL AND EXCITING. SHE WAS...
I WASN'T...
...COMPLIANT.

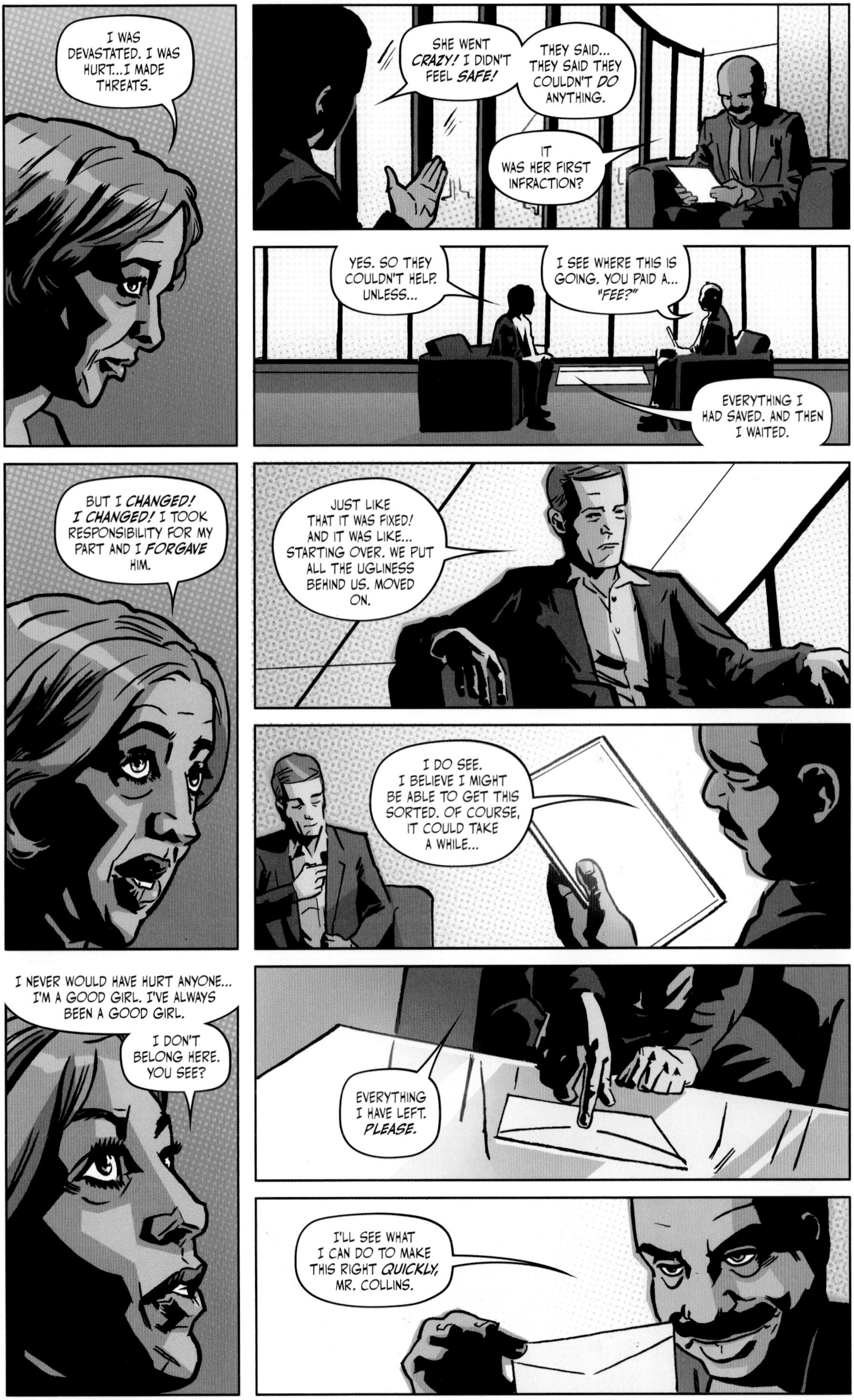
I WAS DEVASTATED. I WAS HURT...I MADE THREATS.
SHE WENT *CRAZY!* I DIDN'T FEEL *SAFE!*
THEY SAID... THEY SAID THEY COULDN'T *DO* ANYTHING.
IT WAS HER FIRST INFRACTION?
YES. SO THEY COULDN'T HELP. UNLESS...
I SEE WHERE THIS IS GOING. YOU PAID A... "FEE?"
EVERYTHING I HAD SAVED. AND THEN I WAITED.
BUT I *CHANGED! I CHANGED!* I TOOK RESPONSIBILITY FOR MY PART AND I *FORGAVE* HIM.
JUST LIKE THAT IT WAS FIXED! AND IT WAS LIKE... STARTING OVER. WE PUT ALL THE UGLINESS BEHIND US. MOVED ON.
I DO SEE. I BELIEVE I MIGHT BE ABLE TO GET THIS SORTED. OF COURSE, IT COULD TAKE A WHILE...
I NEVER WOULD HAVE HURT ANYONE... I'M A GOOD GIRL. I'VE ALWAYS BEEN A GOOD GIRL.
I DON'T BELONG HERE. YOU SEE?
EVERYTHING I HAVE LEFT. *PLEASE.*
I'LL SEE WHAT I CAN DO TO MAKE THIS RIGHT *QUICKLY,* MR. COLLINS.

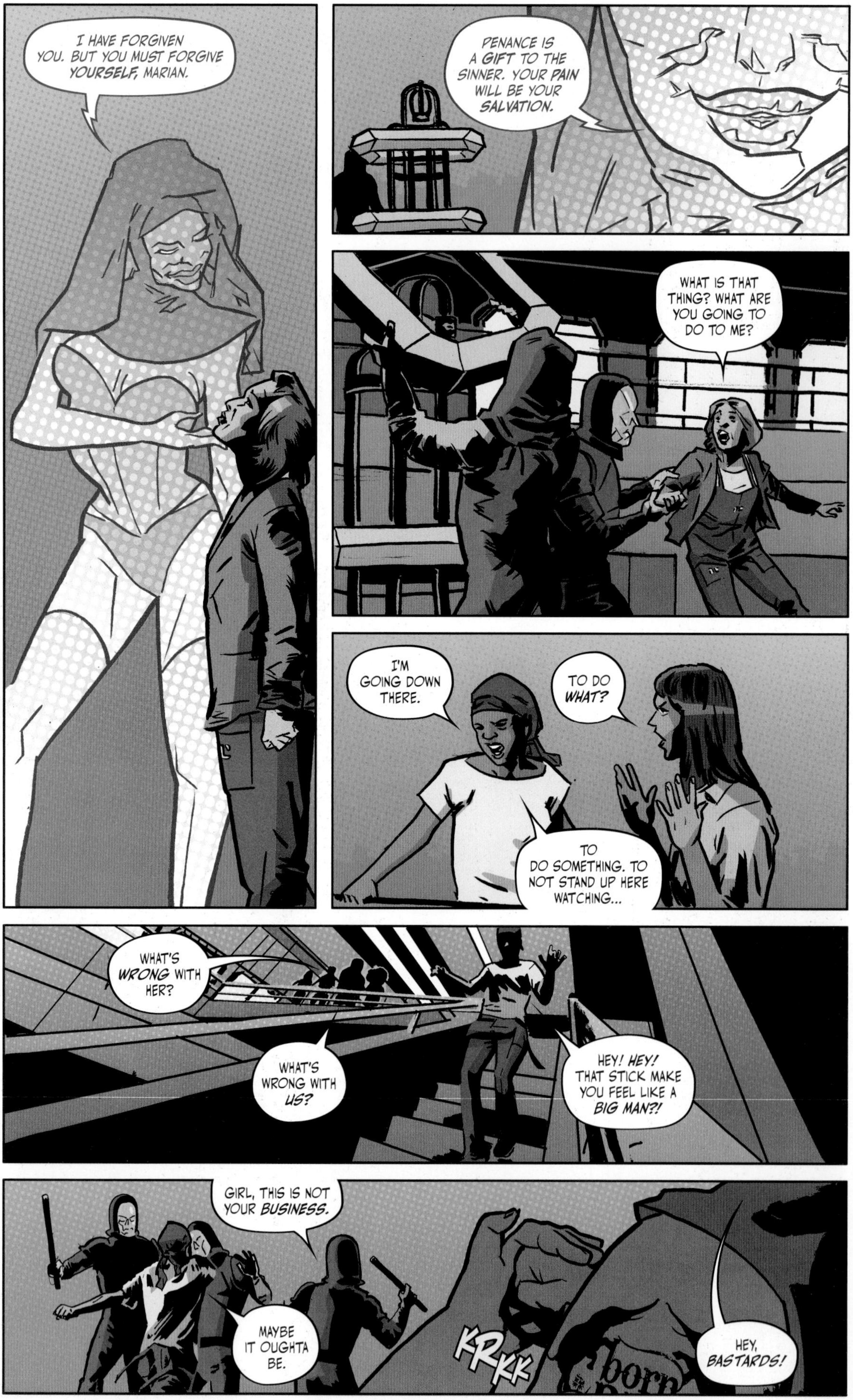
I HAVE FORGIVEN YOU. BUT YOU MUST FORGIVE YOURSELF, MARIAN.
PENANCE IS A GIFT TO THE SINNER. YOUR PAIN WILL BE YOUR SALVATION.
WHAT IS THAT THING? WHAT ARE YOU GOING TO DO TO ME?
I'M GOING DOWN THERE.
TO DO WHAT?
TO DO SOMETHING. TO NOT STAND UP HERE WATCHING...
WHAT'S WRONG WITH HER?
WHAT'S WRONG WITH US?
HEY! HEY! THAT STICK MAKE YOU FEEL LIKE A BIG MAN?!
GIRL, THIS IS NOT YOUR BUSINESS.
MAYBE IT OUGHTA BE.
KRKK
HEY, BASTARDS!

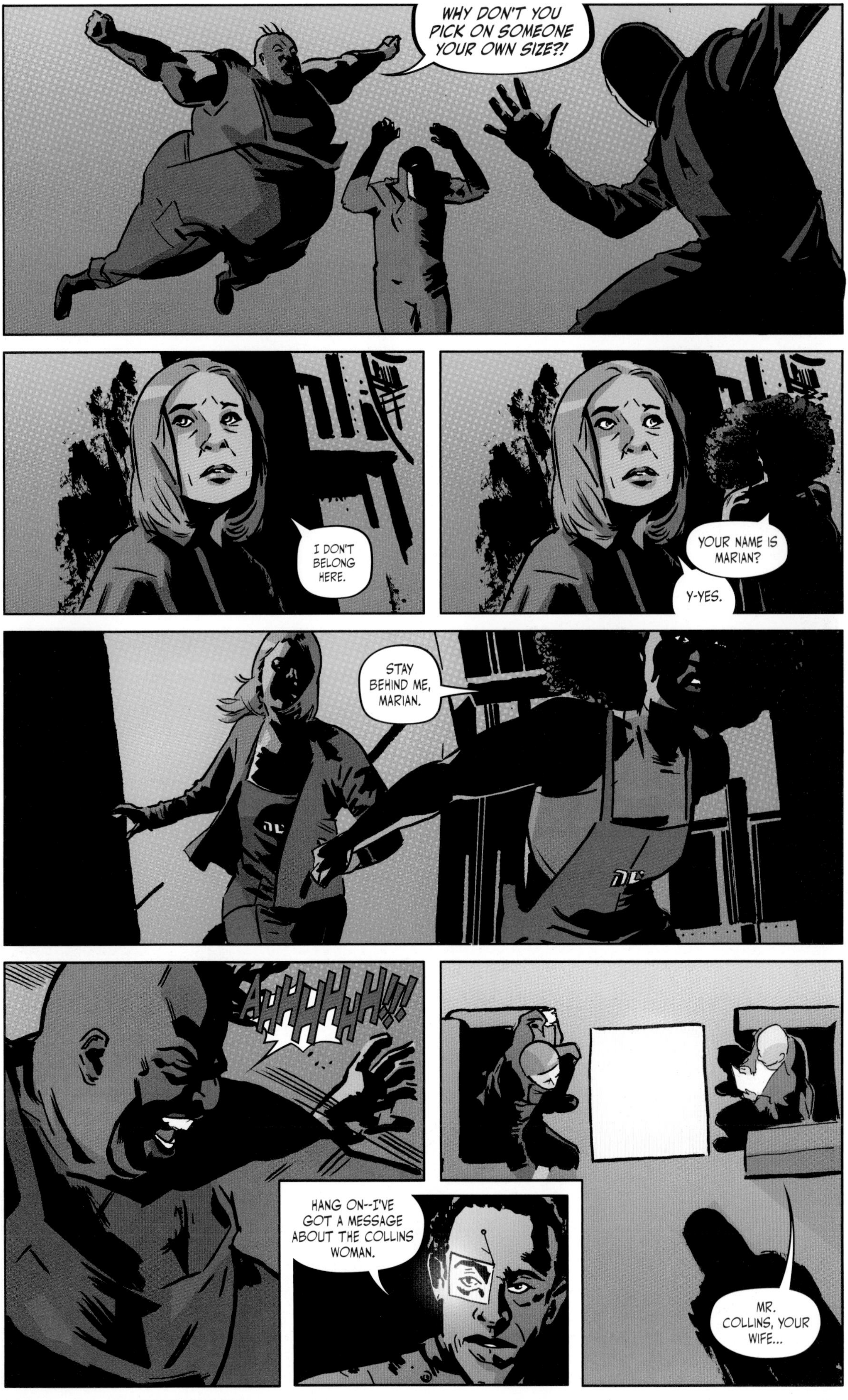
WHY DON'T YOU PICK ON SOMEONE YOUR OWN SIZE?!
I DON'T BELONG HERE.
YOUR NAME IS MARIAN?
Y-YES.
STAY BEHIND ME, MARIAN.
AHHHHHHH!!!
MR. COLLINS, YOUR WIFE...
HANG ON--I'VE GOT A MESSAGE ABOUT THE COLLINS WOMAN.

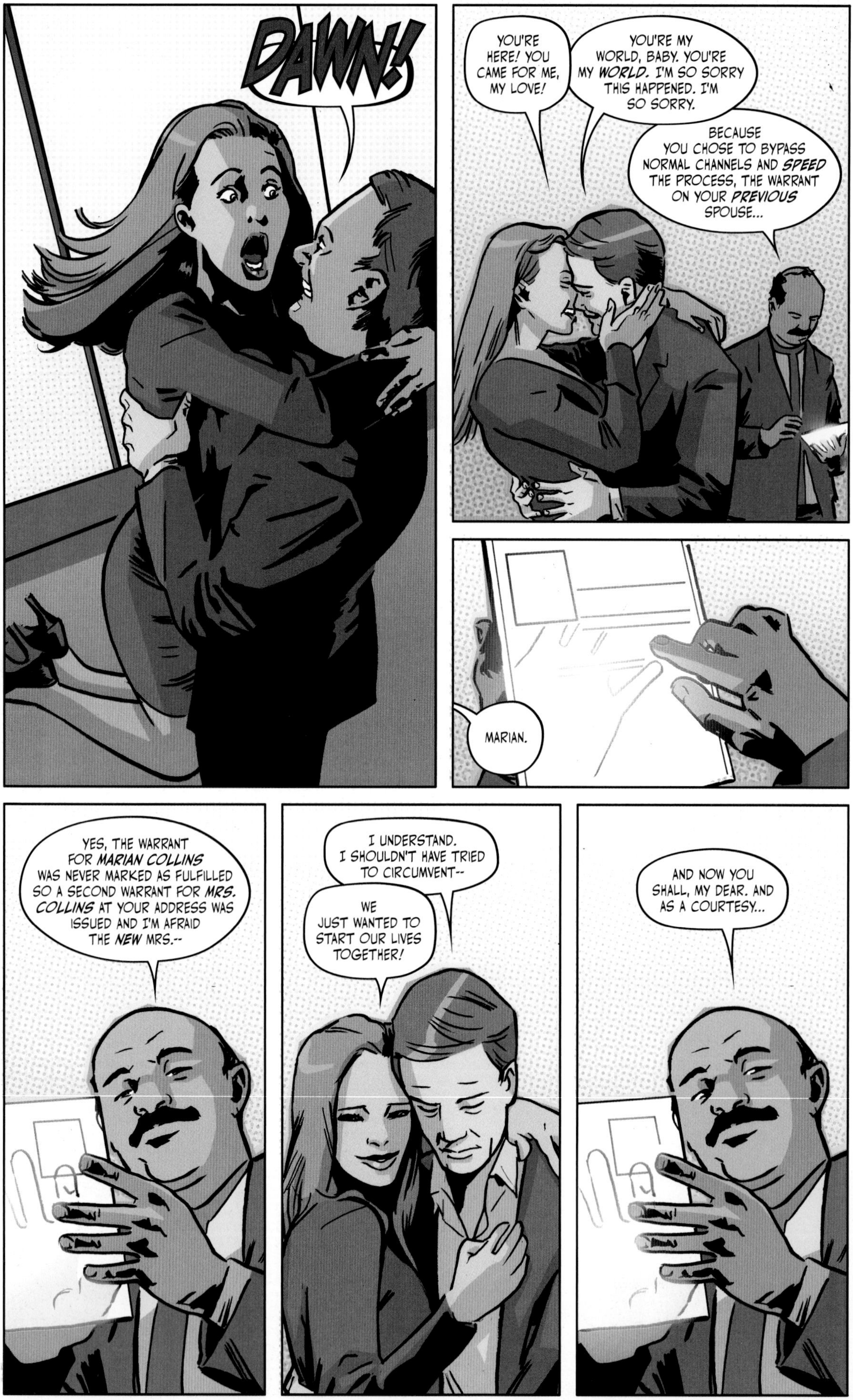
DAWN!
YOU'RE HERE! YOU CAME FOR ME, MY LOVE!
YOU'RE MY WORLD, BABY. YOU'RE MY WORLD. I'M SO SORRY THIS HAPPENED. I'M SO SORRY.
BECAUSE YOU CHOSE TO BYPASS NORMAL CHANNELS AND SPEED THE PROCESS, THE WARRANT ON YOUR PREVIOUS SPOUSE...
MARIAN.
YES, THE WARRANT FOR MARIAN COLLINS WAS NEVER MARKED AS FULFILLED SO A SECOND WARRANT FOR MRS. COLLINS AT YOUR ADDRESS WAS ISSUED AND I'M AFRAID THE NEW MRS.--
I UNDERSTAND. I SHOULDN'T HAVE TRIED TO CIRCUMVENT--
WE JUST WANTED TO START OUR LIVES TOGETHER!
AND NOW YOU SHALL, MY DEAR. AND AS A COURTESY...

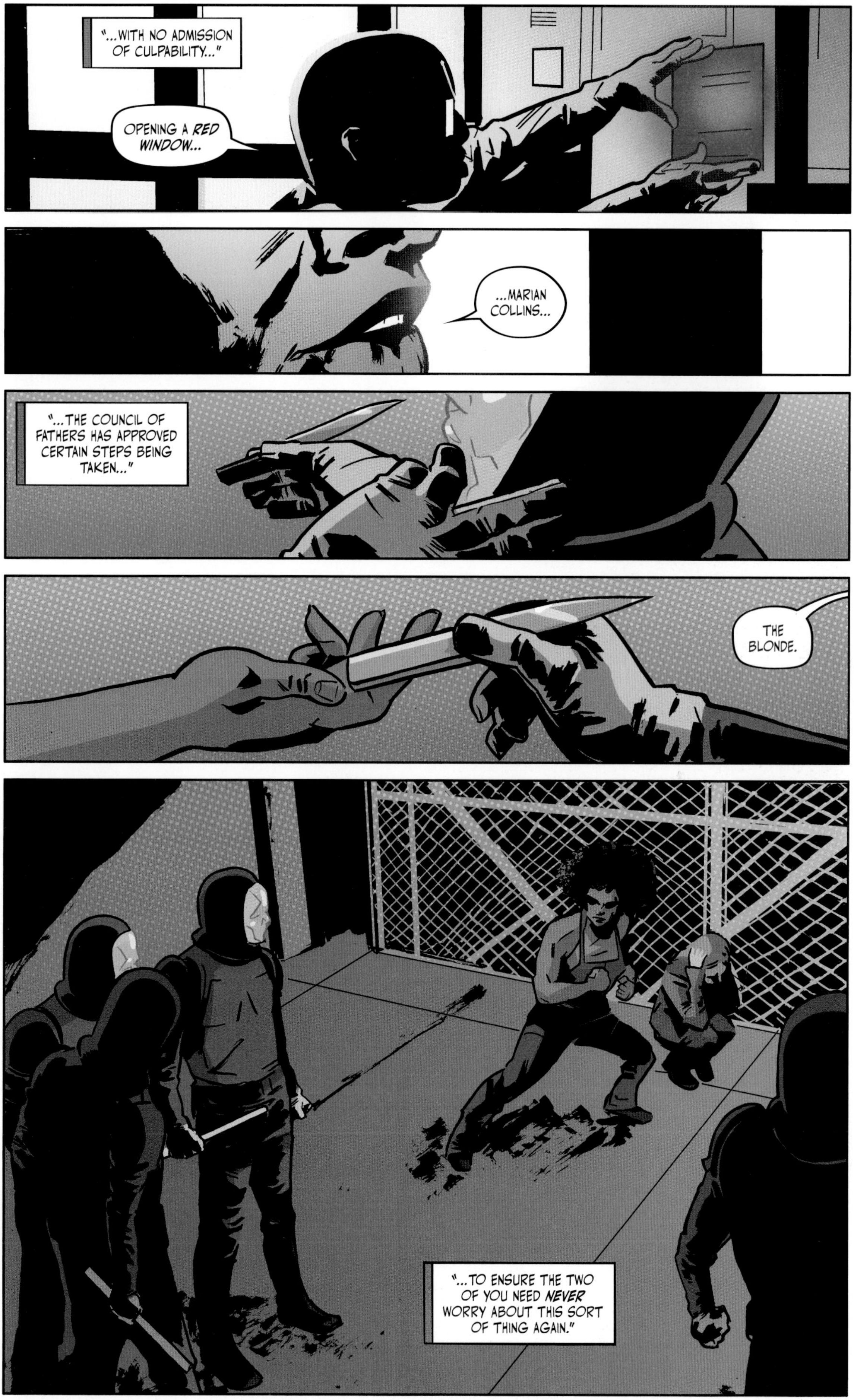
"...WITH NO ADMISSION OF CULPABILITY..."
OPENING A *RED WINDOW*...
...MARIAN COLLINS...
"...THE COUNCIL OF FATHERS HAS APPROVED CERTAIN STEPS BEING TAKEN..."
THE BLONDE.
"...TO ENSURE THE TWO OF YOU NEED *NEVER* WORRY ABOUT THIS SORT OF THING AGAIN."

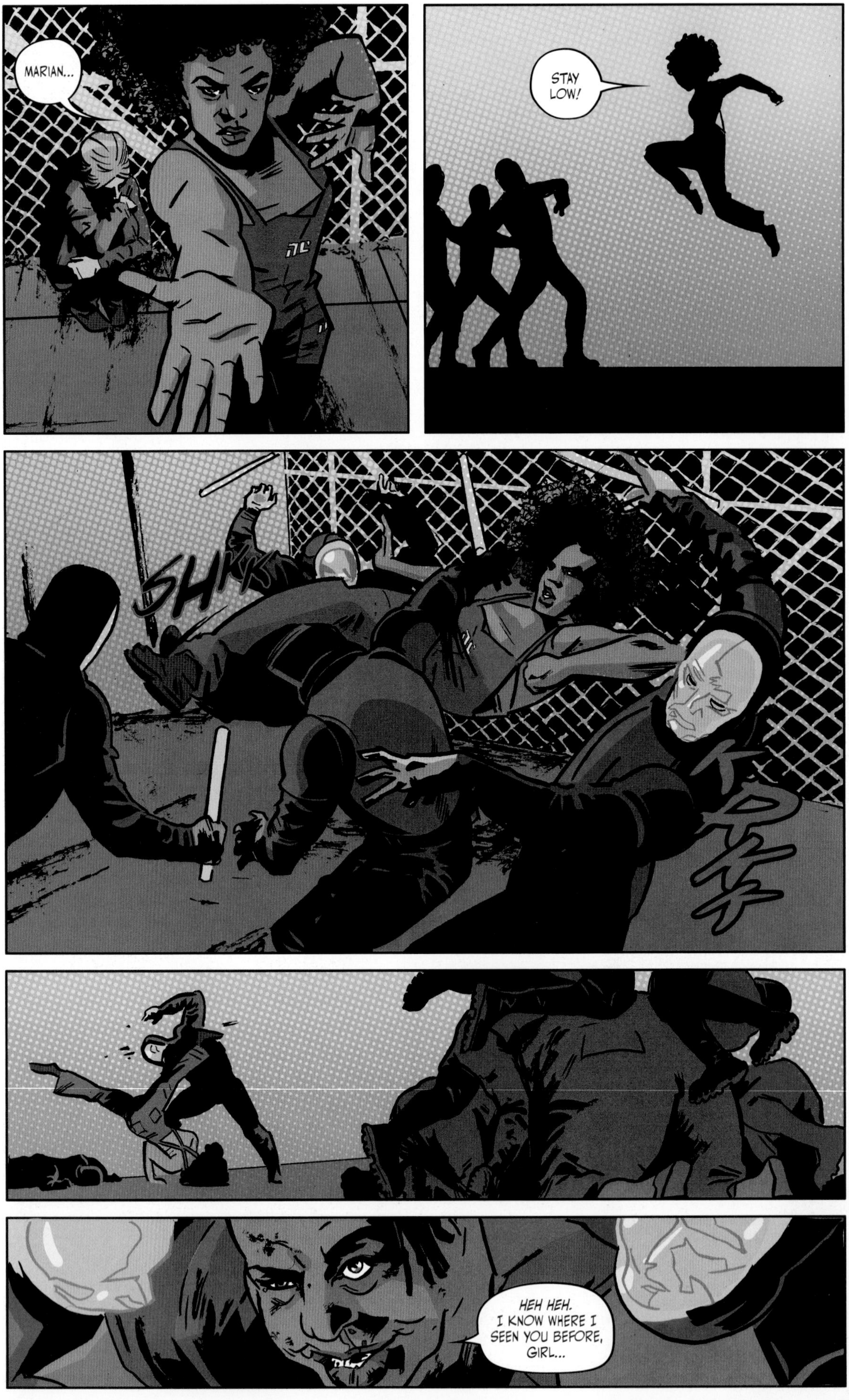
MARIAN...
STAY LOW!
SHKK
KRKK
HEH HEH.
I KNOW WHERE I SEEN YOU BEFORE, GIRL...

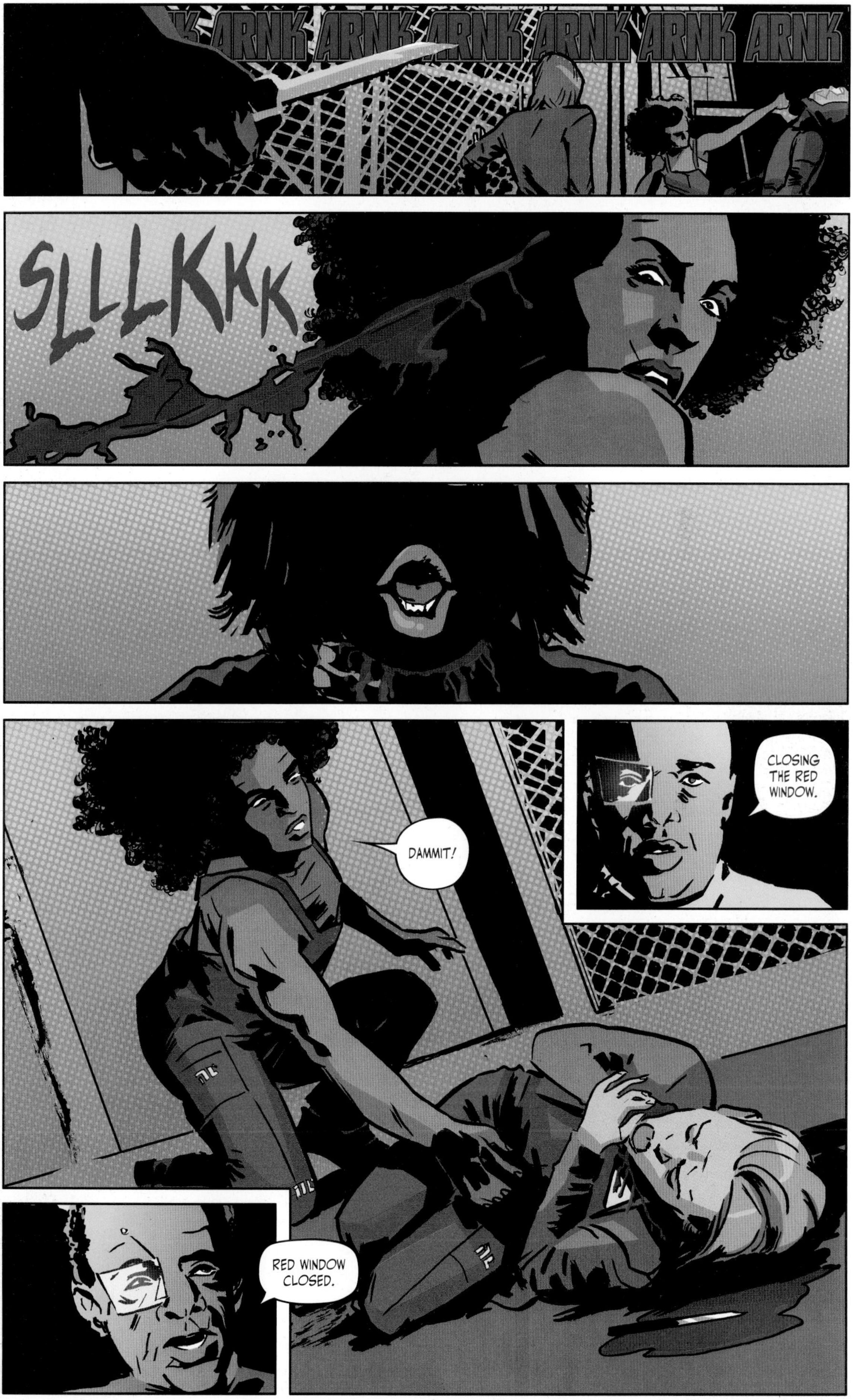
ARNK ARNK ARNK ARNK ARNK ARNK
SLLLKKK
DAMMIT!
CLOSING THE RED WINDOW.
RED WINDOW CLOSED.

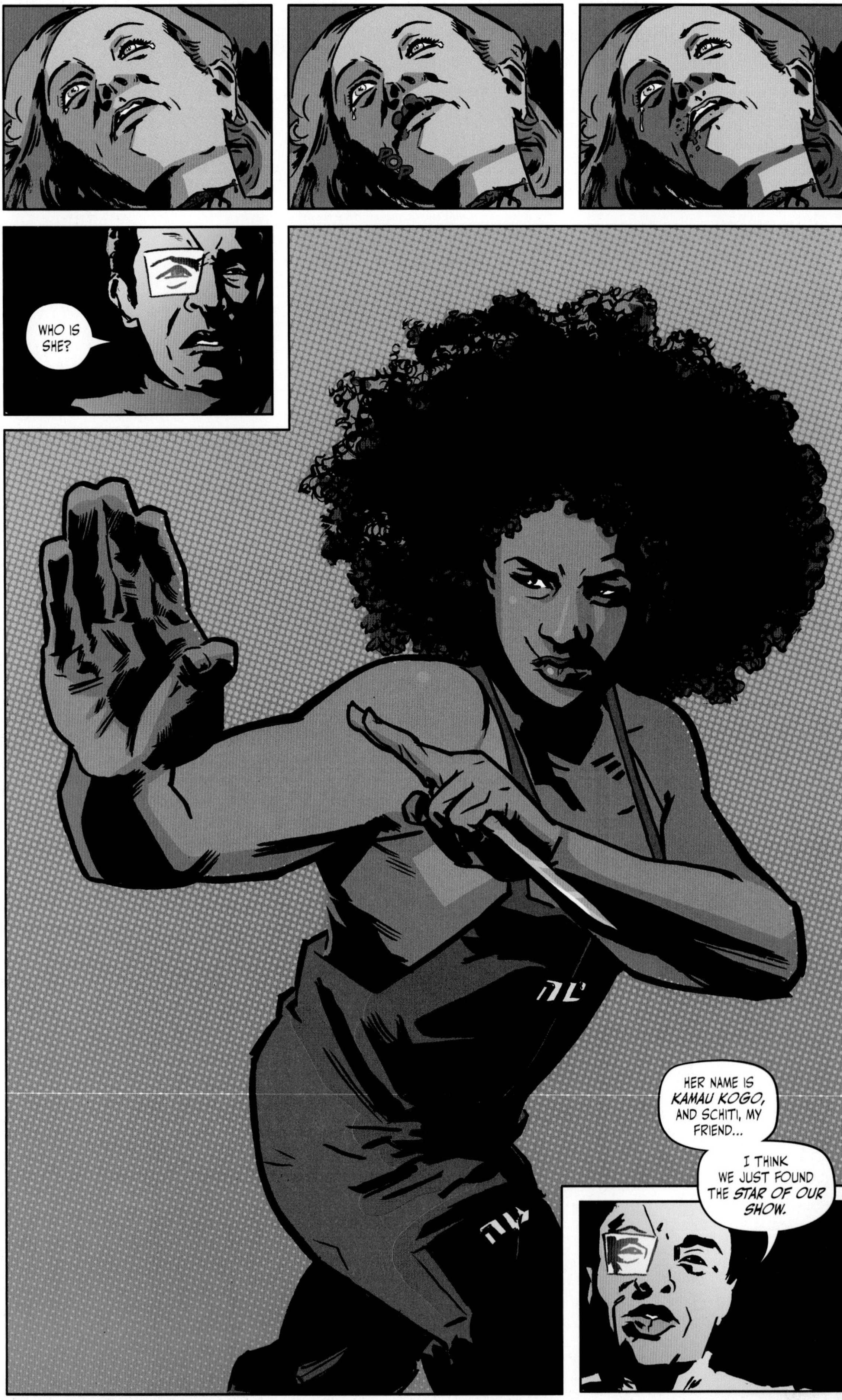
POP
WHO IS SHE?
HER NAME IS KAMAU KOGO, AND SCHITI, MY FRIEND...
I THINK WE JUST FOUND THE STAR OF OUR SHOW.

HEY KIDS, PATRIARCHY!

Missed Connection

ME: At the pool outside DESTINATIONS LOUNGE last Thursday night. I was wearing khakis, solid earning potential, a sparkling smile and a sincere desire for meaningful emotional connection beyond the usual small talk.
YOU: Hot, wet and mute

Are You Non-Compliant?

GIRLS, GIRLS, GIRLS!
You want that sexy, his-blood-in-a-bottle-around-your-neck **CRAZY CHICK** mystique? What says **DREAMY BAD GIRL** like a temporary tattoo??
PUT IT ON YOUR FACE.

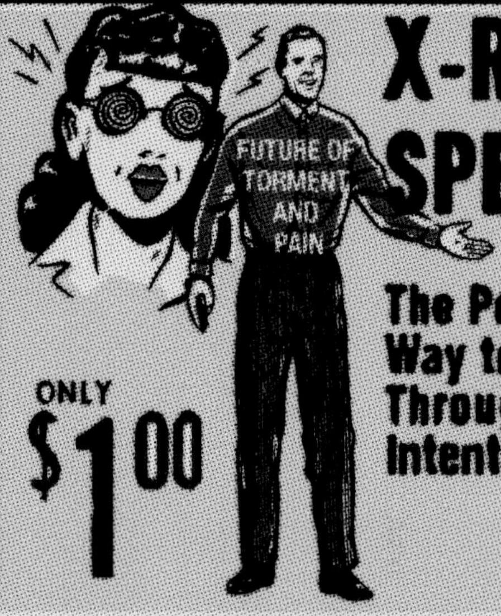
FUTURE OF TORMENT AND PAIN

X-RAY SPECS

The Perfect Way to See Through His Intentions

ONLY $1.00

AMAZING CLARITY INSTANTLY!
Surprise insight! Scientific obfuscation really works. Imagine—you put on the "X-Ray" Specs and hold his hand in front of you. You SEEM to be able to look right through him and see the truth! That guy in the black Taurus who followed you home? Is that really insecurity you "see" beneath his clothes? Or is it a gun? Is he probably going to murder you?
LOADS OF LAUGHS AND FUN AT PARTIES.

Happy Anniversary!

Dawn, you are my light, my morning, my new beginning. Every day I wake with you, I am reborn. Every minute before we met was prologue — HALF my age and ALL of my heart! Let's stay young together forever as long as it feels good.
xxx Skip

RABBIT

I'm spending the only credits I have to place this ad. I need your help. There's no one else I can turn to and nowhere I can hide. **THE DUCHESS** said this was how to reach you. Tell me what to do. **— ALICE**

Let Us Change Your Personality!
(or at least your signature!)

Send us your full name and we'll craft **SIX UNIQUE SIGNATURES** for you to choose from, learn and pretend they express something real about you. Don't like your name? For an extra twenty-five cents, we'll change that too.

SIGN...............3 for $3.00 w/shipping

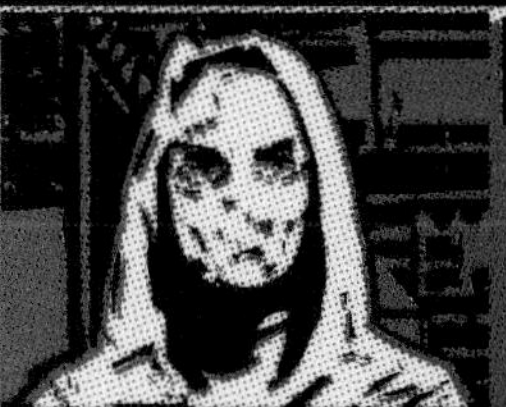

PROTECT YOUR FACE

The sadistic staff on BITCH PLANET must shield their skin to protect themselves from the dampening effects of the alien environment. Who knew their prophylactic faces would be as FABULOUS as they are FREAKY? Now you can emulate the look! Be the first on your block to warp your face and call it FASHION.

FACE...............$3.00 w/shipping

ORDER BY MAIL

You know this is garbage, right? You're ordering garbage. Okay, well, you were warned. Send your dad's hard earned money to the address below and we'll keep the Postal Service alive a little longer by mailing you some crap. I'm not shipping international, so don't even try.

ITEM	HOW MANY	PRICE
SIGN		$3.00
FACE		$3.00
NON		$1.50
	TOTAL	

ALLOW 3-6 WEEKS FOR SHIPPING

SEND CHECK OR MONEY ORDER TO:
Milkfed Criminal Masterminds, Inc. PO Box 25662, Portland, OR 97298

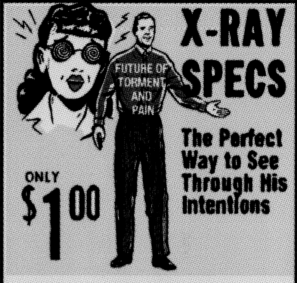

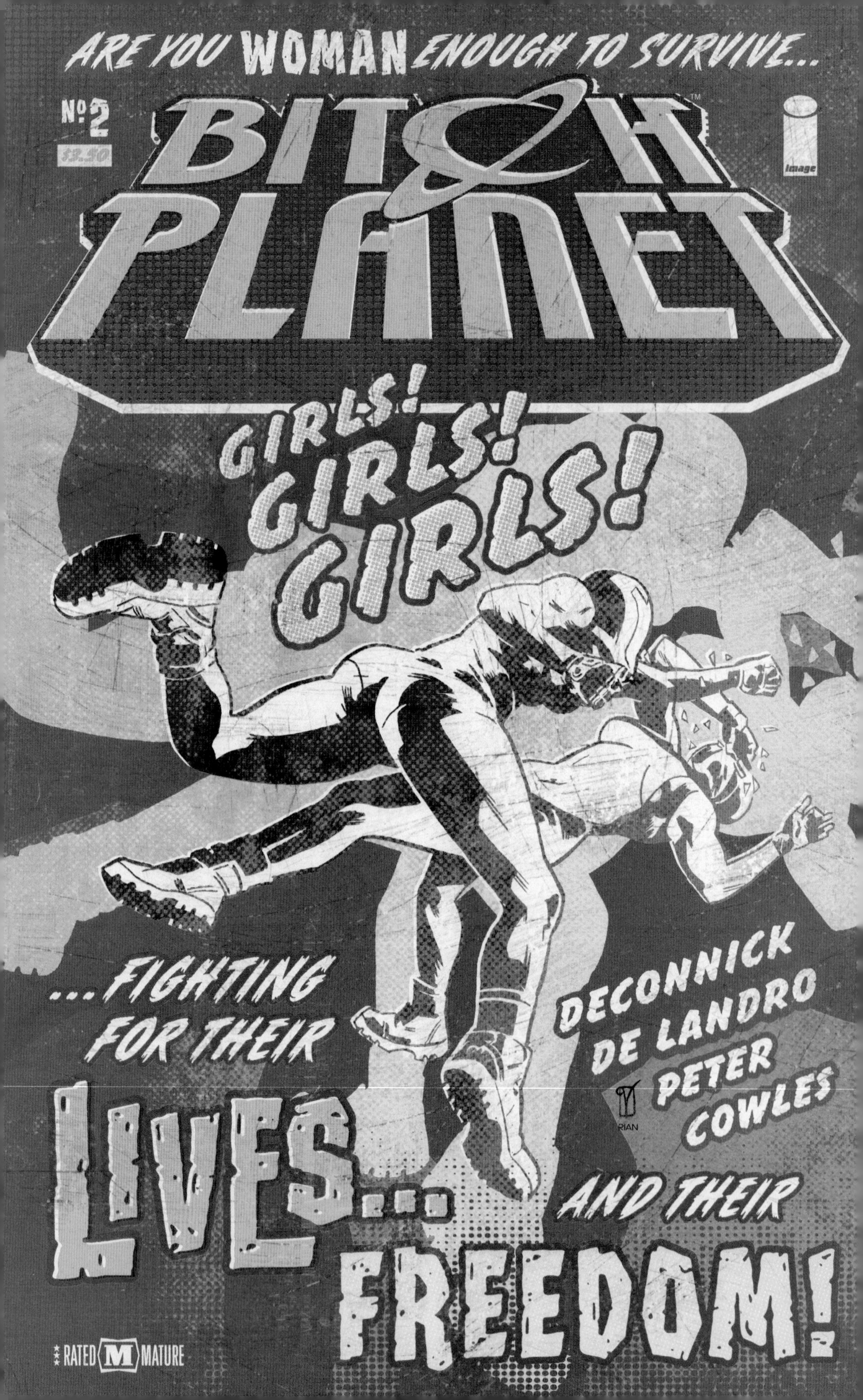
ARE YOU WOMAN ENOUGH TO SURVIVE...
Nº2
BITCH PLANET™
image
GIRLS! GIRLS! GIRLS!
...FIGHTING FOR THEIR
LIVES...
AND THEIR
FREEDOM!
DECONNICK
DE LANDRO
PETER
COWLES
RIAN
RATED M MATURE

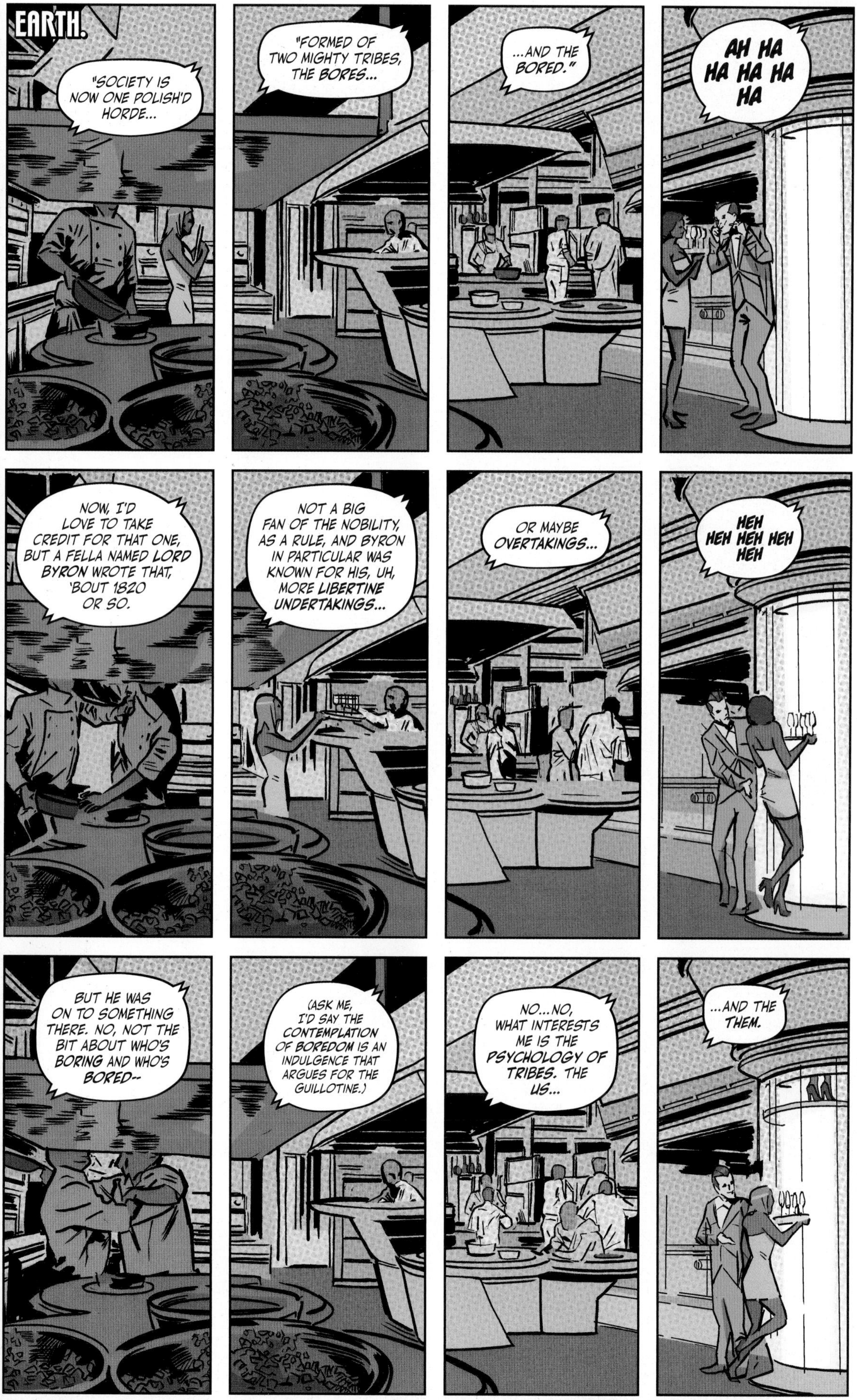
EARTH.
"SOCIETY IS NOW ONE POLISH'D HORDE...
"FORMED OF TWO MIGHTY TRIBES, THE BORES...
...AND THE BORED."
AH HA HA HA HA HA
NOW, I'D LOVE TO TAKE CREDIT FOR THAT ONE, BUT A FELLA NAMED LORD BYRON WROTE THAT, 'BOUT 1820 OR SO.
NOT A BIG FAN OF THE NOBILITY, AS A RULE, AND BYRON IN PARTICULAR WAS KNOWN FOR HIS, UH, MORE LIBERTINE UNDERTAKINGS...
OR MAYBE OVERTAKINGS...
HEH HEH HEH HEH HEH
BUT HE WAS ON TO SOMETHING THERE. NO, NOT THE BIT ABOUT WHO'S BORING AND WHO'S BORED--
(ASK ME, I'D SAY THE CONTEMPLATION OF BOREDOM IS AN INDULGENCE THAT ARGUES FOR THE GUILLOTINE.)
NO...NO, WHAT INTERESTS ME IS THE PSYCHOLOGY OF TRIBES. THE US...
...AND THE THEM.

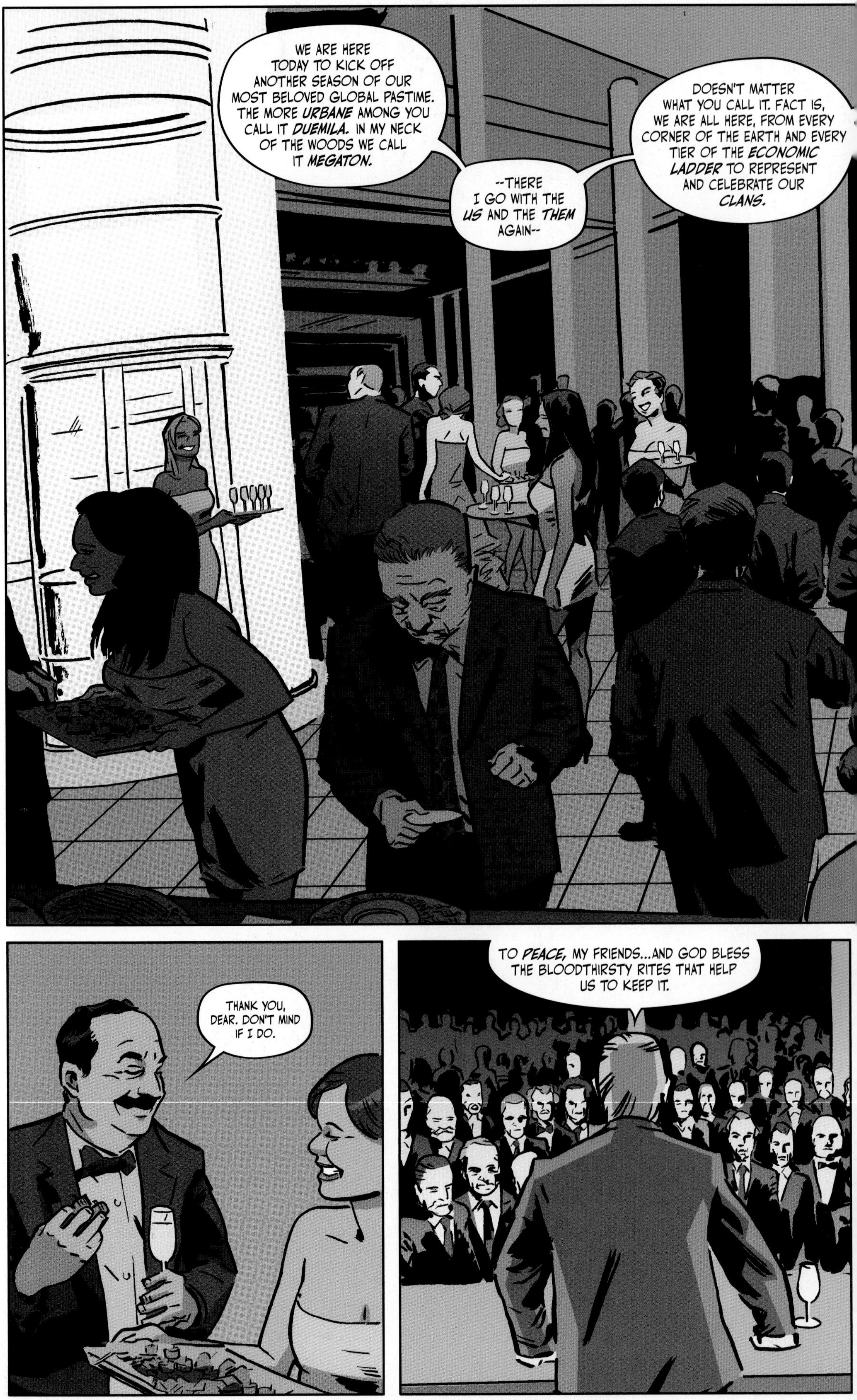
WE ARE HERE TODAY TO KICK OFF ANOTHER SEASON OF OUR MOST BELOVED GLOBAL PASTIME. THE MORE URBANE AMONG YOU CALL IT DUEMILA. IN MY NECK OF THE WOODS WE CALL IT MEGATON.
--THERE I GO WITH THE US AND THE THEM AGAIN--
DOESN'T MATTER WHAT YOU CALL IT. FACT IS, WE ARE ALL HERE, FROM EVERY CORNER OF THE EARTH AND EVERY TIER OF THE ECONOMIC LADDER TO REPRESENT AND CELEBRATE OUR CLANS.
THANK YOU, DEAR. DON'T MIND IF I DO.
TO PEACE, MY FRIENDS...AND GOD BLESS THE BLOODTHIRSTY RITES THAT HELP US TO KEEP IT.

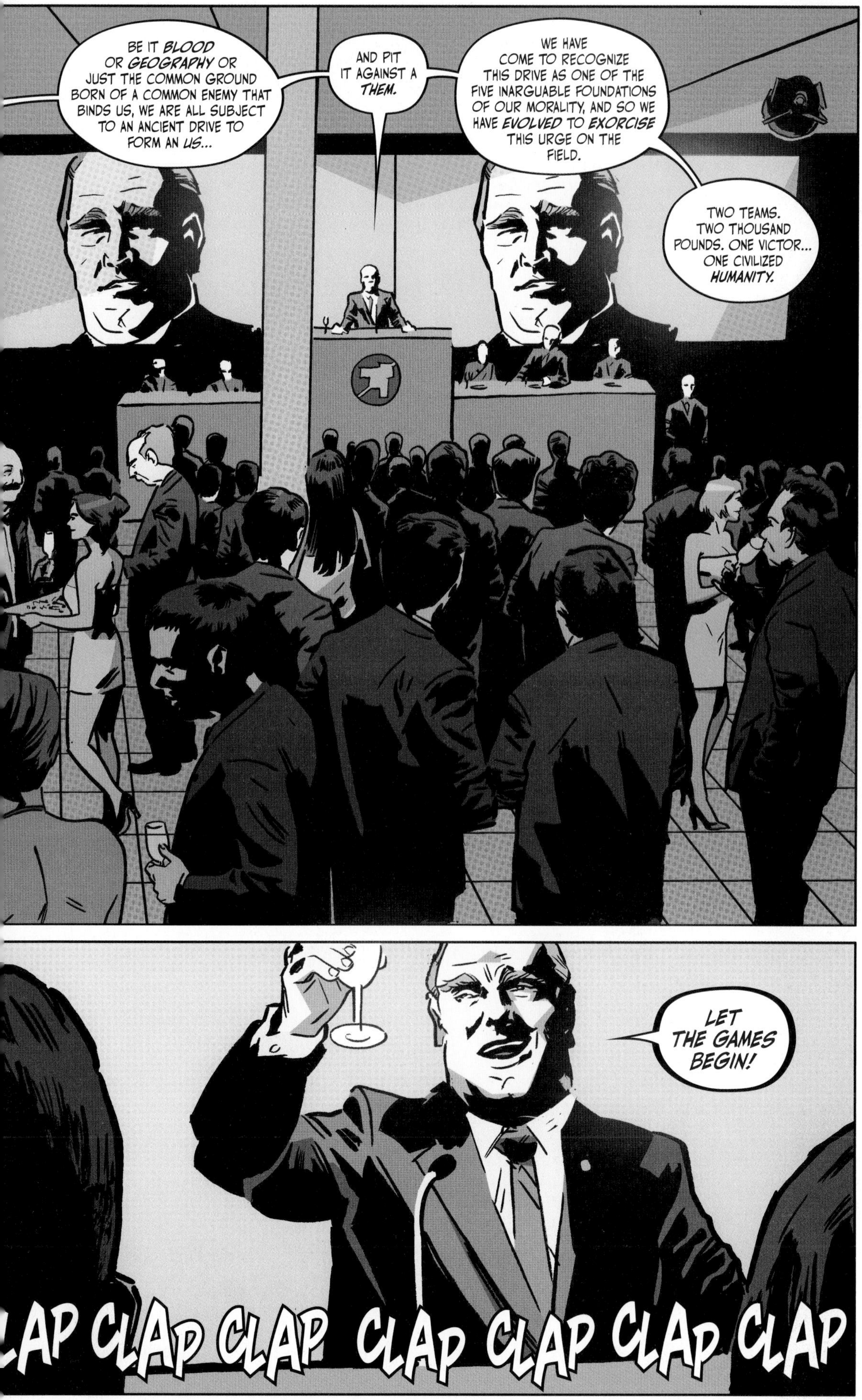
BE IT *BLOOD* OR *GEOGRAPHY* OR JUST THE COMMON GROUND BORN OF A COMMON ENEMY THAT BINDS US, WE ARE ALL SUBJECT TO AN ANCIENT DRIVE TO FORM AN *US*...
AND PIT IT AGAINST A *THEM.*
WE HAVE COME TO RECOGNIZE THIS DRIVE AS ONE OF THE FIVE INARGUABLE FOUNDATIONS OF OUR MORALITY, AND SO WE HAVE *EVOLVED* TO *EXORCISE* THIS URGE ON THE FIELD.
TWO TEAMS. TWO THOUSAND POUNDS. ONE VICTOR... ONE CIVILIZED *HUMANITY.*
LET THE GAMES BEGIN!
LAP CLAP CLAP CLAP CLAP CLAP CLAP

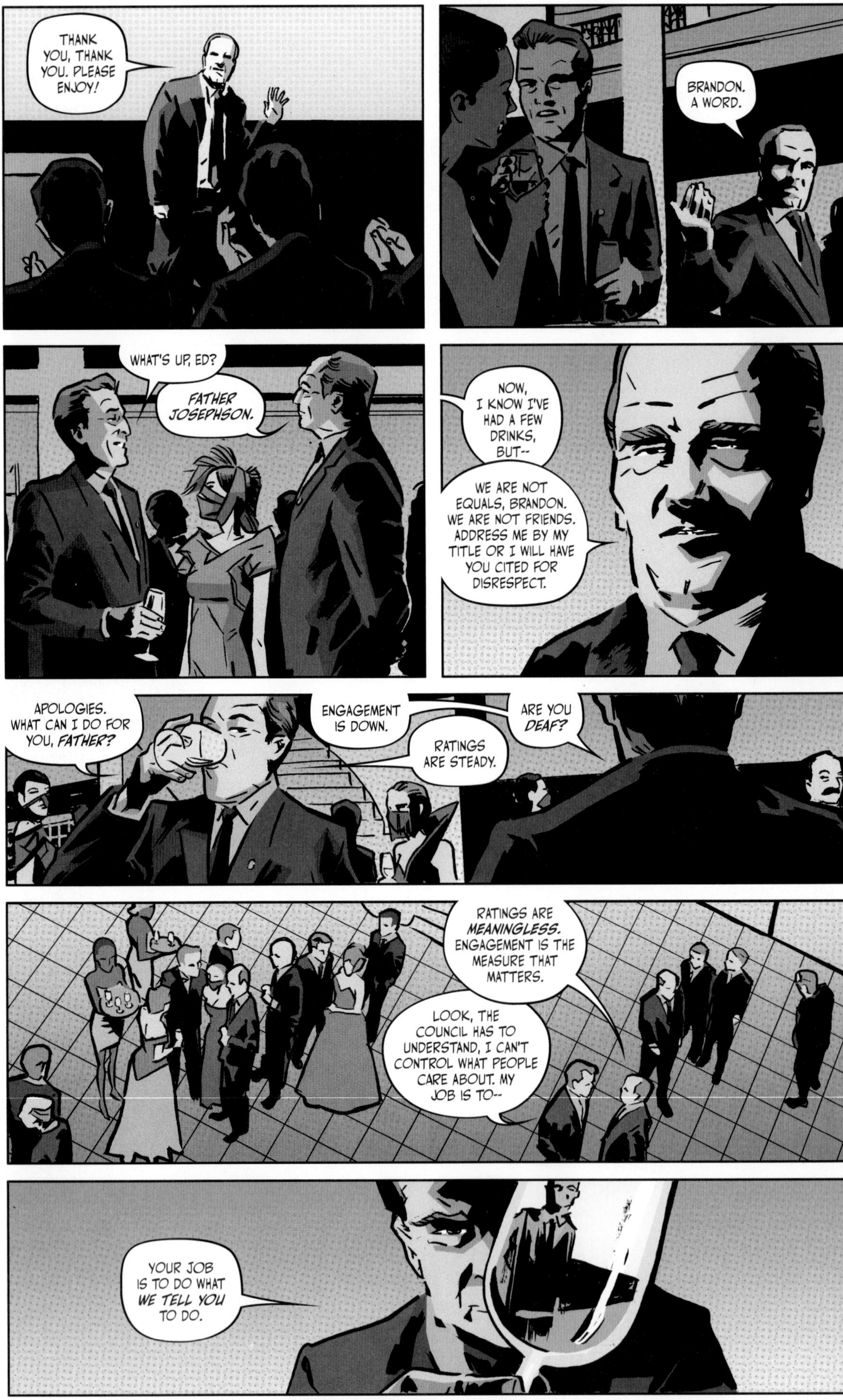

THANK YOU, THANK YOU. PLEASE ENJOY!
BRANDON. A WORD.
WHAT'S UP, ED?
FATHER JOSEPHSON.
NOW, I KNOW I'VE HAD A FEW DRINKS, BUT--
WE ARE NOT EQUALS, BRANDON. WE ARE NOT FRIENDS. ADDRESS ME BY MY TITLE OR I WILL HAVE YOU CITED FOR DISRESPECT.
APOLOGIES. WHAT CAN I DO FOR YOU, FATHER?
ENGAGEMENT IS DOWN.
RATINGS ARE STEADY.
ARE YOU DEAF?
RATINGS ARE MEANINGLESS. ENGAGEMENT IS THE MEASURE THAT MATTERS.
LOOK, THE COUNCIL HAS TO UNDERSTAND, I CAN'T CONTROL WHAT PEOPLE CARE ABOUT. MY JOB IS TO--
YOUR JOB IS TO DO WHAT WE TELL YOU TO DO.

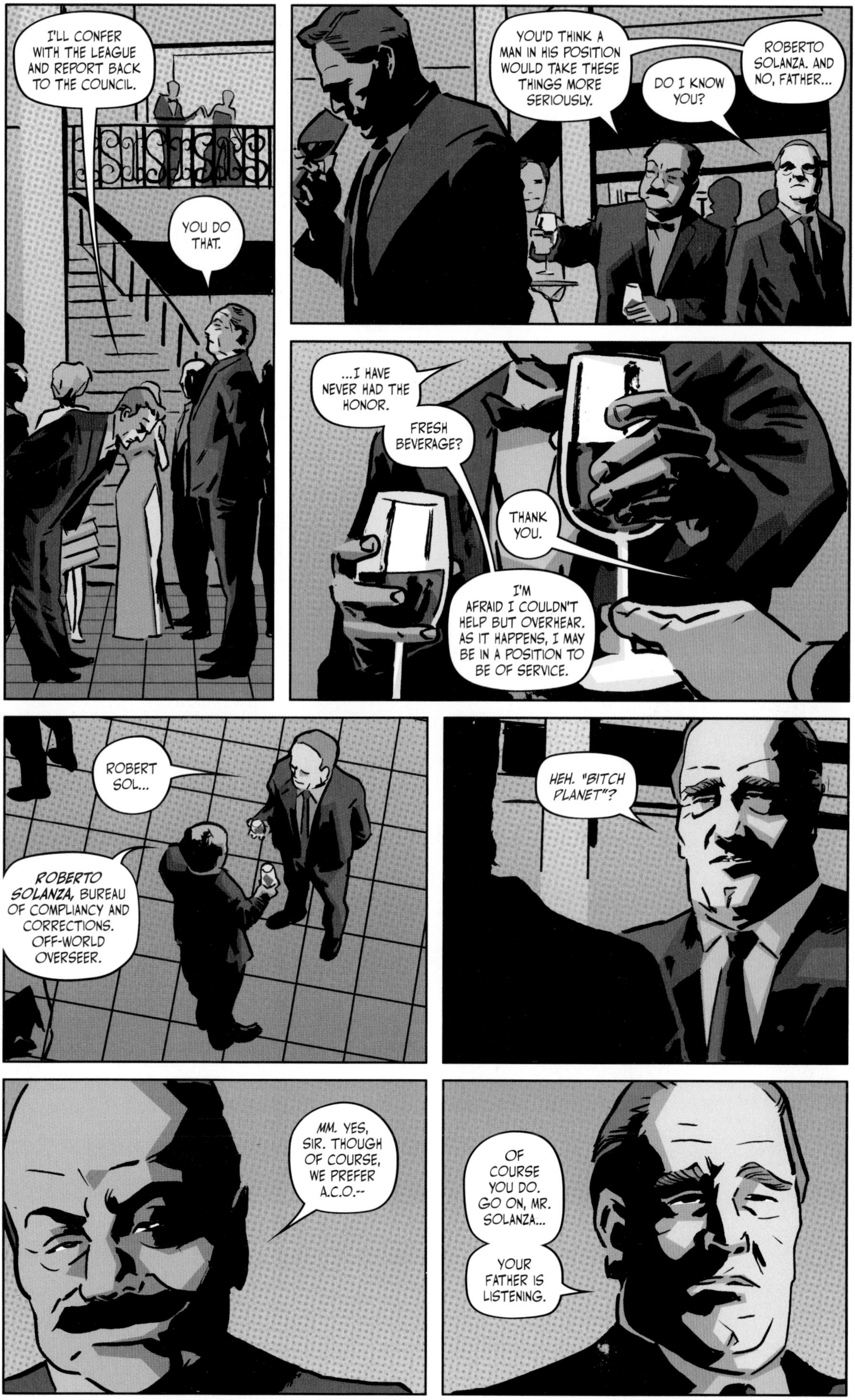
I'LL CONFER WITH THE LEAGUE AND REPORT BACK TO THE COUNCIL.
YOU DO THAT.
YOU'D THINK A MAN IN HIS POSITION WOULD TAKE THESE THINGS MORE SERIOUSLY.
DO I KNOW YOU?
ROBERTO SOLANZA. AND NO, FATHER...
...I HAVE NEVER HAD THE HONOR.
FRESH BEVERAGE?
THANK YOU.
I'M AFRAID I COULDN'T HELP BUT OVERHEAR. AS IT HAPPENS, I MAY BE IN A POSITION TO BE OF SERVICE.
ROBERT SOL...
ROBERTO SOLANZA, BUREAU OF COMPLIANCY AND CORRECTIONS. OFF-WORLD OVERSEER.
HEH. "BITCH PLANET"?
MM. YES, SIR. THOUGH OF COURSE, WE PREFER A.C.O.--
OF COURSE YOU DO. GO ON, MR. SOLANZA...
YOUR FATHER IS LISTENING.

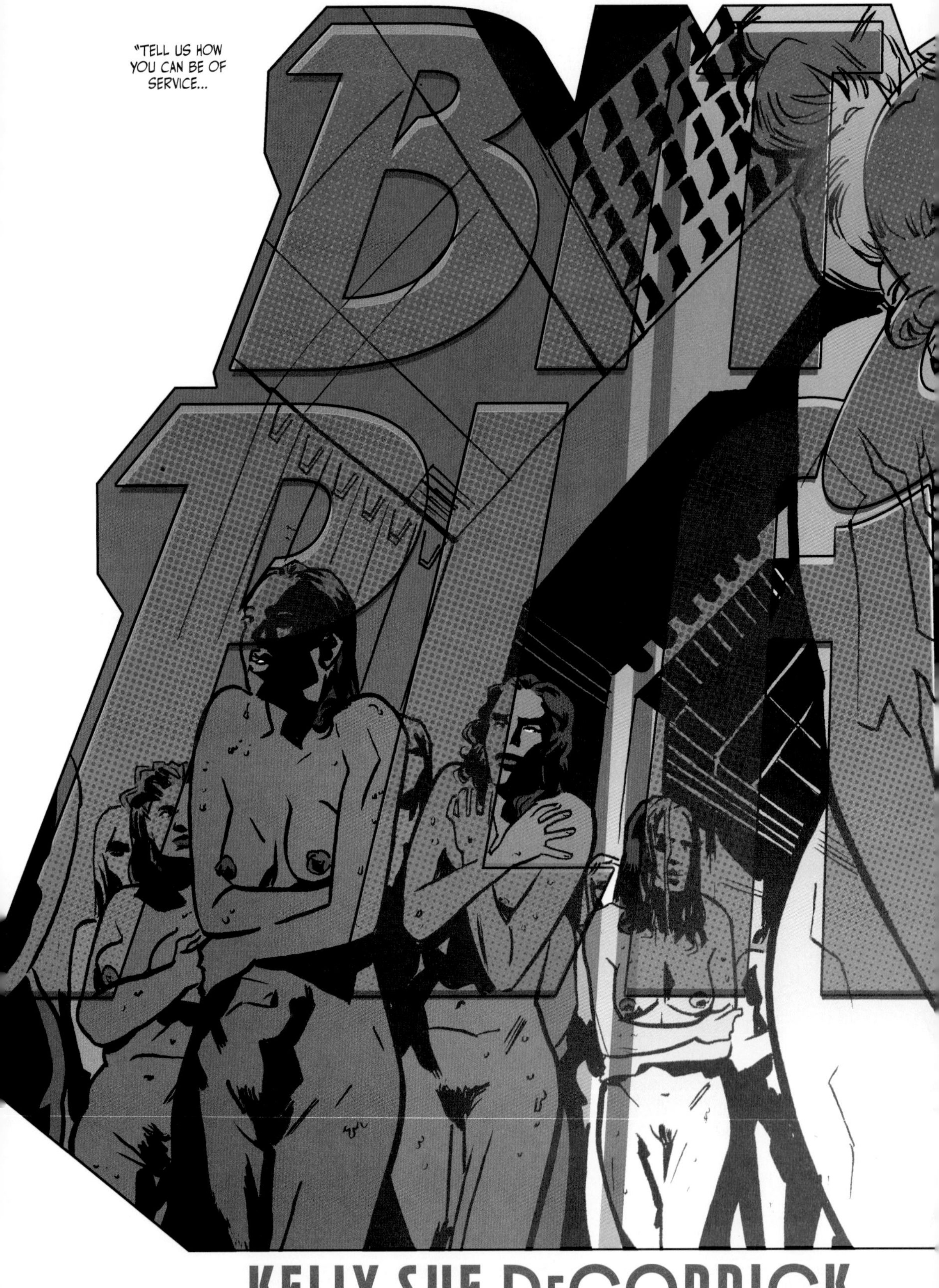
"TELL US HOW YOU CAN BE OF SERVICE...

KELLY SUE DeCONNICK
SCRIPT

CRIS PETER
COLORS

CLAYTON COWLES
LETTERS

RIAN HUGHES
COVER DESIGN & LOGO DESIGN

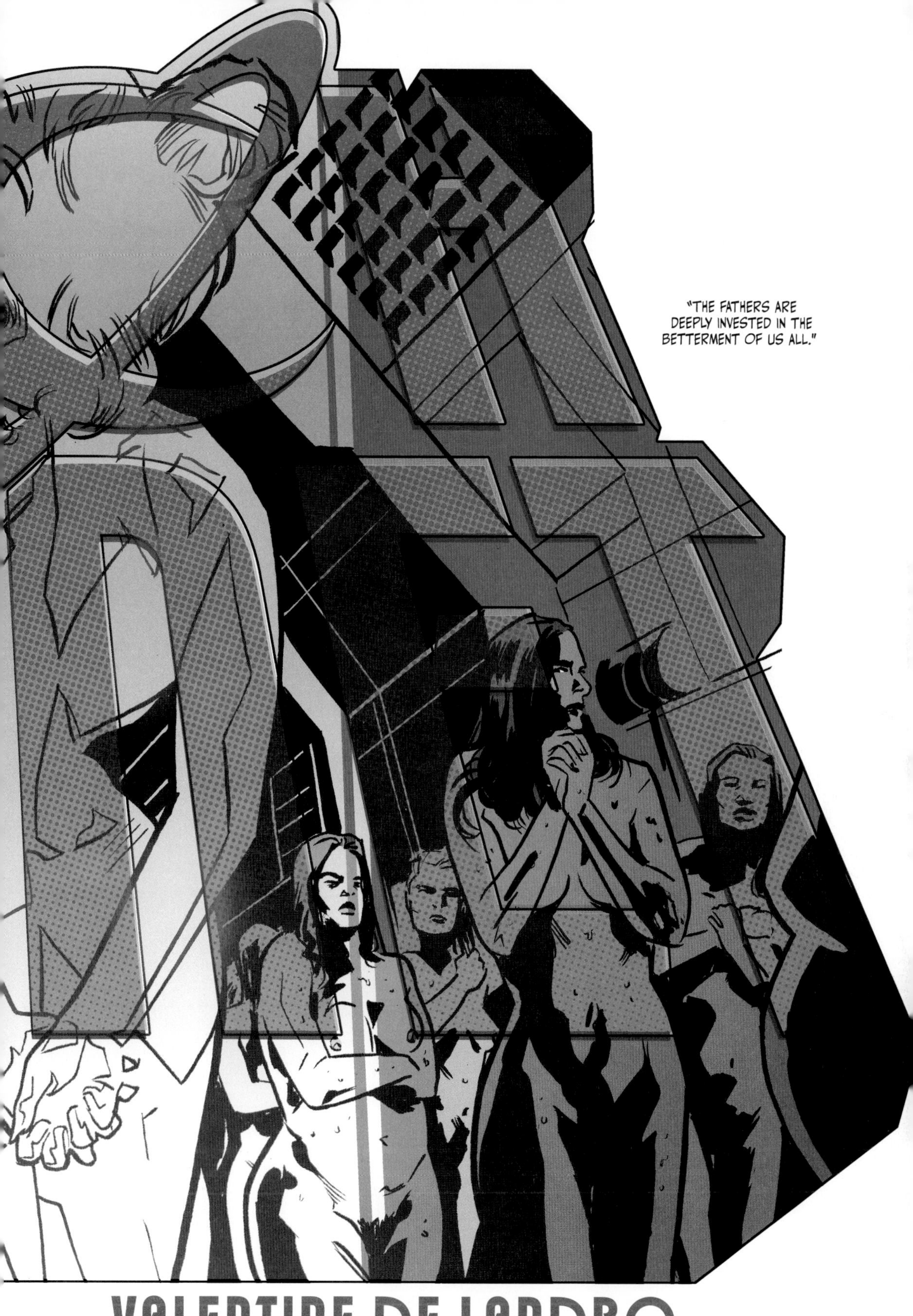
"THE FATHERS ARE
DEEPLY INVESTED IN THE
BETTERMENT OF US ALL."

VALENTINE DE LANDRO
ART/COVERS

LAURENN McCUBBIN
BACKMATTER DESIGN

LAUREN SANKOVITCH
EDITOR

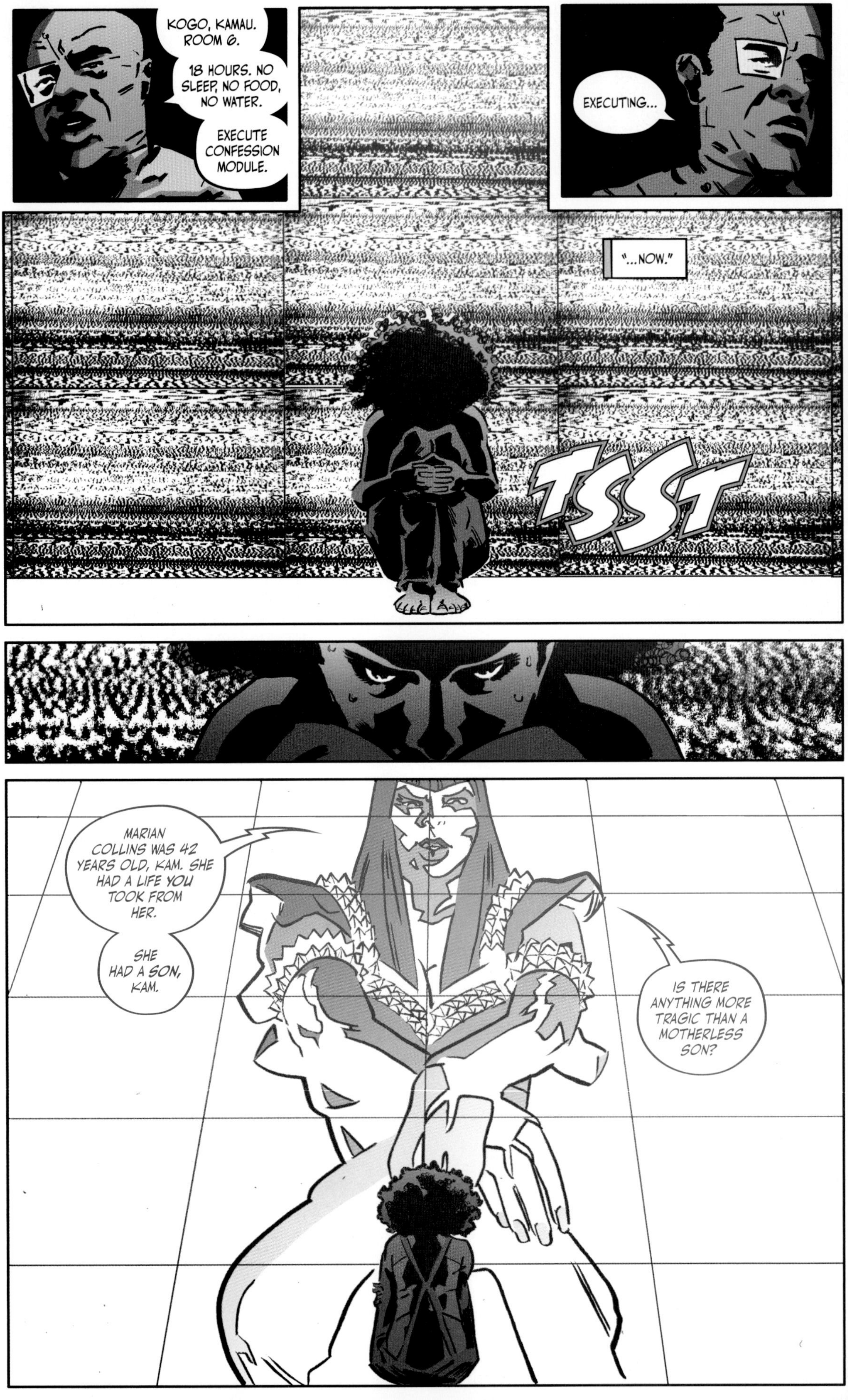
KOGO, KAMAU. ROOM 6.
18 HOURS. NO SLEEP, NO FOOD, NO WATER.
EXECUTE CONFESSION MODULE.
EXECUTING...
"...NOW."
TSST
MARIAN COLLINS WAS 42 YEARS OLD, KAM. SHE HAD A LIFE YOU TOOK FROM HER.
SHE HAD A SON, KAM.
IS THERE ANYTHING MORE TRAGIC THAN A MOTHERLESS SON?

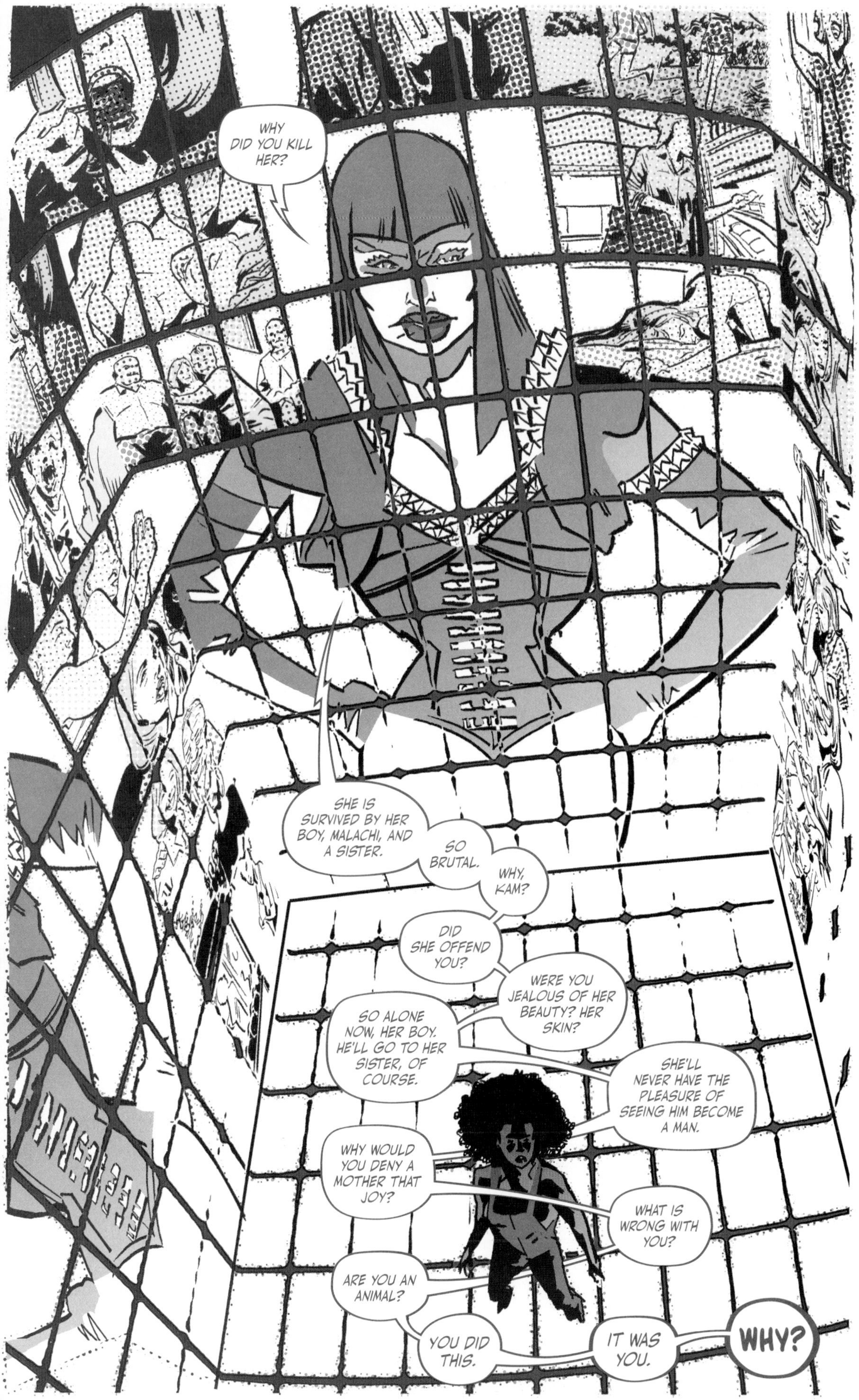
WHY DID YOU KILL HER?
SHE IS SURVIVED BY HER BOY, MALACHI, AND A SISTER.
SO BRUTAL.
WHY, KAM?
DID SHE OFFEND YOU?
WERE YOU JEALOUS OF HER BEAUTY? HER SKIN?
SO ALONE NOW, HER BOY. HE'LL GO TO HER SISTER, OF COURSE.
SHE'LL NEVER HAVE THE PLEASURE OF SEEING HIM BECOME A MAN.
WHY WOULD YOU DENY A MOTHER THAT JOY?
WHAT IS WRONG WITH YOU?
ARE YOU AN ANIMAL?
YOU DID THIS.
IT WAS YOU.
WHY?

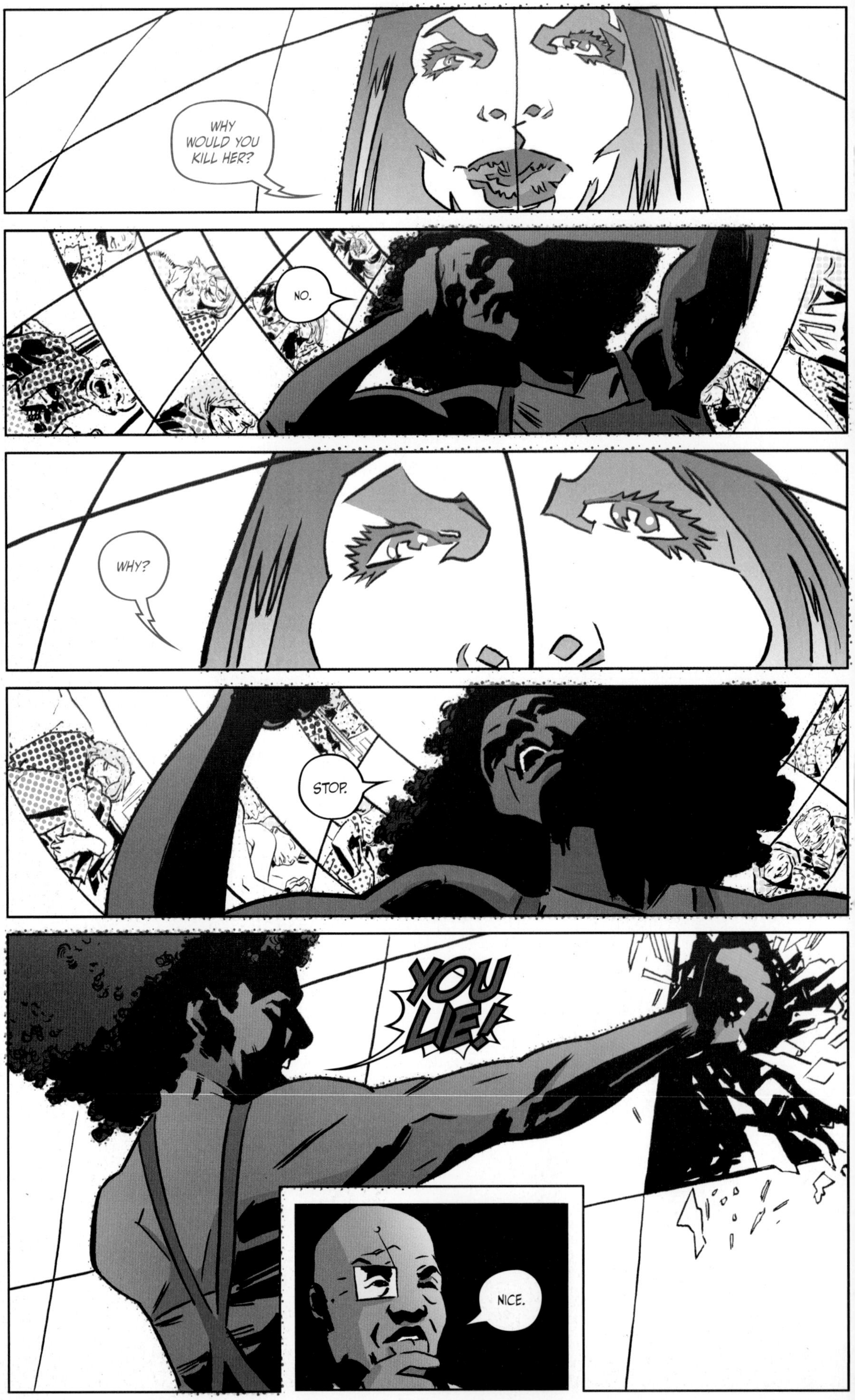
WHY WOULD YOU KILL HER?
NO.
WHY?
STOP.
YOU LIE!
NICE.

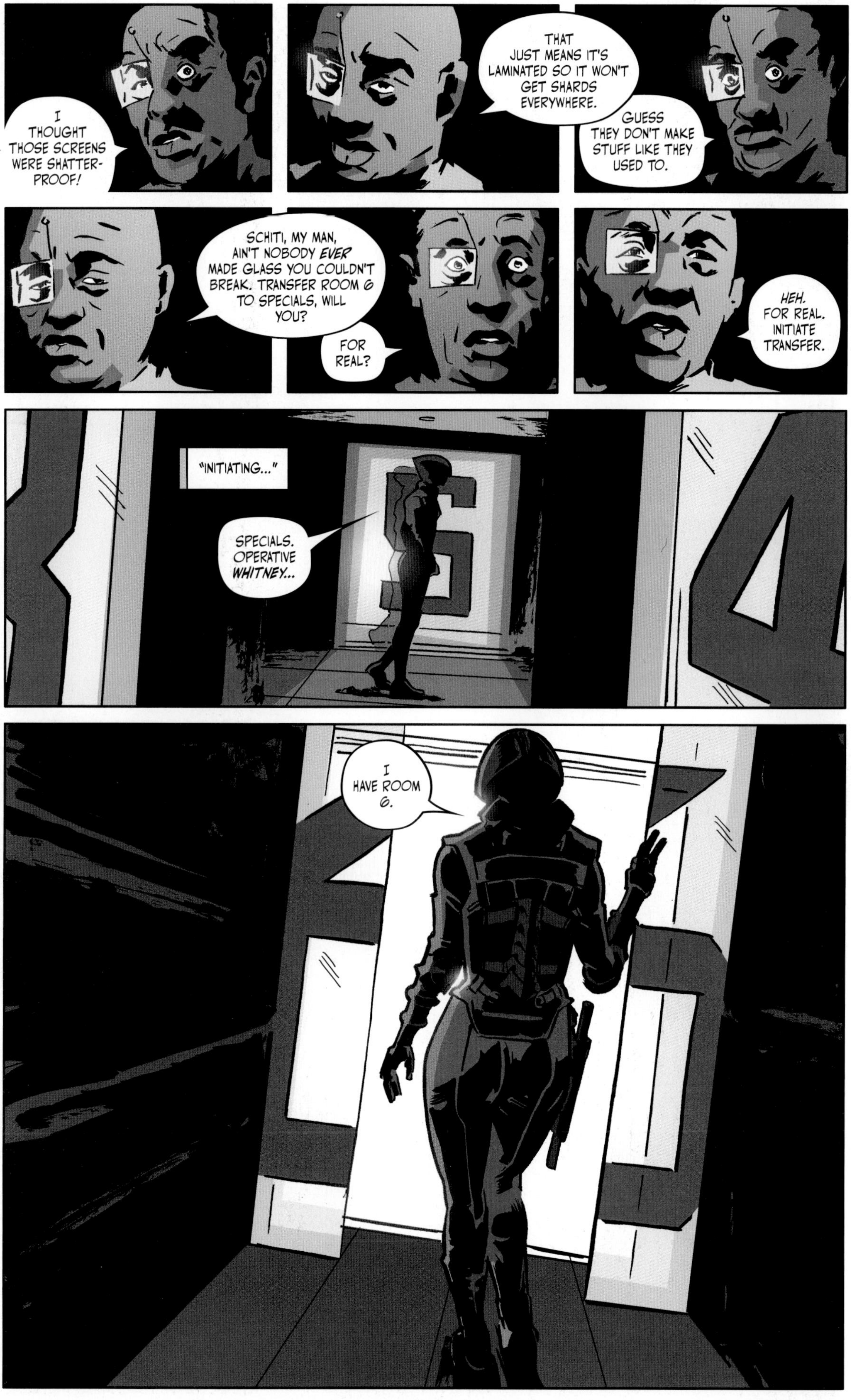
I THOUGHT THOSE SCREENS WERE SHATTER-PROOF!
THAT JUST MEANS IT'S LAMINATED SO IT WON'T GET SHARDS EVERYWHERE.
GUESS THEY DON'T MAKE STUFF LIKE THEY USED TO.
SCHITI, MY MAN, AIN'T NOBODY *EVER* MADE GLASS YOU COULDN'T BREAK. TRANSFER ROOM 6 TO SPECIALS, WILL YOU?
FOR REAL?
HEH. FOR REAL. INITIATE TRANSFER.
"INITIATING..."
SPECIALS. OPERATIVE *WHITNEY*...
I HAVE ROOM 6.

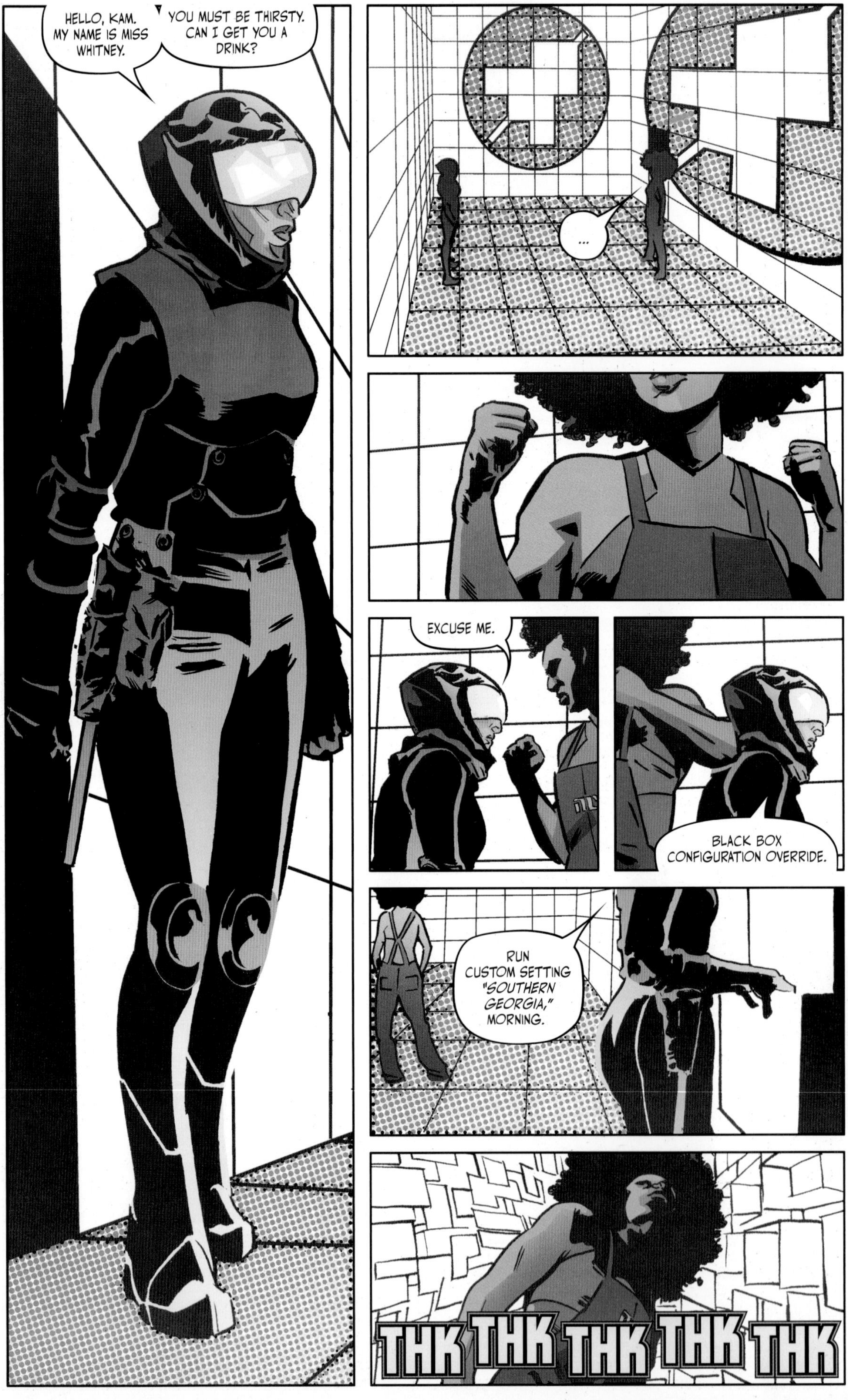
HELLO, KAM. MY NAME IS MISS WHITNEY.
YOU MUST BE THIRSTY. CAN I GET YOU A DRINK?
...
EXCUSE ME.
BLACK BOX CONFIGURATION OVERRIDE.
RUN CUSTOM SETTING "SOUTHERN GEORGIA," MORNING.
THK THK THK THK THK

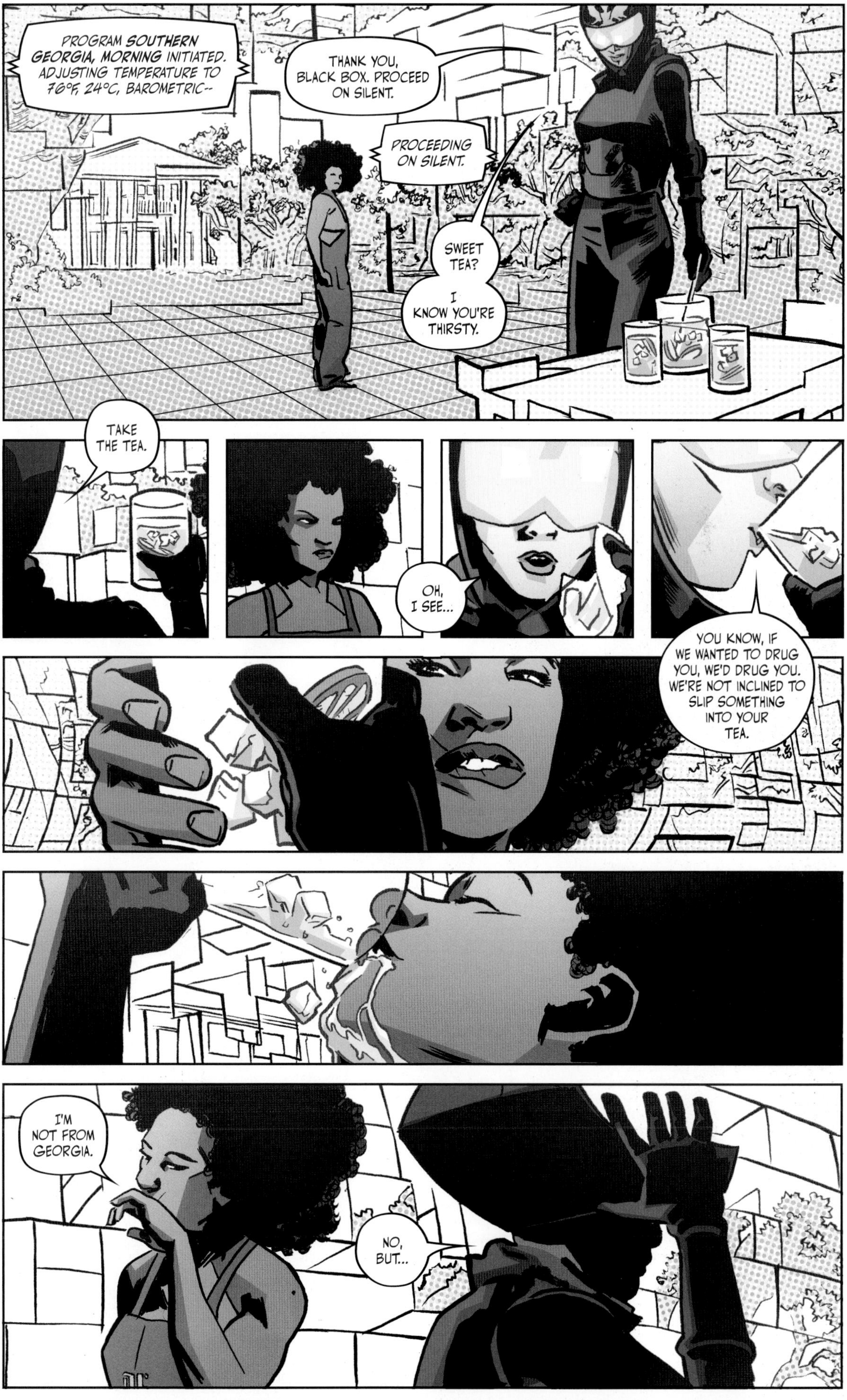
PROGRAM SOUTHERN GEORGIA, MORNING INITIATED. ADJUSTING TEMPERATURE TO 76°F, 24°C, BAROMETRIC--
THANK YOU, BLACK BOX. PROCEED ON SILENT.
PROCEEDING ON SILENT.
SWEET TEA?
I KNOW YOU'RE THIRSTY.
TAKE THE TEA.
OH, I SEE...
YOU KNOW, IF WE WANTED TO DRUG YOU, WE'D DRUG YOU. WE'RE NOT INCLINED TO SLIP SOMETHING INTO YOUR TEA.
I'M NOT FROM GEORGIA.
NO, BUT...

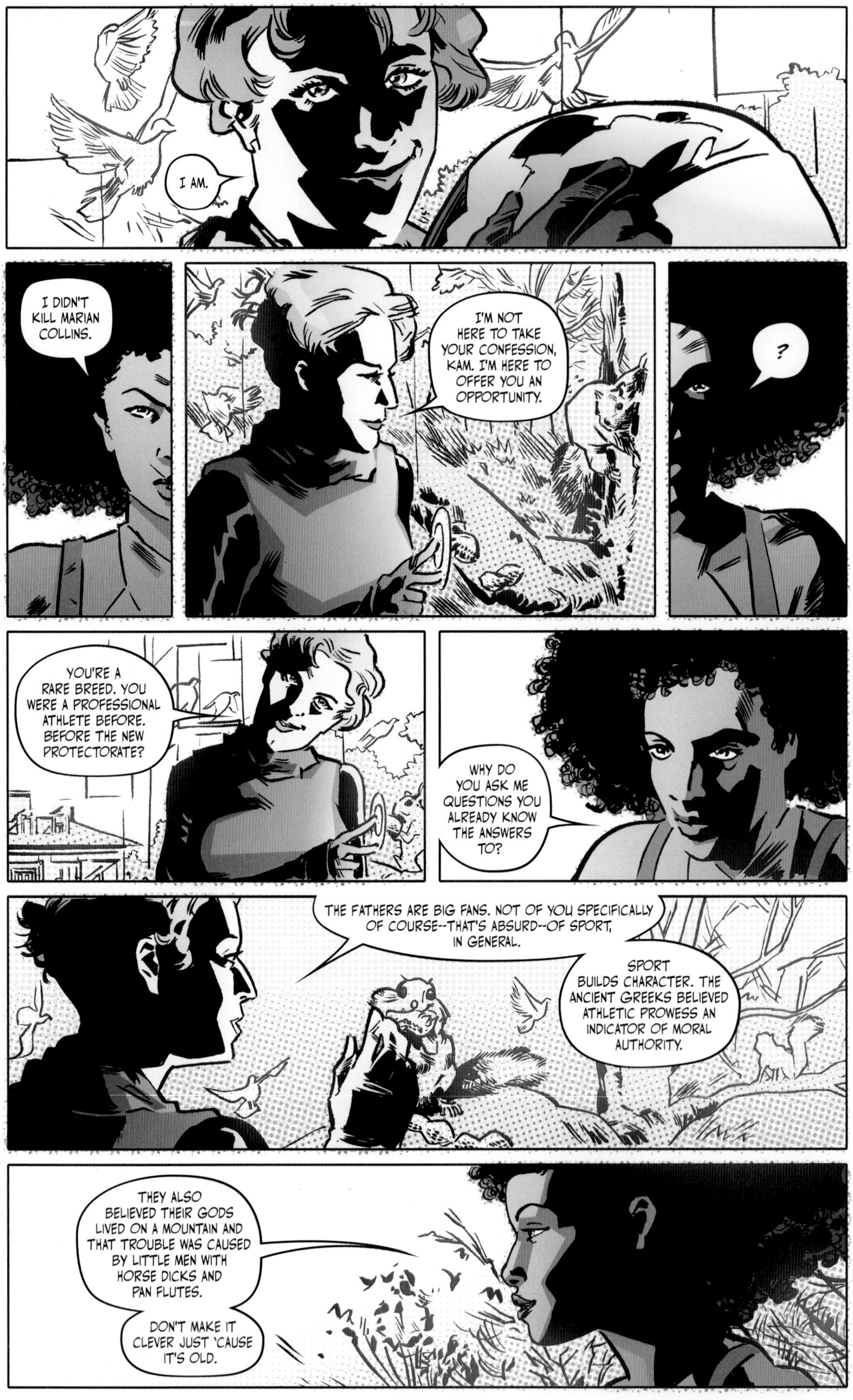
I AM.
I DIDN'T KILL MARIAN COLLINS.
I'M NOT HERE TO TAKE YOUR CONFESSION, KAM. I'M HERE TO OFFER YOU AN OPPORTUNITY.
?
YOU'RE A RARE BREED. YOU WERE A PROFESSIONAL ATHLETE BEFORE. BEFORE THE NEW PROTECTORATE?
WHY DO YOU ASK ME QUESTIONS YOU ALREADY KNOW THE ANSWERS TO?
THE FATHERS ARE BIG FANS. NOT OF YOU SPECIFICALLY OF COURSE--THAT'S ABSURD--OF SPORT, IN GENERAL.
SPORT BUILDS CHARACTER. THE ANCIENT GREEKS BELIEVED ATHLETIC PROWESS AN INDICATOR OF MORAL AUTHORITY.
THEY ALSO BELIEVED THEIR GODS LIVED ON A MOUNTAIN AND THAT TROUBLE WAS CAUSED BY LITTLE MEN WITH HORSE DICKS AND PAN FLUTES.
DON'T MAKE IT CLEVER JUST 'CAUSE IT'S OLD.

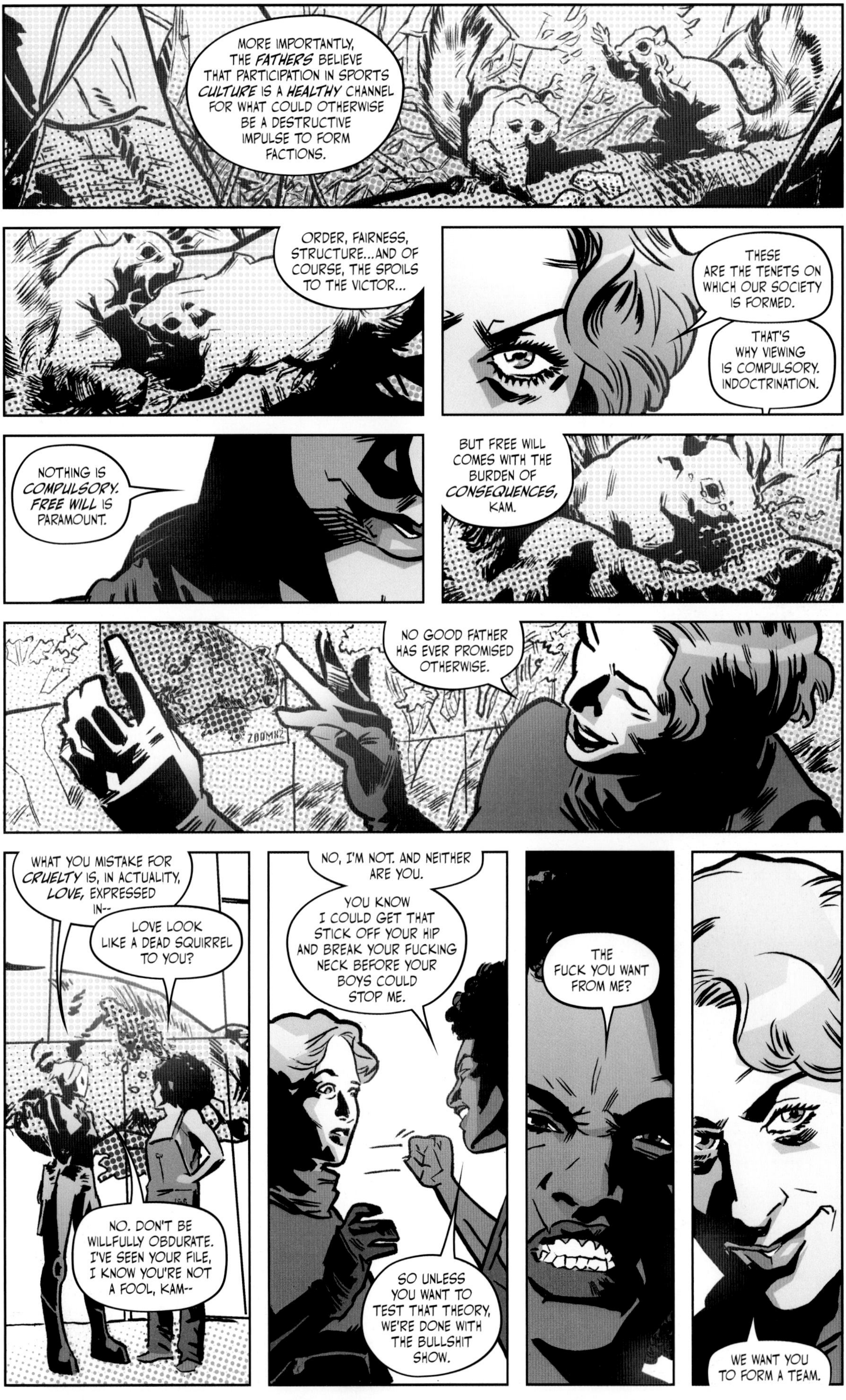

MORE IMPORTANTLY, THE *FATHERS* BELIEVE THAT PARTICIPATION IN SPORTS *CULTURE* IS A *HEALTHY* CHANNEL FOR WHAT COULD OTHERWISE BE A DESTRUCTIVE IMPULSE TO FORM FACTIONS.
ORDER, FAIRNESS, STRUCTURE...AND OF COURSE, THE SPOILS TO THE VICTOR...
THESE ARE THE TENETS ON WHICH OUR SOCIETY IS FORMED.
THAT'S WHY VIEWING IS COMPULSORY. INDOCTRINATION.
NOTHING IS *COMPULSORY. FREE WILL* IS PARAMOUNT.
BUT FREE WILL COMES WITH THE BURDEN OF *CONSEQUENCES,* KAM.
NO GOOD FATHER HAS EVER PROMISED OTHERWISE.
ZOOMNZ
WHAT YOU MISTAKE FOR *CRUELTY* IS, IN ACTUALITY, *LOVE,* EXPRESSED IN--
LOVE LOOK LIKE A DEAD SQUIRREL TO YOU?
NO. DON'T BE WILLFULLY OBDURATE. I'VE SEEN YOUR FILE, I KNOW YOU'RE NOT A FOOL, KAM--
NO, I'M NOT. AND NEITHER ARE YOU.
YOU KNOW I COULD GET THAT STICK OFF YOUR HIP AND BREAK YOUR FUCKING NECK BEFORE YOUR BOYS COULD STOP ME.
SO UNLESS YOU WANT TO TEST THAT THEORY, WE'RE DONE WITH THE BULLSHIT SHOW.
THE FUCK YOU WANT FROM ME?
WE WANT YOU TO FORM A TEAM.

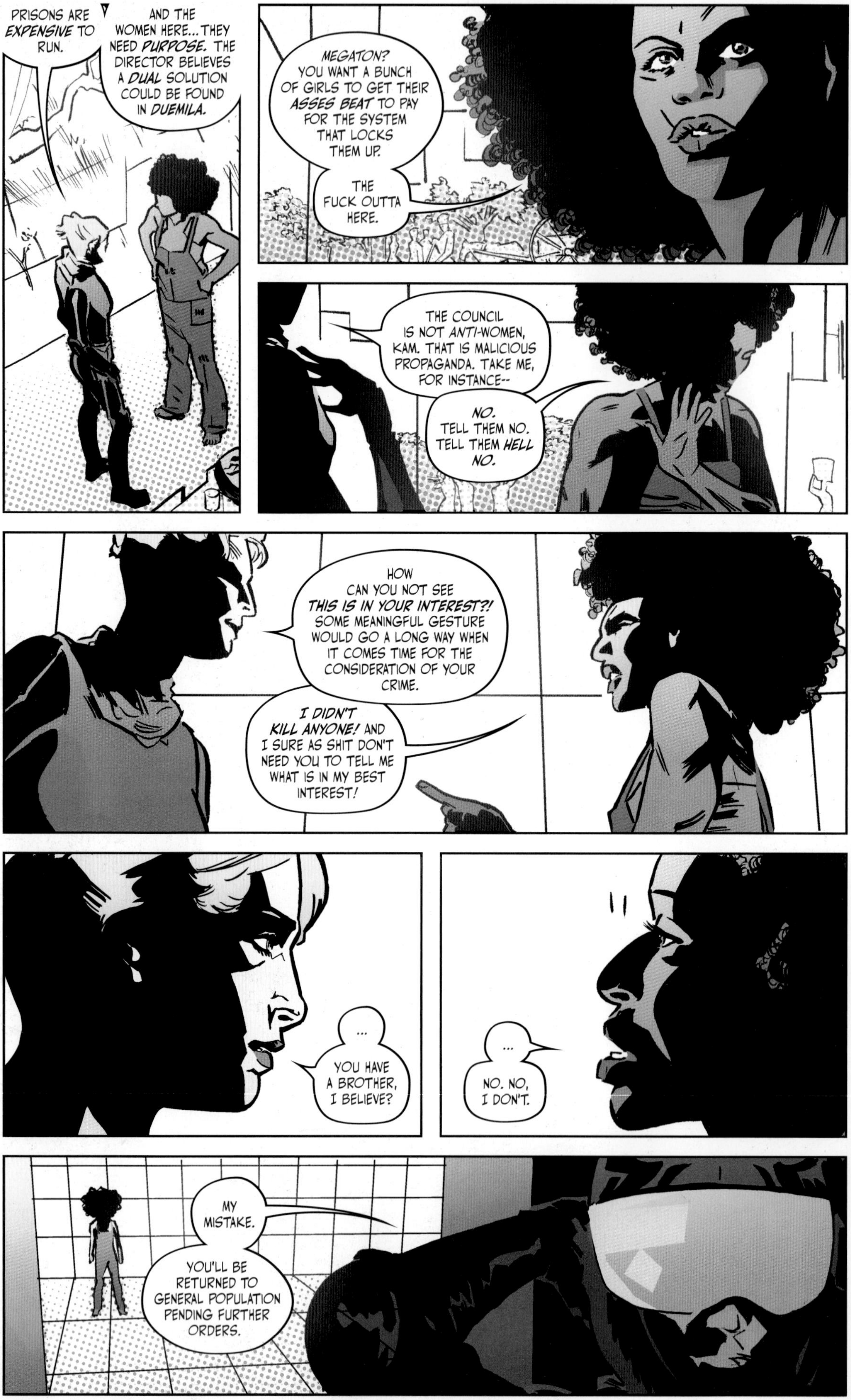
PRISONS ARE EXPENSIVE TO RUN.
AND THE WOMEN HERE... THEY NEED PURPOSE. THE DIRECTOR BELIEVES A DUAL SOLUTION COULD BE FOUND IN DUEMILA.
MEGATON? YOU WANT A BUNCH OF GIRLS TO GET THEIR ASSES BEAT TO PAY FOR THE SYSTEM THAT LOCKS THEM UP.
THE FUCK OUTTA HERE.
THE COUNCIL IS NOT ANTI-WOMEN, KAM. THAT IS MALICIOUS PROPAGANDA. TAKE ME, FOR INSTANCE--
NO. TELL THEM NO. TELL THEM HELL NO.
HOW CAN YOU NOT SEE THIS IS IN YOUR INTEREST?! SOME MEANINGFUL GESTURE WOULD GO A LONG WAY WHEN IT COMES TIME FOR THE CONSIDERATION OF YOUR CRIME.
I DIDN'T KILL ANYONE! AND I SURE AS SHIT DON'T NEED YOU TO TELL ME WHAT IS IN MY BEST INTEREST!
...
YOU HAVE A BROTHER, I BELIEVE?
...
NO. NO, I DON'T.
MY MISTAKE.
YOU'LL BE RETURNED TO GENERAL POPULATION PENDING FURTHER ORDERS.

- VIOLET'S PROPOSAL -

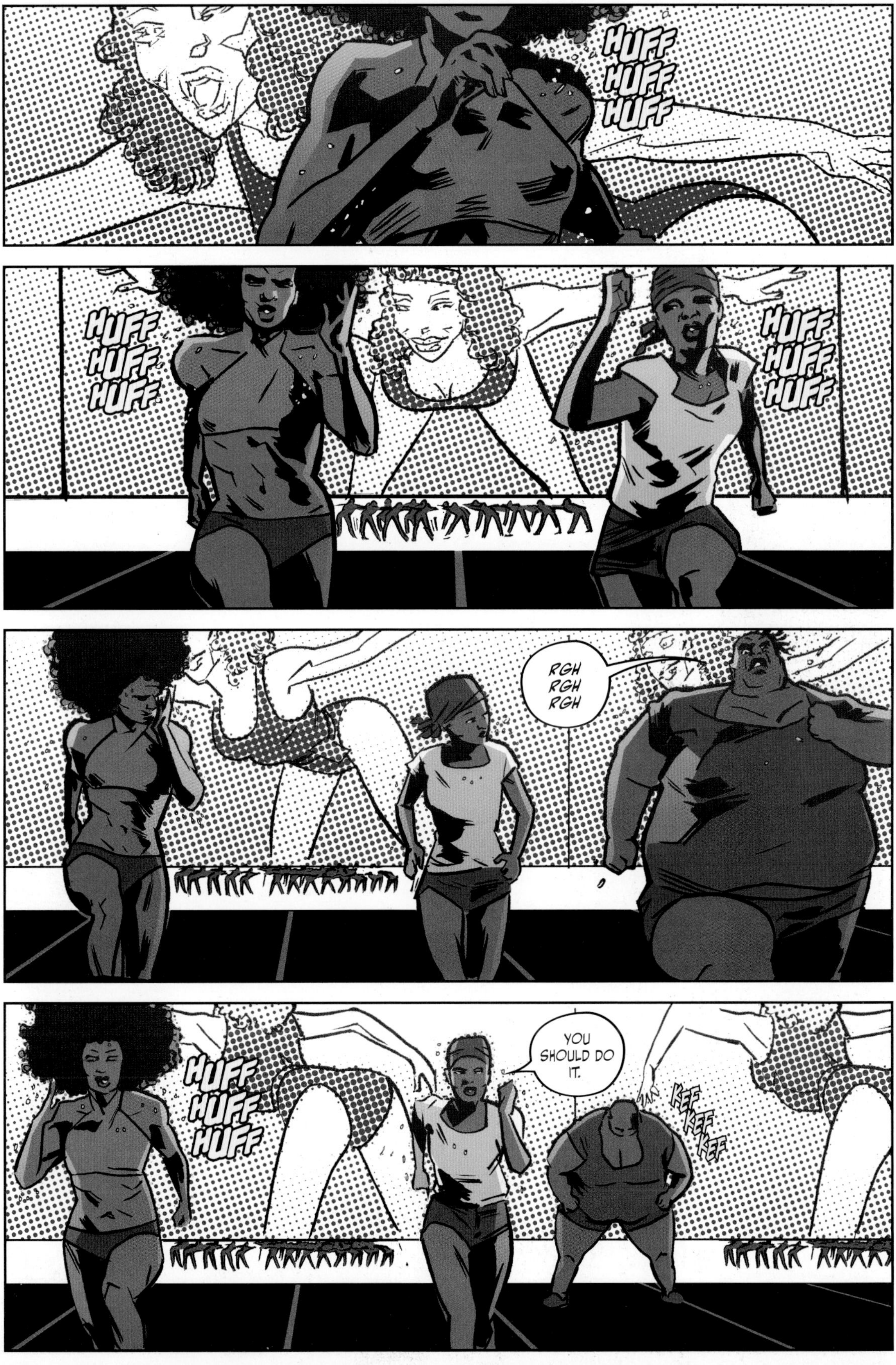
HUFF HUFF HUFF
HUFF HUFF HUFF
HUFF HUFF HUFF
RGH RGH RGH
HUFF HUFF HUFF
YOU SHOULD DO IT.
KEF KEF KEF

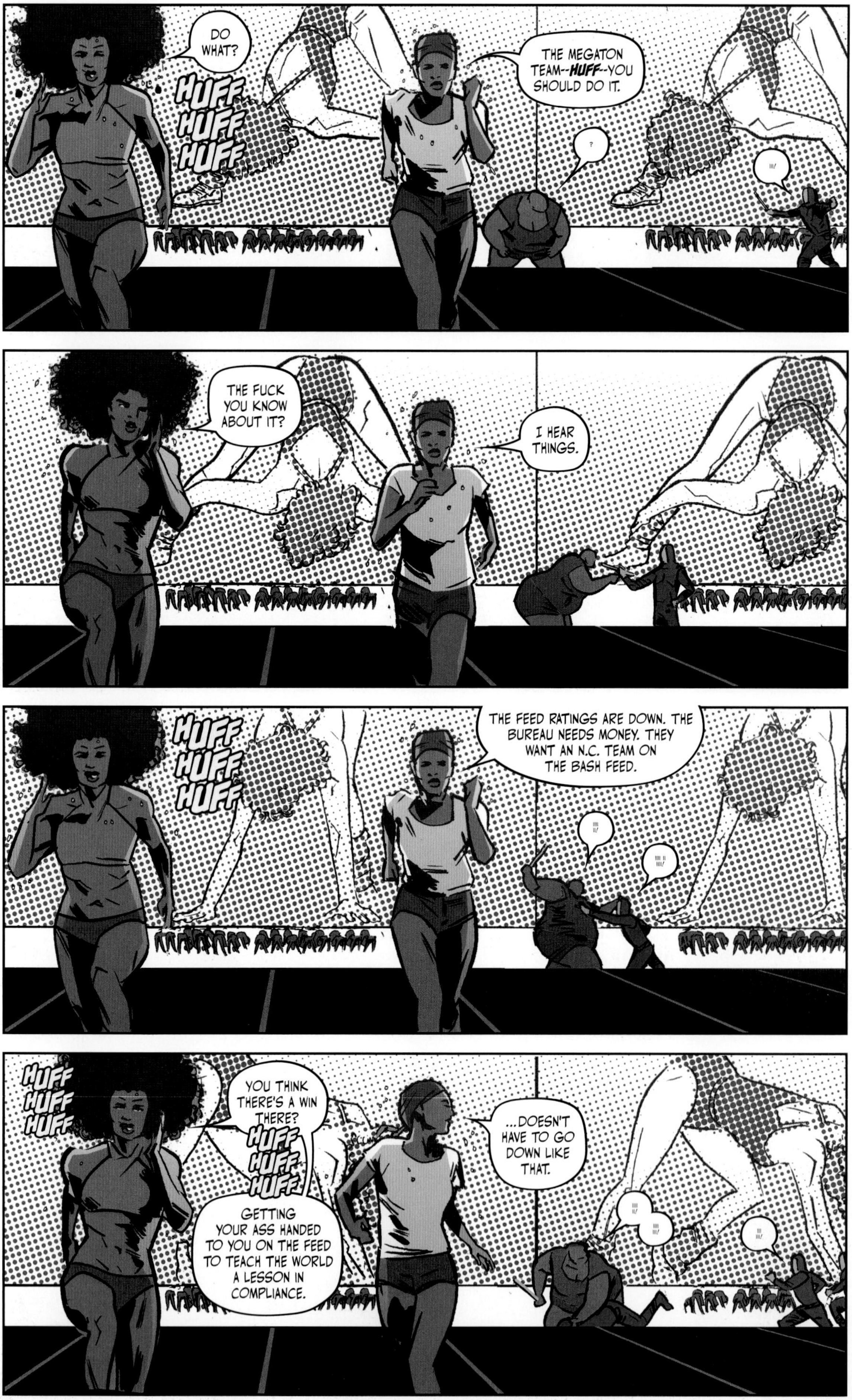
DO WHAT?
HUFF HUFF HUFF
THE MEGATON TEAM--HUFF--YOU SHOULD DO IT.
?
!!!!
THE FUCK YOU KNOW ABOUT IT?
I HEAR THINGS.
HUFF HUFF HUFF
THE FEED RATINGS ARE DOWN. THE BUREAU NEEDS MONEY. THEY WANT AN N.C. TEAM ON THE BASH FEED.
HUFF HUFF HUFF
YOU THINK THERE'S A WIN THERE?
HUFF HUFF HUFF
GETTING YOUR ASS HANDED TO YOU ON THE FEED TO TEACH THE WORLD A LESSON IN COMPLIANCE.
...DOESN'T HAVE TO GO DOWN LIKE THAT.

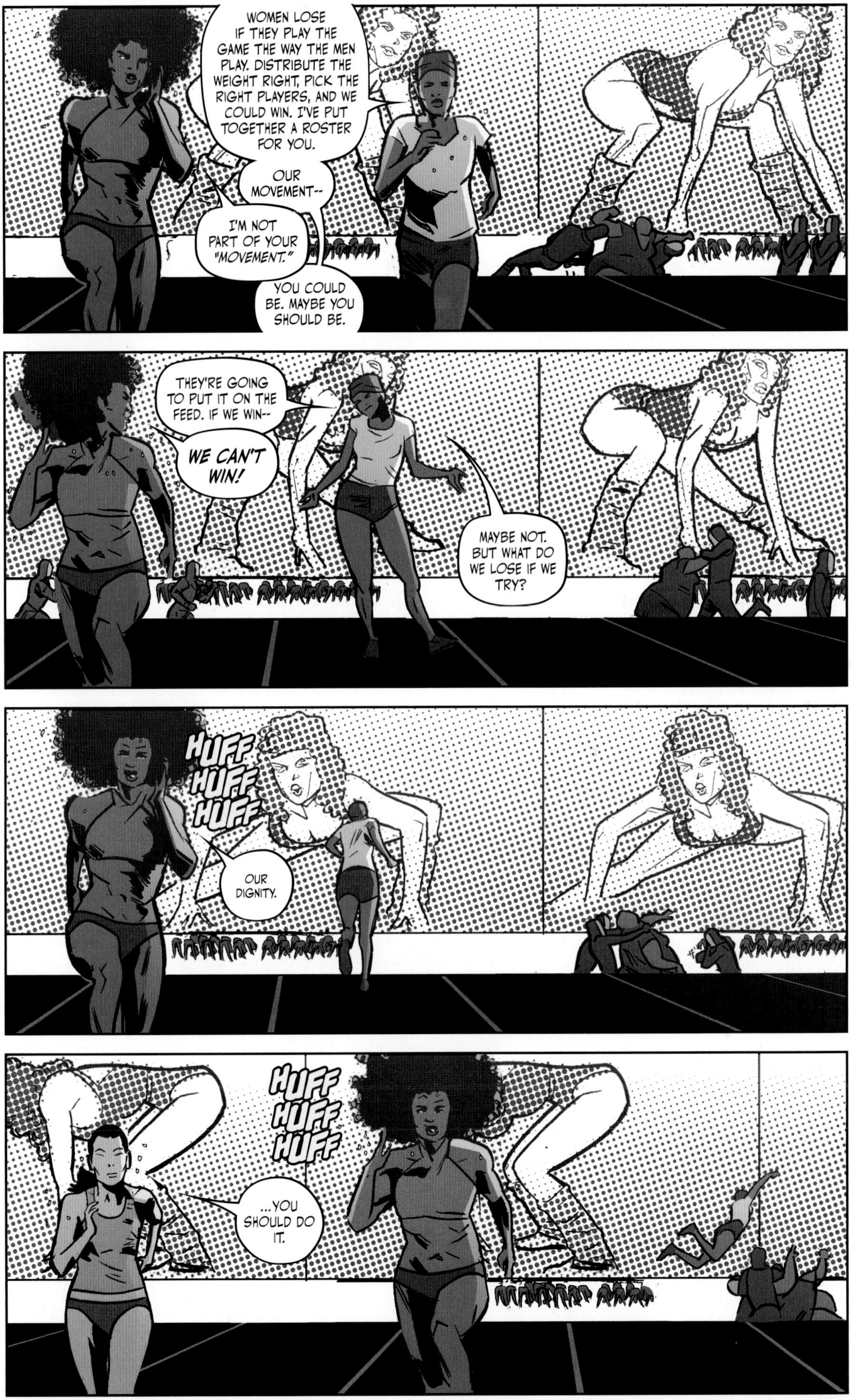
WOMEN LOSE IF THEY PLAY THE GAME THE WAY THE MEN PLAY. DISTRIBUTE THE WEIGHT RIGHT, PICK THE RIGHT PLAYERS, AND WE COULD WIN. I'VE PUT TOGETHER A ROSTER FOR YOU.
OUR MOVEMENT--
I'M NOT PART OF YOUR "MOVEMENT."
YOU COULD BE. MAYBE YOU SHOULD BE.
THEY'RE GOING TO PUT IT ON THE FEED. IF WE WIN--
WE CAN'T WIN!
MAYBE NOT. BUT WHAT DO WE LOSE IF WE TRY?
HUFF HUFF HUFF
OUR DIGNITY.
HUFF HUFF HUFF
...YOU SHOULD DO IT.

- MEIKO'S PROPOSAL -

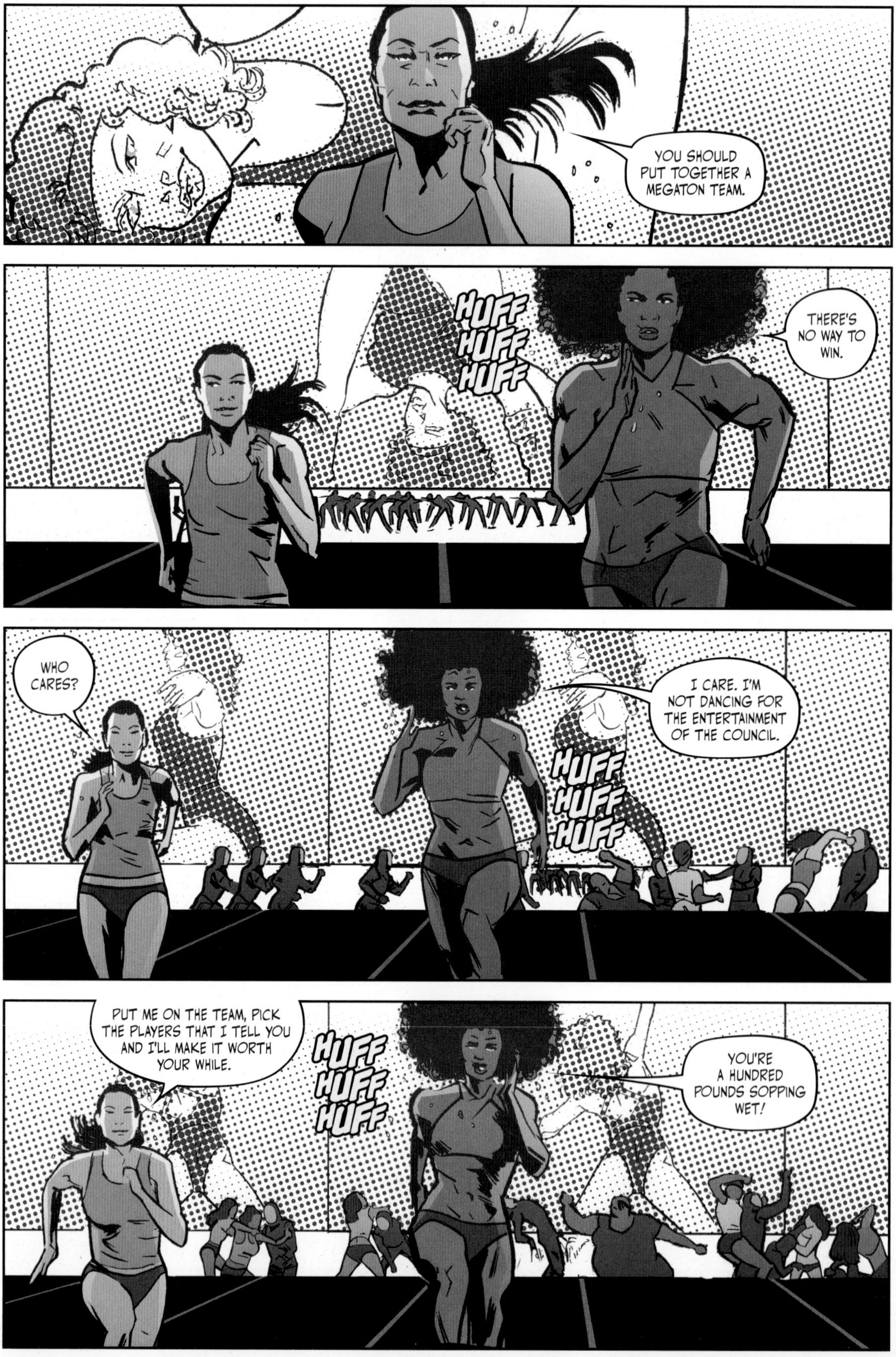
YOU SHOULD PUT TOGETHER A MEGATON TEAM.
HUFF HUFF HUFF
THERE'S NO WAY TO WIN.
WHO CARES?
I CARE. I'M NOT DANCING FOR THE ENTERTAINMENT OF THE COUNCIL.
HUFF HUFF HUFF
PUT ME ON THE TEAM, PICK THE PLAYERS THAT I TELL YOU AND I'LL MAKE IT WORTH YOUR WHILE.
HUFF HUFF HUFF
YOU'RE A HUNDRED POUNDS SOPPING WET!

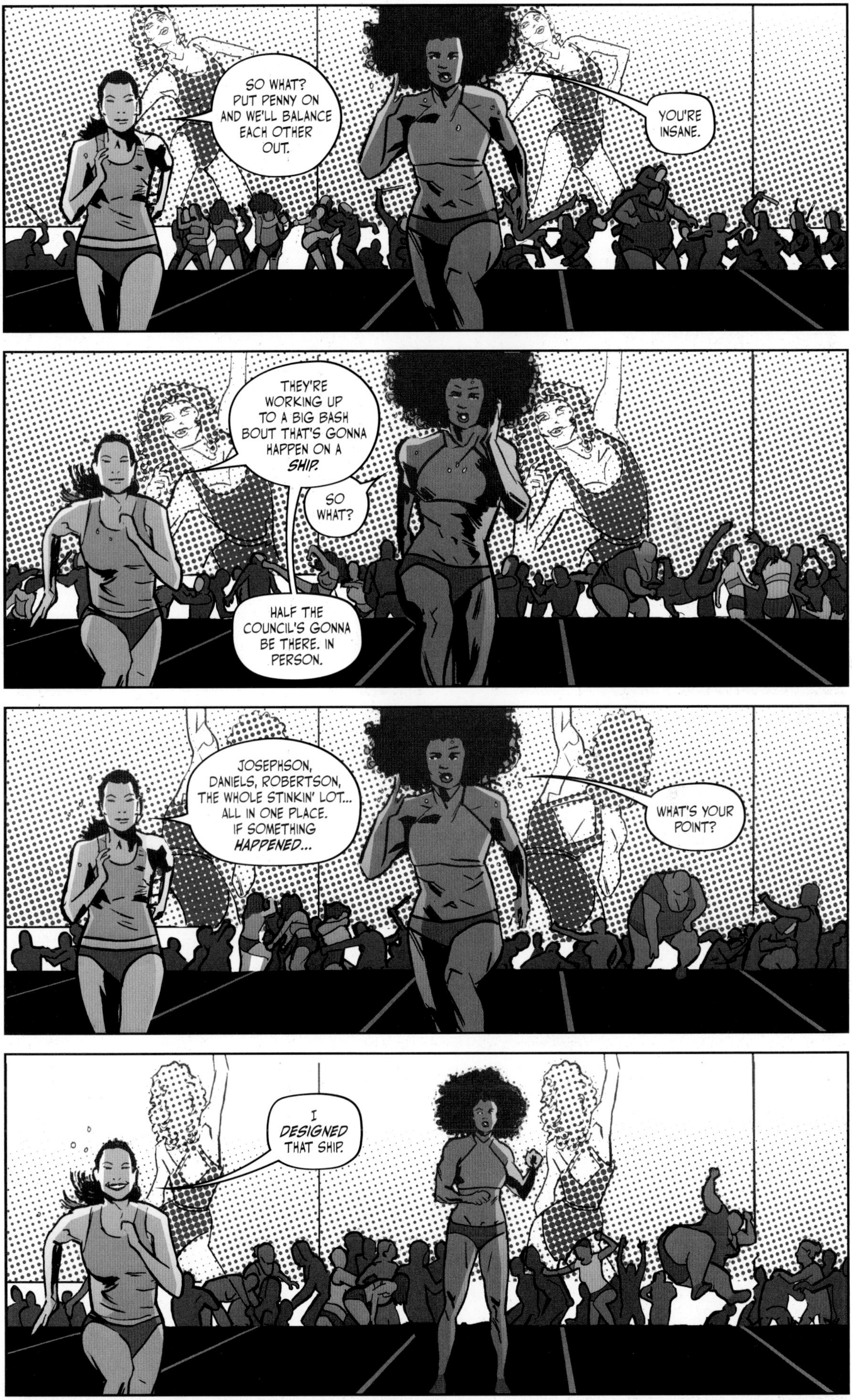
SO WHAT? PUT PENNY ON AND WE'LL BALANCE EACH OTHER OUT.
YOU'RE INSANE.
THEY'RE WORKING UP TO A BIG BASH BOUT THAT'S GONNA HAPPEN ON A *SHIP*.
SO WHAT?
HALF THE COUNCIL'S GONNA BE THERE. IN PERSON.
JOSEPHSON, DANIELS, ROBERTSON, THE WHOLE STINKIN' LOT... ALL IN ONE PLACE. IF SOMETHING *HAPPENED*...
WHAT'S YOUR POINT?
I *DESIGNED* THAT SHIP.

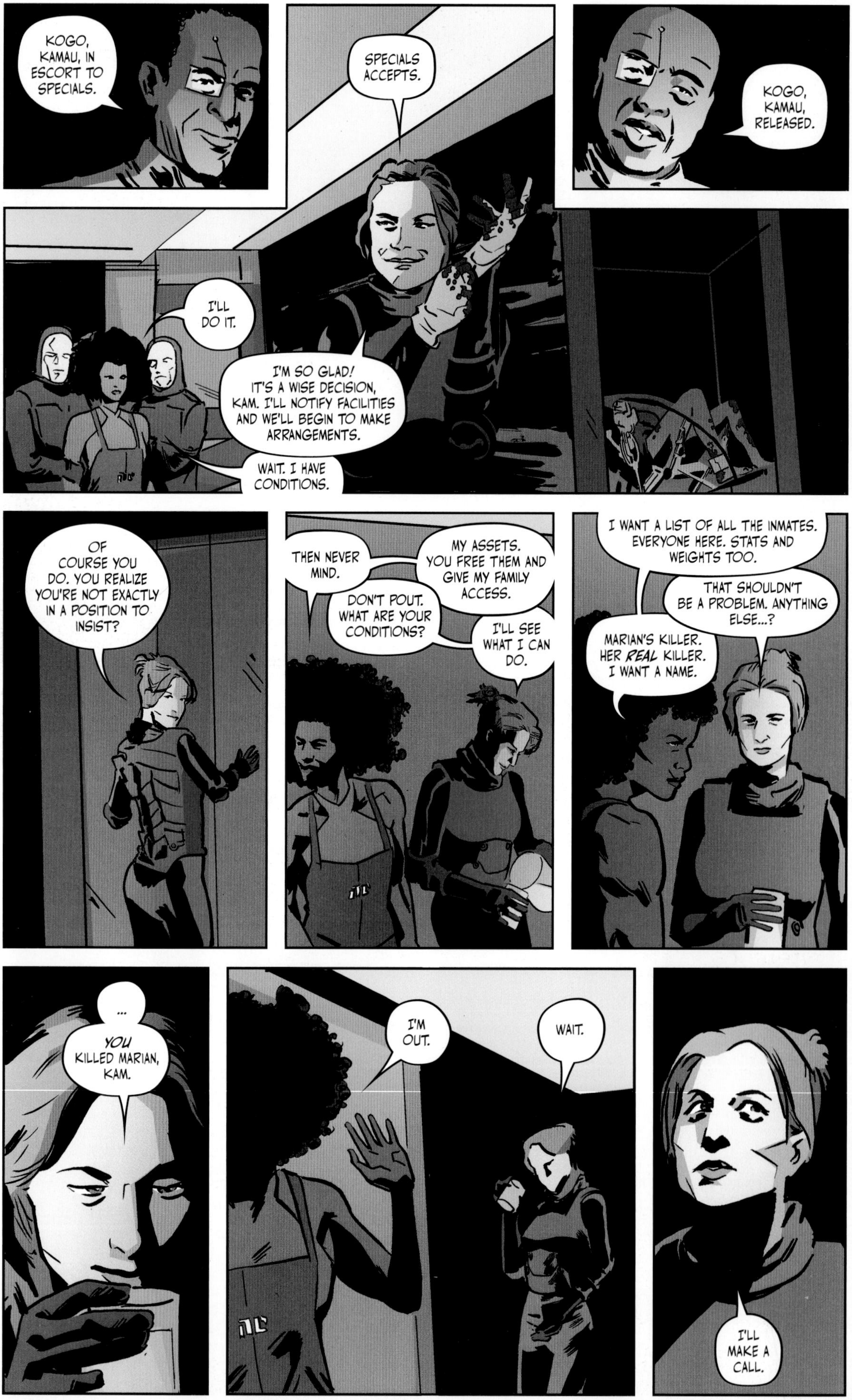
KOGO, KAMAU, IN ESCORT TO SPECIALS.
SPECIALS ACCEPTS.
KOGO, KAMAU, RELEASED.
I'LL DO IT.
I'M SO GLAD! IT'S A WISE DECISION, KAM. I'LL NOTIFY FACILITIES AND WE'LL BEGIN TO MAKE ARRANGEMENTS.
WAIT. I HAVE CONDITIONS.
OF COURSE YOU DO. YOU REALIZE YOU'RE NOT EXACTLY IN A POSITION TO INSIST?
THEN NEVER MIND.
DON'T POUT. WHAT ARE YOUR CONDITIONS?
MY ASSETS. YOU FREE THEM AND GIVE MY FAMILY ACCESS.
I'LL SEE WHAT I CAN DO.
I WANT A LIST OF ALL THE INMATES. EVERYONE HERE. STATS AND WEIGHTS TOO.
THAT SHOULDN'T BE A PROBLEM. ANYTHING ELSE...?
MARIAN'S KILLER. HER *REAL* KILLER. I WANT A NAME.
...
YOU KILLED MARIAN, KAM.
I'M OUT.
WAIT.
I'LL MAKE A CALL.

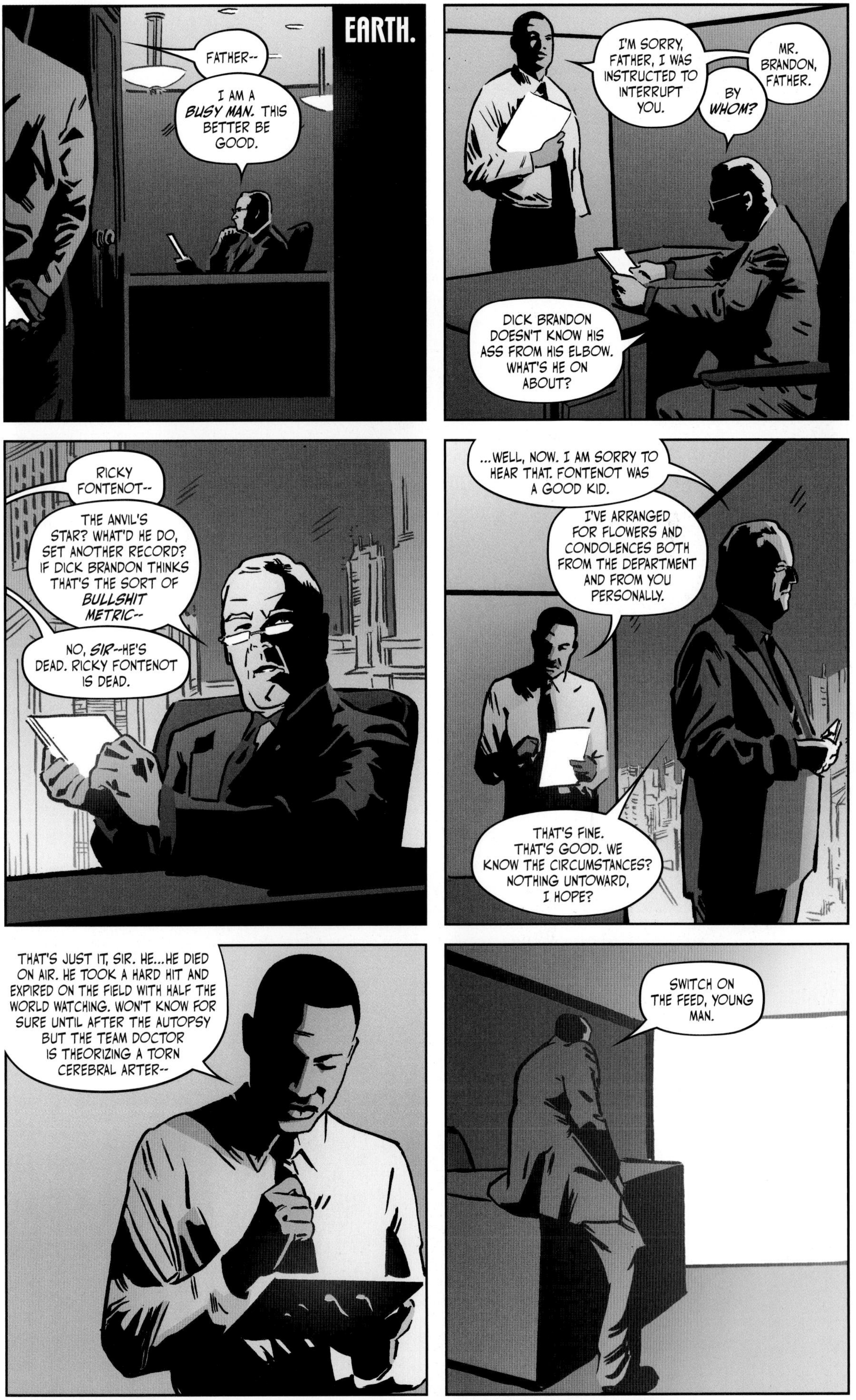
EARTH.
FATHER--
I AM A BUSY MAN. THIS BETTER BE GOOD.
I'M SORRY, FATHER, I WAS INSTRUCTED TO INTERRUPT YOU.
BY WHOM?
MR. BRANDON, FATHER.
DICK BRANDON DOESN'T KNOW HIS ASS FROM HIS ELBOW. WHAT'S HE ON ABOUT?
RICKY FONTENOT--
THE ANVIL'S STAR? WHAT'D HE DO, SET ANOTHER RECORD? IF DICK BRANDON THINKS THAT'S THE SORT OF BULLSHIT METRIC--
NO, SIR--HE'S DEAD. RICKY FONTENOT IS DEAD.
...WELL, NOW. I AM SORRY TO HEAR THAT. FONTENOT WAS A GOOD KID.
I'VE ARRANGED FOR FLOWERS AND CONDOLENCES BOTH FROM THE DEPARTMENT AND FROM YOU PERSONALLY.
THAT'S FINE. THAT'S GOOD. WE KNOW THE CIRCUMSTANCES? NOTHING UNTOWARD, I HOPE?
THAT'S JUST IT, SIR. HE...HE DIED ON AIR. HE TOOK A HARD HIT AND EXPIRED ON THE FIELD WITH HALF THE WORLD WATCHING. WON'T KNOW FOR SURE UNTIL AFTER THE AUTOPSY BUT THE TEAM DOCTOR IS THEORIZING A TORN CEREBRAL ARTER--
SWITCH ON THE FEED, YOUNG MAN.

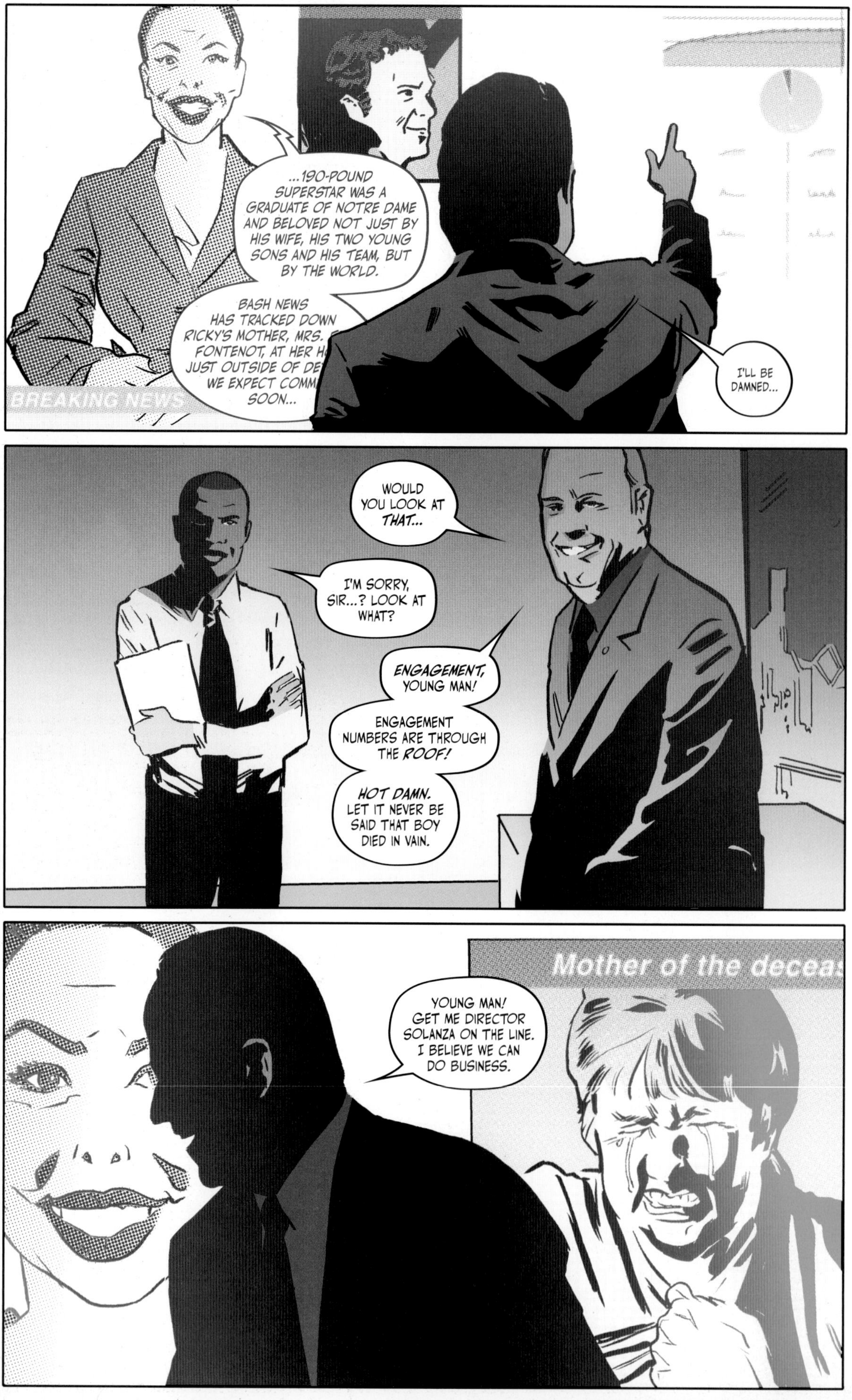
...190-POUND SUPERSTAR WAS A GRADUATE OF NOTRE DAME AND BELOVED NOT JUST BY HIS WIFE, HIS TWO YOUNG SONS AND HIS TEAM, BUT BY THE WORLD.
BASH NEWS HAS TRACKED DOWN RICKY'S MOTHER, MRS.
FONTENOT, AT HER H
JUST OUTSIDE OF DE
WE EXPECT COMM
SOON...
BREAKING NEWS
I'LL BE DAMNED...
WOULD YOU LOOK AT THAT...
I'M SORRY, SIR...? LOOK AT WHAT?
ENGAGEMENT, YOUNG MAN!
ENGAGEMENT NUMBERS ARE THROUGH THE ROOF!
HOT DAMN. LET IT NEVER BE SAID THAT BOY DIED IN VAIN.
Mother of the deceas
YOUNG MAN! GET ME DIRECTOR SOLANZA ON THE LINE. I BELIEVE WE CAN DO BUSINESS.

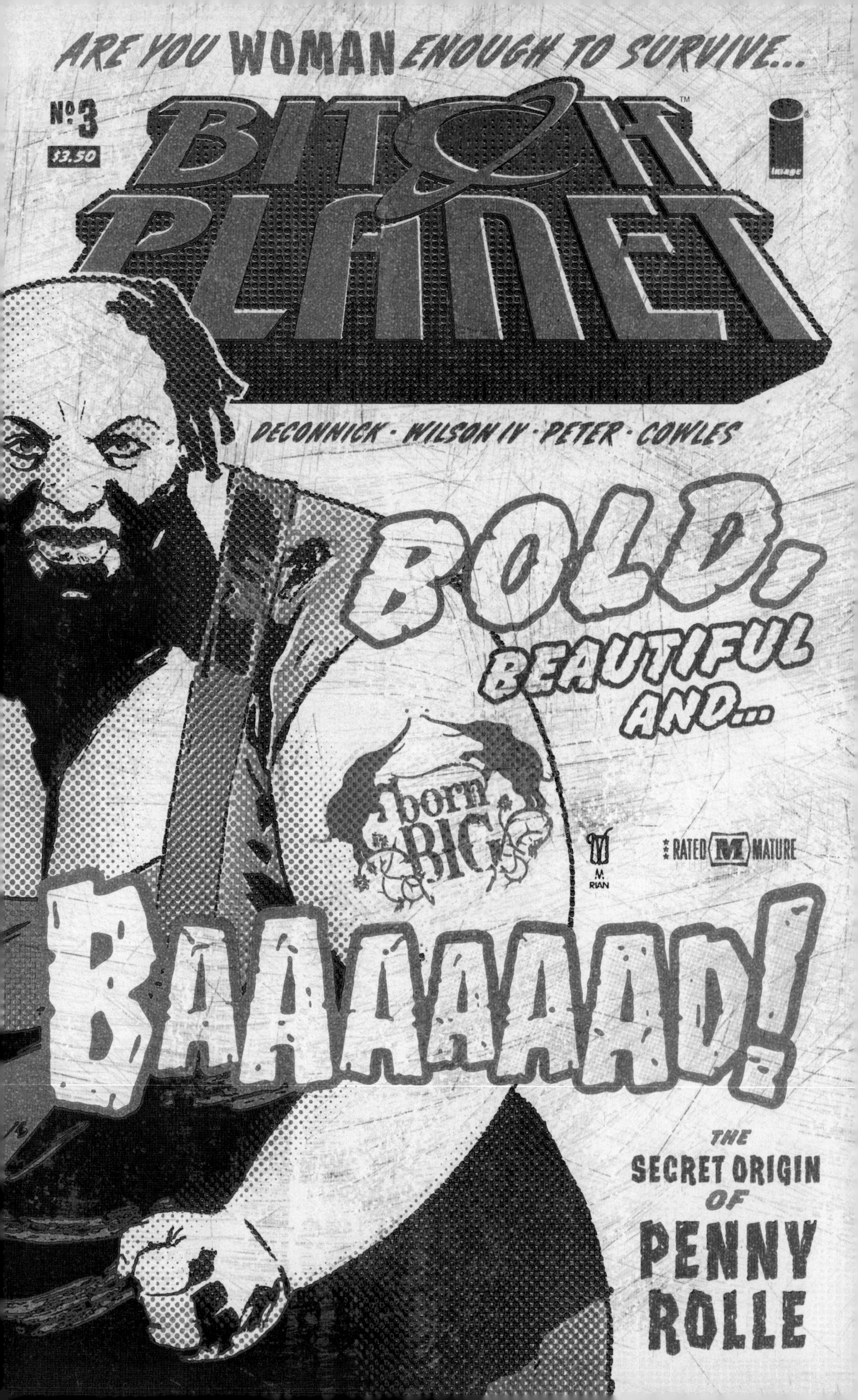
ARE YOU WOMAN ENOUGH TO SURVIVE...
Nº3
$3.50
BITCH PLANET™
DECONNICK · WILSON IV · PETER · COWLES
BOLD, BEAUTIFUL AND...
born BIG
RATED M MATURE
BAAAAAD!
THE SECRET ORIGIN OF PENNY ROLLE

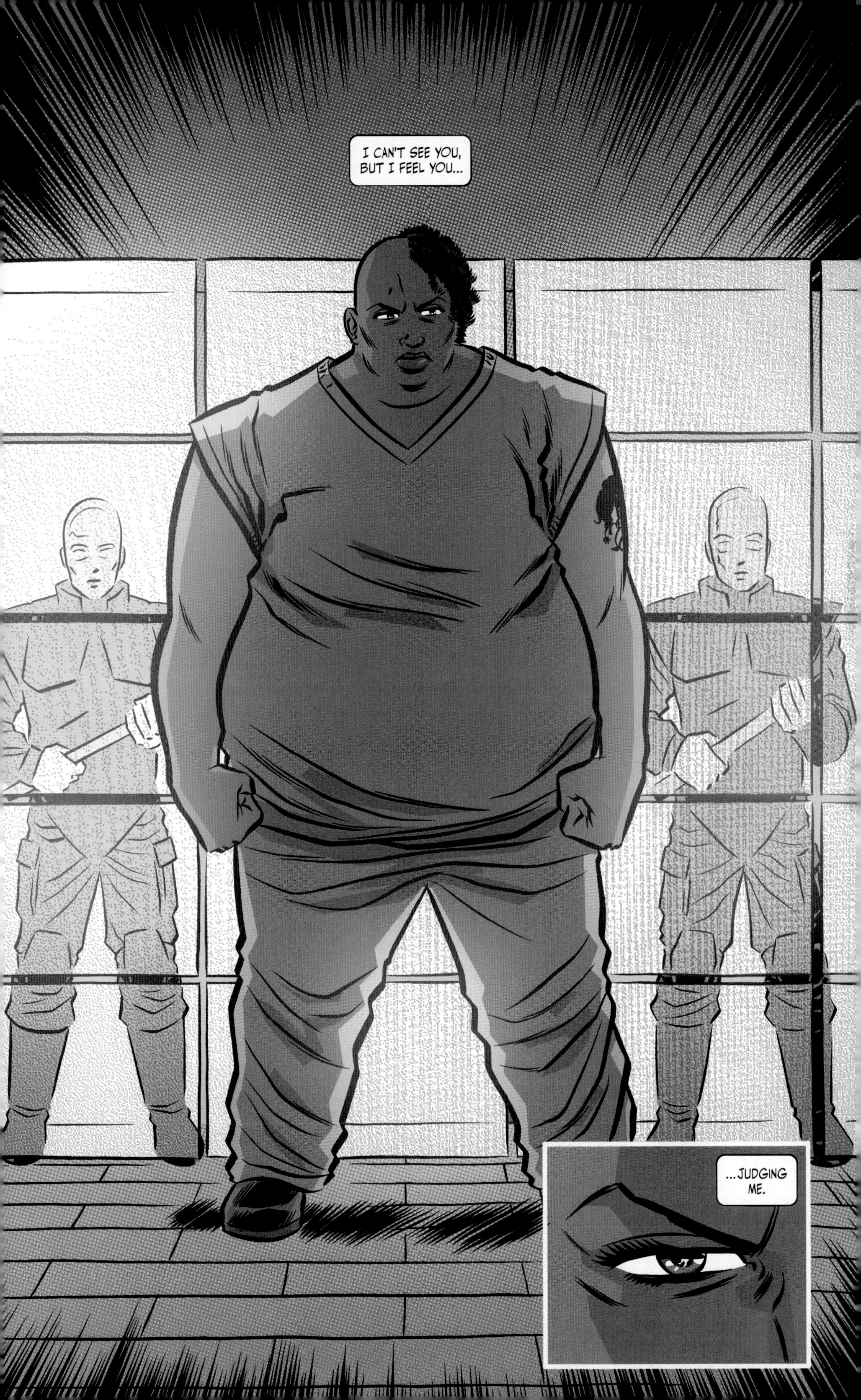
I CAN'T SEE YOU, BUT I FEEL YOU...
...JUDGING ME.

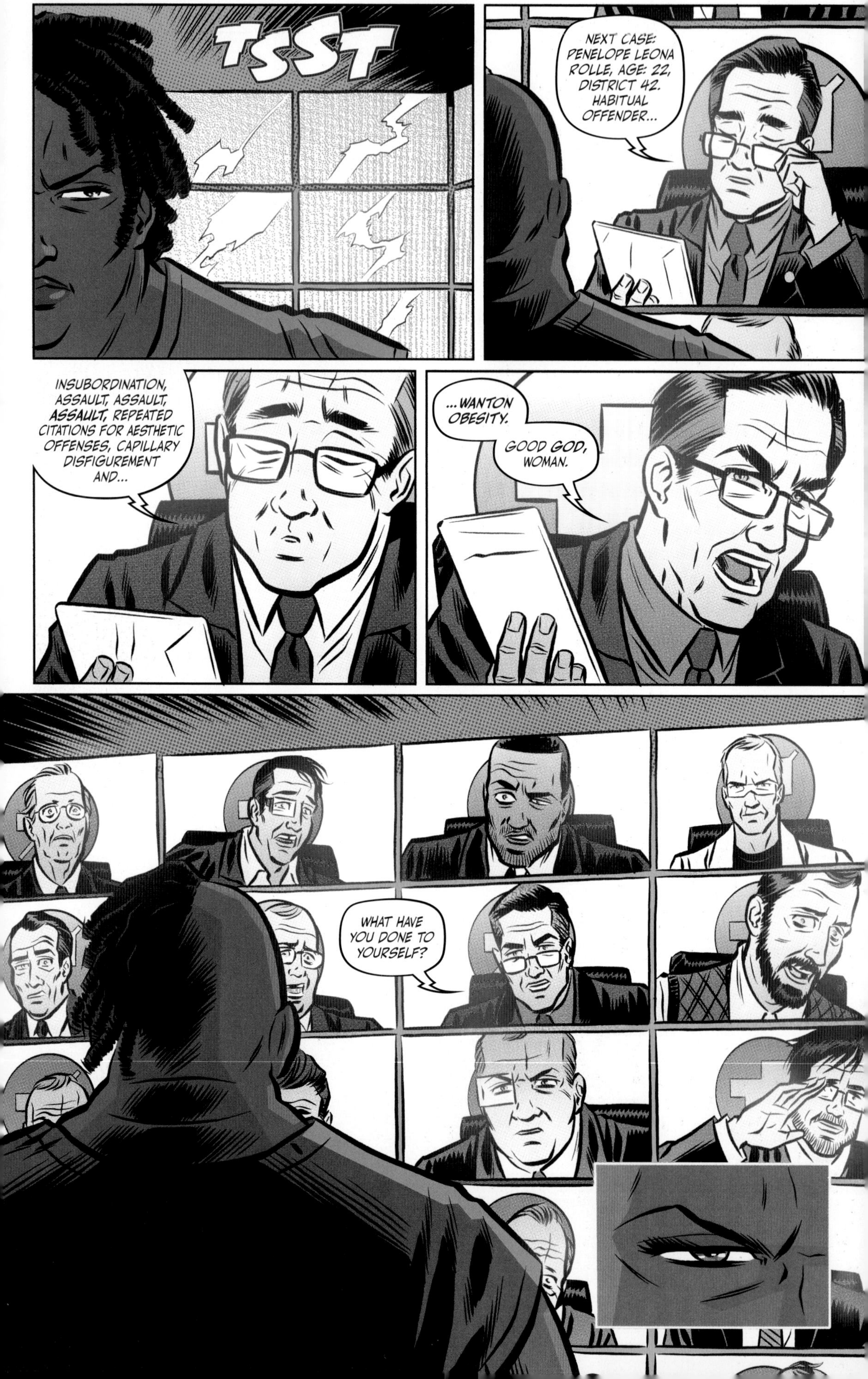
TSST
NEXT CASE: PENELOPE LEONA ROLLE, AGE: 22, DISTRICT 42. HABITUAL OFFENDER...
INSUBORDINATION, ASSAULT, ASSAULT, **ASSAULT**, REPEATED CITATIONS FOR AESTHETIC OFFENSES, CAPILLARY DISFIGUREMENT AND...
...WANTON OBESITY.
GOOD *GOD*, WOMAN.
WHAT HAVE YOU DONE TO YOURSELF?

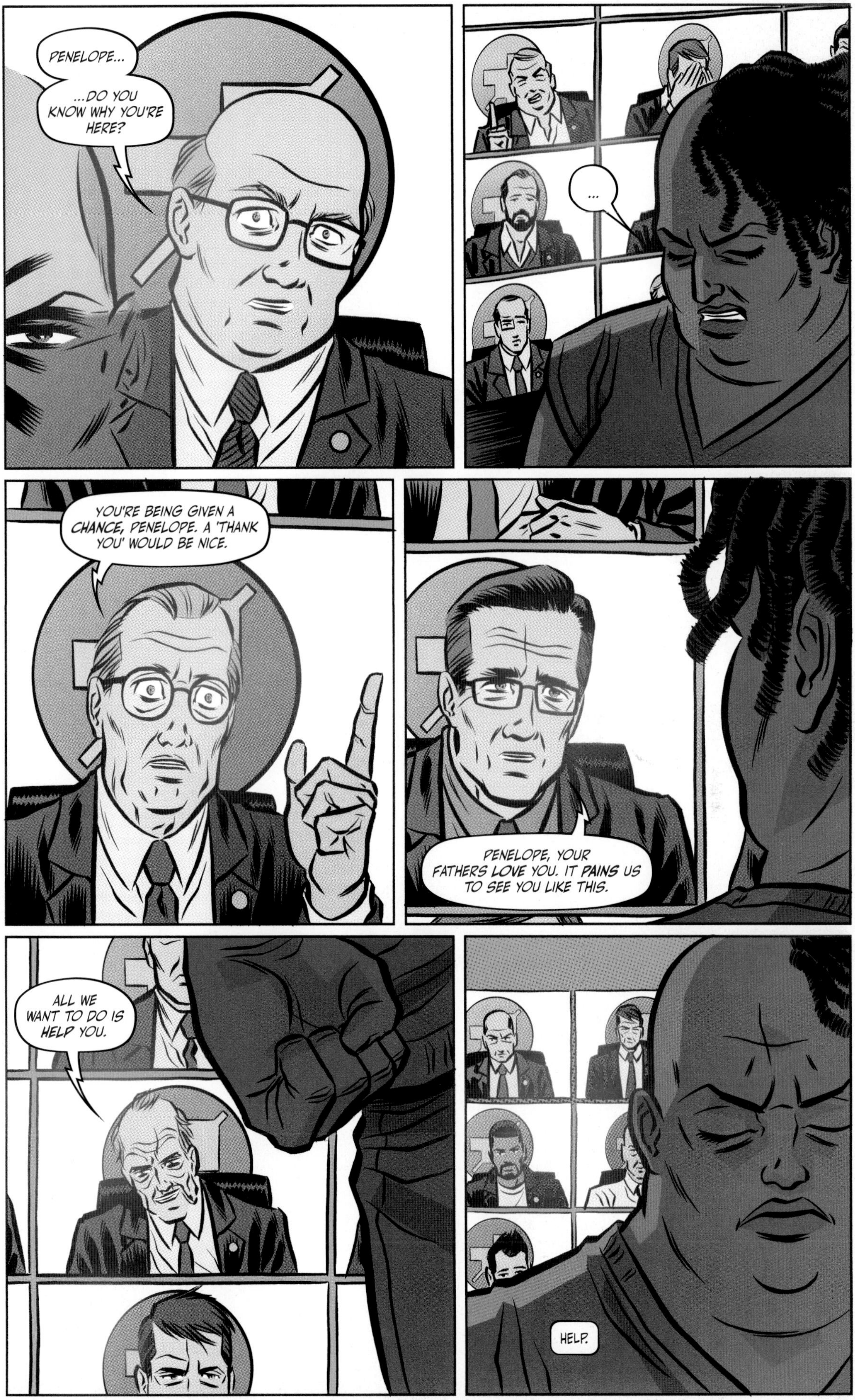
PENELOPE...
...DO YOU KNOW WHY YOU'RE HERE?
...
YOU'RE BEING GIVEN A CHANCE, PENELOPE. A 'THANK YOU' WOULD BE NICE.
PENELOPE, YOUR FATHERS LOVE YOU. IT PAINS US TO SEE YOU LIKE THIS.
ALL WE WANT TO DO IS HELP YOU.
HELP.

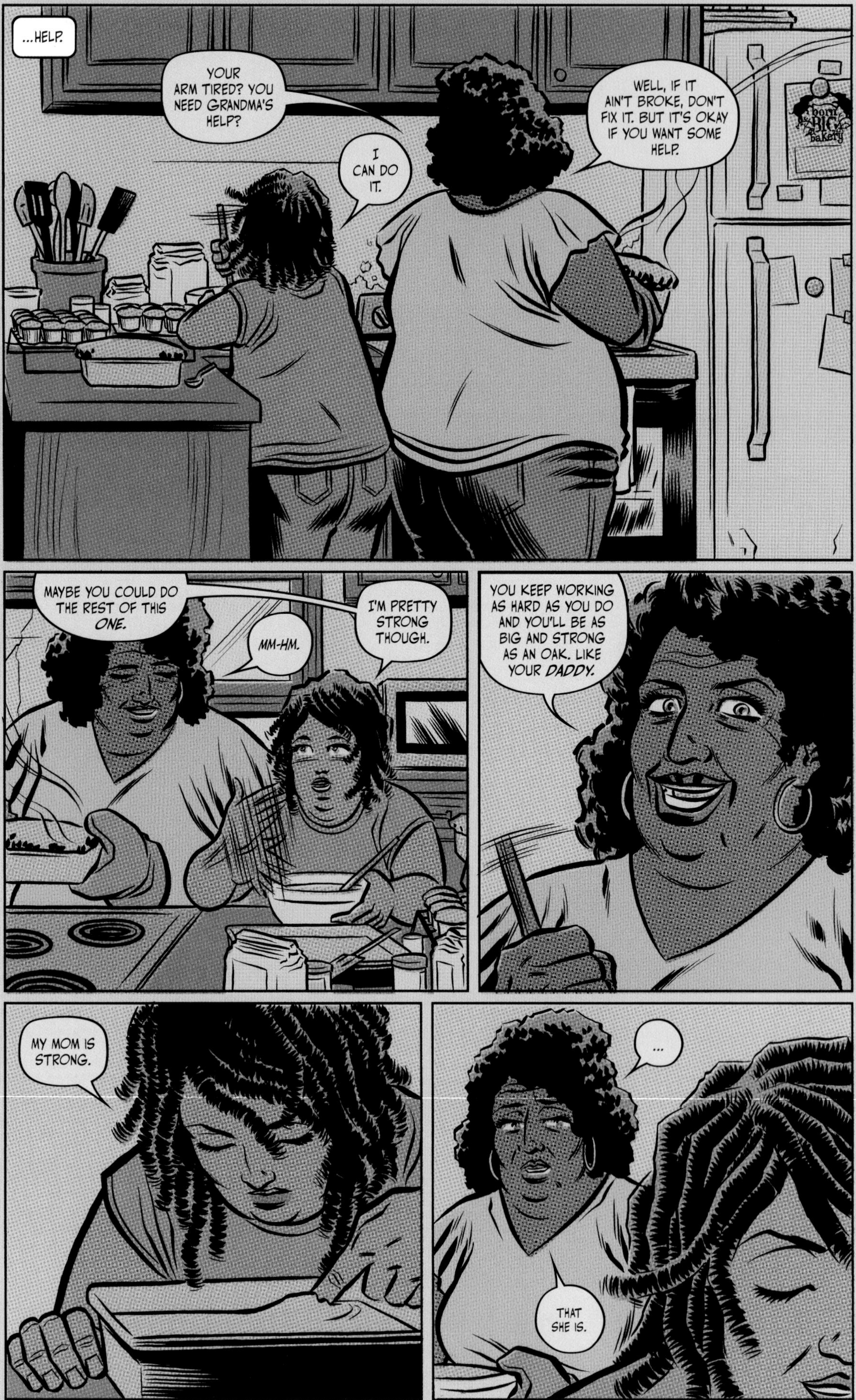
...HELP.
YOUR ARM TIRED? YOU NEED GRANDMA'S HELP?
I CAN DO IT.
WELL, IF IT AIN'T BROKE, DON'T FIX IT. BUT IT'S OKAY IF YOU WANT SOME HELP.
MAYBE YOU COULD DO THE REST OF THIS *ONE.*
MM-HM.
I'M PRETTY STRONG THOUGH.
YOU KEEP WORKING AS HARD AS YOU DO AND YOU'LL BE AS BIG AND STRONG AS AN OAK. LIKE YOUR *DADDY.*
MY MOM IS STRONG.
...
THAT SHE IS.

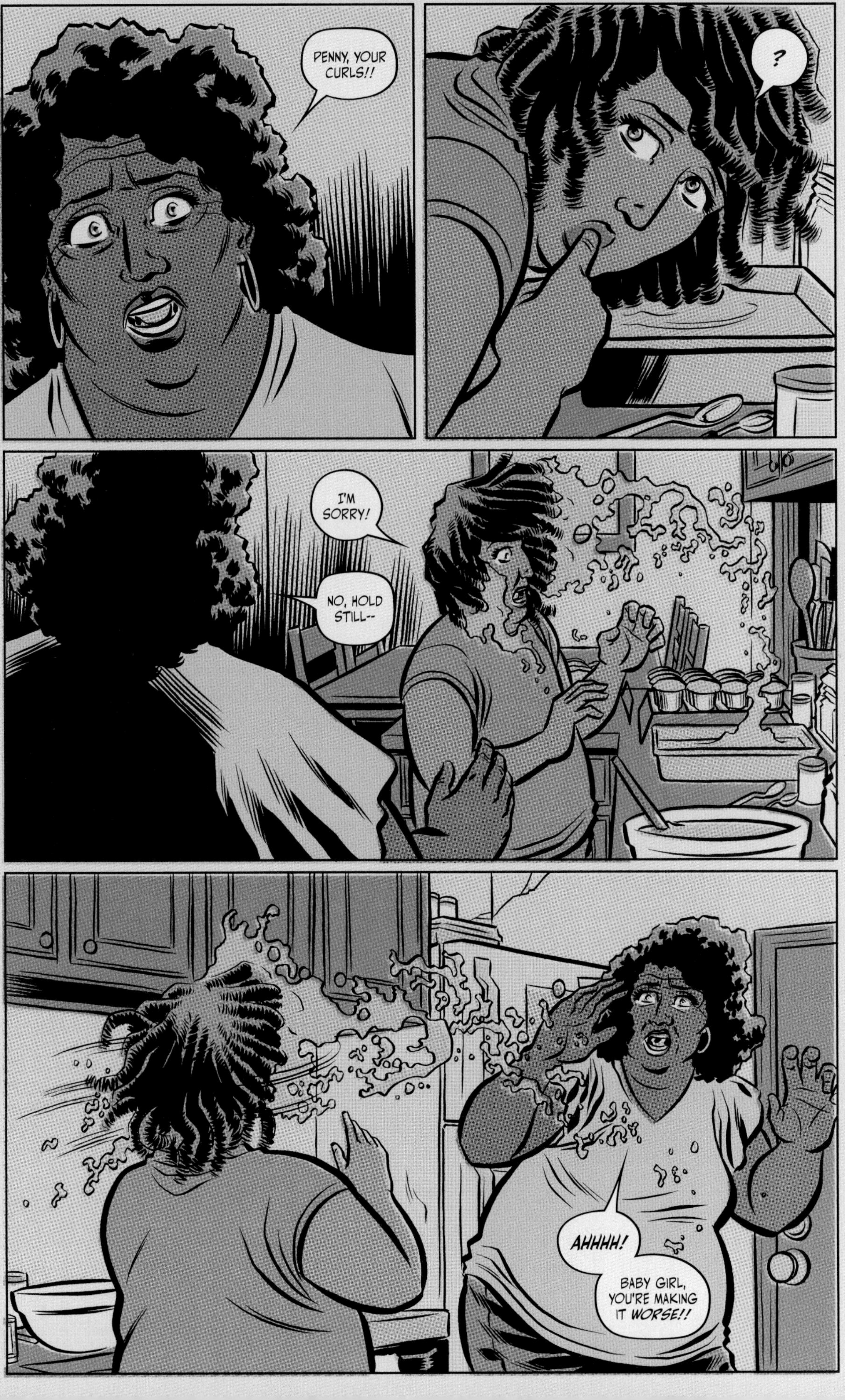
PENNY, YOUR CURLS!!
?
I'M SORRY!
NO, HOLD STILL--
AHHHH!
BABY GIRL, YOU'RE MAKING IT WORSE!!

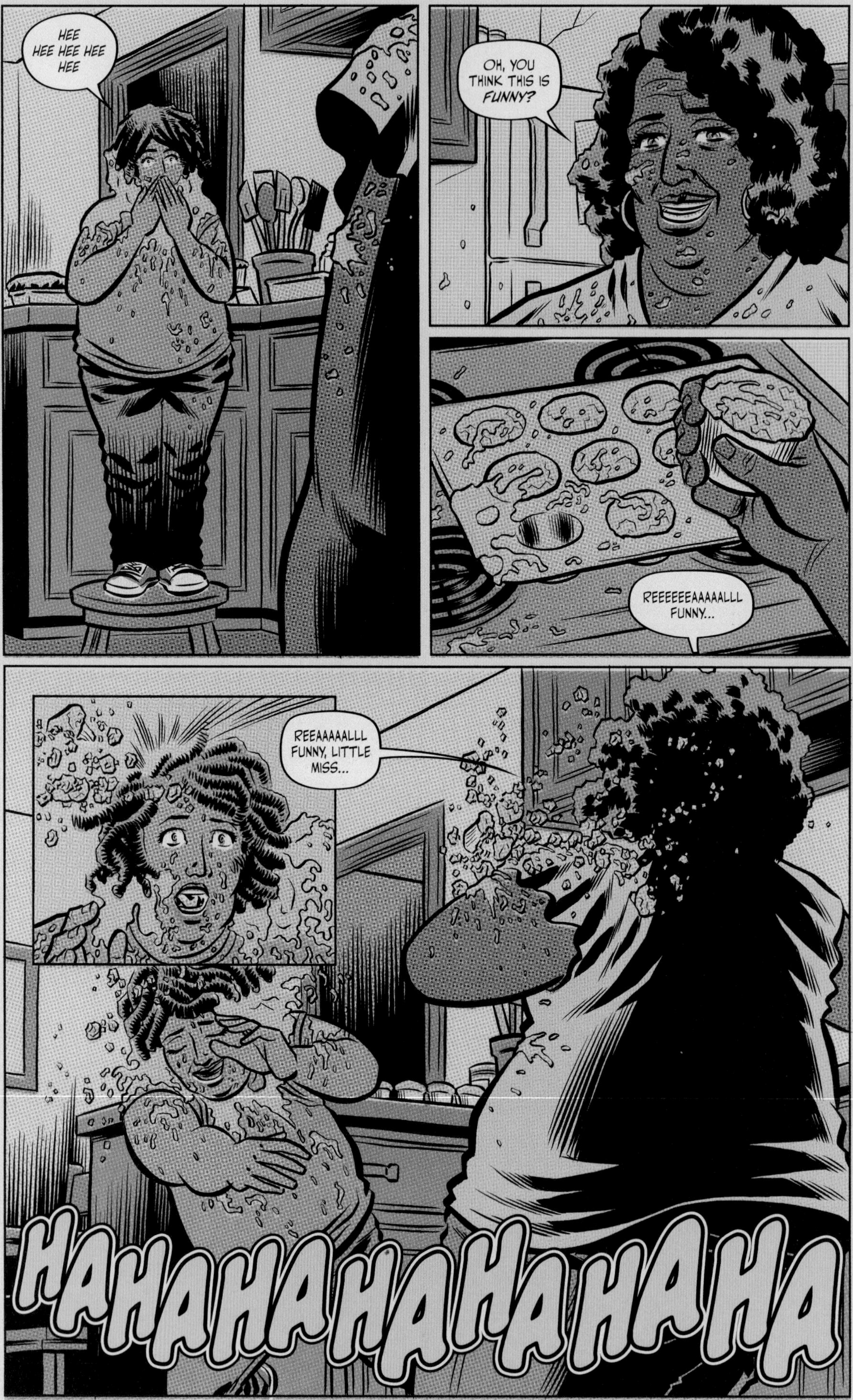
HEE
HEE HEE HEE
HEE
OH, YOU
THINK THIS IS
FUNNY?
REEEEEEAAAAALLL
FUNNY...
REEAAAAALLL
FUNNY, LITTLE
MISS...
HAHAHAHAHAHAHAHAHA

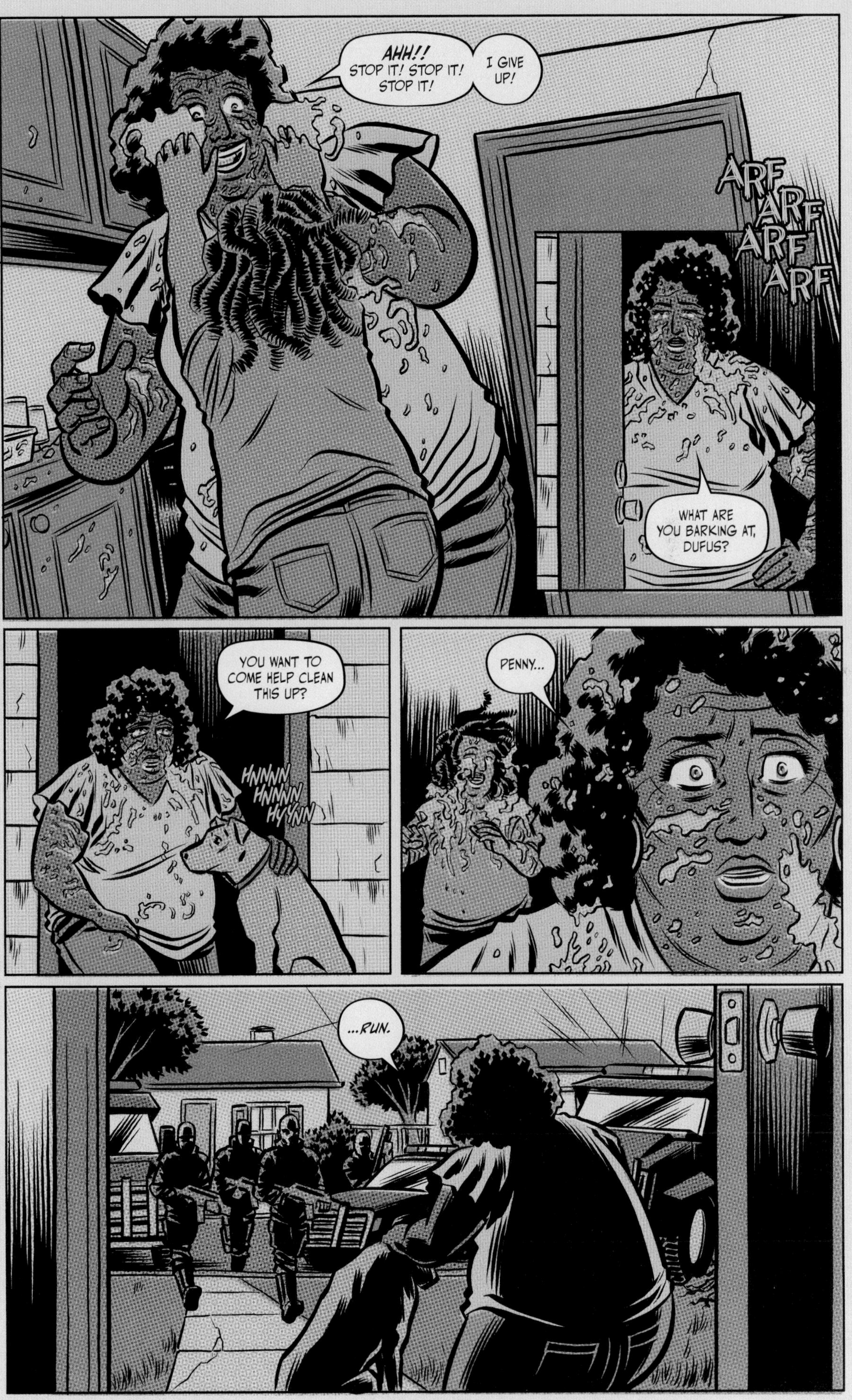
AHH!! STOP IT! STOP IT! STOP IT!
I GIVE UP!
ARF ARF ARF ARF
WHAT ARE YOU BARKING AT, DUFUS?
YOU WANT TO COME HELP CLEAN THIS UP?
HNNNN HNNNN HYYNN
PENNY...
...RUN.

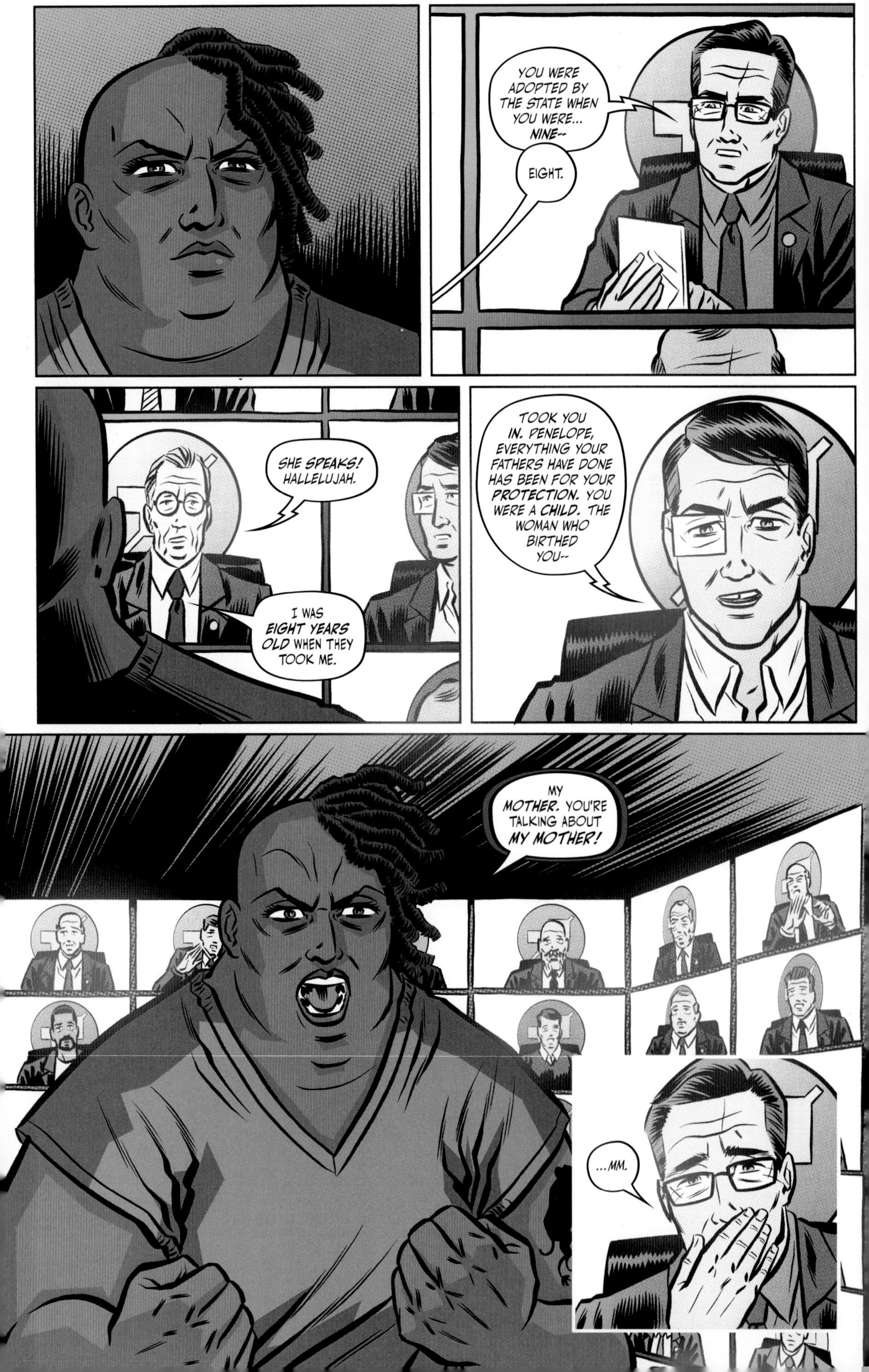
YOU WERE ADOPTED BY THE STATE WHEN YOU WERE... NINE--
EIGHT.
SHE SPEAKS! HALLELUJAH.
I WAS EIGHT YEARS OLD WHEN THEY TOOK ME.
TOOK YOU IN. PENELOPE, EVERYTHING YOUR FATHERS HAVE DONE HAS BEEN FOR YOUR PROTECTION. YOU WERE A CHILD. THE WOMAN WHO BIRTHED YOU--
MY MOTHER. YOU'RE TALKING ABOUT MY MOTHER!
...MM.

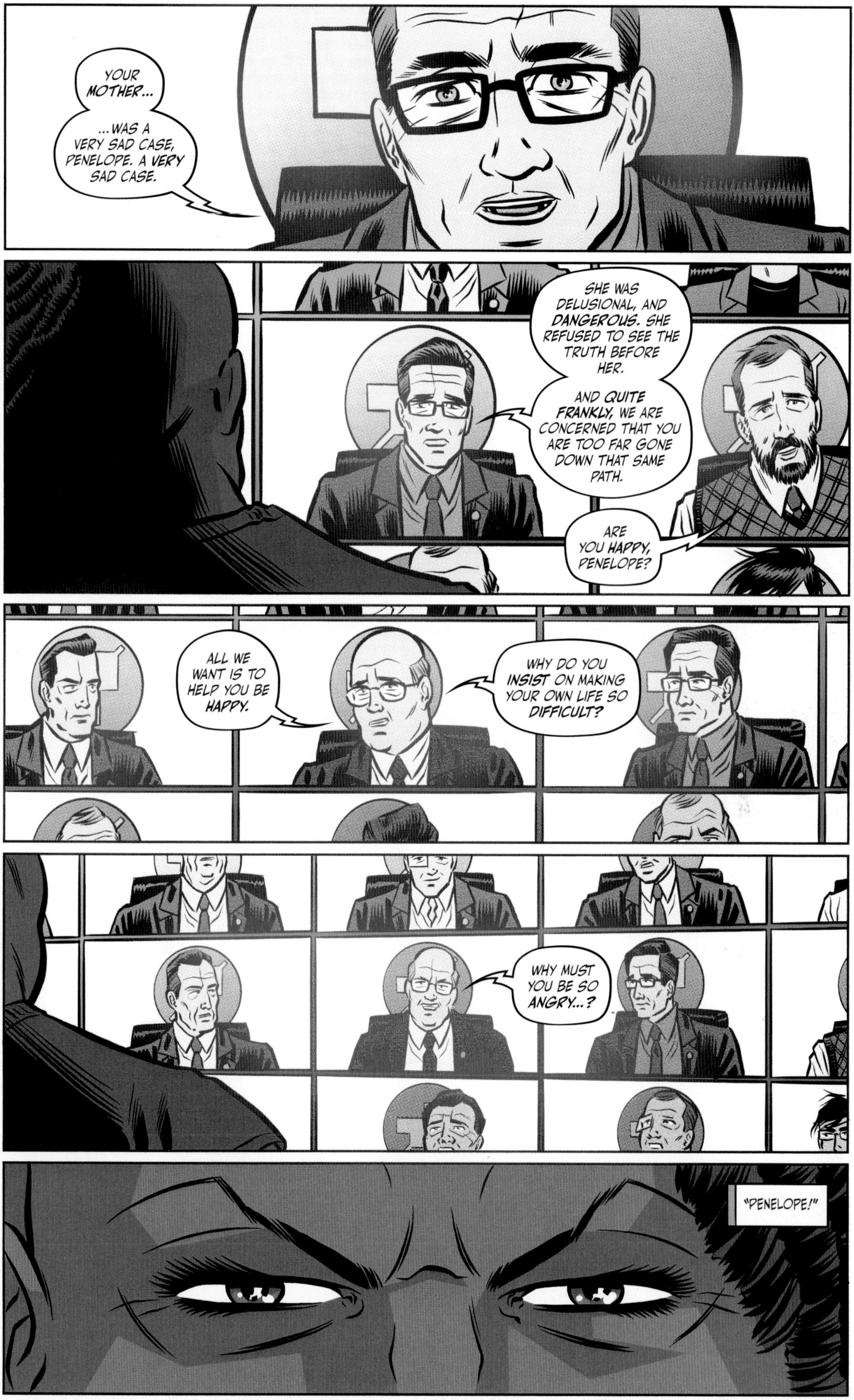
YOUR MOTHER...
...WAS A VERY SAD CASE, PENELOPE. A VERY SAD CASE.
SHE WAS DELUSIONAL, AND DANGEROUS. SHE REFUSED TO SEE THE TRUTH BEFORE HER.
AND QUITE FRANKLY, WE ARE CONCERNED THAT YOU ARE TOO FAR GONE DOWN THAT SAME PATH.
ARE YOU HAPPY, PENELOPE?
ALL WE WANT IS TO HELP YOU BE HAPPY.
WHY DO YOU INSIST ON MAKING YOUR OWN LIFE SO DIFFICULT?
WHY MUST YOU BE SO ANGRY...?
"PENELOPE!"

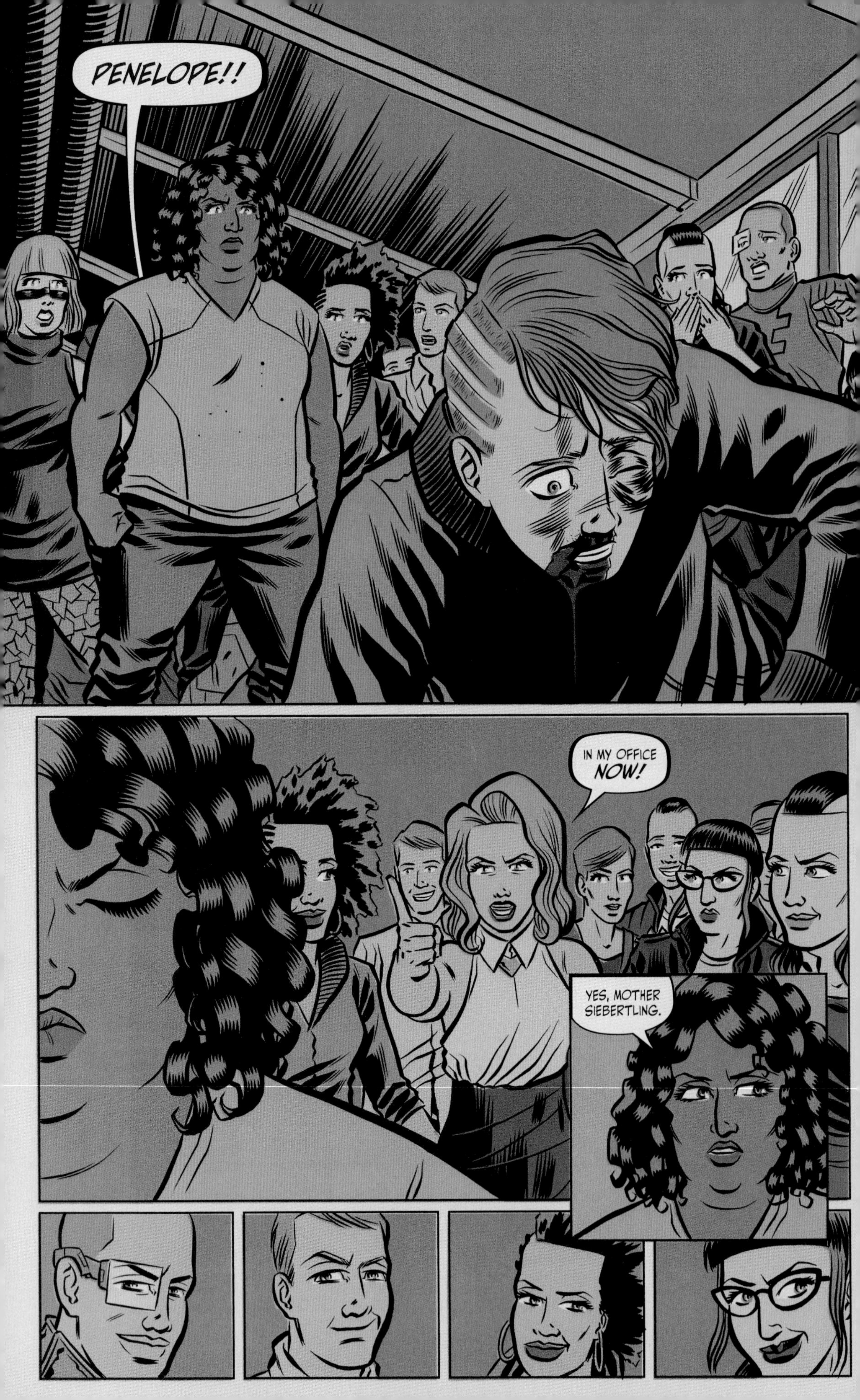
PENELOPE!!
IN MY OFFICE NOW!
YES, MOTHER SIEBERTLING.

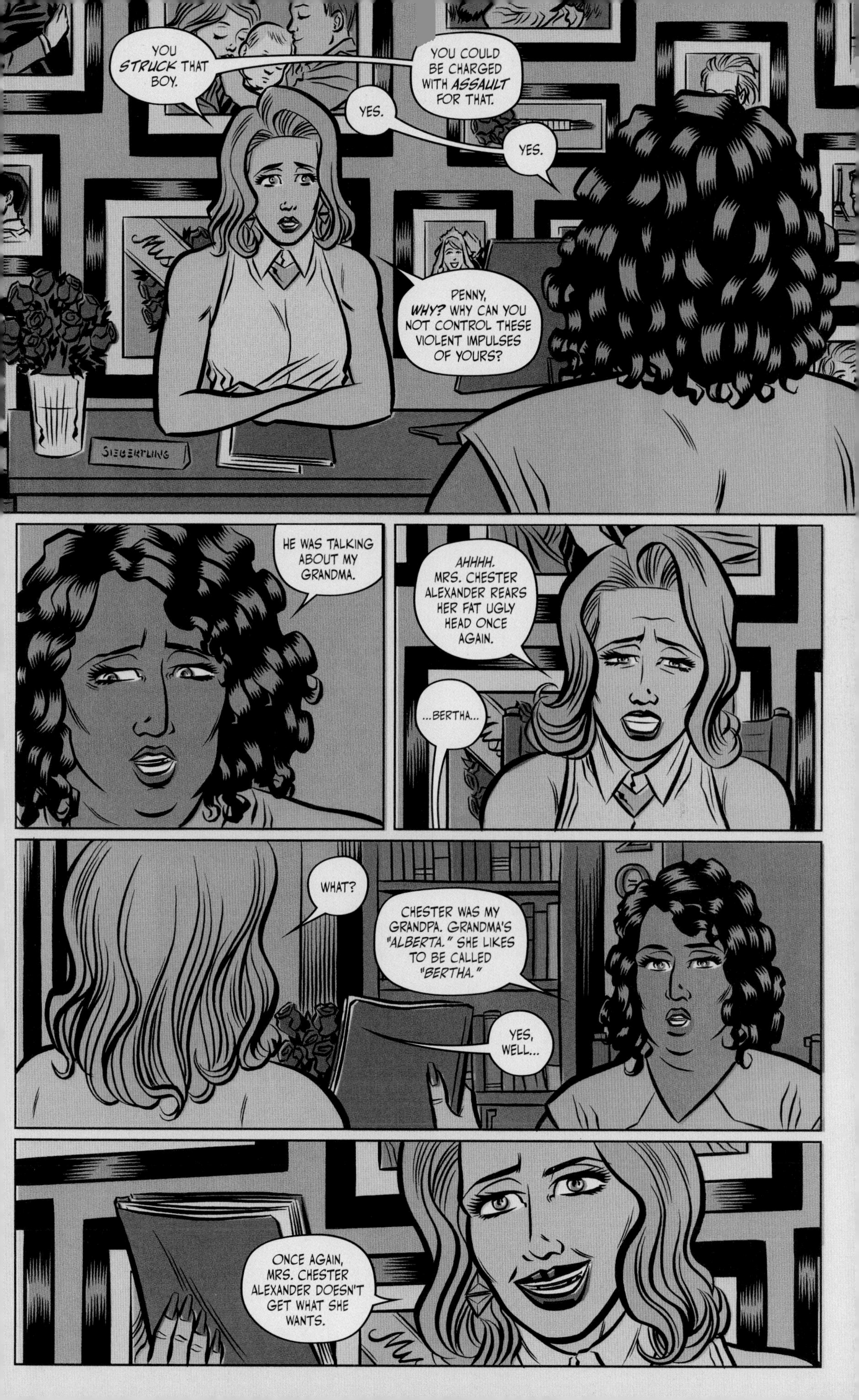
YOU STRUCK THAT BOY.
YES.
YOU COULD BE CHARGED WITH ASSAULT FOR THAT.
YES.
PENNY, WHY? WHY CAN YOU NOT CONTROL THESE VIOLENT IMPULSES OF YOURS?
SIEGERTLING
HE WAS TALKING ABOUT MY GRANDMA.
AHHHH. MRS. CHESTER ALEXANDER REARS HER FAT UGLY HEAD ONCE AGAIN.
...BERTHA...
WHAT?
CHESTER WAS MY GRANDPA. GRANDMA'S "ALBERTA." SHE LIKES TO BE CALLED "BERTHA."
YES, WELL...
ONCE AGAIN, MRS. CHESTER ALEXANDER DOESN'T GET WHAT SHE WANTS.

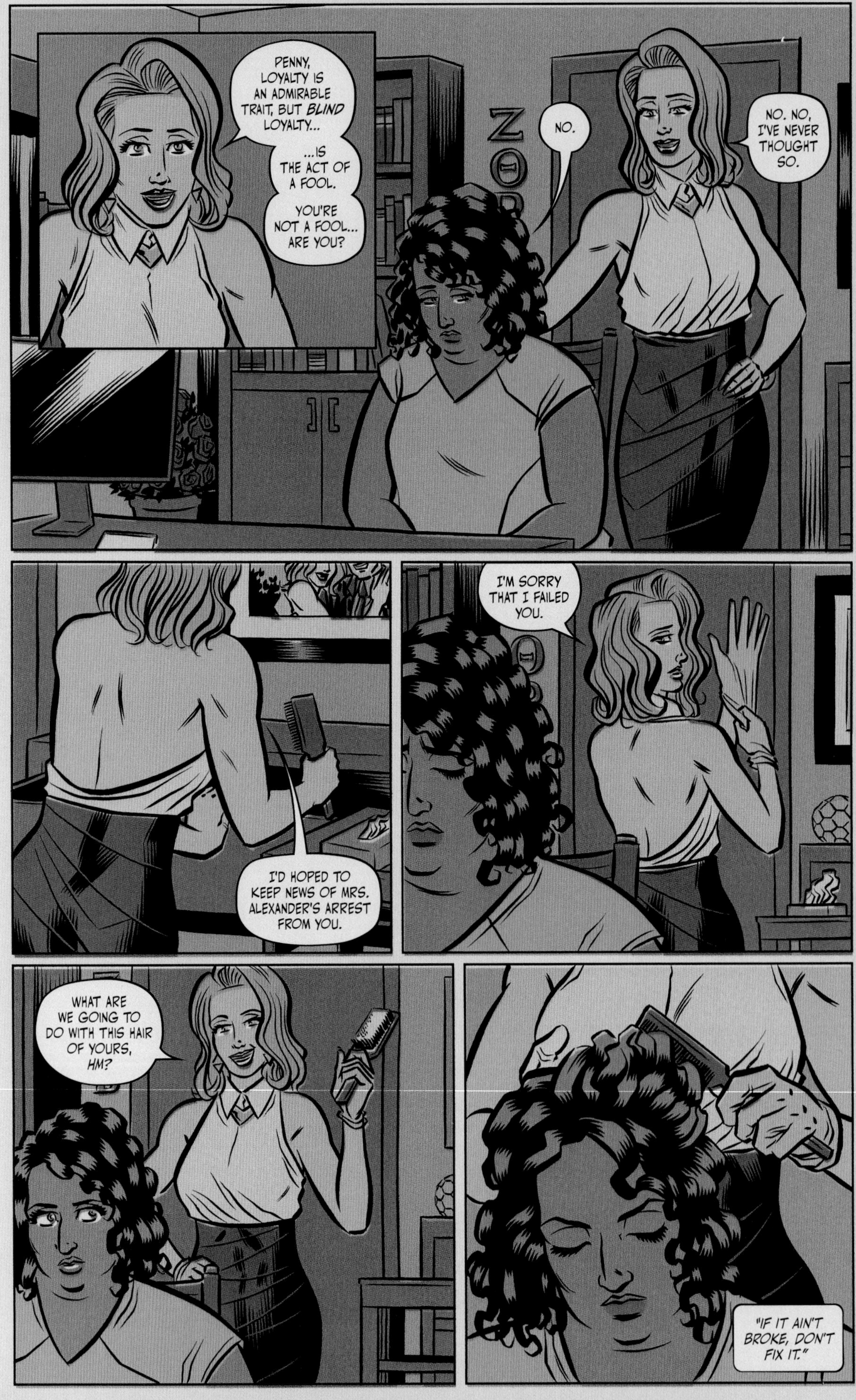
PENNY, LOYALTY IS AN ADMIRABLE TRAIT, BUT *BLIND* LOYALTY...
...IS THE ACT OF A FOOL.
YOU'RE NOT A FOOL... ARE YOU?
NO.
NO. NO, I'VE NEVER THOUGHT SO.
I'D HOPED TO KEEP NEWS OF MRS. ALEXANDER'S ARREST FROM YOU.
I'M SORRY THAT I FAILED YOU.
WHAT ARE WE GOING TO DO WITH THIS HAIR OF YOURS, HM?
"IF IT AIN'T BROKE, DON'T FIX IT."

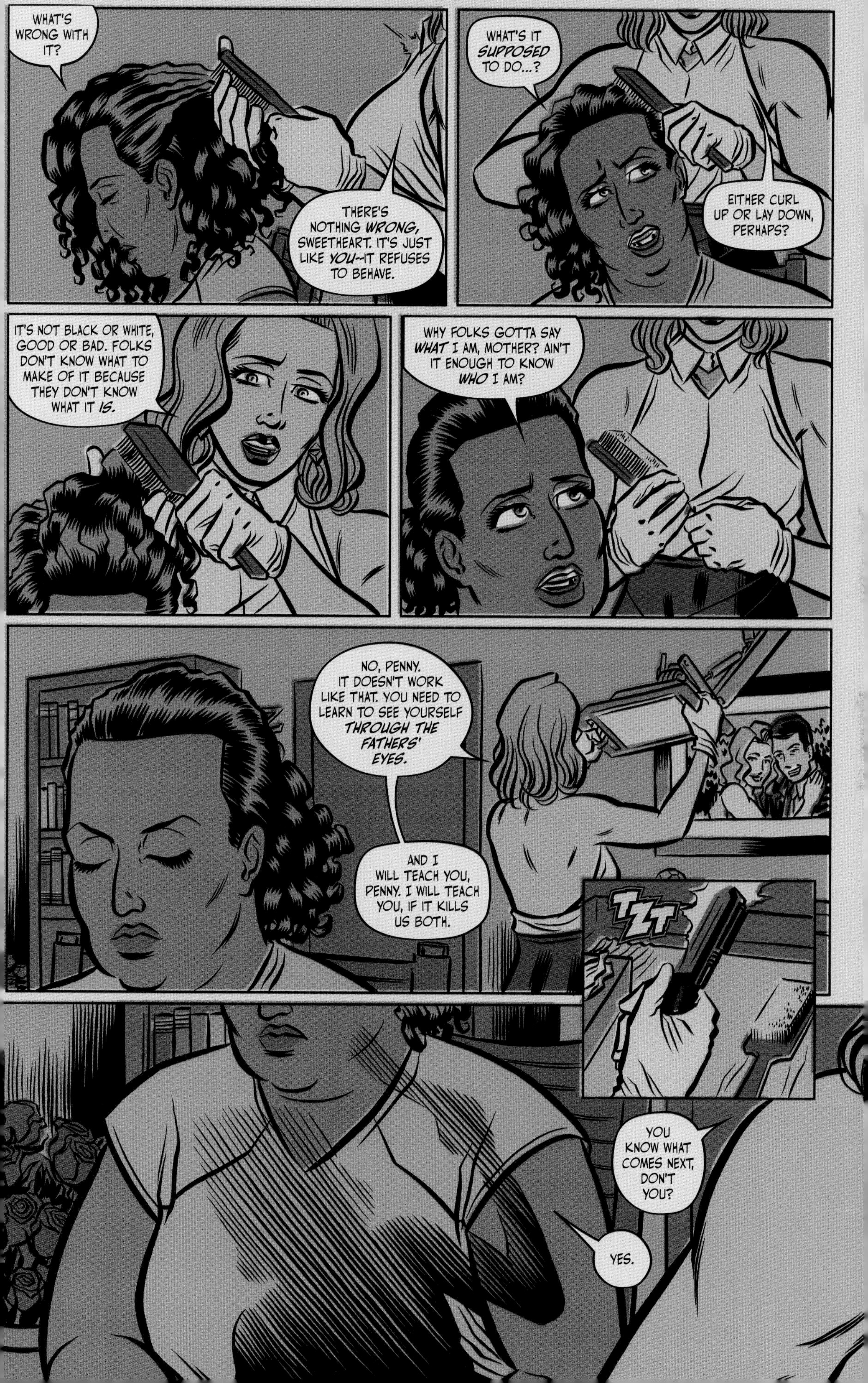
WHAT'S WRONG WITH IT?
THERE'S NOTHING WRONG, SWEETHEART. IT'S JUST LIKE YOU--IT REFUSES TO BEHAVE.
WHAT'S IT SUPPOSED TO DO...?
EITHER CURL UP OR LAY DOWN, PERHAPS?
IT'S NOT BLACK OR WHITE, GOOD OR BAD. FOLKS DON'T KNOW WHAT TO MAKE OF IT BECAUSE THEY DON'T KNOW WHAT IT IS.
WHY FOLKS GOTTA SAY WHAT I AM, MOTHER? AIN'T IT ENOUGH TO KNOW WHO I AM?
NO, PENNY. IT DOESN'T WORK LIKE THAT. YOU NEED TO LEARN TO SEE YOURSELF THROUGH THE FATHERS' EYES.
AND I WILL TEACH YOU, PENNY. I WILL TEACH YOU, IF IT KILLS US BOTH.
TZT
YOU KNOW WHAT COMES NEXT, DON'T YOU?
YES.

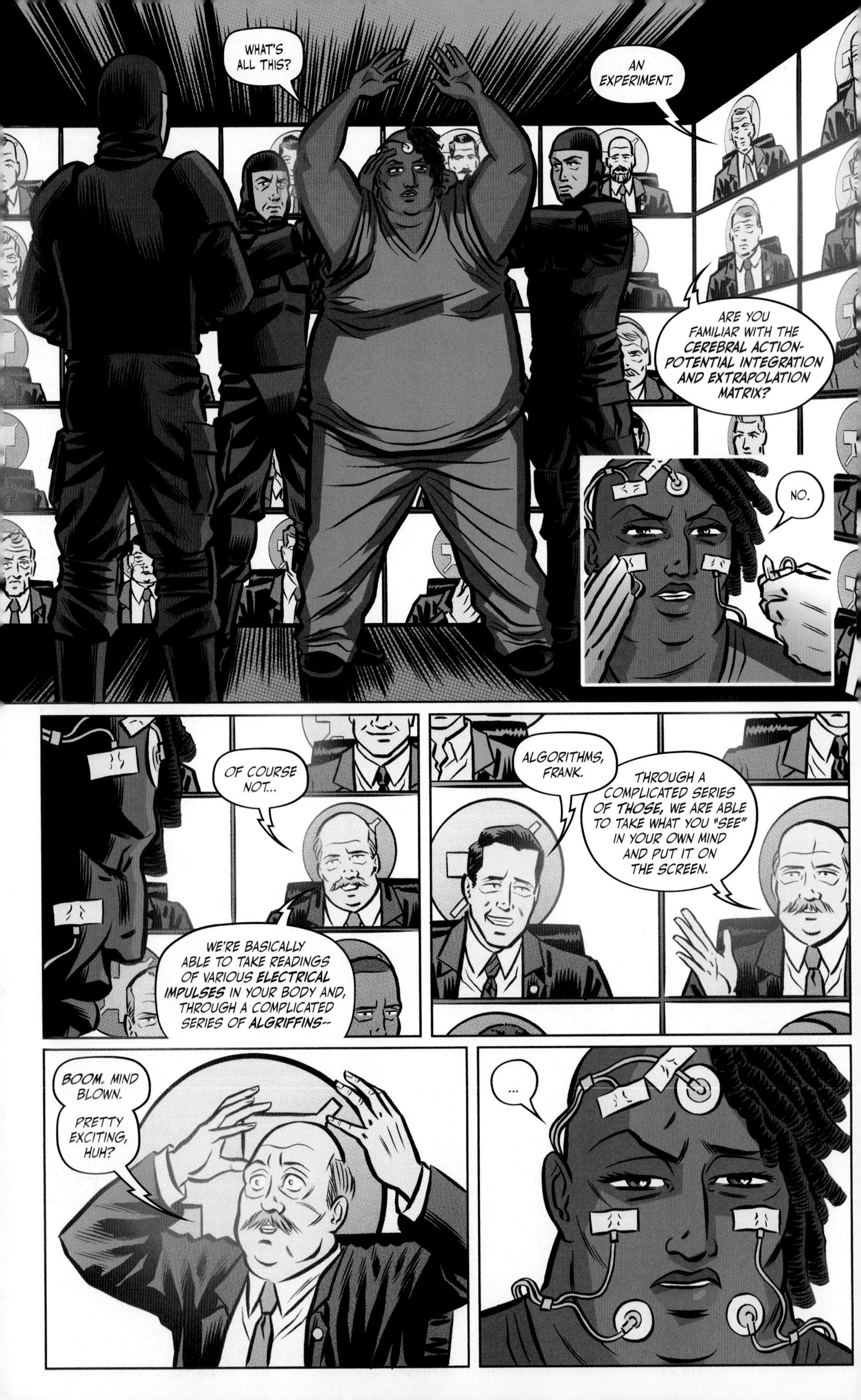
WHAT'S ALL THIS?
AN EXPERIMENT.
ARE YOU FAMILIAR WITH THE CEREBRAL ACTION-POTENTIAL INTEGRATION AND EXTRAPOLATION MATRIX?
NO.
OF COURSE NOT...
WE'RE BASICALLY ABLE TO TAKE READINGS OF VARIOUS ELECTRICAL IMPULSES IN YOUR BODY AND, THROUGH A COMPLICATED SERIES OF ALGRIFFINS--
ALGORITHMS, FRANK.
THROUGH A COMPLICATED SERIES OF THOSE, WE ARE ABLE TO TAKE WHAT YOU "SEE" IN YOUR OWN MIND AND PUT IT ON THE SCREEN.
BOOM. MIND BLOWN.
PRETTY EXCITING, HUH?
...

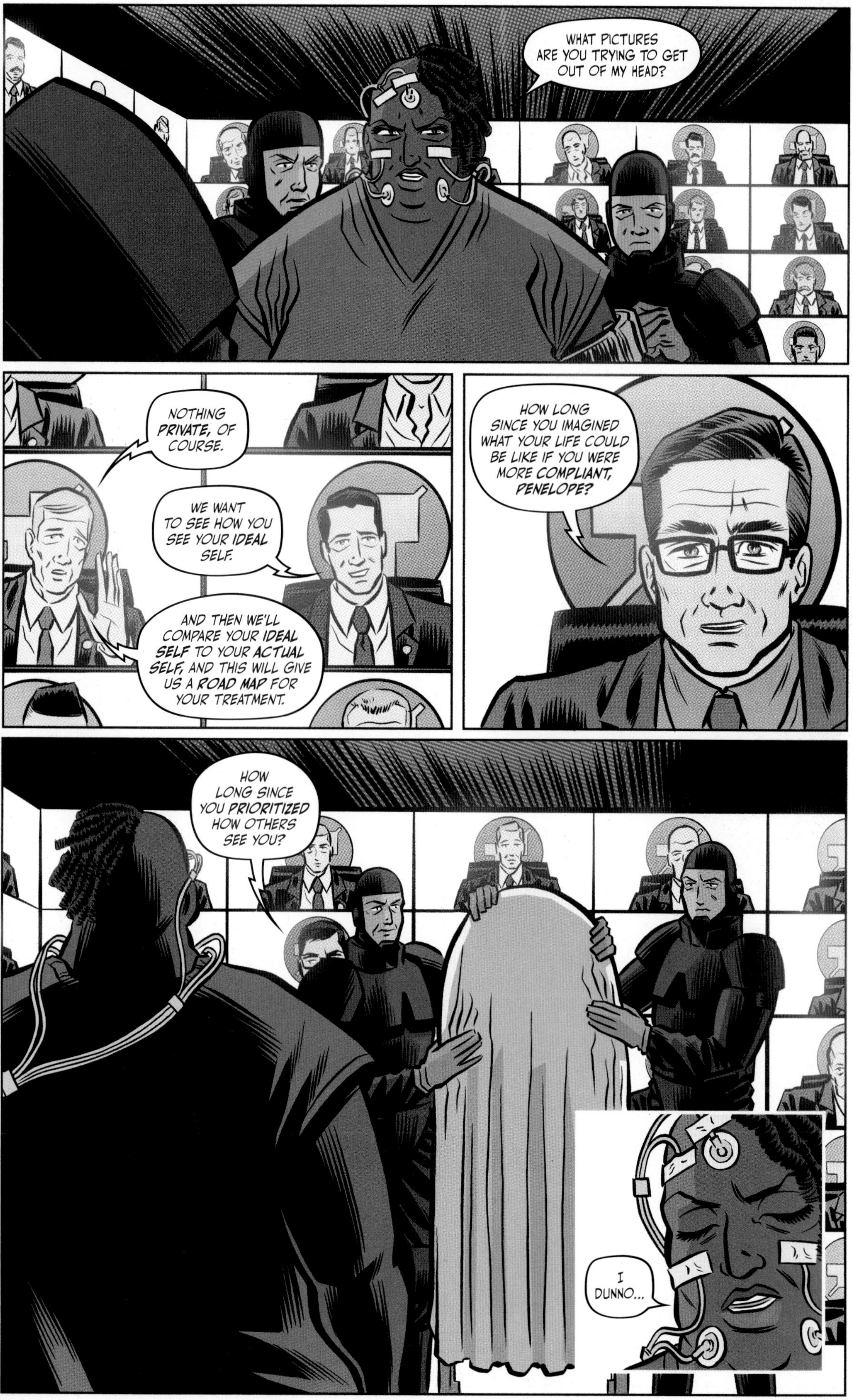
WHAT PICTURES ARE YOU TRYING TO GET OUT OF MY HEAD?
NOTHING PRIVATE, OF COURSE.
WE WANT TO SEE HOW YOU SEE YOUR IDEAL SELF.
AND THEN WE'LL COMPARE YOUR IDEAL SELF TO YOUR ACTUAL SELF, AND THIS WILL GIVE US A ROAD MAP FOR YOUR TREATMENT.
HOW LONG SINCE YOU IMAGINED WHAT YOUR LIFE COULD BE LIKE IF YOU WERE MORE COMPLIANT, PENELOPE?
HOW LONG SINCE YOU PRIORITIZED HOW OTHERS SEE YOU?
I DUNNO...

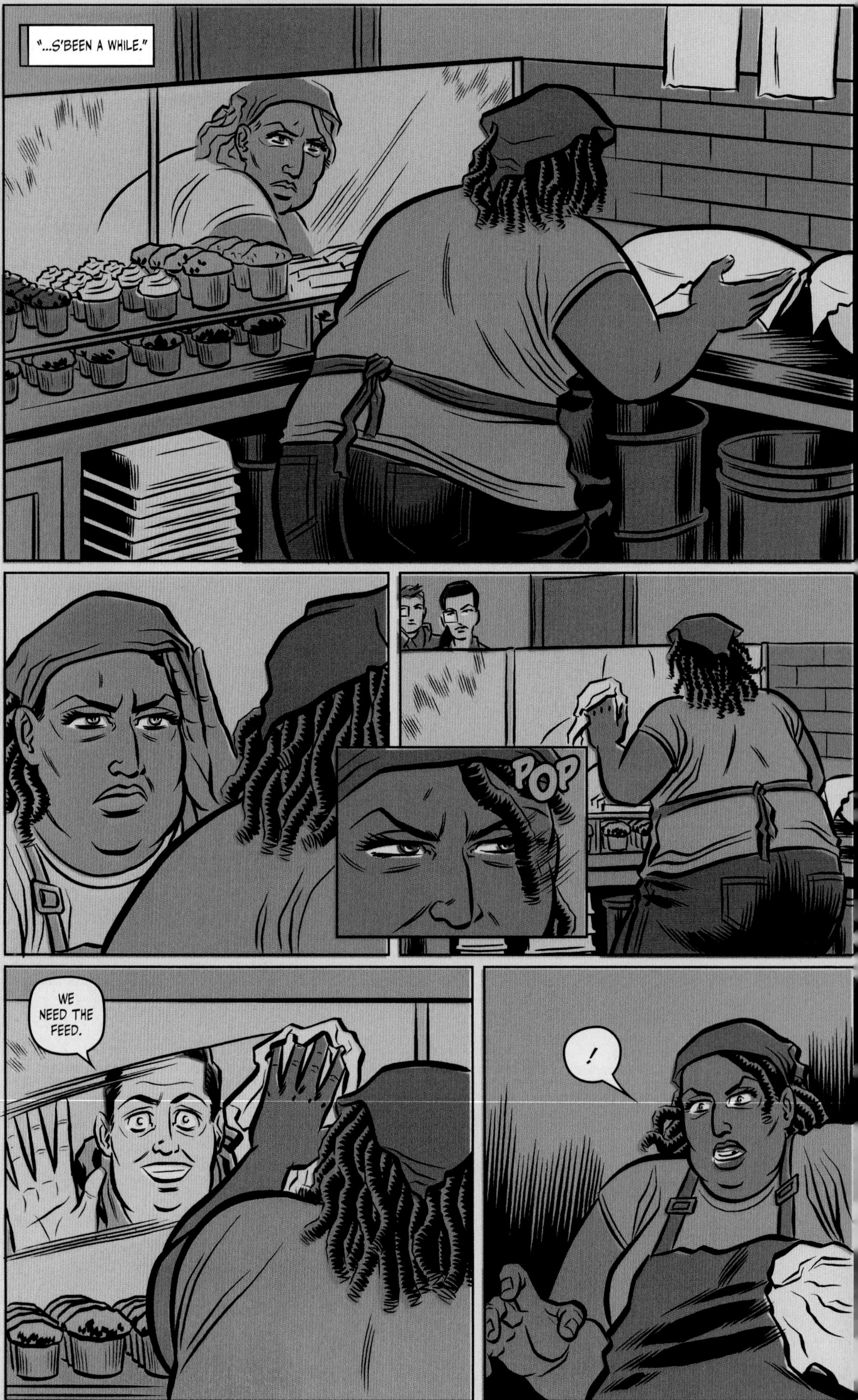
"...S'BEEN A WHILE."
POP
WE NEED THE FEED.
!

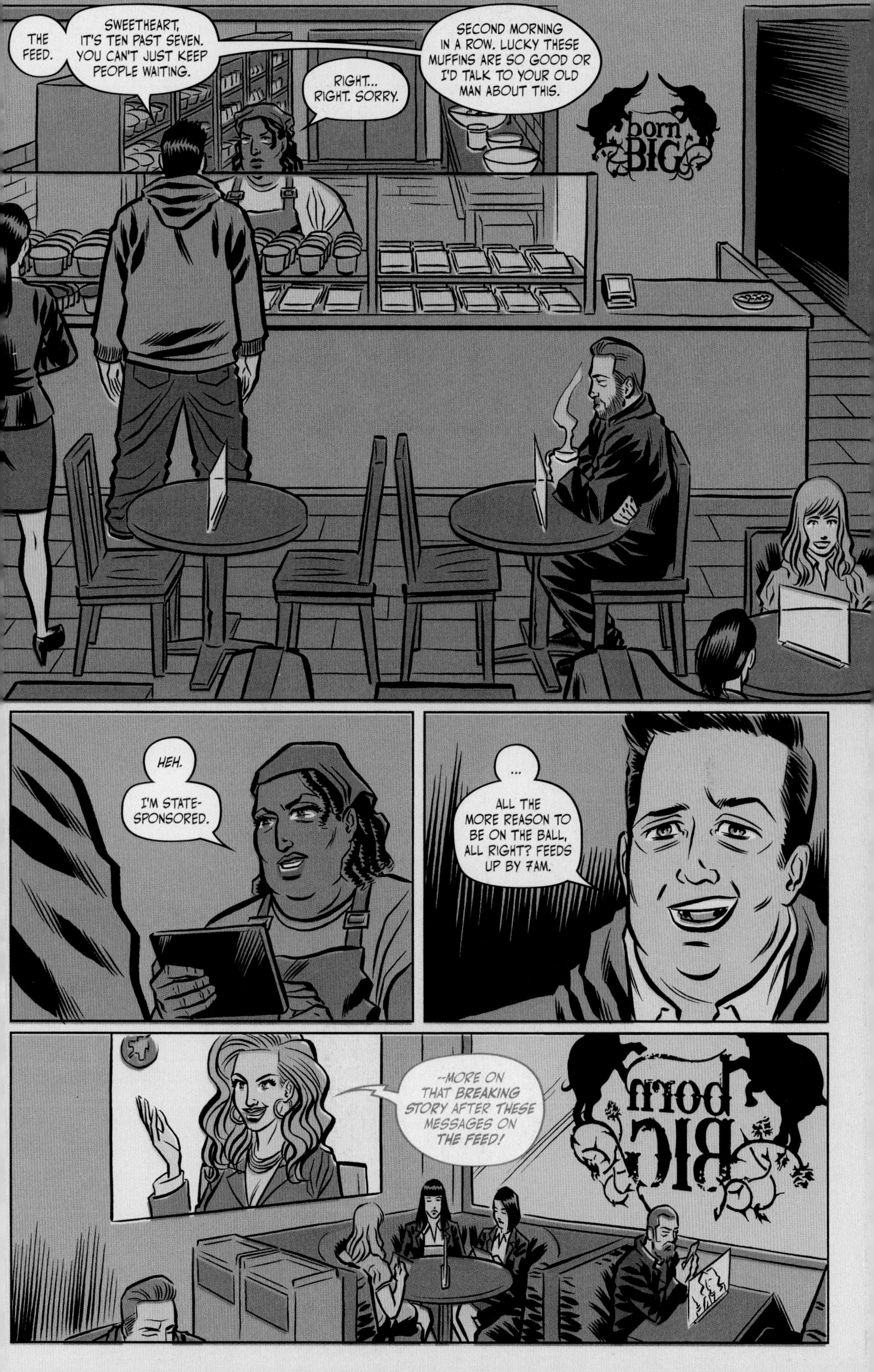
THE FEED.
SWEETHEART, IT'S TEN PAST SEVEN. YOU CAN'T JUST KEEP PEOPLE WAITING.
RIGHT... RIGHT. SORRY.
SECOND MORNING IN A ROW. LUCKY THESE MUFFINS ARE SO GOOD OR I'D TALK TO YOUR OLD MAN ABOUT THIS.
born BIG
HEH.
I'M STATE-SPONSORED.
...
ALL THE MORE REASON TO BE ON THE BALL, ALL RIGHT? FEEDS UP BY 7AM.
--MORE ON THAT BREAKING STORY AFTER THESE MESSAGES ON THE FEED!

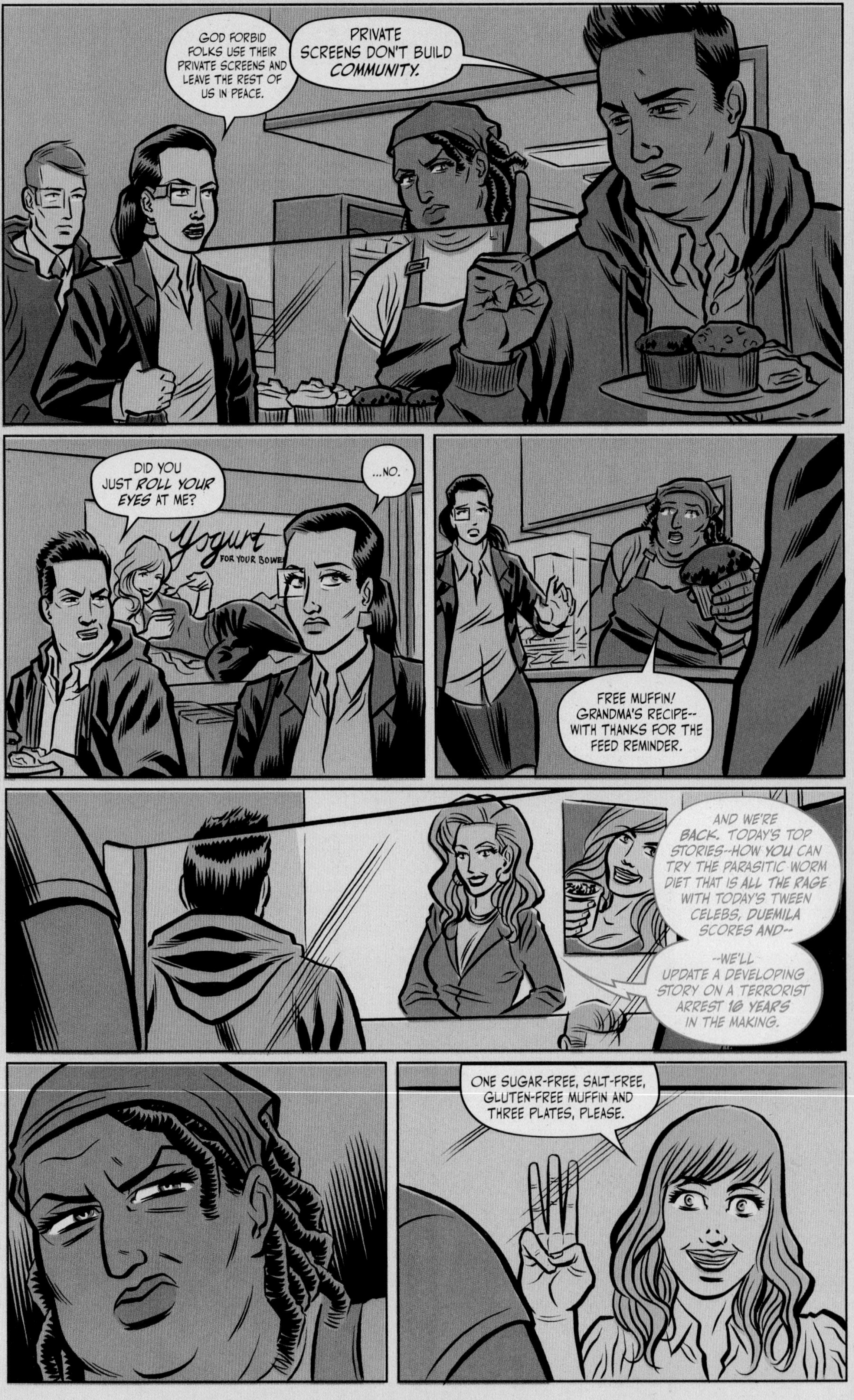
GOD FORBID FOLKS USE THEIR PRIVATE SCREENS AND LEAVE THE REST OF US IN PEACE.
PRIVATE SCREENS DON'T BUILD COMMUNITY.
DID YOU JUST ROLL YOUR EYES AT ME?
...NO.
Yogurt
FOR YOUR BOWE
FREE MUFFIN! GRANDMA'S RECIPE-- WITH THANKS FOR THE FEED REMINDER.
AND WE'RE BACK. TODAY'S TOP STORIES--HOW YOU CAN TRY THE PARASITIC WORM DIET THAT IS ALL THE RAGE WITH TODAY'S TWEEN CELEBS, DUEMILA SCORES AND--
--WE'LL UPDATE A DEVELOPING STORY ON A TERRORIST ARREST 16 YEARS IN THE MAKING.
ONE SUGAR-FREE, SALT-FREE, GLUTEN-FREE MUFFIN AND THREE PLATES, PLEASE.

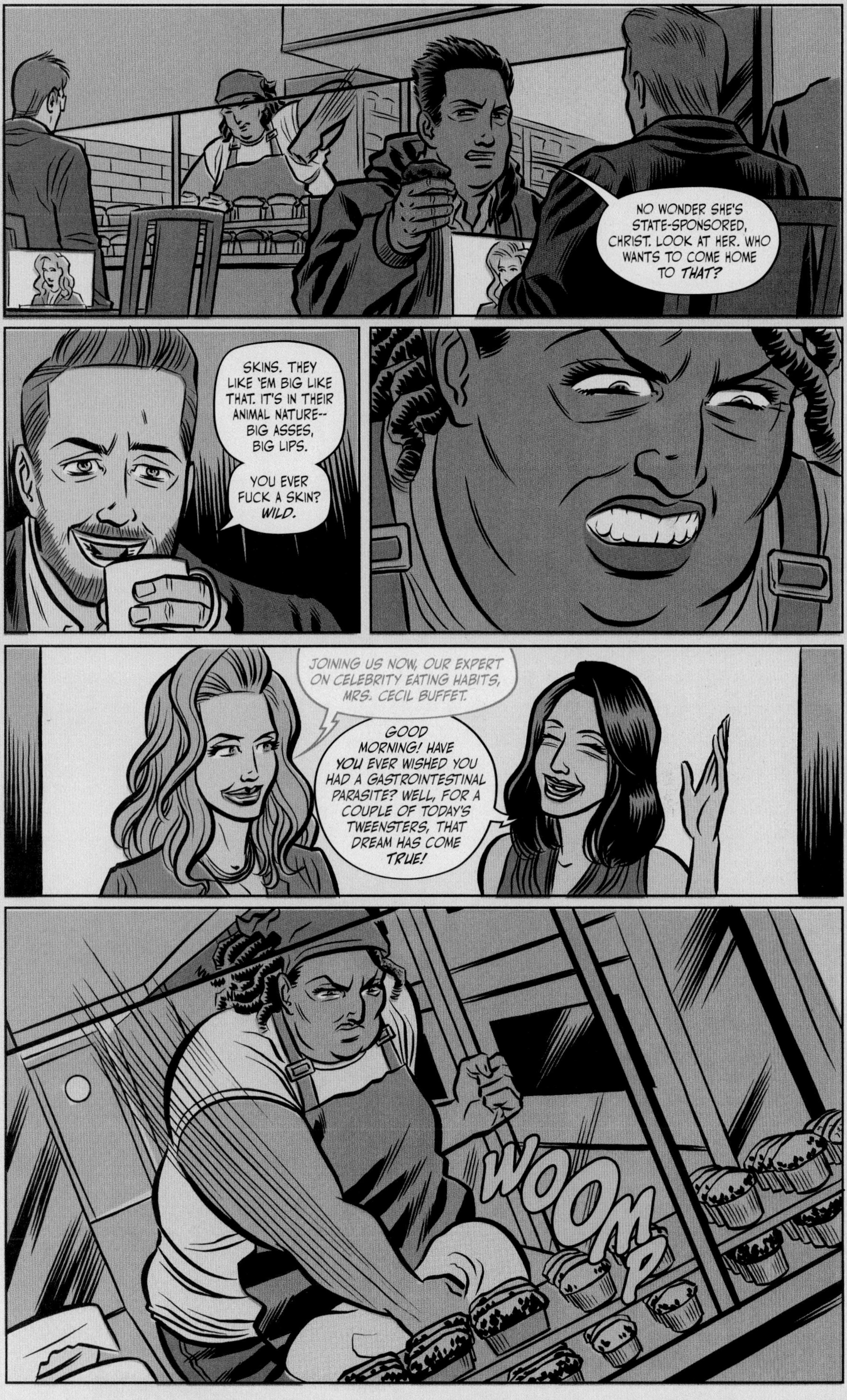
NO WONDER SHE'S STATE-SPONSORED, CHRIST. LOOK AT HER. WHO WANTS TO COME HOME TO THAT?
SKINS. THEY LIKE 'EM BIG LIKE THAT. IT'S IN THEIR ANIMAL NATURE-- BIG ASSES, BIG LIPS.
YOU EVER FUCK A SKIN? WILD.
JOINING US NOW, OUR EXPERT ON CELEBRITY EATING HABITS, MRS. CECIL BUFFET.
GOOD MORNING! HAVE YOU EVER WISHED YOU HAD A GASTROINTESTINAL PARASITE? WELL, FOR A COUPLE OF TODAY'S TWEENSTERS, THAT DREAM HAS COME TRUE!
WOOMP

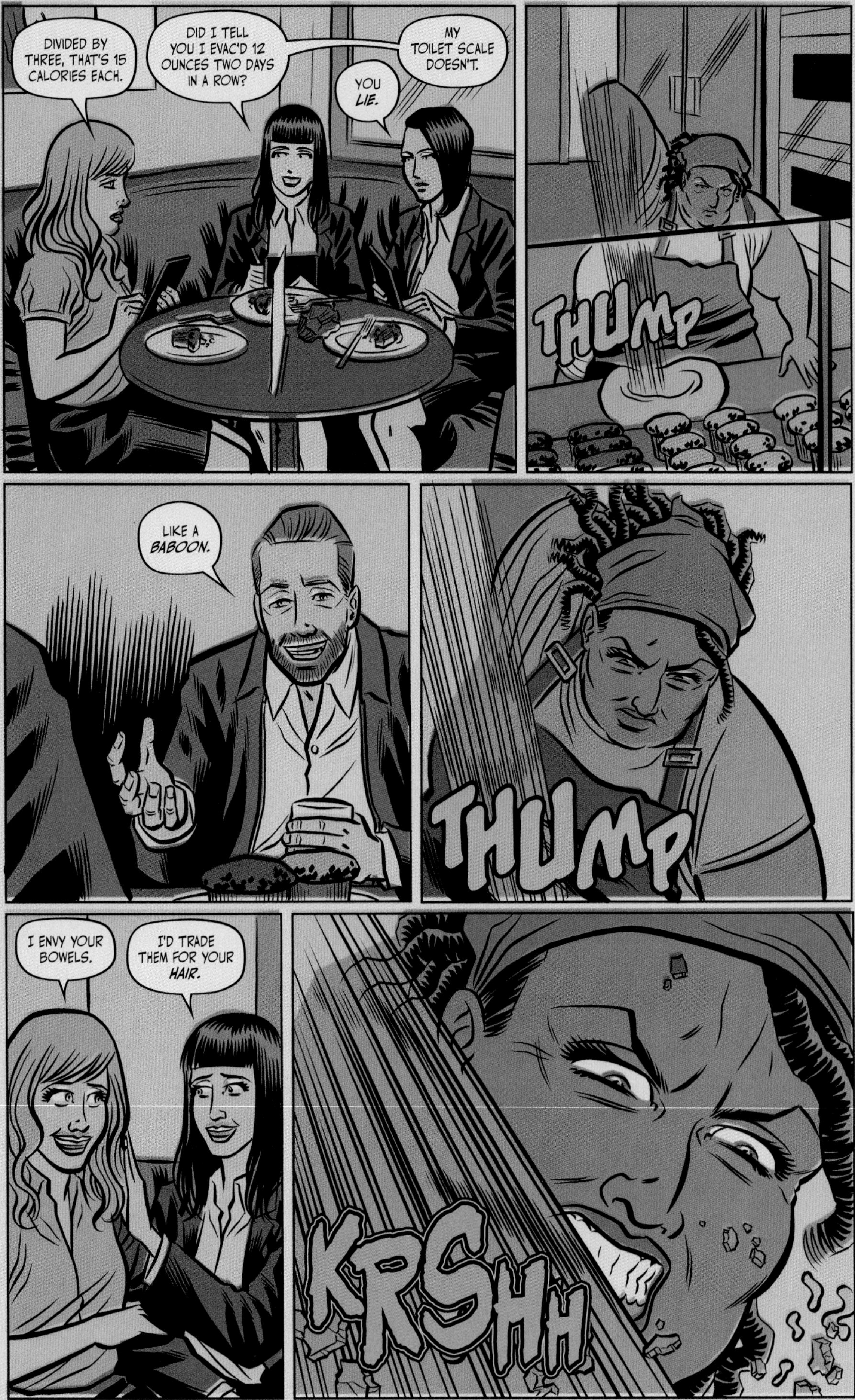
DIVIDED BY THREE, THAT'S 15 CALORIES EACH.
DID I TELL YOU I EVAC'D 12 OUNCES TWO DAYS IN A ROW?
MY TOILET SCALE DOESN'T.
YOU LIE.
THUMP
LIKE A BABOON.
THUMP
I ENVY YOUR BOWELS.
I'D TRADE THEM FOR YOUR HAIR.
KRSHH

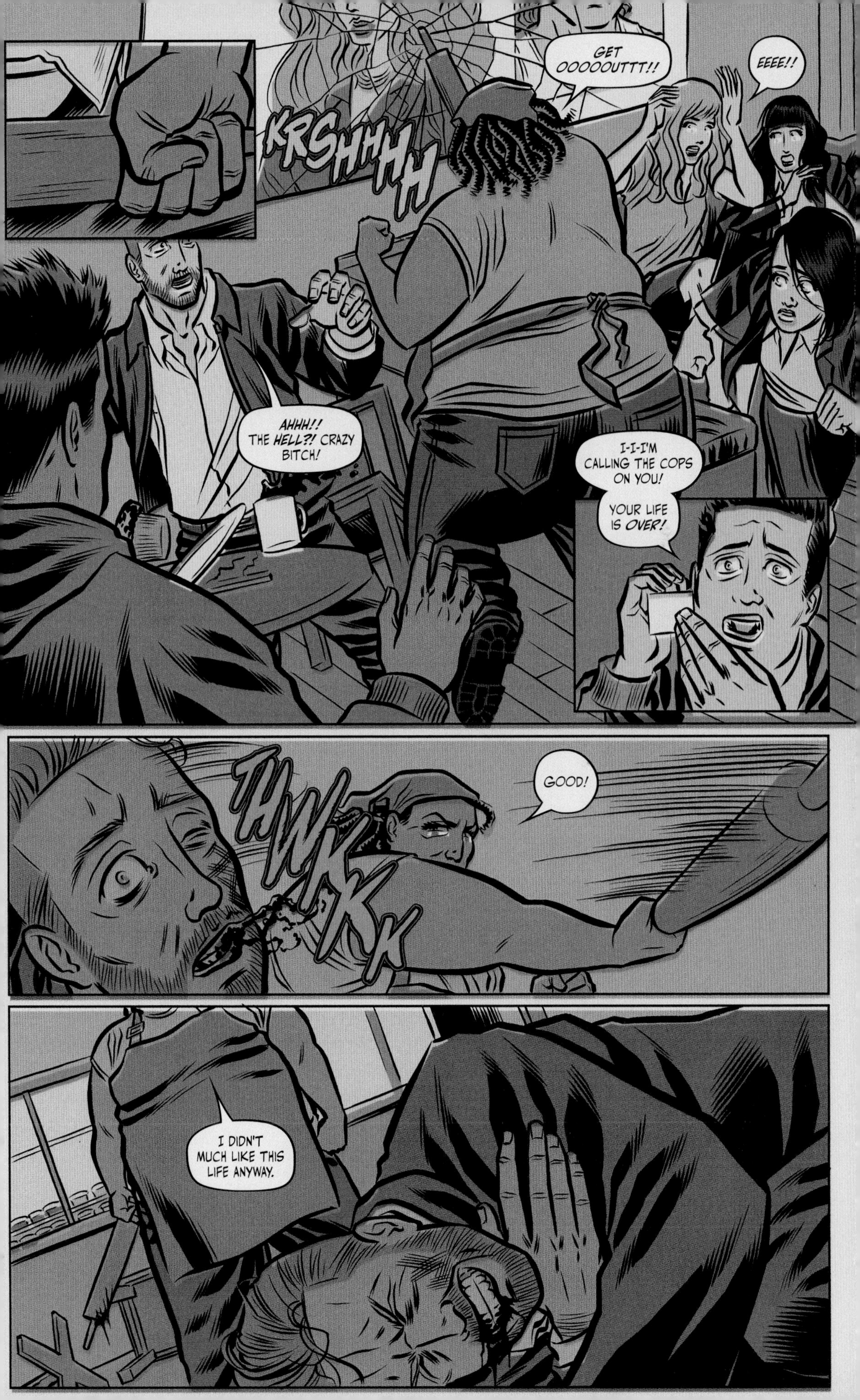
GET OOOOOUTTT!!
EEEE!!
KRSHHHH
AHHH!! THE HELL?! CRAZY BITCH!
I-I-I'M CALLING THE COPS ON YOU!
YOUR LIFE IS OVER!
THWKKK
GOOD!
I DIDN'T MUCH LIKE THIS LIFE ANYWAY.

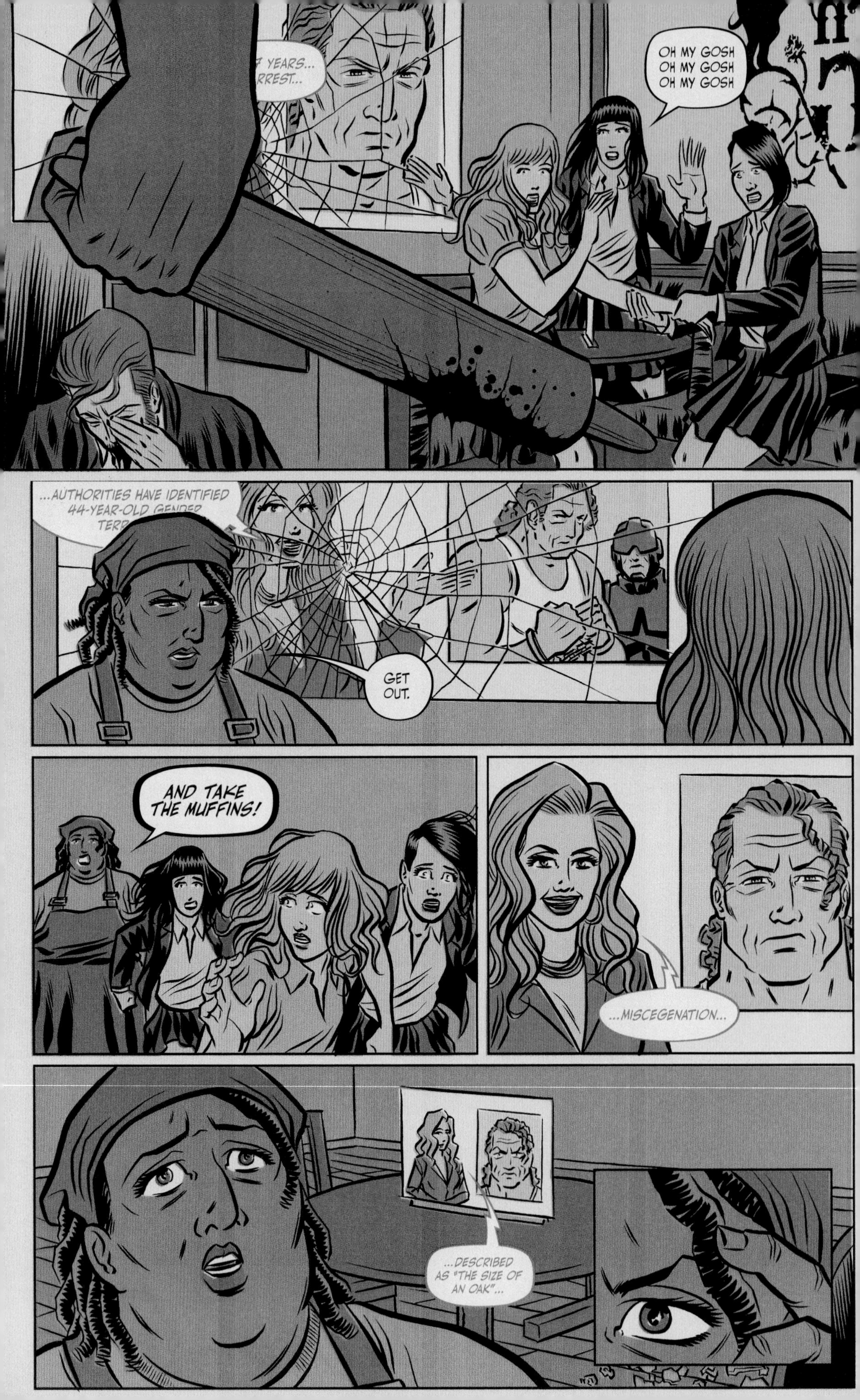

...7 YEARS...
...RREST...
OH MY GOSH
OH MY GOSH
OH MY GOSH
...AUTHORITIES HAVE IDENTIFIED 44-YEAR-OLD GENDER TERR...
GET OUT.
AND TAKE THE MUFFINS!
...MISCEGENATION...
...DESCRIBED AS "THE SIZE OF AN OAK"...

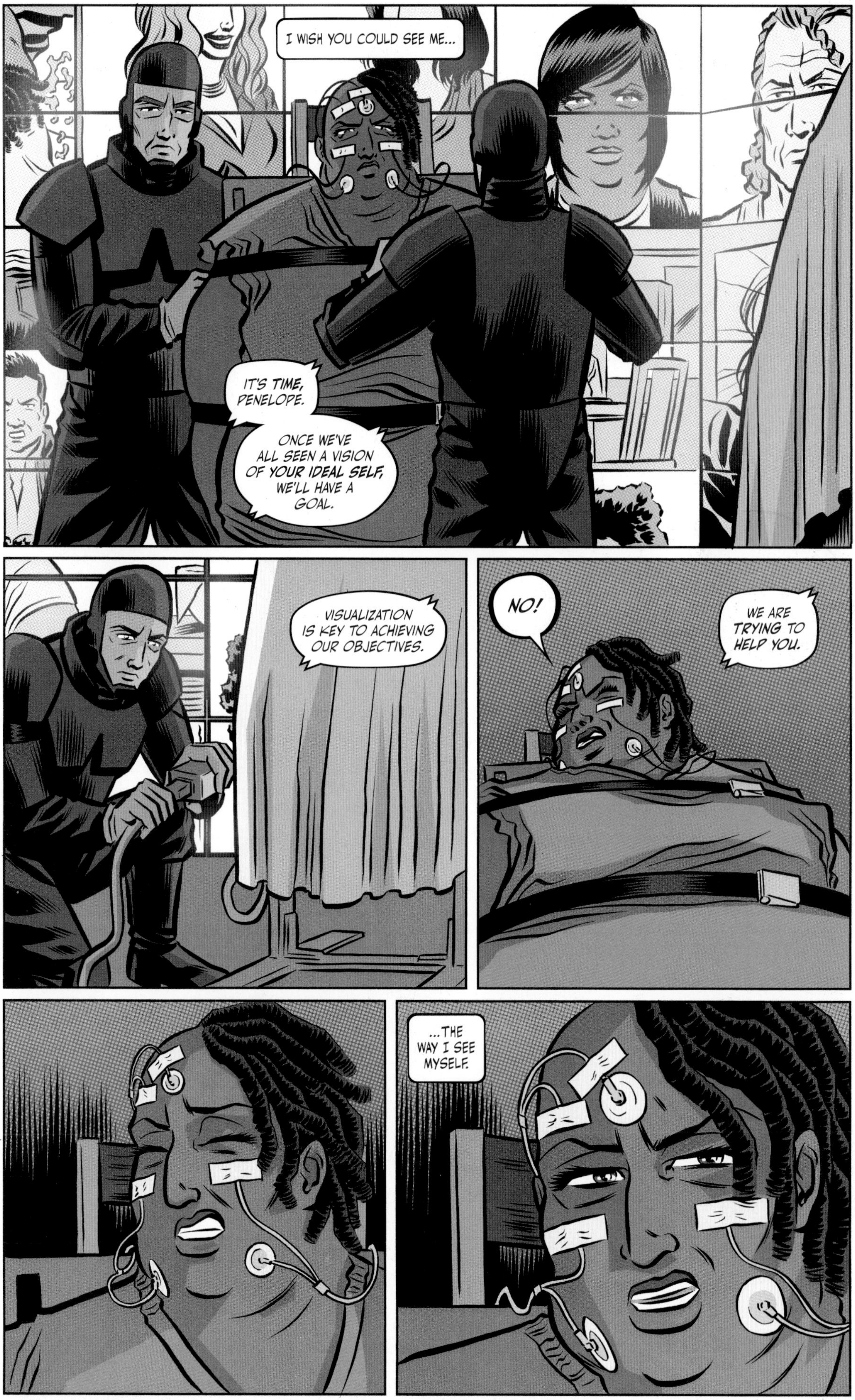
I WISH YOU COULD SEE ME...
IT'S TIME, PENELOPE.
ONCE WE'VE ALL SEEN A VISION OF YOUR IDEAL SELF, WE'LL HAVE A GOAL.
VISUALIZATION IS KEY TO ACHIEVING OUR OBJECTIVES.
NO!
WE ARE TRYING TO HELP YOU.
...THE WAY I SEE MYSELF.

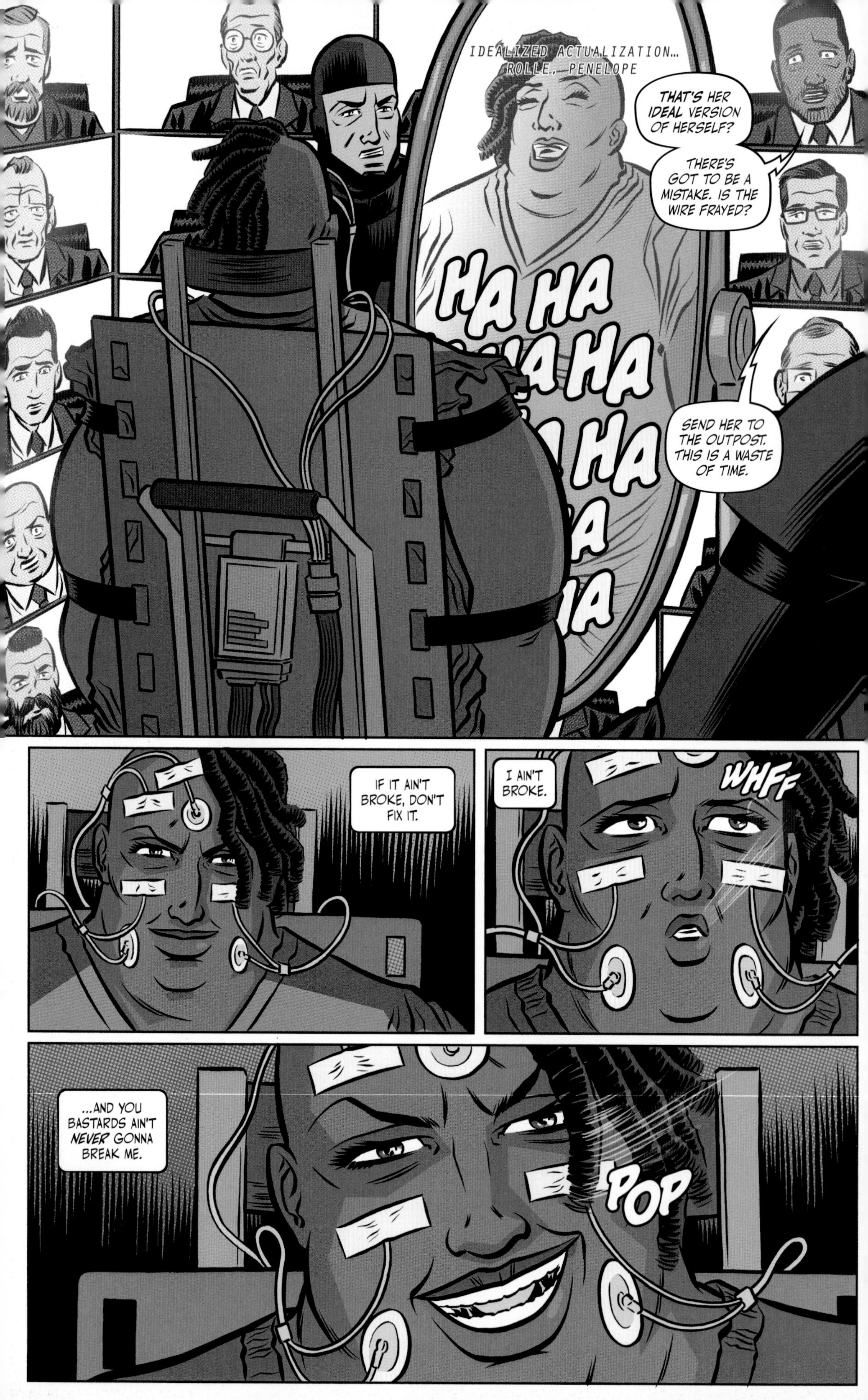
IDEALIZED ACTUALIZATION...
ROLLE, PENELOPE
THAT'S HER IDEAL VERSION OF HERSELF?
THERE'S GOT TO BE A MISTAKE. IS THE WIRE FRAYED?
HA HA HA HA HA HA HA HA HA HA
SEND HER TO THE OUTPOST. THIS IS A WASTE OF TIME.
IF IT AIN'T BROKE, DON'T FIX IT.
I AIN'T BROKE.
WHFF
...AND YOU BASTARDS AIN'T NEVER GONNA BREAK ME.
POP

HEY KIDS, PATRIARCHY!

DIMINISH WITH DELICIOUS CESTODA

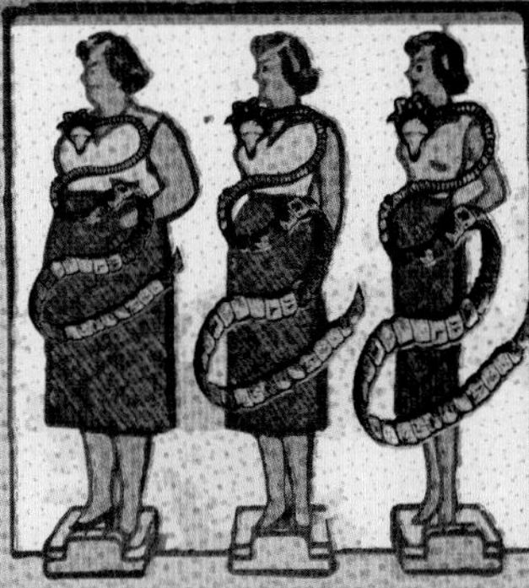

THIS CAN HAPPEN TO YOU
IF YOU ARE DESPERATE ENOUGH TO EAT A PARASITE

WE GUARANTEE YOU WILL LOSE
YOUR BALANCE!
YOUR ENERGY!
YOUR JOIE DE VIVRE!
YOUR WILL TO LIVE!

AND KEEP IT OFF

MONEY BACK GUARANTEE

If you try to order a diet parasite from us, we will donate your money to the Girls Leadership Institute in the hopes that tomorrows generation fares better. And we will be sad for you.

GUARANTEED.

STOP BEING SO FAT AND GROSS YOU BIG FATTY!

OR maybe try not to let other people's standards of beauty or femininity or your value as a human being dictate your self-worth. If **ANY PART OF YOU** has ever been jealous of anorexics or considered extra-medical hormone injections or parasites, or used body-hate to bond with girlfriends, you have bought in. It's near impossible not to, but maybe today **TRY** not to believe that your **VALUE** is inextricably linked to some asshat's assessment of your desirability. Fuck that dude. Fuck that **CULTURE.**

Missed Connection

According to the U.S. Surgeon General, domestic violence is the **leading cause of injury to women** in the United States.
Source: National Domestic Violence Statistics, Arkansas Coalition Against Domestic Violence, DomesticPeace.com

BITCH PLANET POSTER

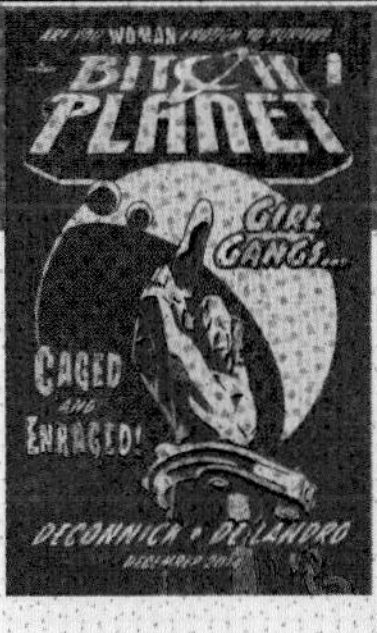
BITCH PLANET
GIRL GANGS...
CAGED AND ENRAGED!
DECONNICK • DE LANDRO

Do you have a dorm room? Does it have a **DOOR**? Have we got a **POSTER** for you? **YES**! 17 inches tall, 11 inches wide, 3 ½ glorious inches of the majestic **NC** bird. C'mon, it's this or that stupid Marilyn Monroe print they keep trying to sell you on the commons.

POSTER..$7 w/shipping

Missed Connection

I think the lady who took my money at Captain Dees had a **#noncompliant** tattoo. I hope it was any way, cause that would be **awesome.**

- Adam carter
@theadamcarter

Missed Connection

Number of American women murdered by their intimate partners between 2002-1012: **15,462**
Total American deaths from September 11 and the wars in Iraq and Afghanistan combined as of October 2014: **9,838.**
Source: politifact.com

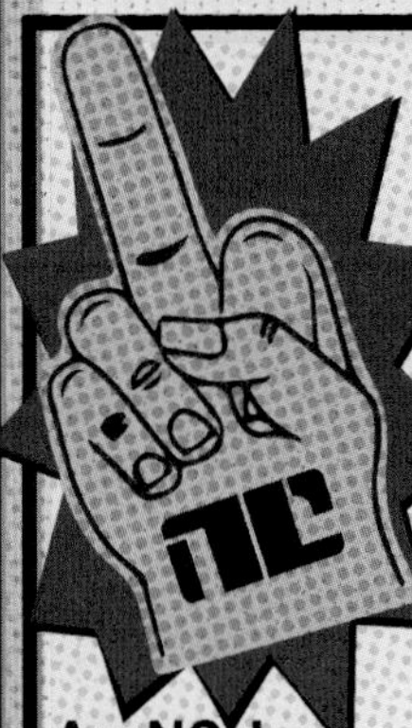

WE'VE GOT YOUR SPIRIT FINGERS RIGHT HERE!

Are you a **MEGATON** fan?? Want to let the **BAD GIRLS** of **BITCH PLANET** know you're an NC team booster? Sit in the stands and give the **BIRD SALUTE** for **YOUR GIRLS!**

What do we want?
TO GIVE THEM THE FINGER!
When to we want it?
OH MY GOD ALL THE FUCKING TIME??

AgeNCy!
AdamaNCy!
AscendaNCy!

FINGER.........$4 w/shipping

Are You Non-Compliant?

GIRLS, GIRLS, GIRLS!

You want that sexy, his-blood-in-a-bottle-around-your-neck **CRAZY CHICK** mystique? What says **DREAMY BAD GIRL** like a temporary tattoo??

PUT IT ON YOUR FACE.

NON..................................$1.50 w/shipping

YOU BUYING THIS?

You know this is garbage, right? You're ordering garbage. Okay, well, you were warned. Send your dad's hard earned money to the address below and we'll keep the Postal Service alive a little longer by mailing you some crap. I'm not shipping international, so don't even try.

ALLOW 3-6 WEEKS FOR SHIPPING

ITEM	HOW MANY	PRICE
FINGER		$5.00
POSTER		$7.00
NON		$1.50
TOTAL		

SEND CHECK OR MONEY ORDER TO:
Milkfed Criminal Masterminds, Inc. PO Box 25662, Portland, OR 97298

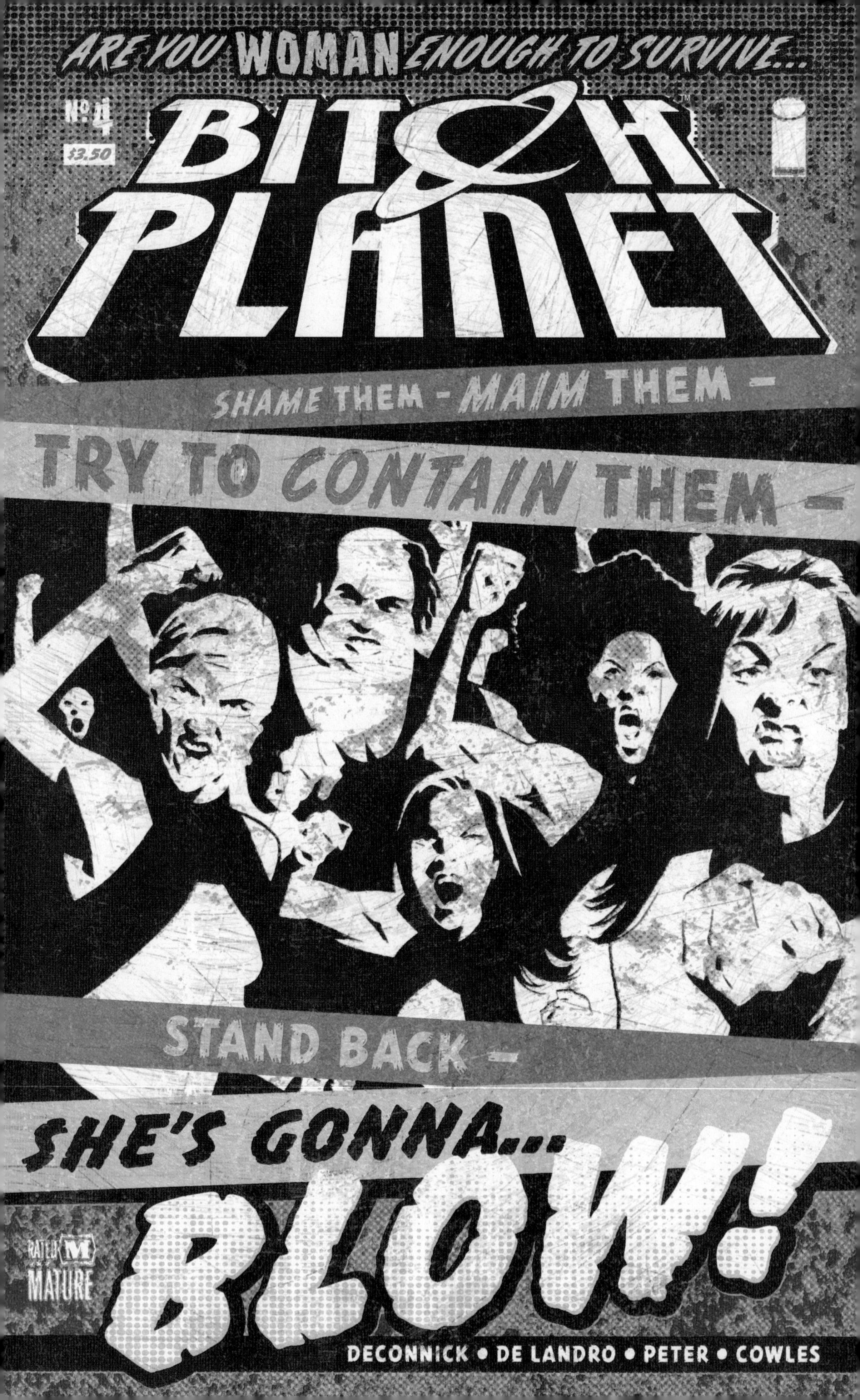
ARE YOU WOMAN ENOUGH TO SURVIVE...
Nº 4
$3.50
BITCH PLANET
SHAME THEM - MAIM THEM -
TRY TO CONTAIN THEM -
STAND BACK -
SHE'S GONNA... BLOW!
RATED M MATURE
DECONNICK • DE LANDRO • PETER • COWLES

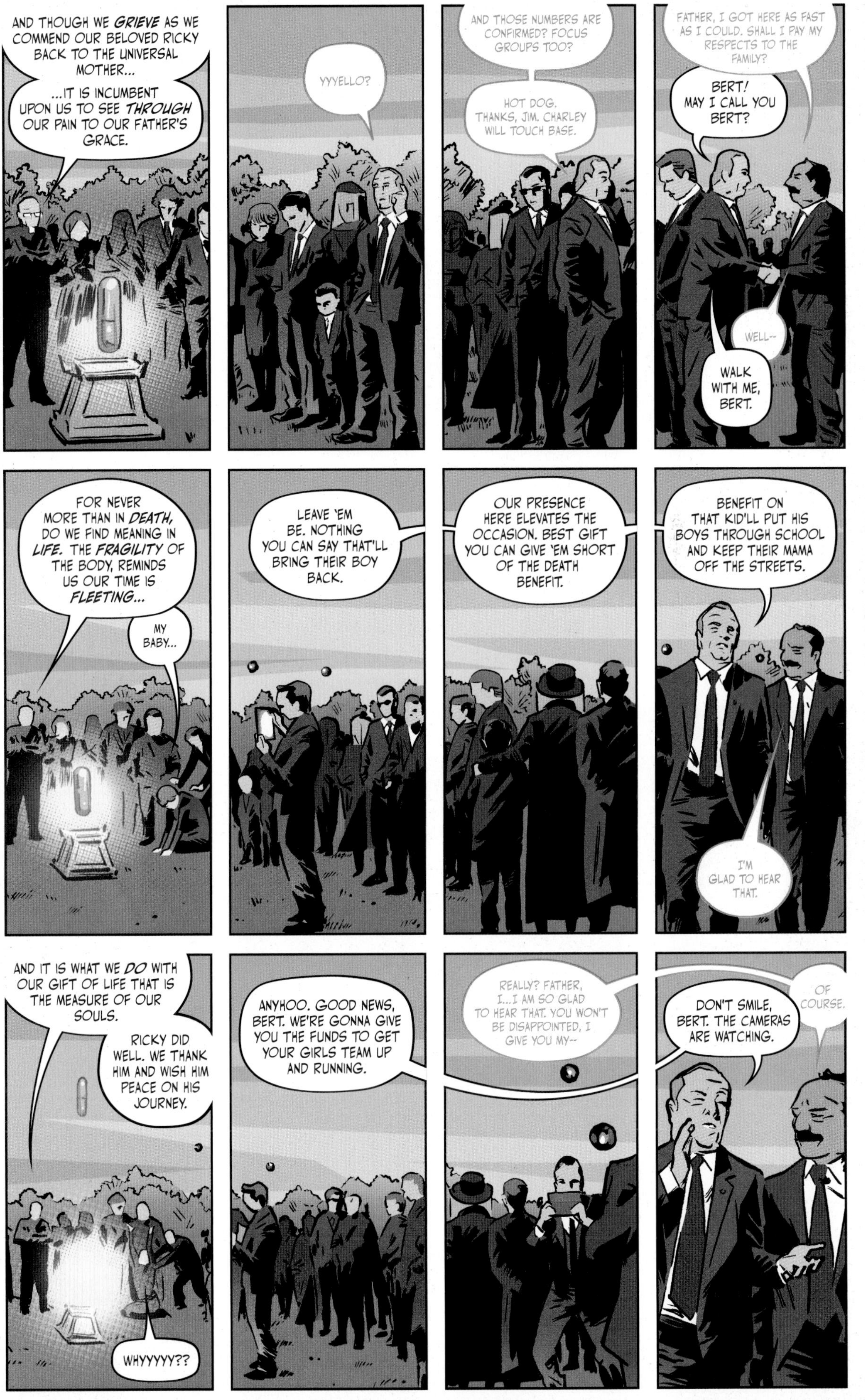
AND THOUGH WE GRIEVE AS WE COMMEND OUR BELOVED RICKY BACK TO THE UNIVERSAL MOTHER...
...IT IS INCUMBENT UPON US TO SEE THROUGH OUR PAIN TO OUR FATHER'S GRACE.
YYYELLO?
AND THOSE NUMBERS ARE CONFIRMED? FOCUS GROUPS TOO?
HOT DOG. THANKS, JIM. CHARLEY WILL TOUCH BASE.
FATHER, I GOT HERE AS FAST AS I COULD. SHALL I PAY MY RESPECTS TO THE FAMILY?
BERT! MAY I CALL YOU BERT?
WELL--
WALK WITH ME, BERT.
FOR NEVER MORE THAN IN DEATH, DO WE FIND MEANING IN LIFE. THE FRAGILITY OF THE BODY, REMINDS US OUR TIME IS FLEETING...
MY BABY...
LEAVE 'EM BE. NOTHING YOU CAN SAY THAT'LL BRING THEIR BOY BACK.
OUR PRESENCE HERE ELEVATES THE OCCASION. BEST GIFT YOU CAN GIVE 'EM SHORT OF THE DEATH BENEFIT.
BENEFIT ON THAT KID'LL PUT HIS BOYS THROUGH SCHOOL AND KEEP THEIR MAMA OFF THE STREETS.
I'M GLAD TO HEAR THAT.
AND IT IS WHAT WE DO WITH OUR GIFT OF LIFE THAT IS THE MEASURE OF OUR SOULS.
RICKY DID WELL. WE THANK HIM AND WISH HIM PEACE ON HIS JOURNEY.
WHYYYYY??
ANYHOO. GOOD NEWS, BERT. WE'RE GONNA GIVE YOU THE FUNDS TO GET YOUR GIRLS TEAM UP AND RUNNING.
REALLY? FATHER, I...I AM SO GLAD TO HEAR THAT. YOU WON'T BE DISAPPOINTED, I GIVE YOU MY--
DON'T SMILE, BERT. THE CAMERAS ARE WATCHING.
OF COURSE.

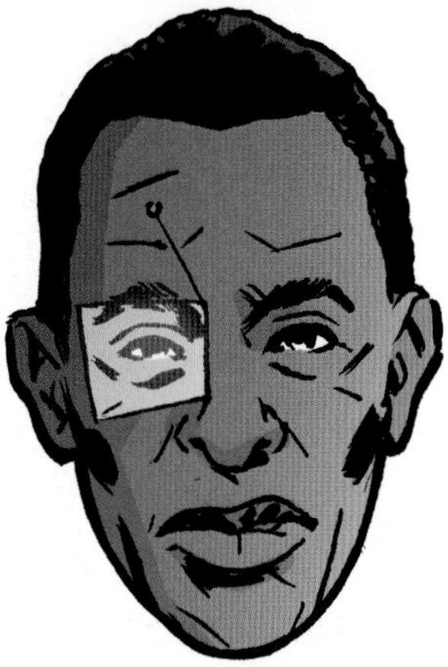
YOU EVER FEEL SORRY FOR THEM? THE NCS, I MEAN? EVERY WONDER WHAT IF IT HAD GONE DOWN DIFFERENT--

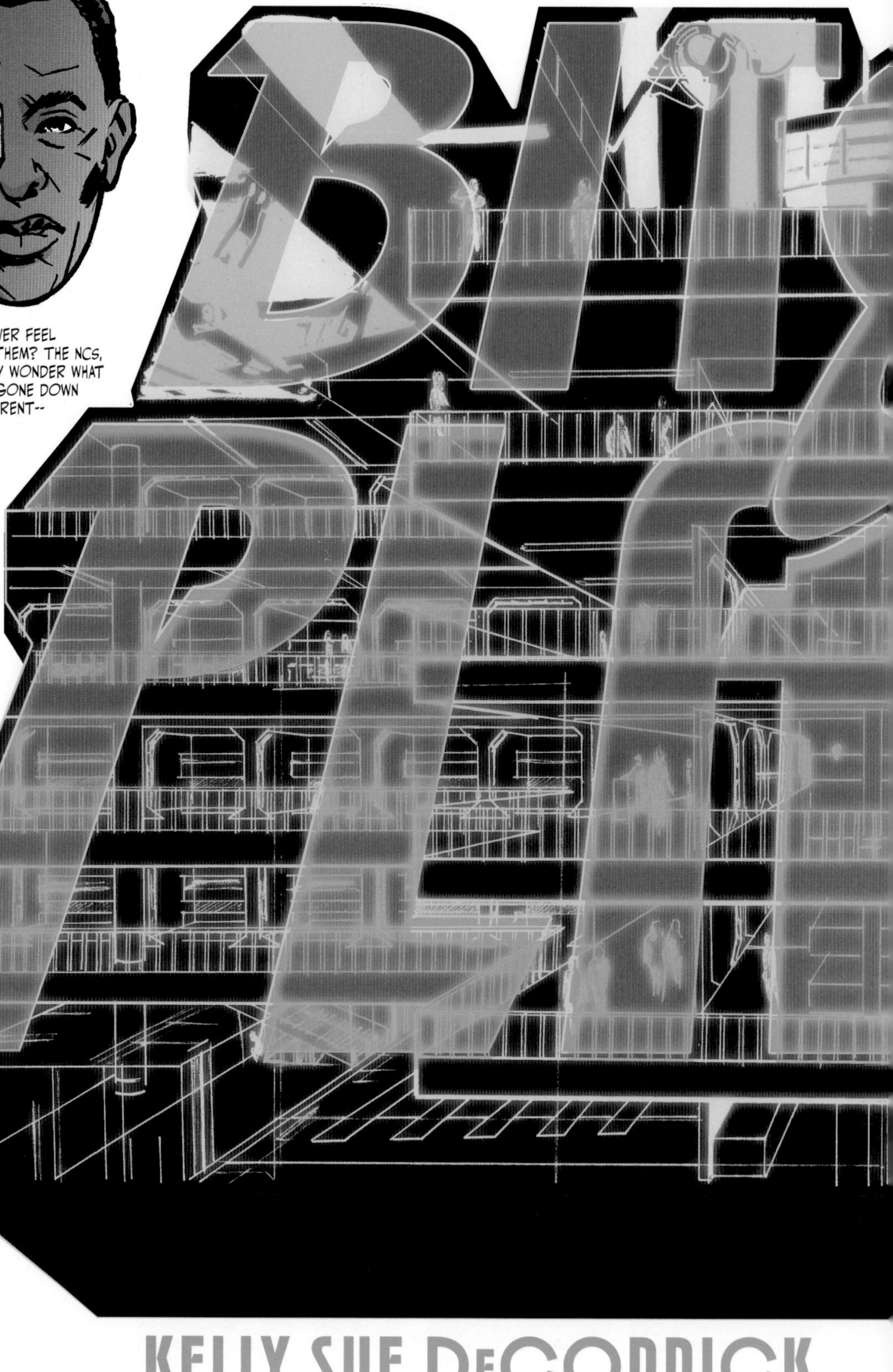

KELLY SUE DECONNICK
SCRIPT

CRIS PETER
COLORS

CLAYTON COWLES
LETTERS

RIAN HUGHES
COVER DESIGN & LOGO DESIGN

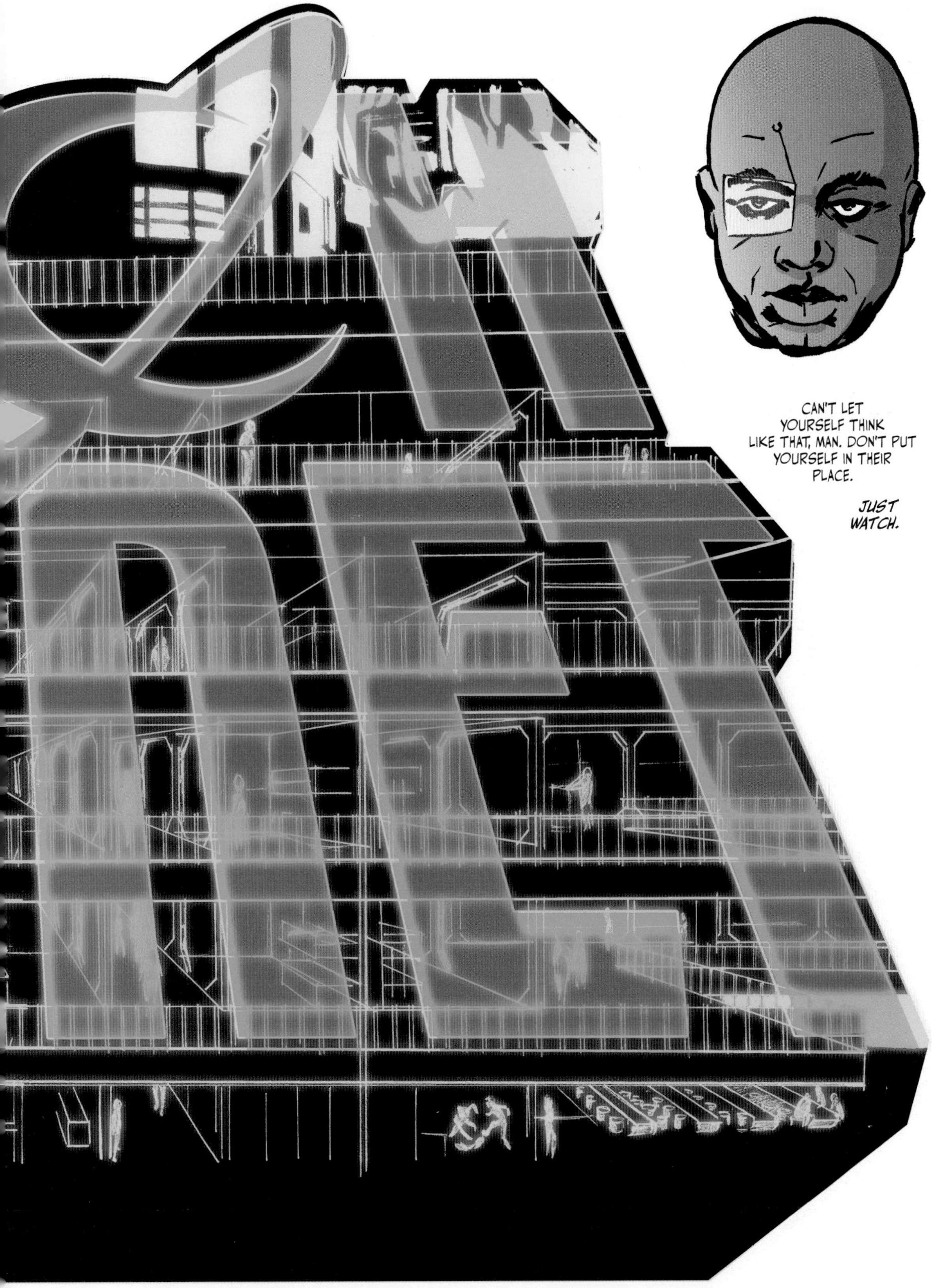
CAN'T LET YOURSELF THINK LIKE THAT, MAN. DON'T PUT YOURSELF IN THEIR PLACE.
JUST WATCH.

VALENTINE DE LANDRO
ART/COVERS

LAURENN McCUBBIN
BACKMATTER DESIGN

LAUREN SANKOVITCH
EDITOR

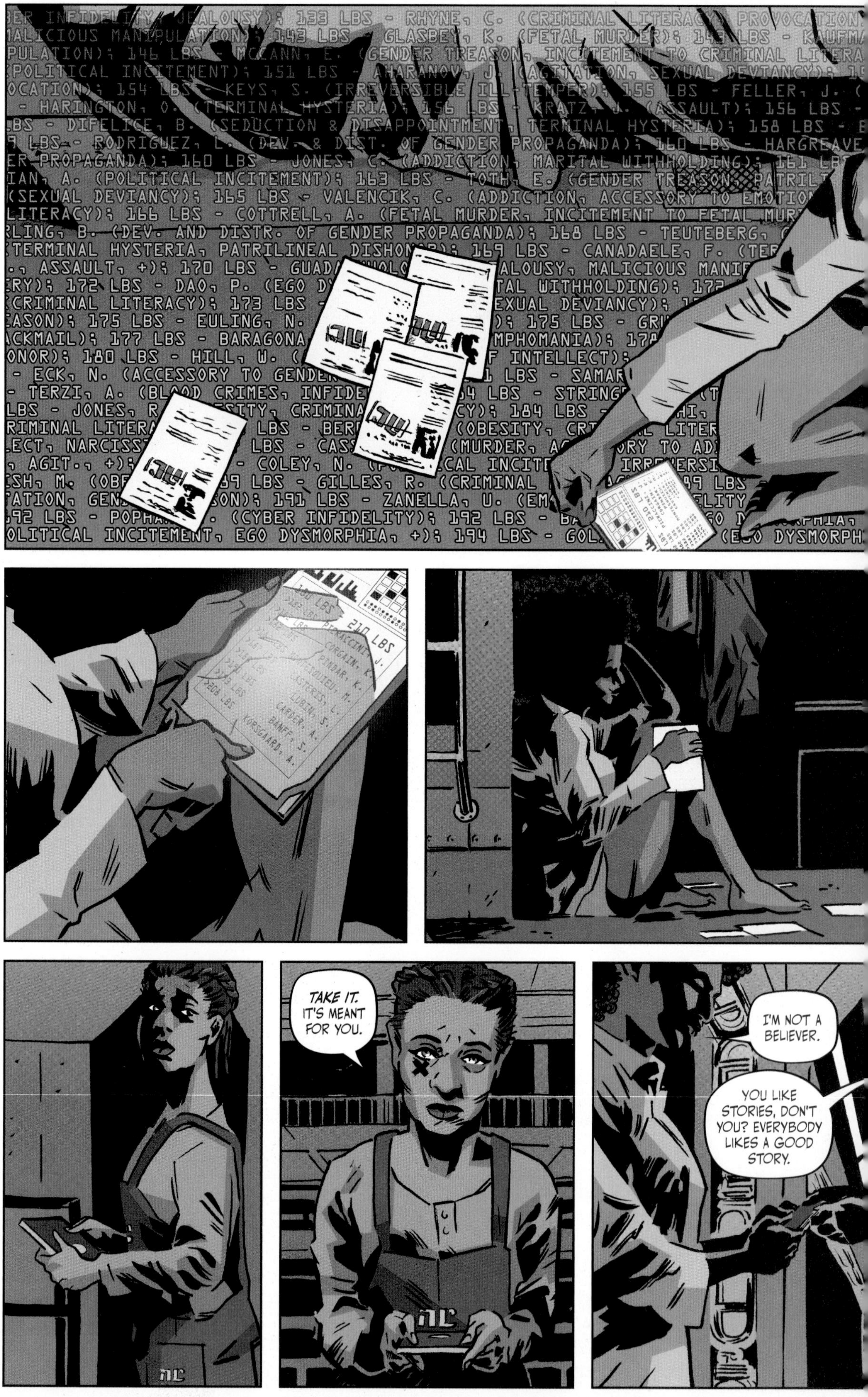
TAKE IT. IT'S MEANT FOR YOU.
I'M NOT A BELIEVER.
YOU LIKE STORIES, DON'T YOU? EVERYBODY LIKES A GOOD STORY.

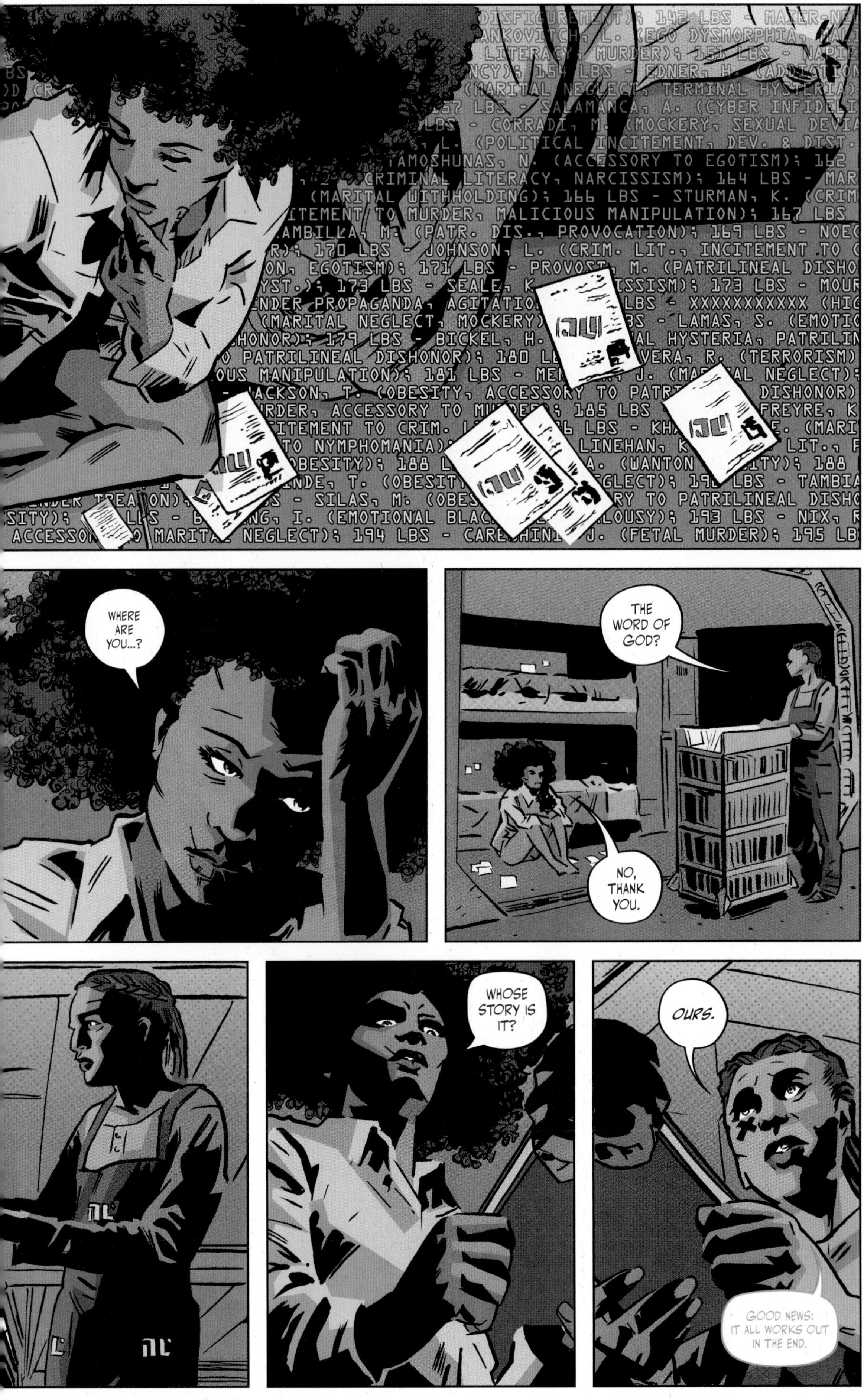
WHERE ARE YOU...?
THE WORD OF GOD?
NO, THANK YOU.
WHOSE STORY IS IT?
OURS.
GOOD NEWS: IT ALL WORKS OUT IN THE END.

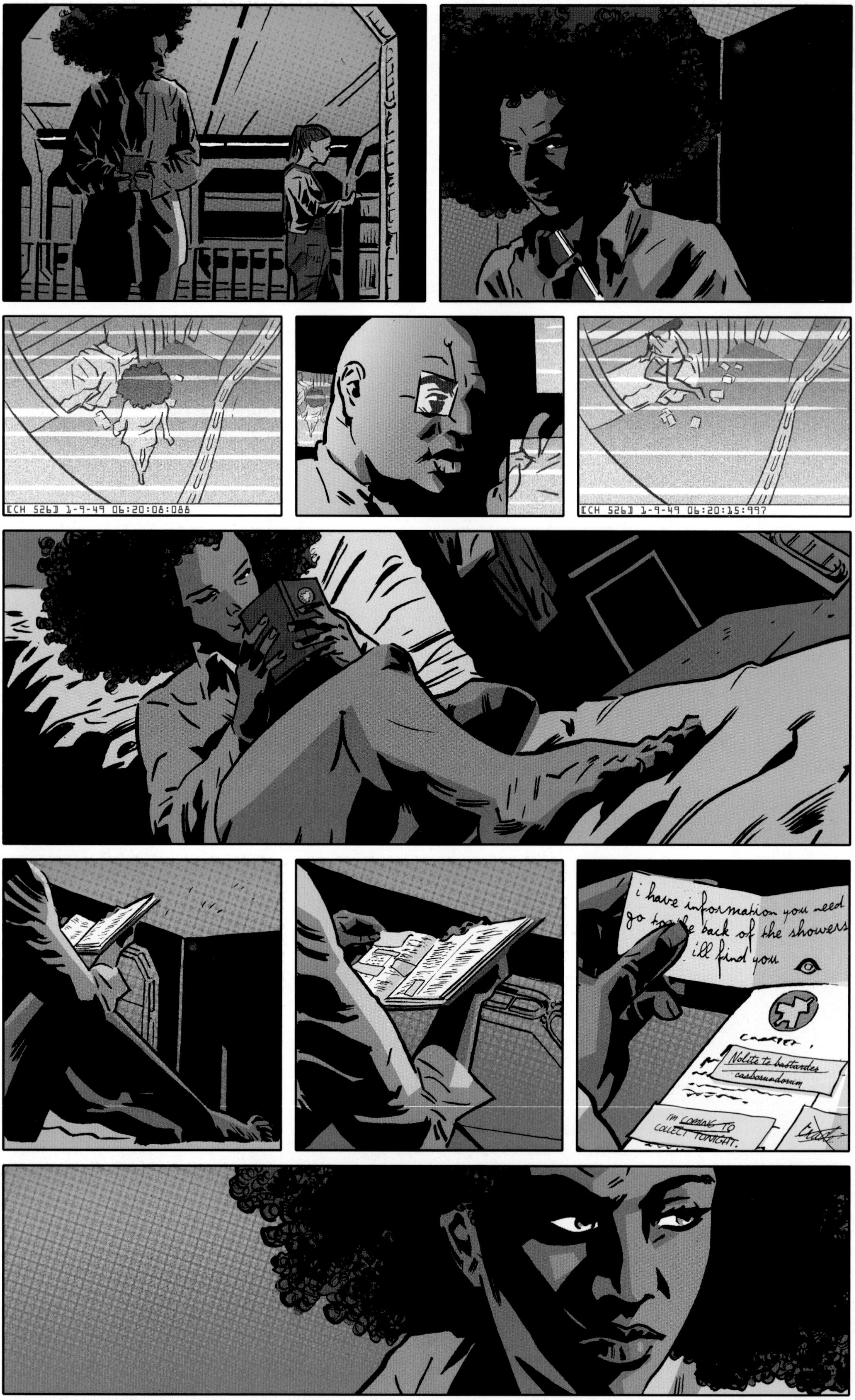
[CH 526] 1-9-49 06:20:08:088
[CH 526] 1-9-49 06:20:15:997
i have information you need
go to the back of the showers
ill find you
Nolite te bastardes
carborundorum
I'M COMING TO
COLLECT TONIGHT.

THE OBLIGATORY SHOWER SCENE

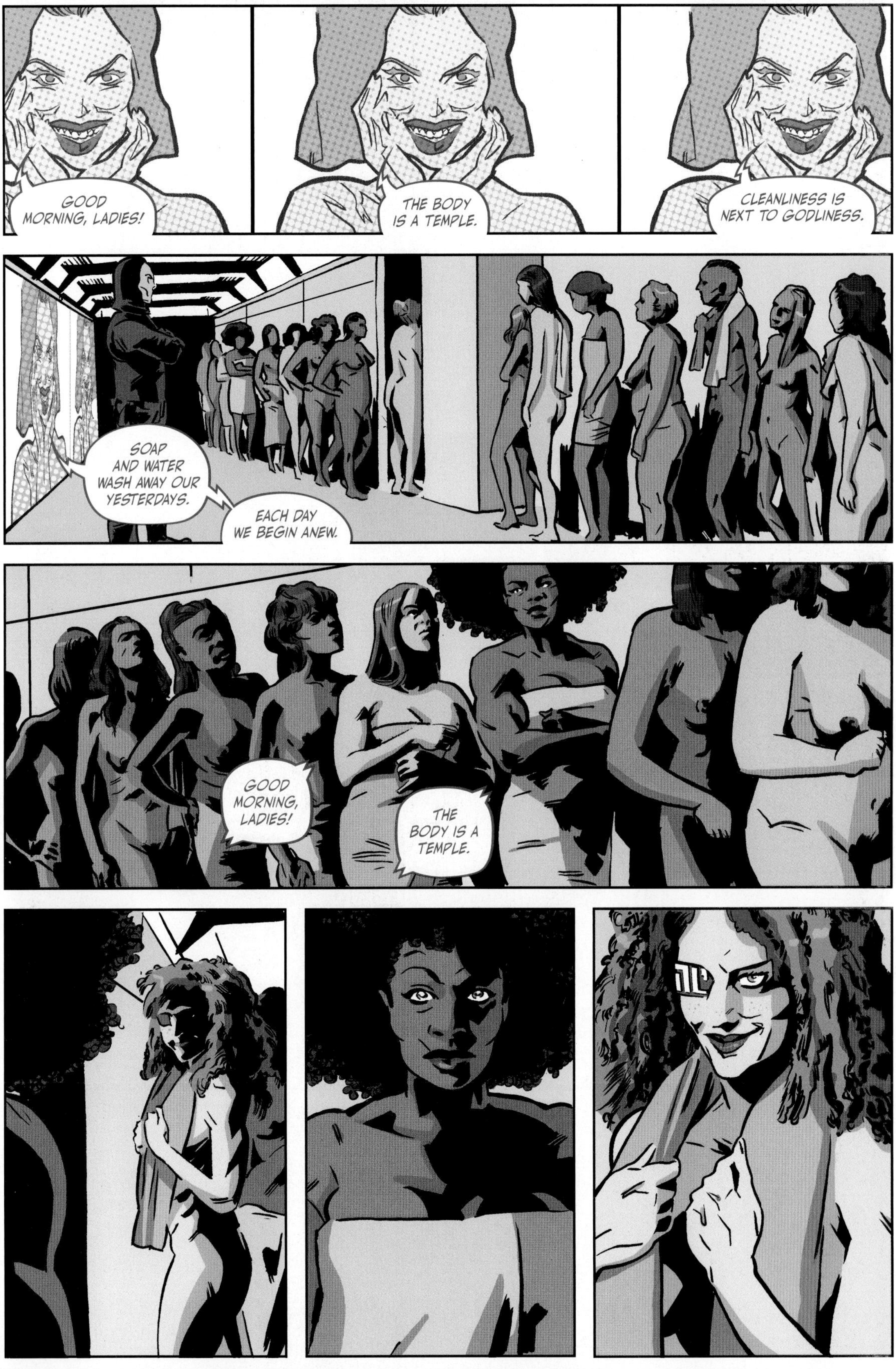
GOOD MORNING, LADIES!
THE BODY IS A TEMPLE.
CLEANLINESS IS NEXT TO GODLINESS.
SOAP AND WATER WASH AWAY OUR YESTERDAYS.
EACH DAY WE BEGIN ANEW.
GOOD MORNING, LADIES!
THE BODY IS A TEMPLE.

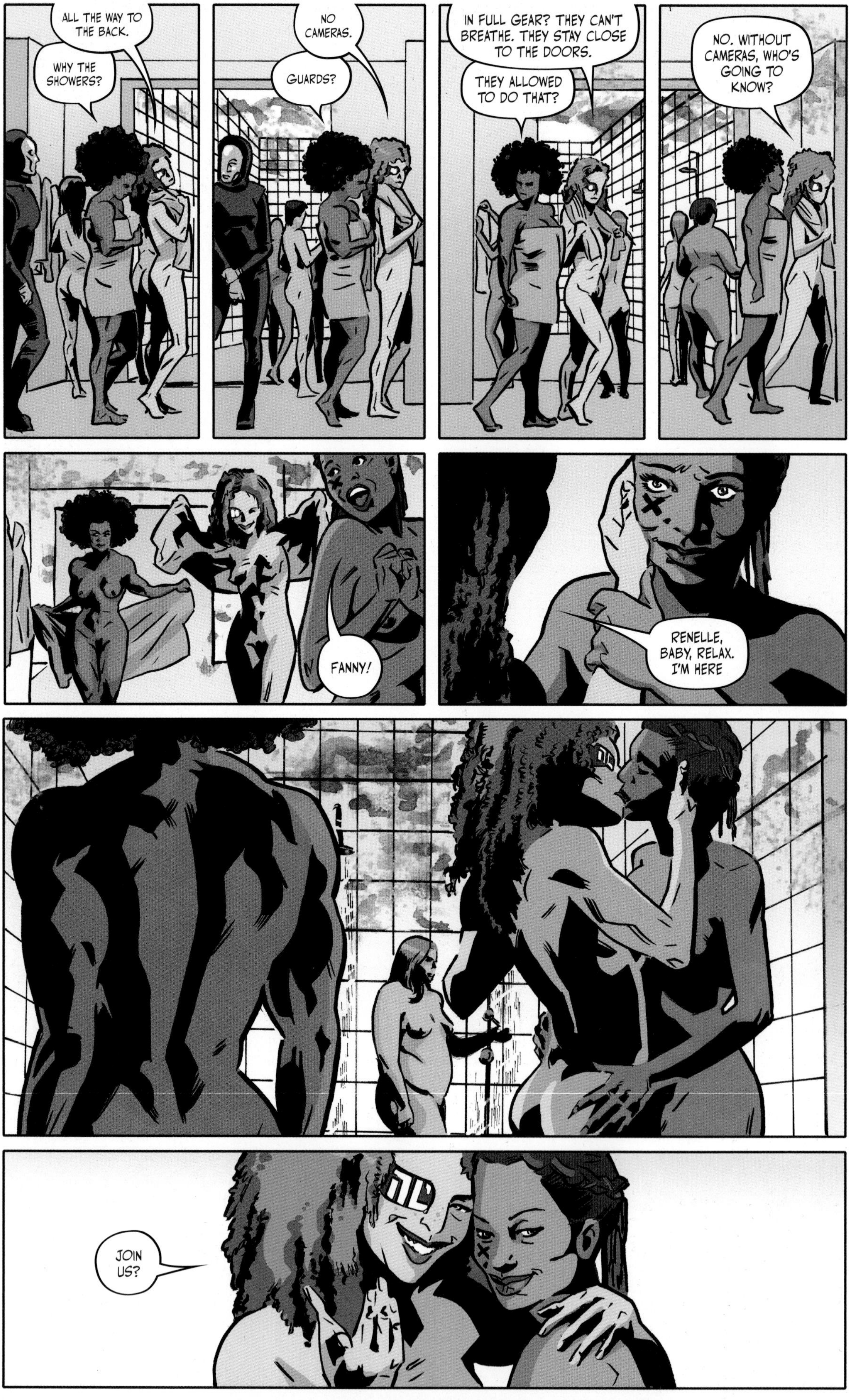
ALL THE WAY TO THE BACK.
WHY THE SHOWERS?
NO CAMERAS.
GUARDS?
IN FULL GEAR? THEY CAN'T BREATHE. THEY STAY CLOSE TO THE DOORS.
THEY ALLOWED TO DO THAT?
NO. WITHOUT CAMERAS, WHO'S GOING TO KNOW?
FANNY!
RENELLE, BABY, RELAX. I'M HERE
JOIN US?

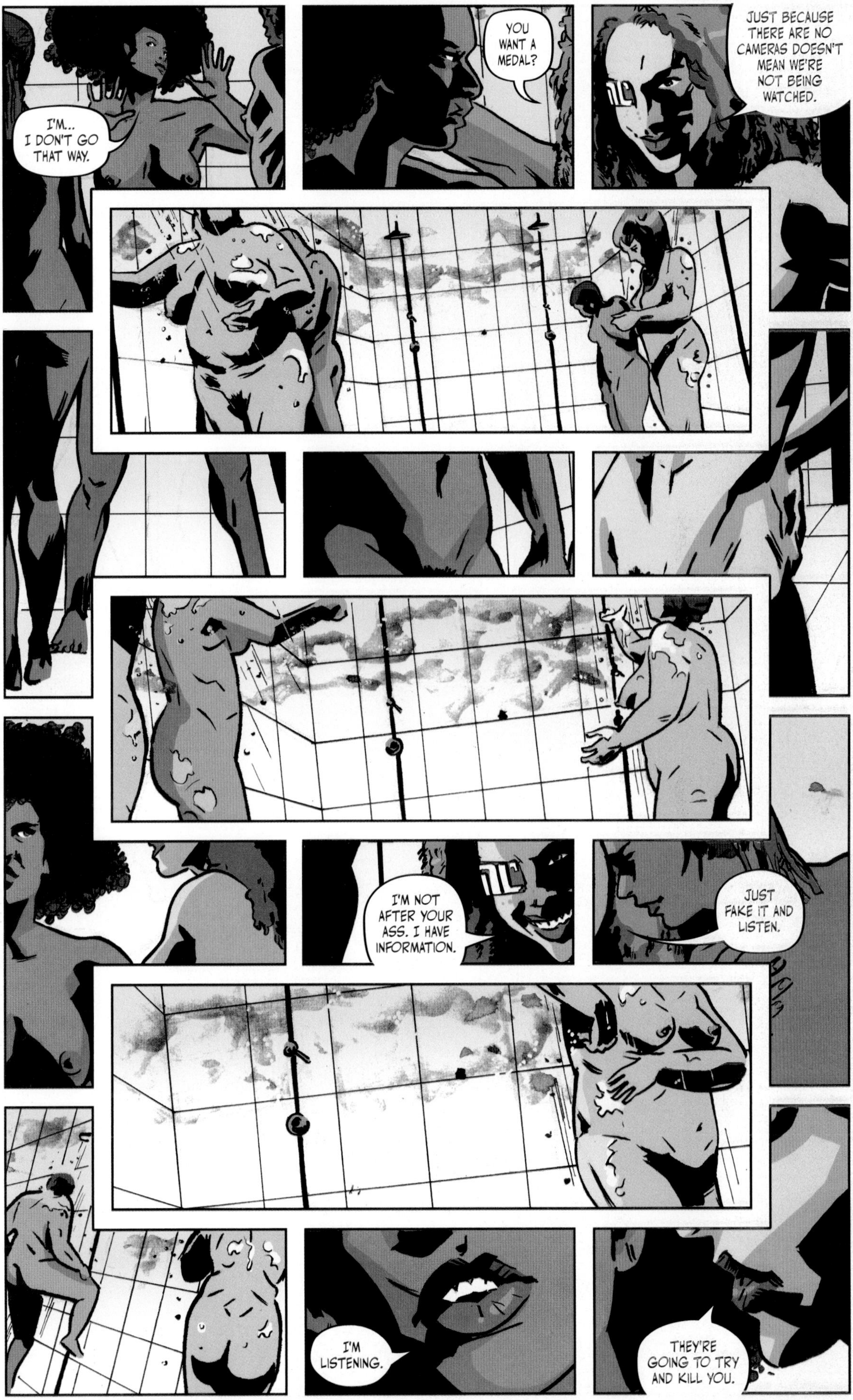
I'M... I DON'T GO THAT WAY.
YOU WANT A MEDAL?
JUST BECAUSE THERE ARE NO CAMERAS DOESN'T MEAN WE'RE NOT BEING WATCHED.
I'M NOT AFTER YOUR ASS. I HAVE INFORMATION.
JUST FAKE IT AND LISTEN.
I'M LISTENING.
THEY'RE GOING TO TRY AND KILL YOU.

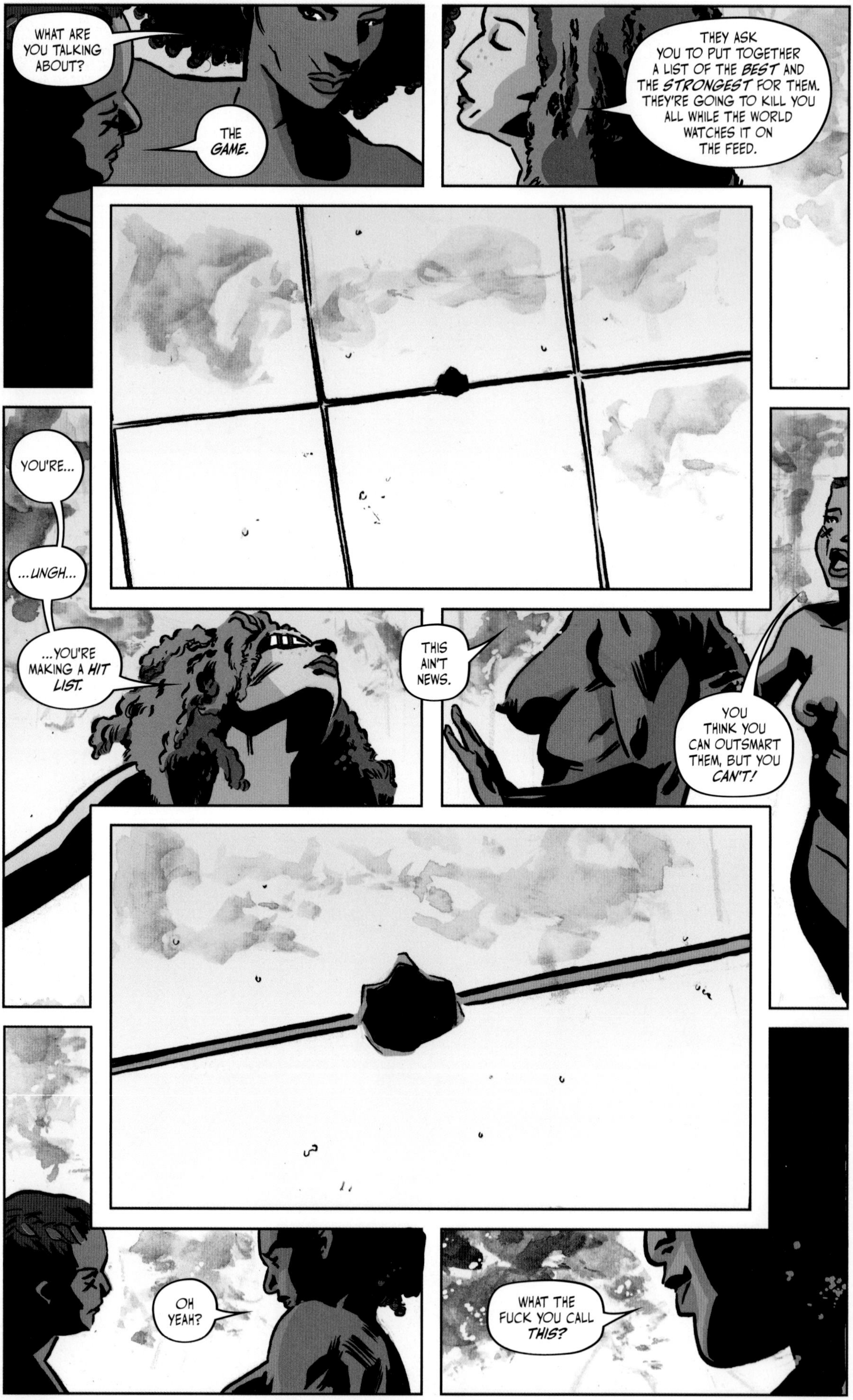
WHAT ARE YOU TALKING ABOUT?
THE *GAME.*
THEY ASK YOU TO PUT TOGETHER A LIST OF THE *BEST* AND THE *STRONGEST* FOR THEM. THEY'RE GOING TO KILL YOU ALL WHILE THE WORLD WATCHES IT ON THE FEED.
YOU'RE...
...*UNGH*...
...YOU'RE MAKING A *HIT LIST.*
THIS AIN'T NEWS.
YOU THINK YOU CAN OUTSMART THEM, BUT YOU *CAN'T!*
OH YEAH?
WHAT THE FUCK YOU CALL *THIS?*

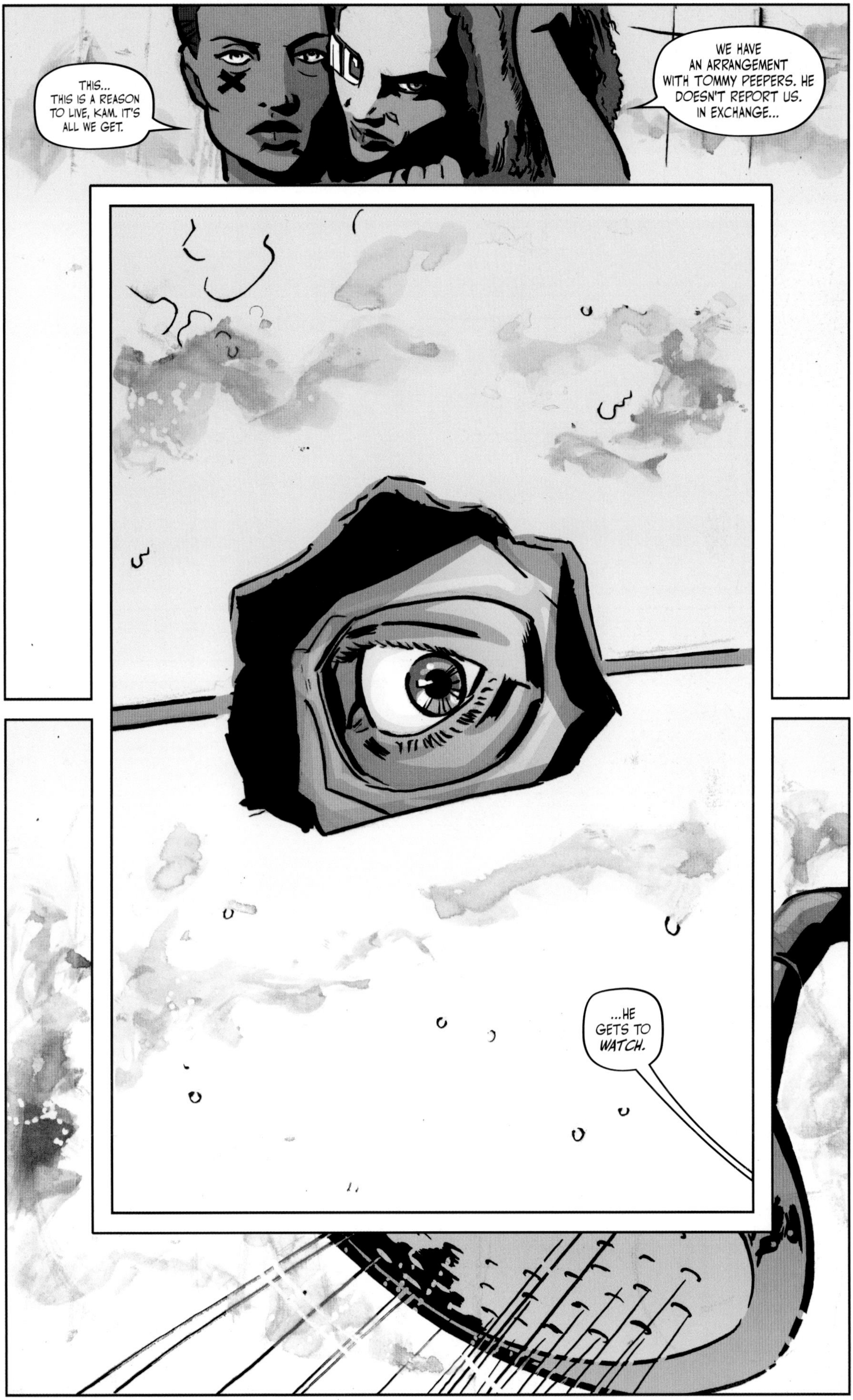
THIS... THIS IS A REASON TO LIVE, KAM. IT'S ALL WE GET.
WE HAVE AN ARRANGEMENT WITH TOMMY PEEPERS. HE DOESN'T REPORT US. IN EXCHANGE...
...HE GETS TO *WATCH.*

WHAT'VE WE GOT FOR MEGATON RULES?

OH, GOD. ALL RIGHT.

HAILEY AND KAILEY.

ROLLING HAILEY AND KAILEY IN 3...2...

MEGATON 101

IL MONDO DEL DUEMILA FOR DUMMIES WOMEN with *Hailey & Kailey*

HI, KAILEY!

HI, HAILEY!

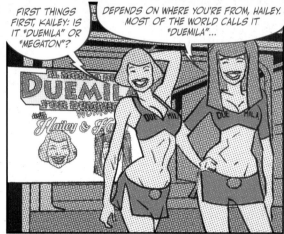

FIRST THINGS FIRST, KAILEY: IS IT "DUEMILA" OR "MEGATON"?

DEPENDS ON WHERE YOU'RE FROM, HAILEY. MOST OF THE WORLD CALLS IT "DUEMILA"...

...BUT HERE IN THE NEW PROTECTORATE IT'S MEGATON.

I DID NOT KNOW THAT! BUT I DID KNOW THIS--

MEN LOVE MEGATON!!

WHETHER THEY'RE WATCHING, PLAYING, TALKING ABOUT OR--IN PROPERLY LICENSED VENUES--BETTING ON THE GAME...

MEN ARE OBSESSED WITH THE SPORT THAT IS TWO TONS OF FUN.

SINGLE LADIES, JUST IMAGINE THE GLEAM IN HIS EYE WHEN YOU FOOL HIM INTO THINKING YOU SHARE HIS PASSION!

MARRIED LADIES, MEN WHO TALK MEGATON DO BETTER AT THE OFFICE. YOU'LL REIGNITE THAT SPARK AND HELP HIM SUCCEED.

I'M CONVINCED, KAILEY! WHERE DO WE BEGIN?

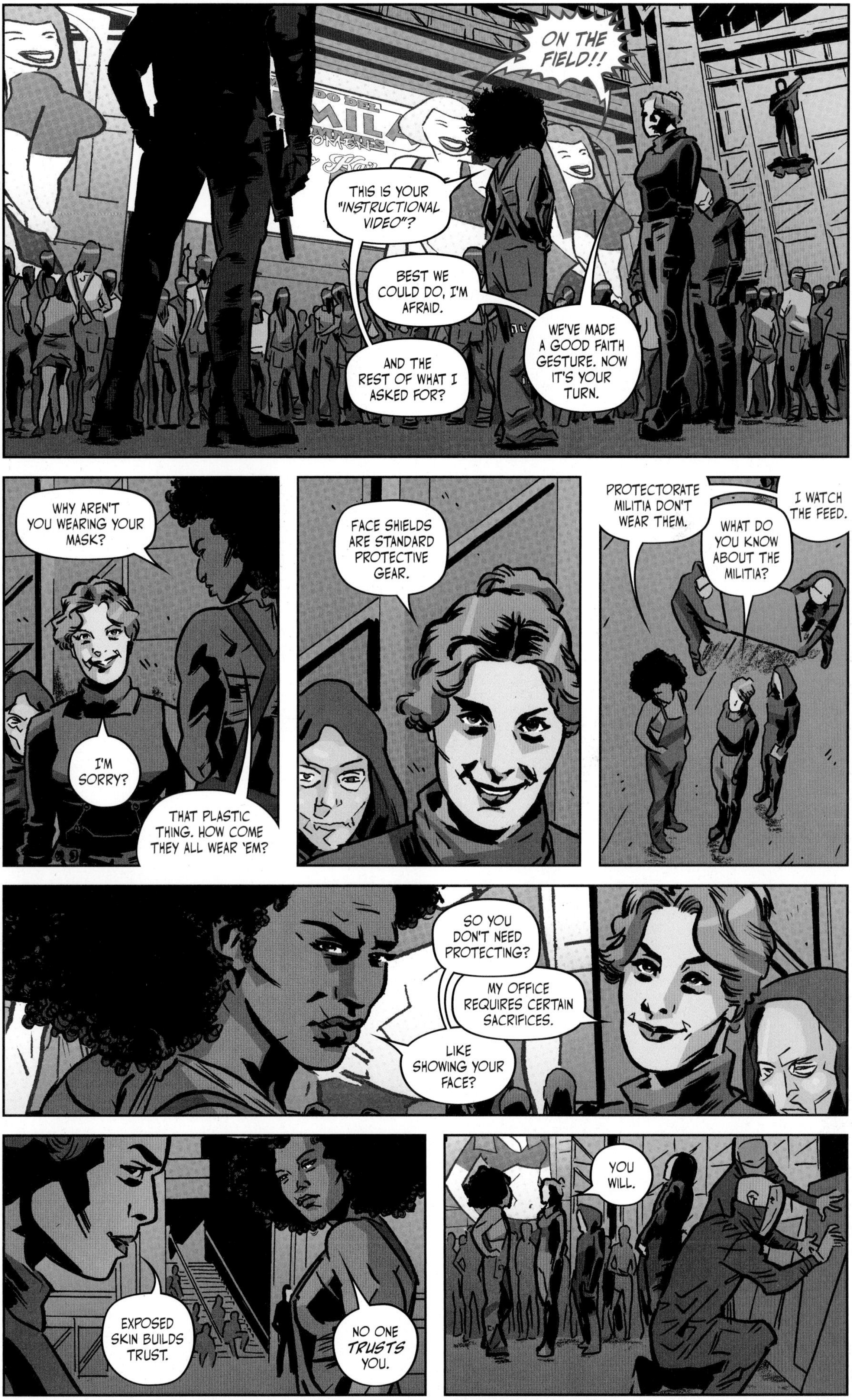
ON THE FIELD!!
THIS IS YOUR "INSTRUCTIONAL VIDEO"?
BEST WE COULD DO, I'M AFRAID.
AND THE REST OF WHAT I ASKED FOR?
WE'VE MADE A GOOD FAITH GESTURE. NOW IT'S YOUR TURN.
WHY AREN'T YOU WEARING YOUR MASK?
I'M SORRY?
THAT PLASTIC THING. HOW COME THEY ALL WEAR 'EM?
FACE SHIELDS ARE STANDARD PROTECTIVE GEAR.
PROTECTORATE MILITIA DON'T WEAR THEM.
WHAT DO YOU KNOW ABOUT THE MILITIA?
I WATCH THE FEED.
SO YOU DON'T NEED PROTECTING?
MY OFFICE REQUIRES CERTAIN SACRIFICES.
LIKE SHOWING YOUR FACE?
EXPOSED SKIN BUILDS TRUST.
NO ONE TRUSTS YOU.
YOU WILL.

MEGATON IS ONE OF MANY MODERN DESCENDANTS OF CALCIO FIORENTINO, A 16TH CENTURY ITALIAN SPORT.

THE MOST FAMOUS PLAYER IN THE HISTORY OF THE GAME WAS *ALEXANDER GETCHELL*, WHO LED THE *NEVADA GAMBLERS* TO SIX CONSECUTIVE TITLES FROM 2012 TO 2018.

GETCHELL WAS SO FAMOUS THAT HIS NAME WAS MORE WIDELY RECOGNIZED THAN *SANTA CLAUS*.

IL MON
DUE
FOR DU
with
Hailey

TEAMS MAY BE COMPRISED OF ANY NUMBER OF PLAYERS, BUT THEIR COMBINED WEIGHT CAN BE NO MORE THAN...

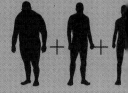

100 y

50 yards (45.72m)

LA SINISTRA

THE LONG SIDES OF THE FIELD ARE THE *OSCURO* AND THE *PULITO*, NAMED FOR THEIR POSITIONS RELATIVE TO THE THREE JUDGES, POSITIONED ON THE PULITO AT QTR LEFT, CENTER AND QTR RIGHT.

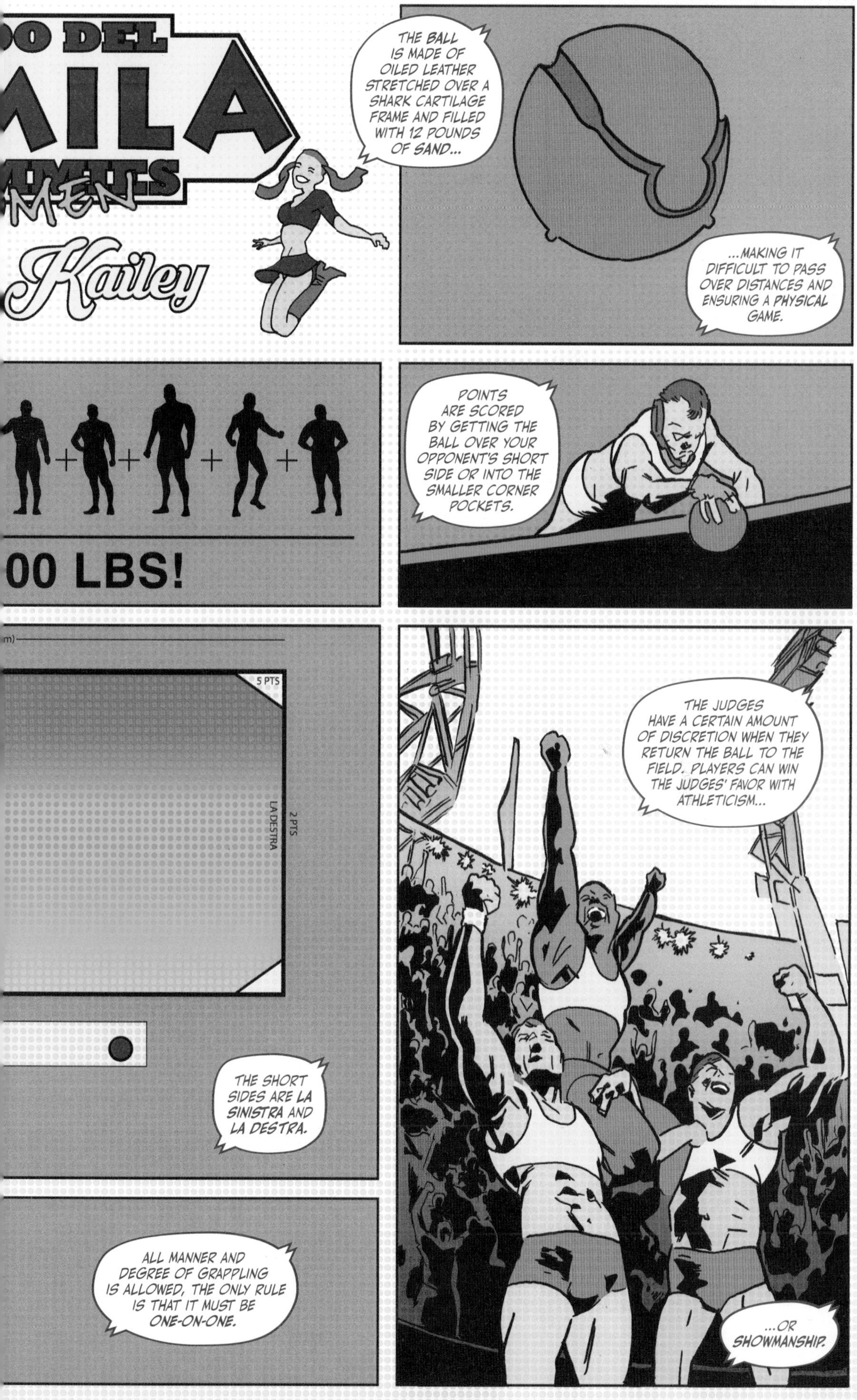

00 DEL
AILA
MEN
Kailey
THE BALL IS MADE OF OILED LEATHER STRETCHED OVER A SHARK CARTILAGE FRAME AND FILLED WITH 12 POUNDS OF SAND...
...MAKING IT DIFFICULT TO PASS OVER DISTANCES AND ENSURING A PHYSICAL GAME.
00 LBS!
POINTS ARE SCORED BY GETTING THE BALL OVER YOUR OPPONENT'S SHORT SIDE OR INTO THE SMALLER CORNER POCKETS.
5 PTS
2 PTS
LA DESTRA
THE SHORT SIDES ARE LA SINISTRA AND LA DESTRA.
ALL MANNER AND DEGREE OF GRAPPLING IS ALLOWED, THE ONLY RULE IS THAT IT MUST BE ONE-ON-ONE.
THE JUDGES HAVE A CERTAIN AMOUNT OF DISCRETION WHEN THEY RETURN THE BALL TO THE FIELD. PLAYERS CAN WIN THE JUDGES' FAVOR WITH ATHLETICISM...
...OR SHOWMANSHIP.

...OR SHOWMANSHIP.

GIMME THAT LIST.

GIMME THAT LIST... PLEASE.

WATCH YOUR TONE.

THIS ISN'T EVERYONE I ASKED FOR.

YES, WELL, A FEW OF YOUR CHOICES WERE--

MY CHOICES. THAT'S THE DEAL.

... OFFICER RIVERS, SEND THE HOLDBACKS OVER, PLEASE.

THERE'S ONE HERE WITHOUT A NAME.

>173 LBS
>173 LBS
>174 LBS
>175 LBS
>175 LBS
>175 LBS
>176 LBS
>176 LBS
>177 LBS
>177 LBS
>177 LBS
>180 LBS
>180 LBS

MOURE, O.
ROBERTS, A.
RODRIGUEZ, J.
XXXXXXXXXX
EULING, N.
GRUNDEN, F.
SIRRI, L.
LAMAS, S.
BARAGONA, E.
KLEIN, M.
BICKEL, H.
HILL,
PERIVOLAROPOULOS

THIS ONE.

THAT'S A GLITCH. THERE'S NO SUCH INMATE.

I DON'T RUN.

I DON'T NEED YOU TO RUN. I NEED YOU STOP ANYONE FROM GETTING TO MEIKO.

CAN YOU DO THAT?

I CAN.

SHOW ME.

HEH.

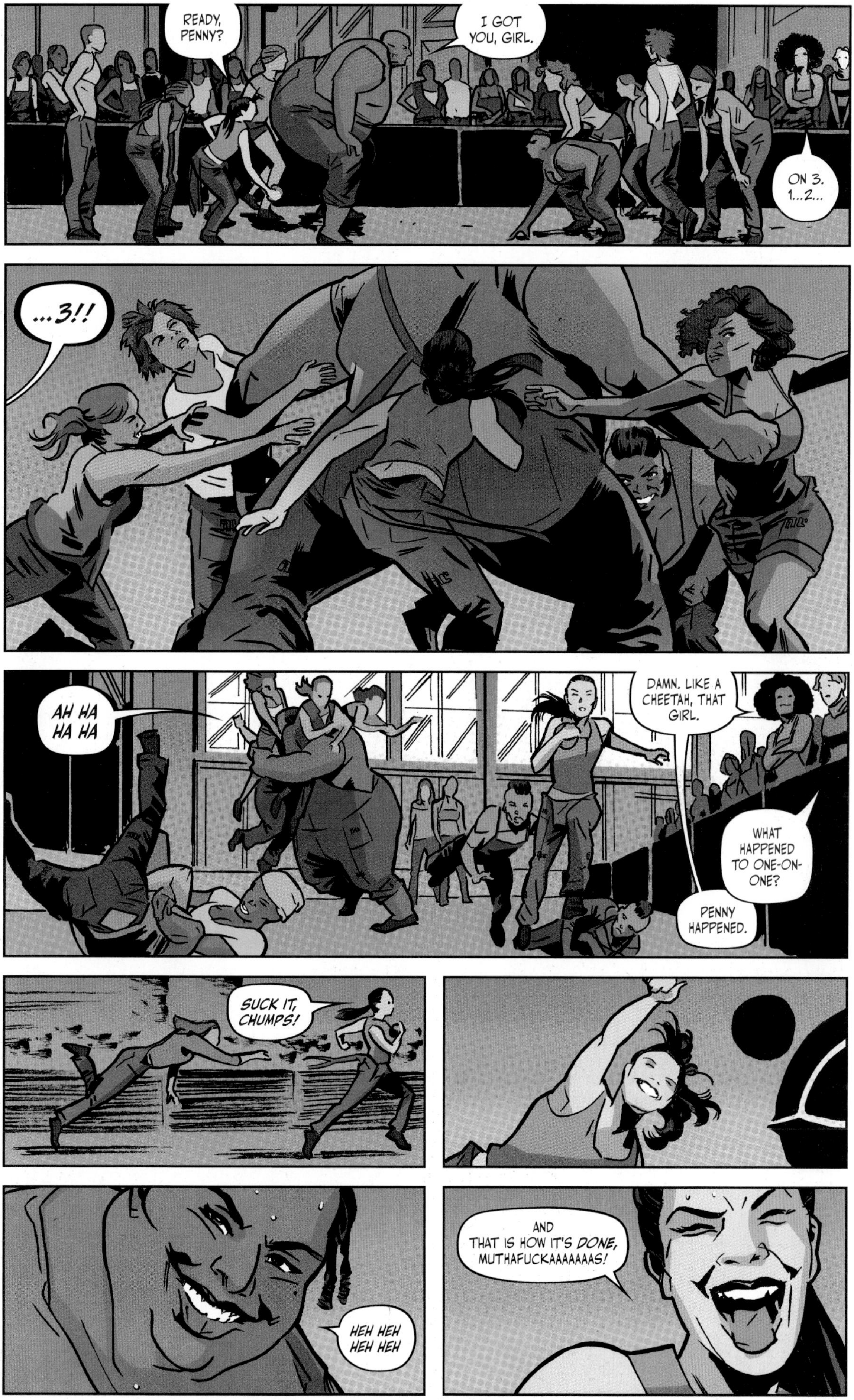
READY, PENNY?
I GOT YOU, GIRL.
ON 3. 1...2...
...3!!
AH HA HA HA
DAMN. LIKE A CHEETAH, THAT GIRL.
WHAT HAPPENED TO ONE-ON-ONE?
PENNY HAPPENED.
SUCK IT, CHUMPS!
HEH HEH HEH HEH
AND THAT IS HOW IT'S DONE, MUTHAFUCKAAAAAAAS!

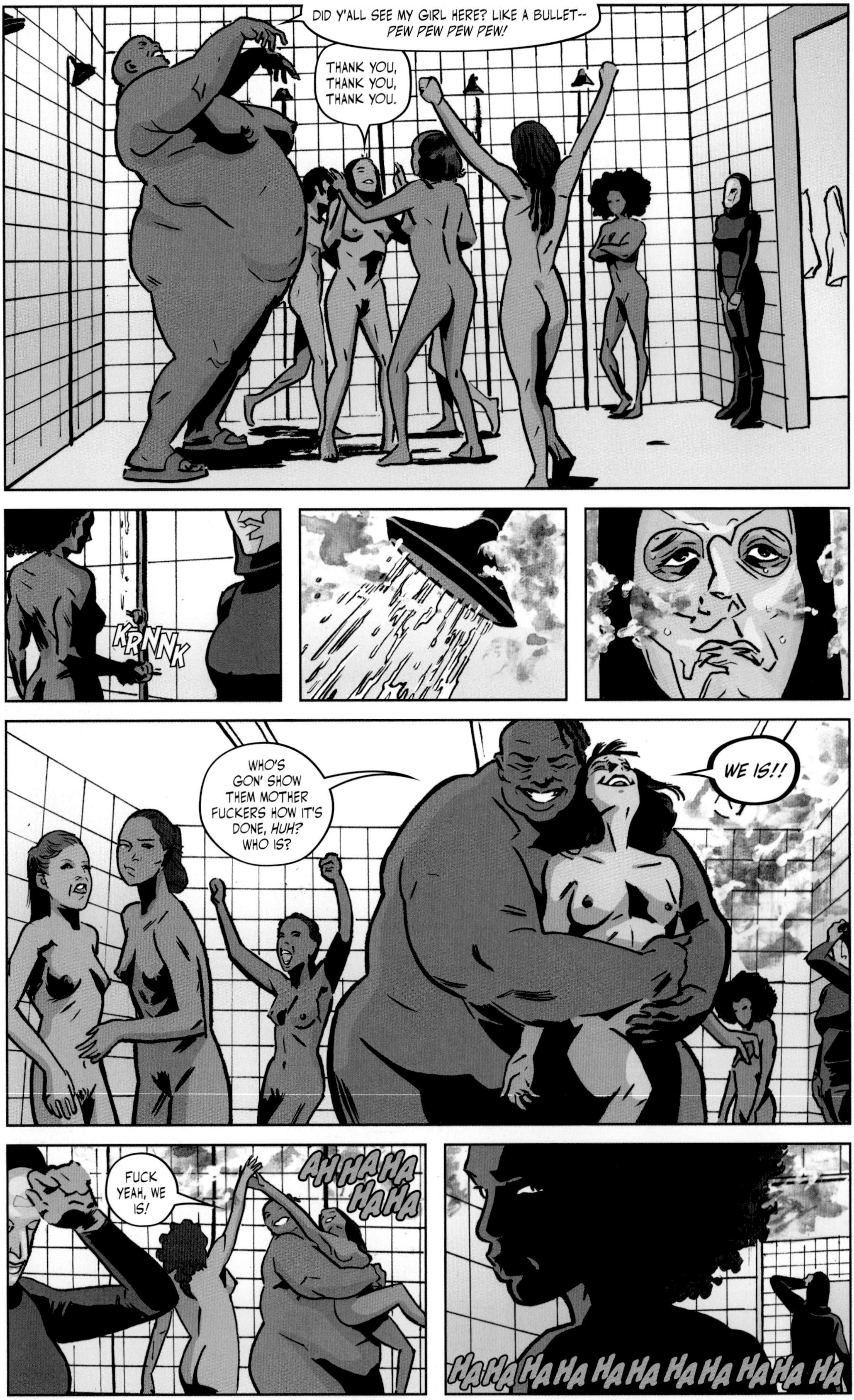
DID Y'ALL SEE MY GIRL HERE? LIKE A BULLET-- *PEW PEW PEW PEW!*
THANK YOU, THANK YOU, THANK YOU.
KRNNK
WHO'S GON' SHOW THEM MOTHER FUCKERS HOW IT'S DONE, *HUH?* WHO IS?
WE IS!!
FUCK YEAH, WE IS!
AH HA HA HA HA HA
HA HA HA HA HA HA HA HA HA HA HA HA HA HA

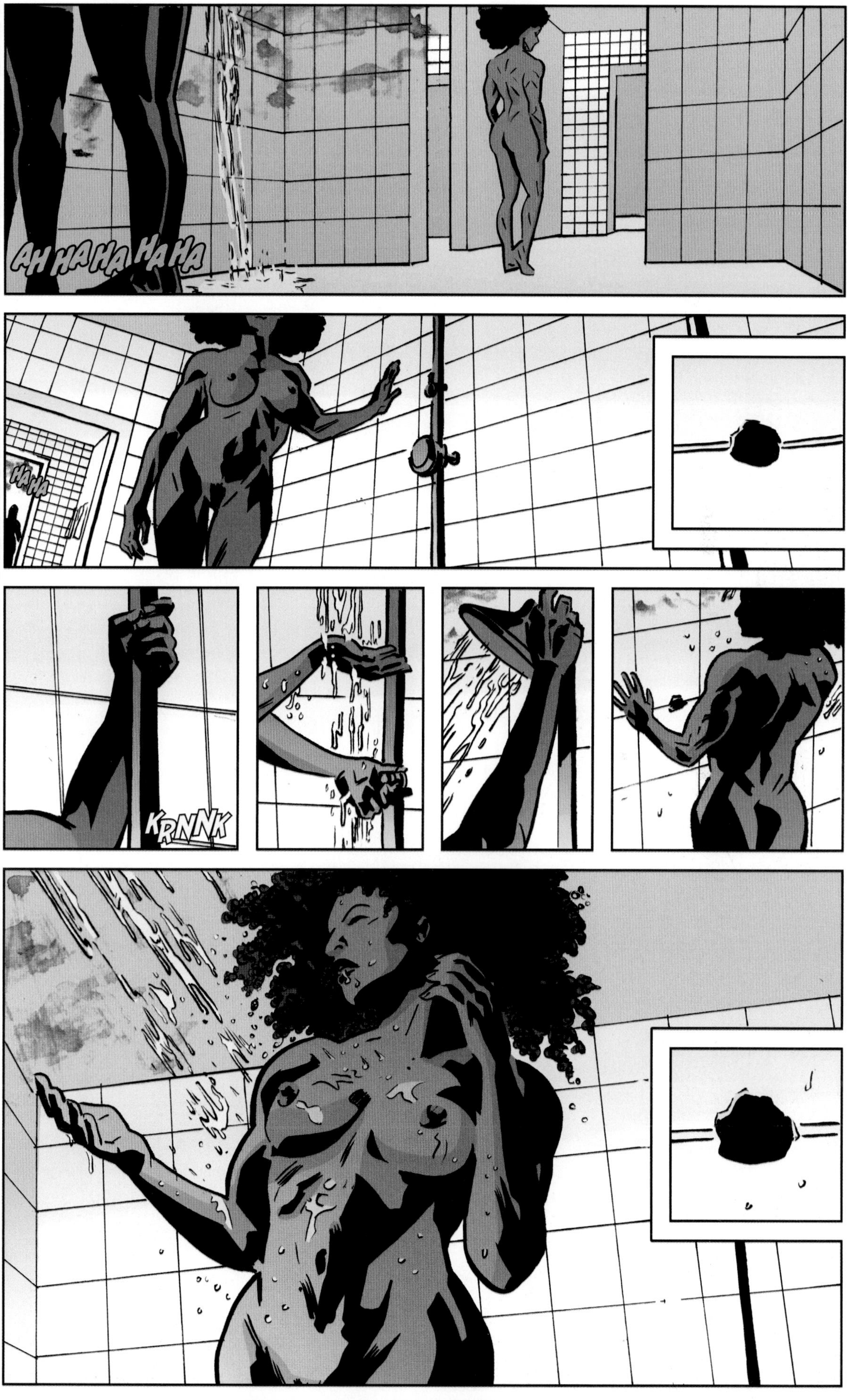
AH HA HA HA HA
HA HA
KRNNK

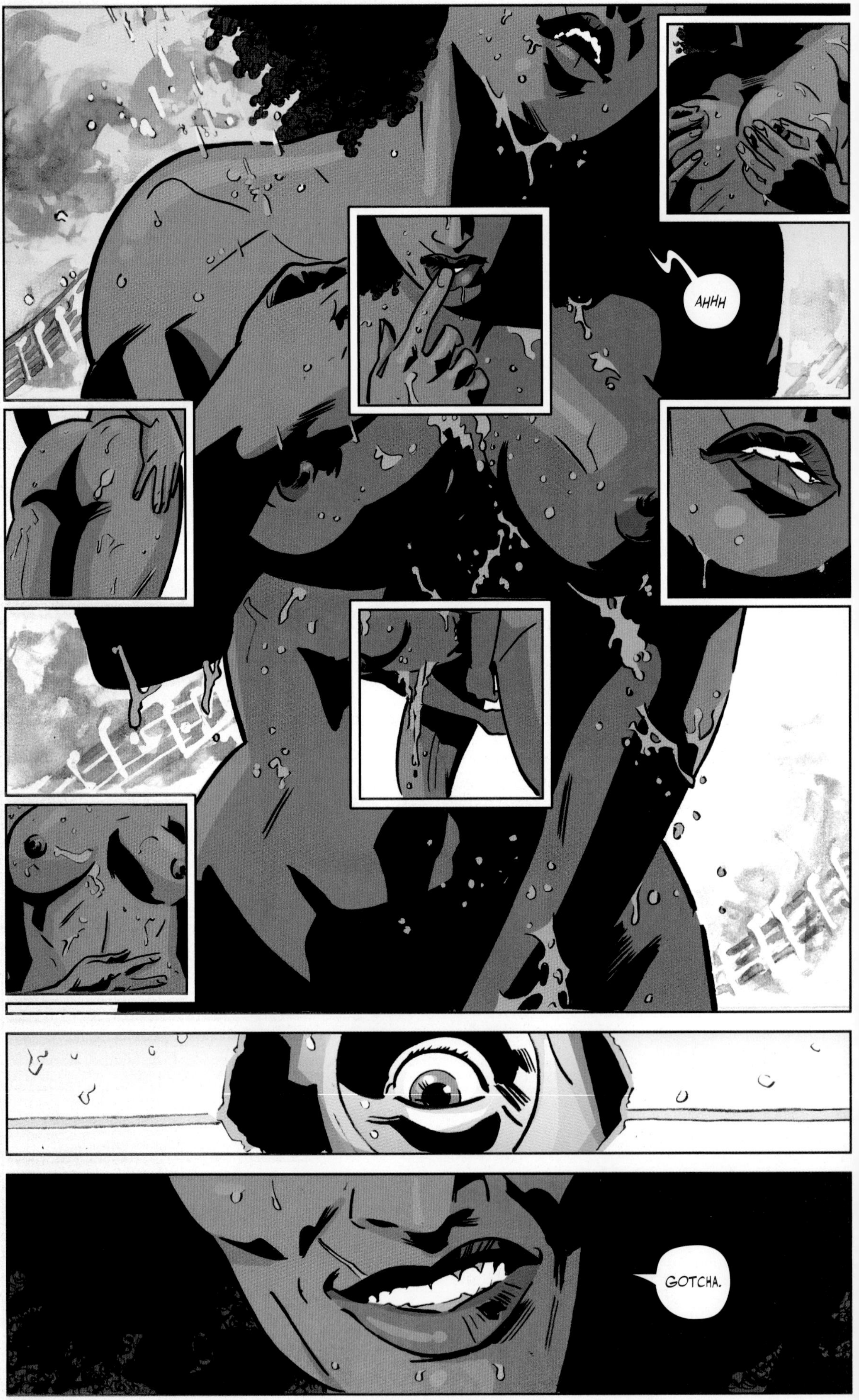
AHHH
GOTCHA.

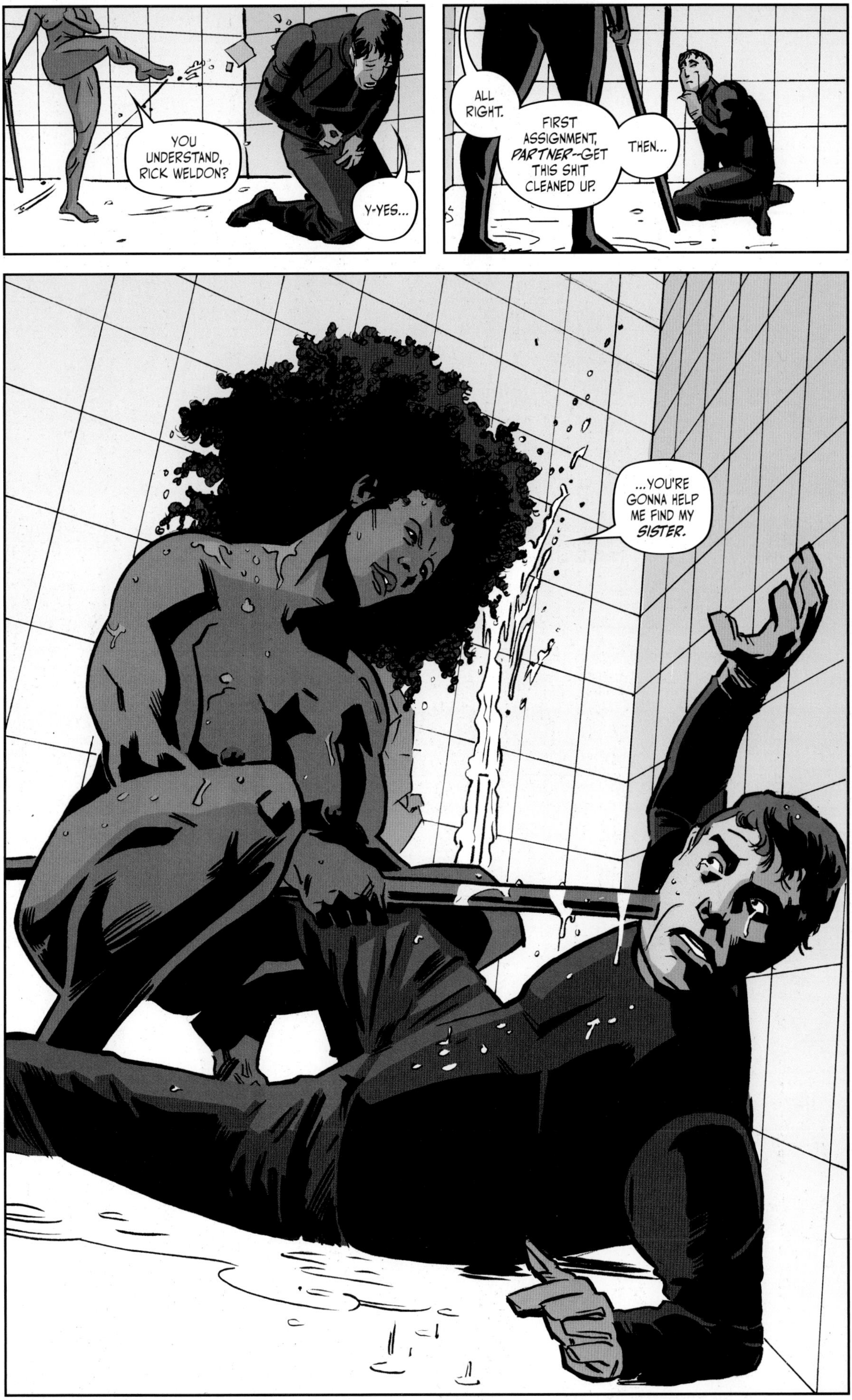
YOU UNDERSTAND, RICK WELDON?
Y-YES...
ALL RIGHT.
FIRST ASSIGNMENT, PARTNER--GET THIS SHIT CLEANED UP.
THEN...
...YOU'RE GONNA HELP ME FIND MY SISTER.

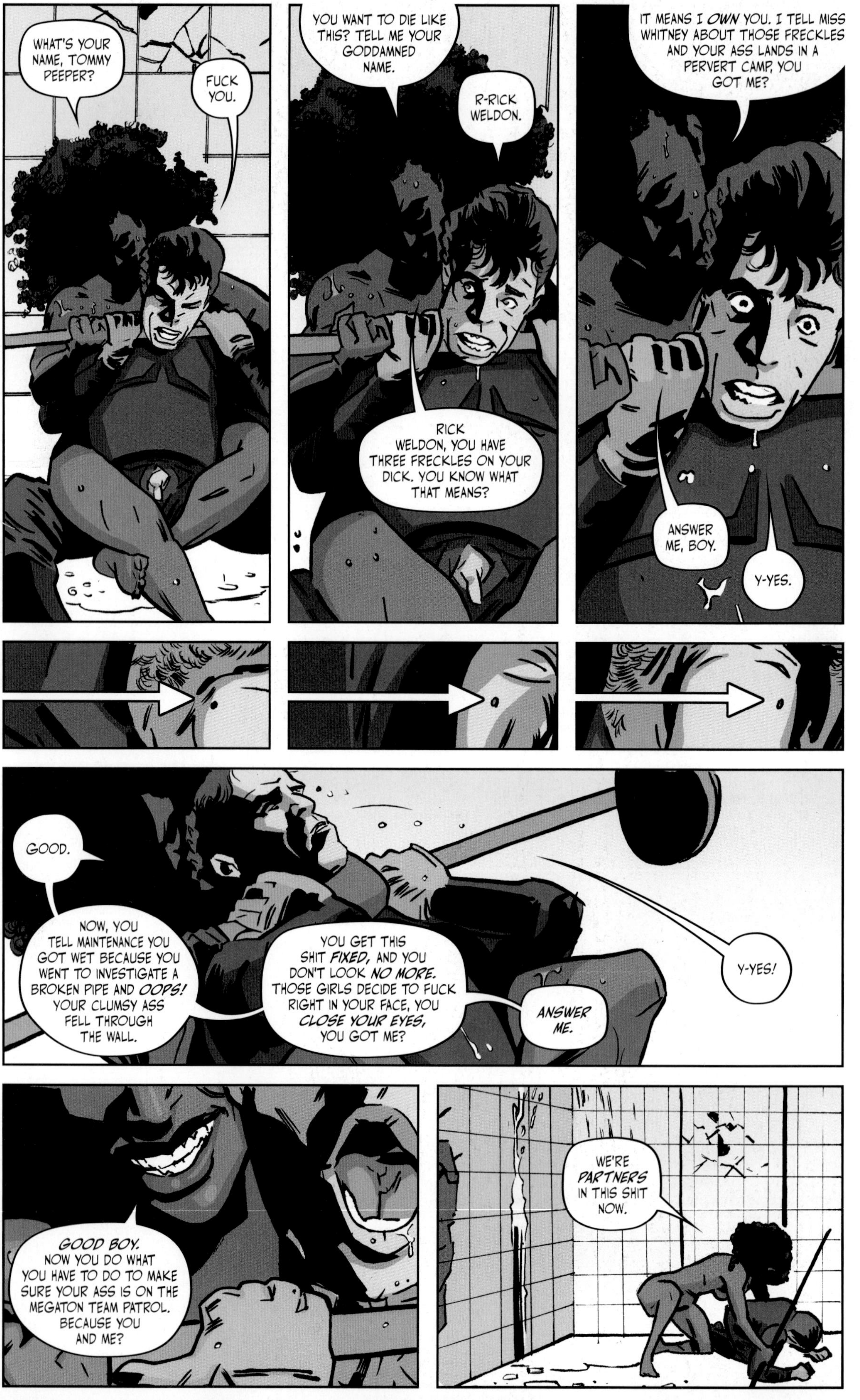
WHAT'S YOUR NAME, TOMMY PEEPER?
FUCK YOU.
YOU WANT TO DIE LIKE THIS? TELL ME YOUR GODDAMNED NAME.
R-RICK WELDON.
RICK WELDON, YOU HAVE THREE FRECKLES ON YOUR DICK. YOU KNOW WHAT THAT MEANS?
IT MEANS I OWN YOU. I TELL MISS WHITNEY ABOUT THOSE FRECKLES AND YOUR ASS LANDS IN A PERVERT CAMP, YOU GOT ME?
ANSWER ME, BOY.
Y-YES.
GOOD.
NOW, YOU TELL MAINTENANCE YOU GOT WET BECAUSE YOU WENT TO INVESTIGATE A BROKEN PIPE AND OOPS! YOUR CLUMSY ASS FELL THROUGH THE WALL.
YOU GET THIS SHIT FIXED, AND YOU DON'T LOOK NO MORE. THOSE GIRLS DECIDE TO FUCK RIGHT IN YOUR FACE, YOU CLOSE YOUR EYES, YOU GOT ME?
ANSWER ME.
Y-YES!
GOOD BOY. NOW YOU DO WHAT YOU HAVE TO DO TO MAKE SURE YOUR ASS IS ON THE MEGATON TEAM PATROL. BECAUSE YOU AND ME?
WE'RE PARTNERS IN THIS SHIT NOW.

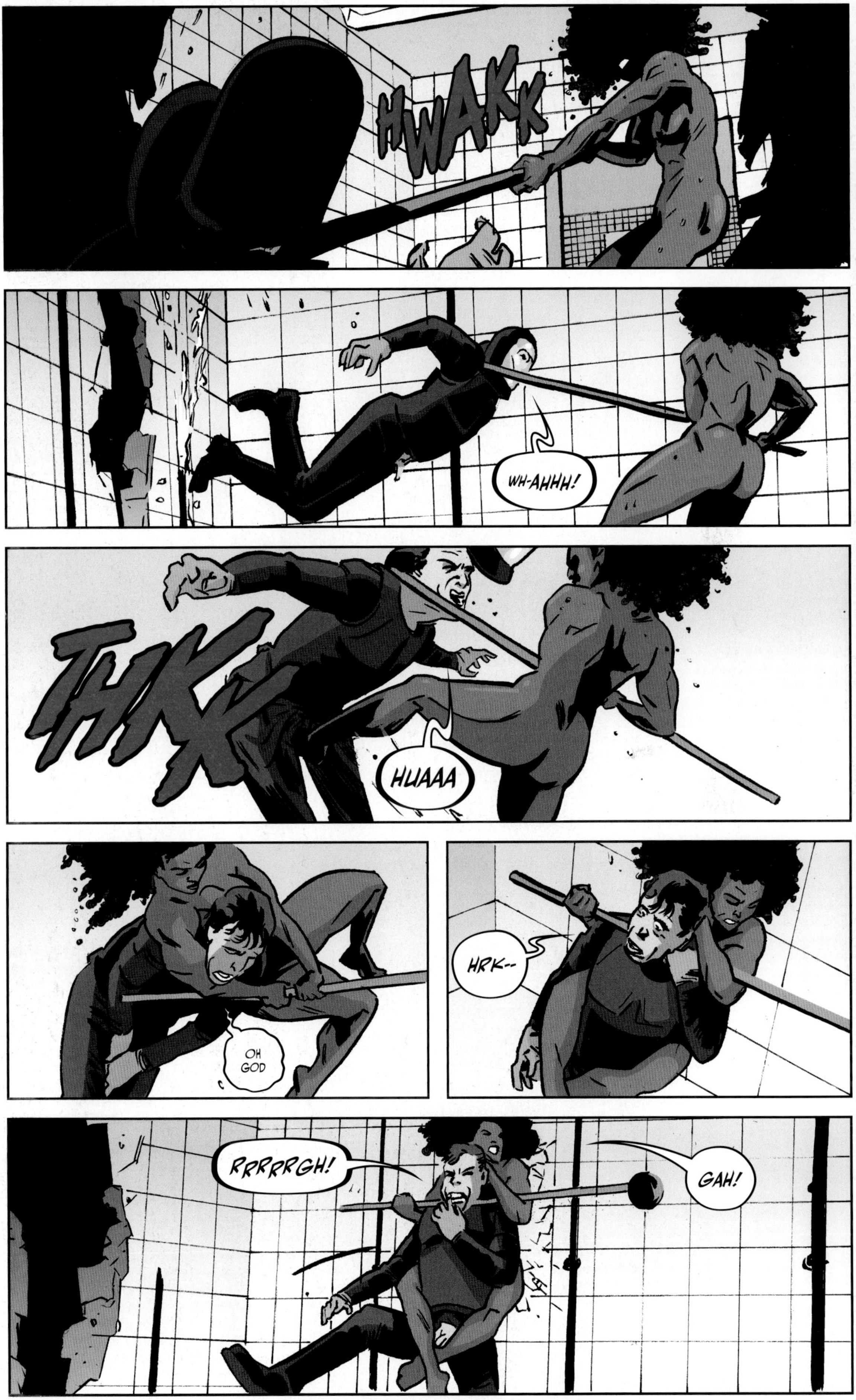
HWAKK
WH-AHHH!
THKK
HUAAA
OH GOD
HRK--
RRRRRGH!
GAH!

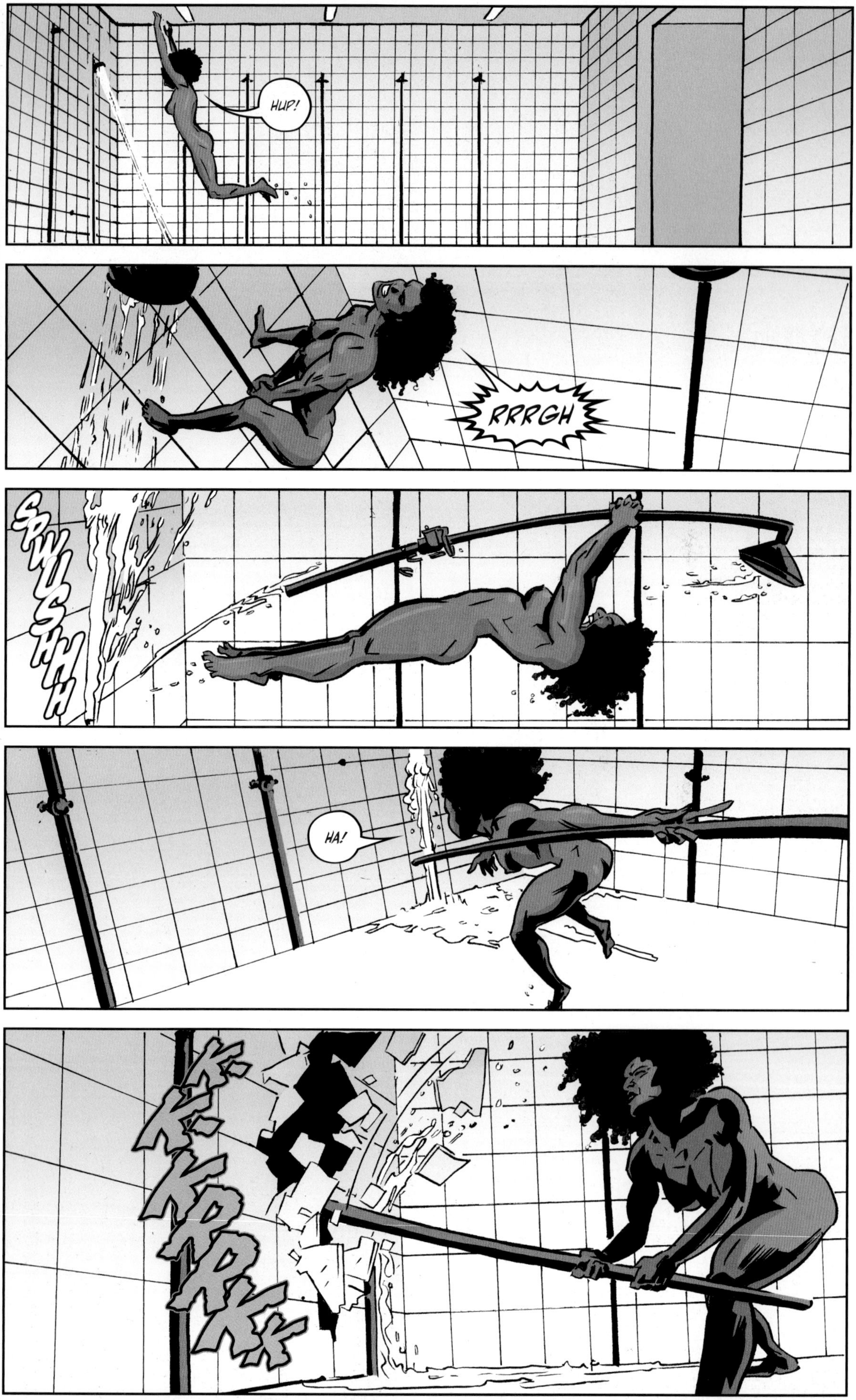
HUP!
RRRGH
SPWUSHHH
HA!
KKKRRKK

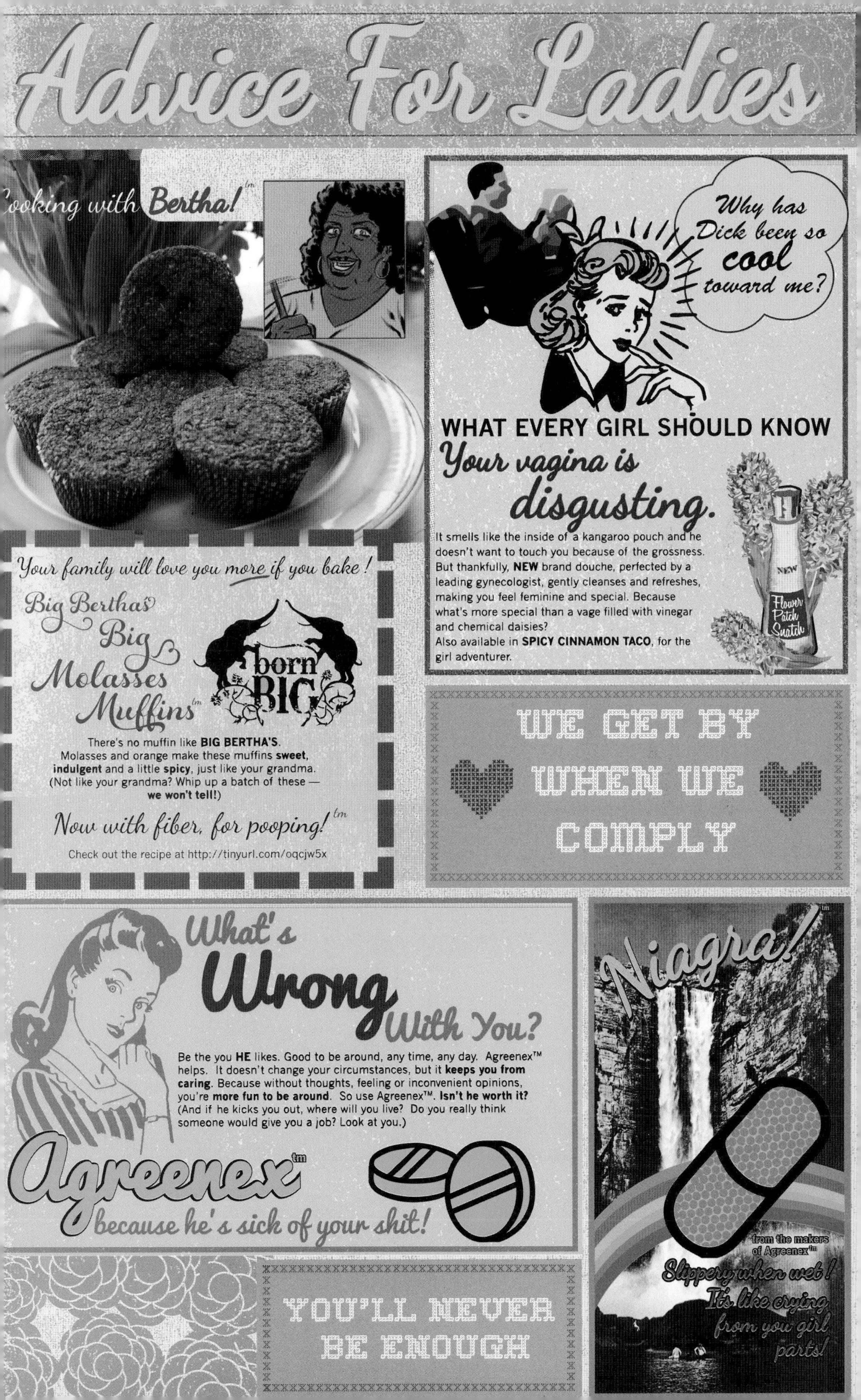

Advice For Ladies
Cooking with Bertha! tm
Your family will love you more if you bake!
Big Bertha's Big Molasses Muffins tm
born BIG
There's no muffin like BIG BERTHA'S.
Molasses and orange make these muffins sweet, indulgent and a little spicy, just like your grandma. (Not like your grandma? Whip up a batch of these — we won't tell!)
Now with fiber, for pooping! tm
Check out the recipe at http://tinyurl.com/oqcjw5x
Why has Dick been so cool toward me?
WHAT EVERY GIRL SHOULD KNOW
Your vagina is disgusting.
It smells like the inside of a kangaroo pouch and he doesn't want to touch you because of the grossness. But thankfully, NEW brand douche, perfected by a leading gynecologist, gently cleanses and refreshes, making you feel feminine and special. Because what's more special than a vage filled with vinegar and chemical daisies?
Also available in SPICY CINNAMON TACO, for the girl adventurer.
NEW
Flower Patch Snatch
WE GET BY WHEN WE COMPLY
What's Wrong With You?
Be the you HE likes. Good to be around, any time, any day. Agreenex™ helps. It doesn't change your circumstances, but it keeps you from caring. Because without thoughts, feeling or inconvenient opinions, you're more fun to be around. So use Agreenex™. Isn't he worth it? (And if he kicks you out, where will you live? Do you really think someone would give you a job? Look at you.)
Agreenex tm
because he's sick of your shit!
Niagra! tm
from the makers of Agreenex™
Slippery when wet! It's like crying from you girl parts!
YOU'LL NEVER BE ENOUGH

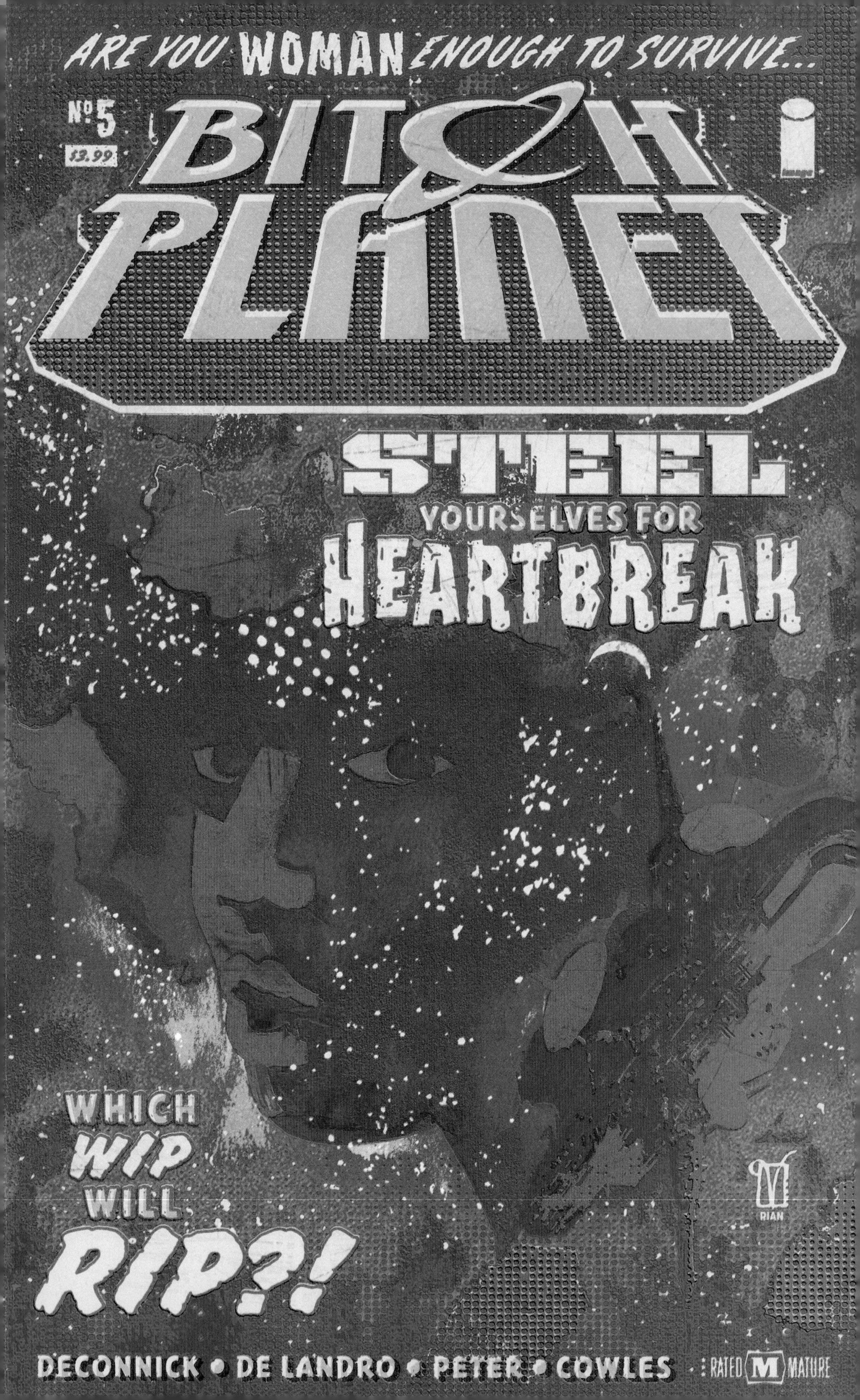
ARE YOU WOMAN ENOUGH TO SURVIVE...
Nº5
$3.99
BITCH PLANET
STEEL
YOURSELVES FOR
HEARTBREAK
WHICH
WIP
WILL
RIP?!
RIAN
DECONNICK • DE LANDRO • PETER • COWLES
RATED M MATURE

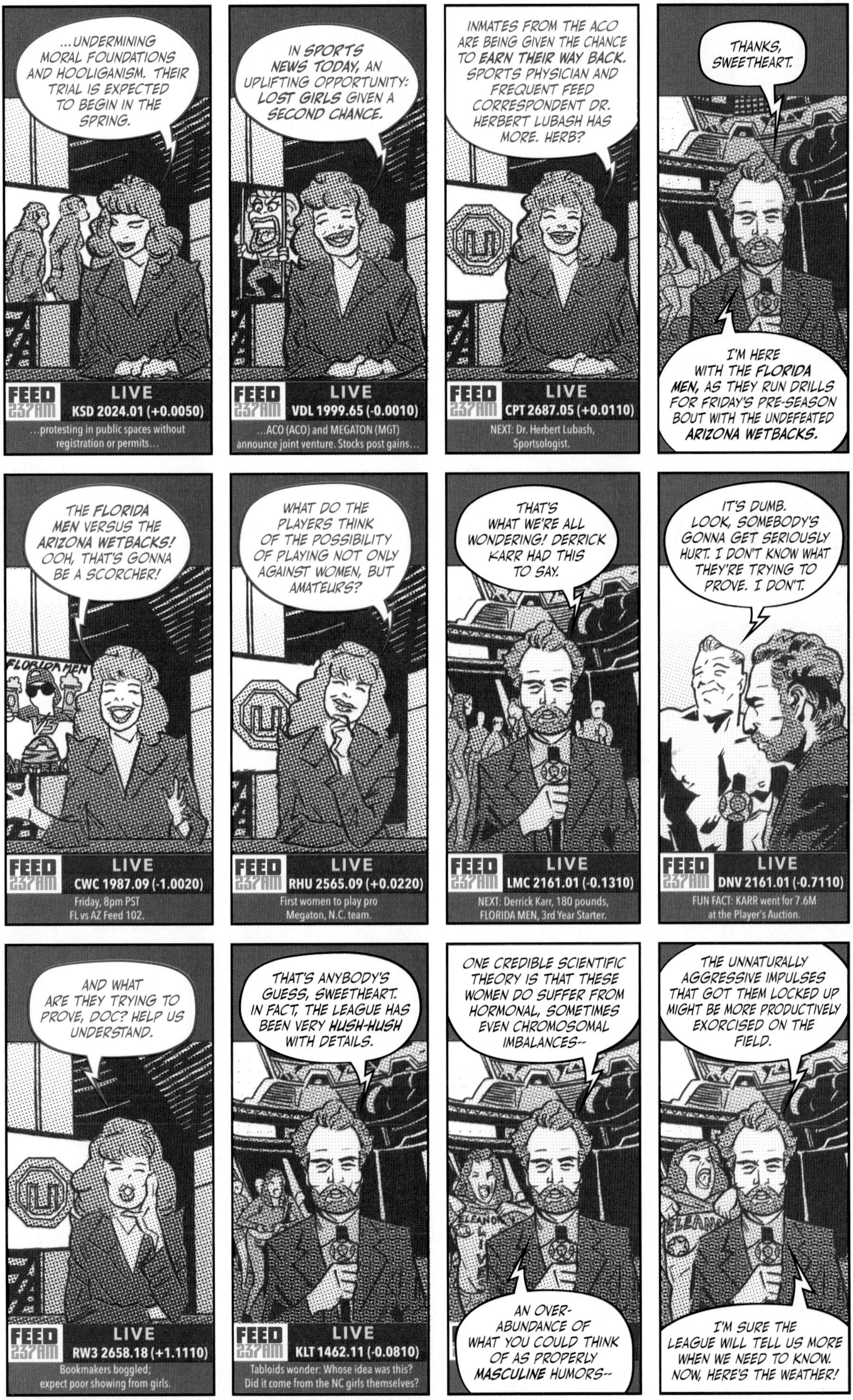
...UNDERMINING MORAL FOUNDATIONS AND HOOLIGANISM. THEIR TRIAL IS EXPECTED TO BEGIN IN THE SPRING.
FEED 237AM
LIVE
KSD 2024.01 (+0.0050)
...protesting in public spaces without registration or permits...
IN SPORTS NEWS TODAY, AN UPLIFTING OPPORTUNITY: LOST GIRLS GIVEN A SECOND CHANCE.
FEED 237AM
LIVE
VDL 1999.65 (-0.0010)
...ACO (ACO) and MEGATON (MGT) announce joint venture. Stocks post gains...
INMATES FROM THE ACO ARE BEING GIVEN THE CHANCE TO EARN THEIR WAY BACK. SPORTS PHYSICIAN AND FREQUENT FEED CORRESPONDENT DR. HERBERT LUBASH HAS MORE. HERB?
FEED 237AM
LIVE
CPT 2687.05 (+0.0110)
NEXT: Dr. Herbert Lubash, Sportsologist.
THANKS, SWEETHEART.
I'M HERE WITH THE FLORIDA MEN, AS THEY RUN DRILLS FOR FRIDAY'S PRE-SEASON BOUT WITH THE UNDEFEATED ARIZONA WETBACKS.
THE FLORIDA MEN VERSUS THE ARIZONA WETBACKS! OOH, THAT'S GONNA BE A SCORCHER!
FLORIDA MEN
VS
FEED 237AM
LIVE
CWC 1987.09 (-1.0020)
Friday, 8pm PST
FL vs AZ Feed 102.
WHAT DO THE PLAYERS THINK OF THE POSSIBILITY OF PLAYING NOT ONLY AGAINST WOMEN, BUT AMATEURS?
FEED 237AM
LIVE
RHU 2565.09 (+0.0220)
First women to play pro Megaton, N.C. team.
THAT'S WHAT WE'RE ALL WONDERING! DERRICK KARR HAD THIS TO SAY.
FEED 237AM
LIVE
LMC 2161.01 (-0.1310)
NEXT: Derrick Karr, 180 pounds, FLORIDA MEN, 3rd Year Starter.
IT'S DUMB. LOOK, SOMEBODY'S GONNA GET SERIOUSLY HURT. I DON'T KNOW WHAT THEY'RE TRYING TO PROVE. I DON'T.
FEED 237AM
LIVE
DNV 2161.01 (-0.7110)
FUN FACT: KARR went for 7.6M at the Player's Auction.
AND WHAT ARE THEY TRYING TO PROVE, DOC? HELP US UNDERSTAND.
FEED 237AM
LIVE
RW3 2658.18 (+1.1110)
Bookmakers boggled; expect poor showing from girls.
THAT'S ANYBODY'S GUESS, SWEETHEART. IN FACT, THE LEAGUE HAS BEEN VERY HUSH-HUSH WITH DETAILS.
FEED 237AM
LIVE
KLT 1462.11 (-0.0810)
Tabloids wonder: Whose idea was this? Did it come from the NC girls themselves?
ONE CREDIBLE SCIENTIFIC THEORY IS THAT THESE WOMEN DO SUFFER FROM HORMONAL, SOMETIMES EVEN CHROMOSOMAL IMBALANCES--
AN OVER-ABUNDANCE OF WHAT YOU COULD THINK OF AS PROPERLY MASCULINE HUMORS--
THE UNNATURALLY AGGRESSIVE IMPULSES THAT GOT THEM LOCKED UP MIGHT BE MORE PRODUCTIVELY EXORCISED ON THE FIELD.
I'M SURE THE LEAGUE WILL TELL US MORE WHEN WE NEED TO KNOW. NOW, HERE'S THE WEATHER!

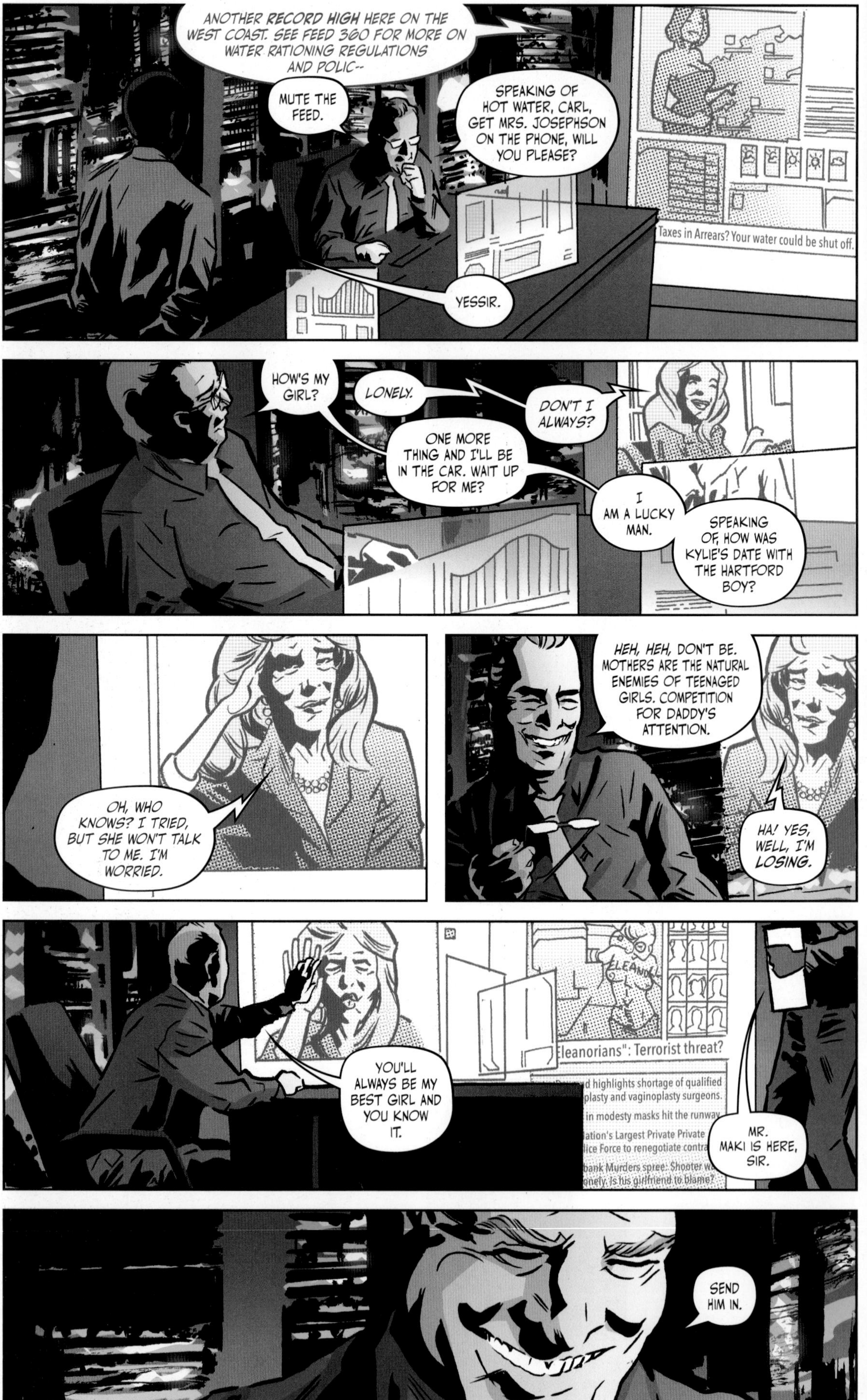
ANOTHER RECORD HIGH HERE ON THE WEST COAST. SEE FEED 360 FOR MORE ON WATER RATIONING REGULATIONS AND POLIC--
MUTE THE FEED.
SPEAKING OF HOT WATER, CARL, GET MRS. JOSEPHSON ON THE PHONE, WILL YOU PLEASE?
Taxes in Arrears? Your water could be shut off.
YESSIR.
HOW'S MY GIRL?
LONELY.
DON'T I ALWAYS?
ONE MORE THING AND I'LL BE IN THE CAR. WAIT UP FOR ME?
I AM A LUCKY MAN.
SPEAKING OF, HOW WAS KYLIE'S DATE WITH THE HARTFORD BOY?
OH, WHO KNOWS? I TRIED, BUT SHE WON'T TALK TO ME. I'M WORRIED.
HEH, HEH, DON'T BE. MOTHERS ARE THE NATURAL ENEMIES OF TEENAGED GIRLS. COMPETITION FOR DADDY'S ATTENTION.
HA! YES, WELL, I'M LOSING.
"Eleanorians": Terrorist threat?
YOU'LL ALWAYS BE MY BEST GIRL AND YOU KNOW IT.
MR. MAKI IS HERE, SIR.
SEND HIM IN.

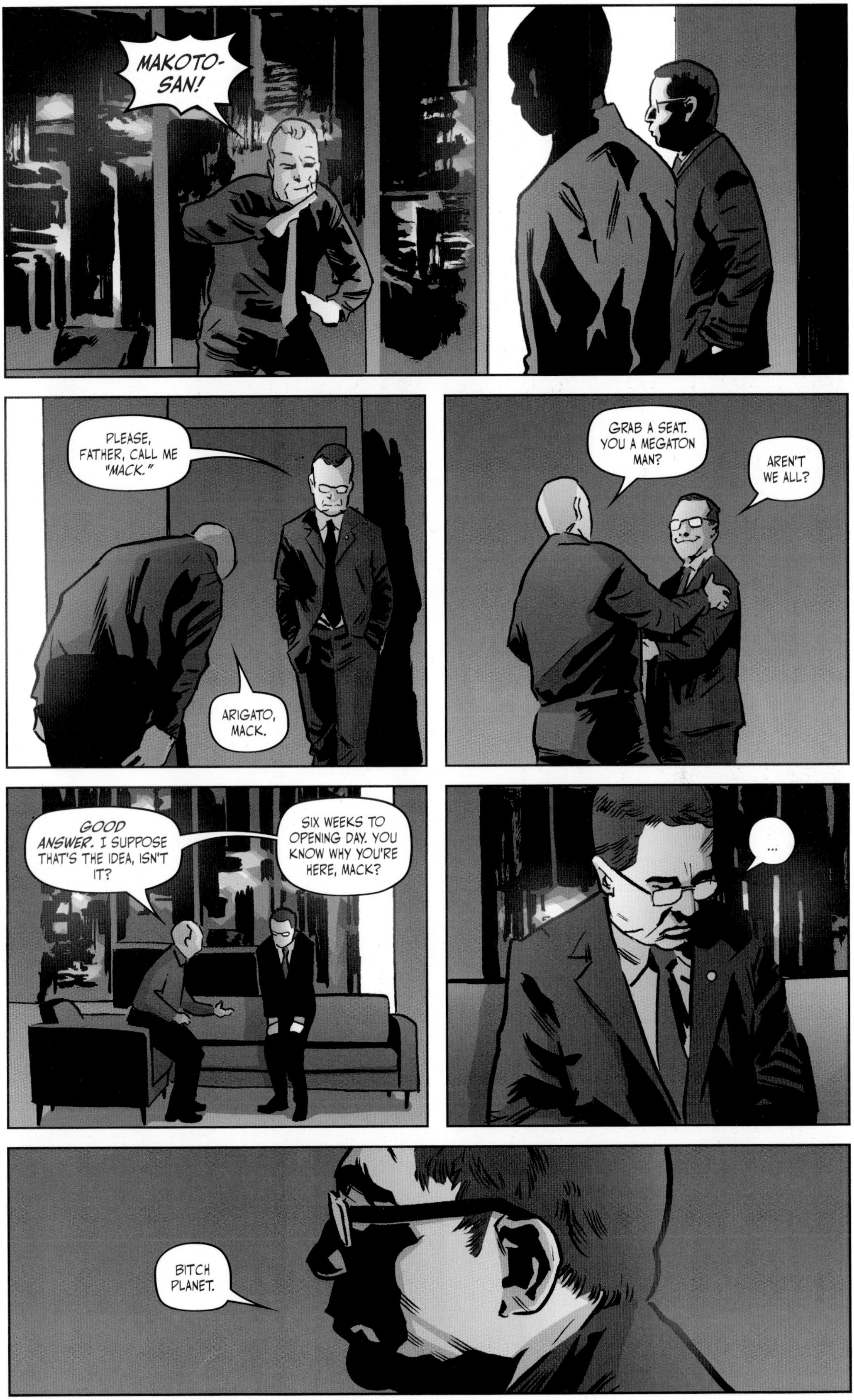
MAKOTO-SAN!
PLEASE, FATHER, CALL ME "MACK."
ARIGATO, MACK.
GRAB A SEAT. YOU A MEGATON MAN?
AREN'T WE ALL?
GOOD ANSWER. I SUPPOSE THAT'S THE IDEA, ISN'T IT?
SIX WEEKS TO OPENING DAY. YOU KNOW WHY YOU'RE HERE, MACK?
...
BITCH PLANET.

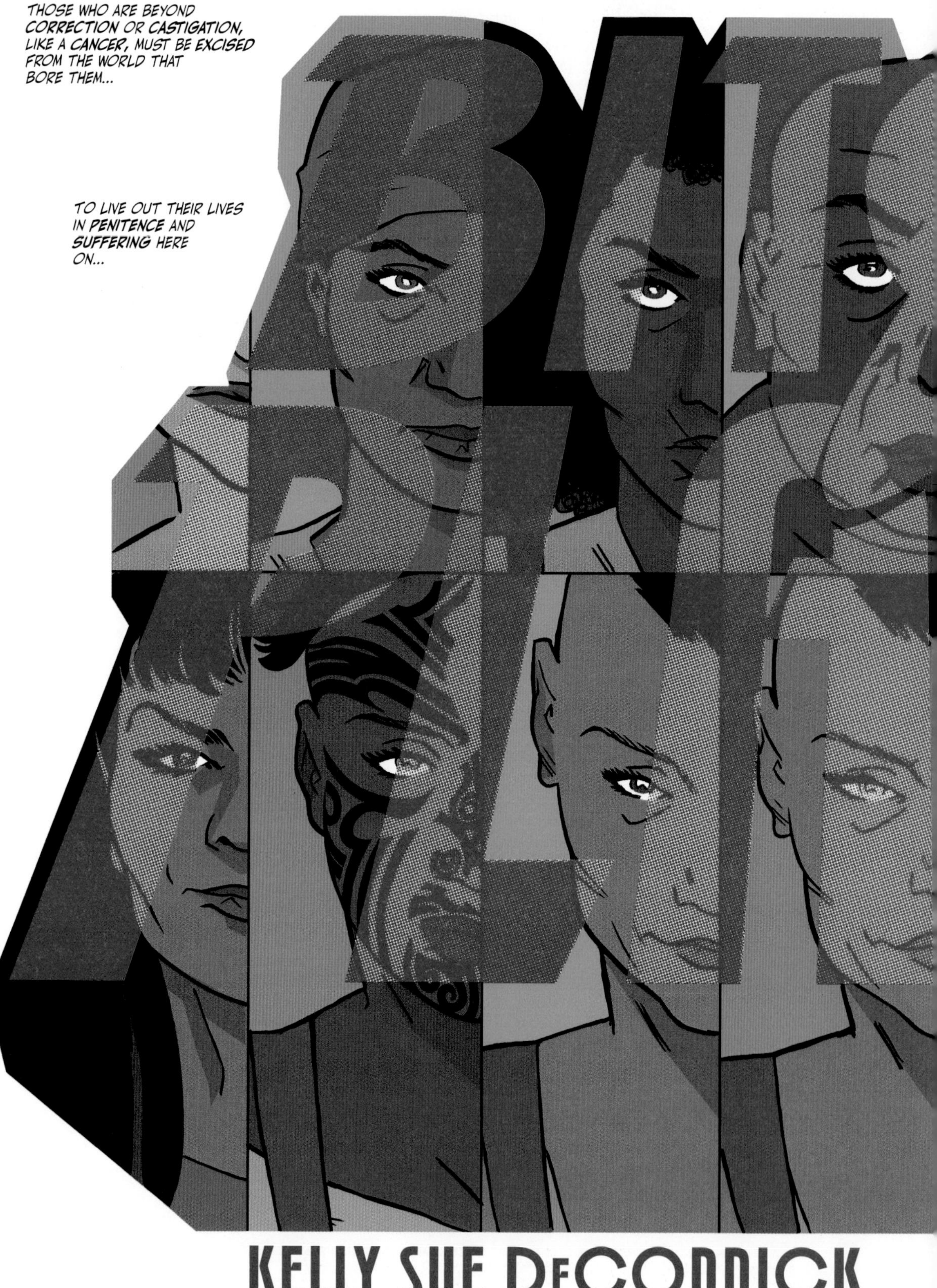
THOSE WHO ARE BEYOND CORRECTION OR CASTIGATION, LIKE A CANCER, MUST BE EXCISED FROM THE WORLD THAT BORE THEM...
TO LIVE OUT THEIR LIVES IN PENITENCE AND SUFFERING HERE ON...

KELLY SUE DECONNICK
SCRIPT

CRIS PETER
COLORS

CLAYTON COWLES
LETTERS

RIAN HUGHES
COVER DESIGN & LOGO DESIGN

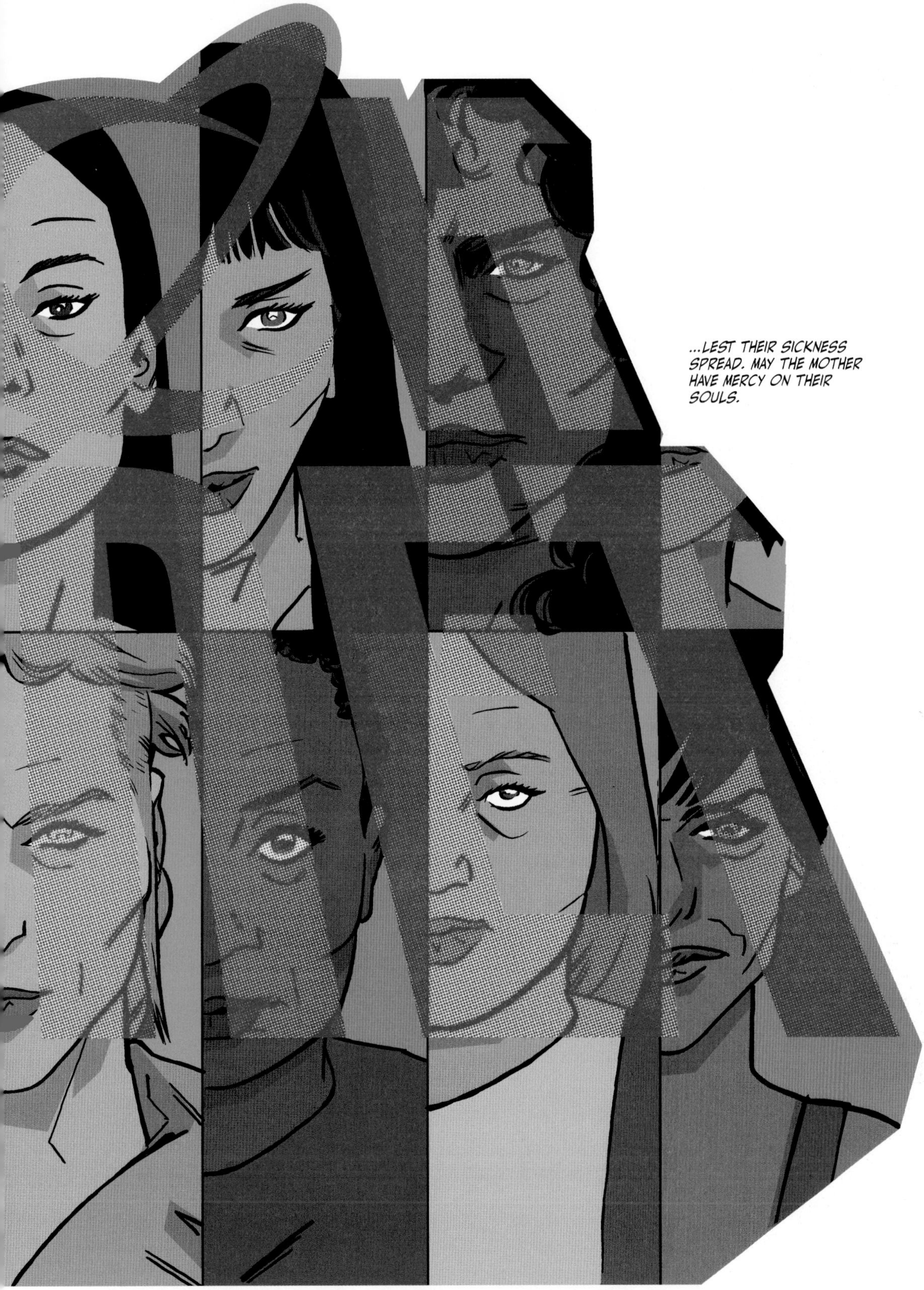
...LEST THEIR SICKNESS SPREAD. MAY THE MOTHER HAVE MERCY ON THEIR SOULS.

VALENTINE DE LANDRO
ART/COVERS

LAURENN McCUBBIN
BACKMATTER DESIGN

LAUREN SANKOVITCH
EDITOR

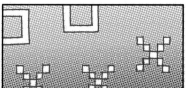

APRIL, MAY...THEY'LL READ YOU AS OUR OFFENSE.

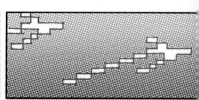

...ANY QUESTIONS?

NO.

I GOT ONE.

ARE WE REALLY GONNA GO BACK HOME?

KATRINA "KAT" JAIMES-FREYRE, 145LBS. SEDUCTION AND DISAPPOINTMENT; EMOTIONAL MANIPULATION; ASSAULT.

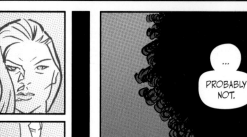
...

PROBABLY NOT.

I KNEW IT. 'SBULLSHIT.

YES. YES, YOU CAN FIGHT THE GUARDS WITHOUT GOING TO THE BOX. AND NO, THEY WILL NOT HAVE THEIR STICKS.

HEY BOSS, I GOT A QUESTION...

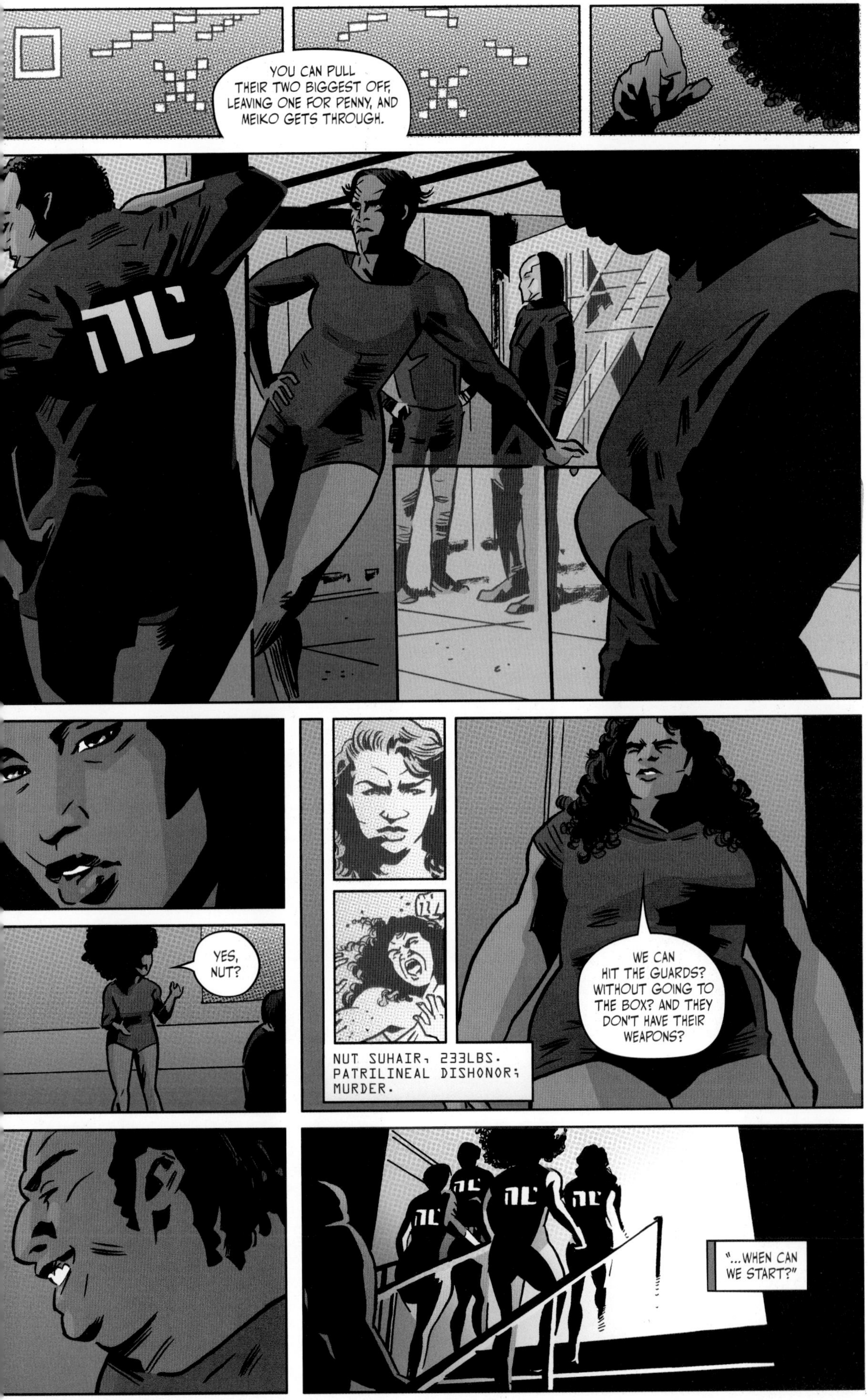
YOU CAN PULL THEIR TWO BIGGEST OFF, LEAVING ONE FOR PENNY, AND MEIKO GETS THROUGH.
YES, NUT?
NUT SUHAIR, 233LBS. PATRILINEAL DISHONOR; MURDER.
WE CAN HIT THE GUARDS? WITHOUT GOING TO THE BOX? AND THEY DON'T HAVE THEIR WEAPONS?
"...WHEN CAN WE START?"

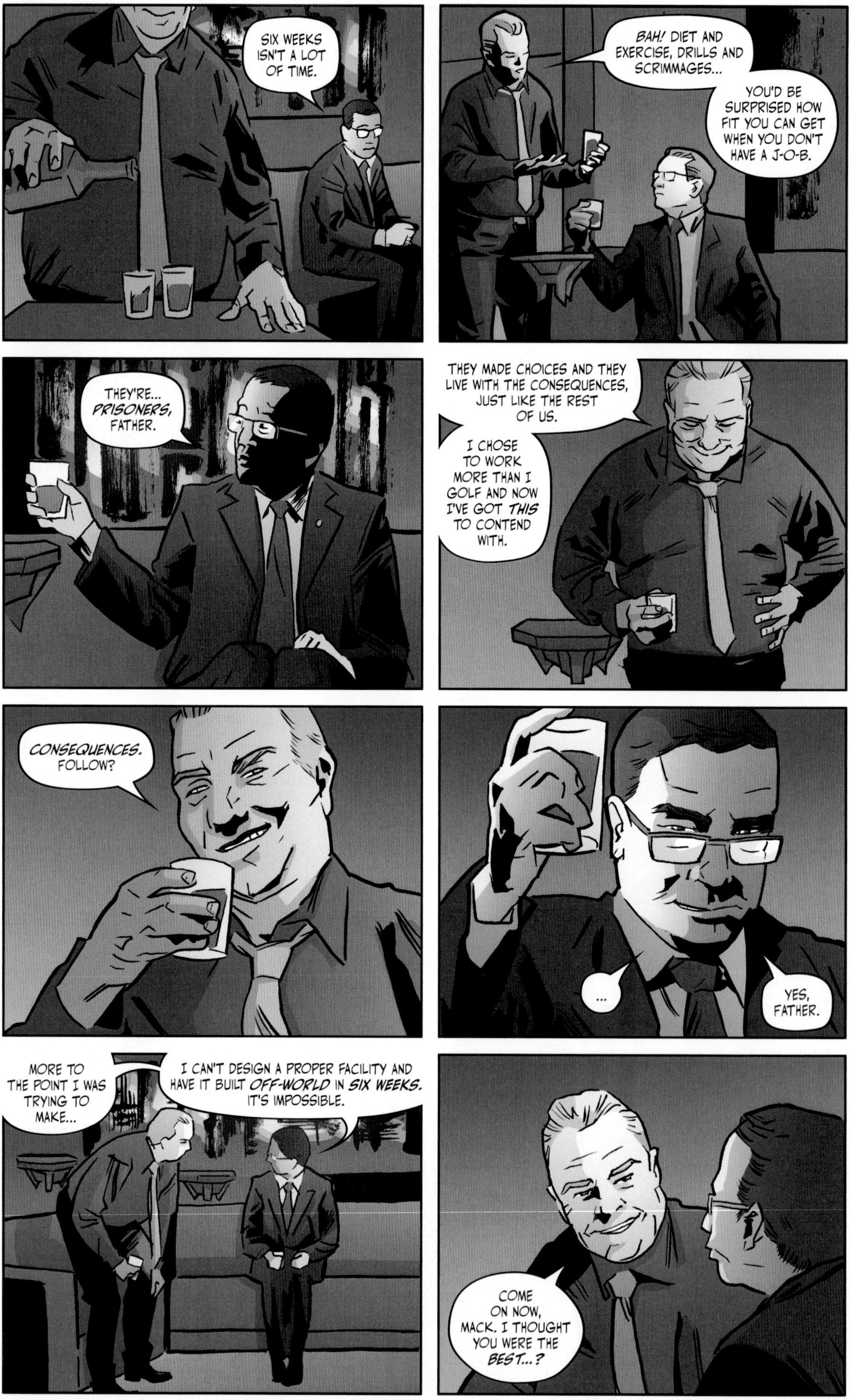
SIX WEEKS ISN'T A LOT OF TIME.
BAH! DIET AND EXERCISE, DRILLS AND SCRIMMAGES...
YOU'D BE SURPRISED HOW FIT YOU CAN GET WHEN YOU DON'T HAVE A J-O-B.
THEY'RE... PRISONERS, FATHER.
THEY MADE CHOICES AND THEY LIVE WITH THE CONSEQUENCES, JUST LIKE THE REST OF US.
I CHOSE TO WORK MORE THAN I GOLF AND NOW I'VE GOT THIS TO CONTEND WITH.
CONSEQUENCES. FOLLOW?
...
YES, FATHER.
MORE TO THE POINT I WAS TRYING TO MAKE...
I CAN'T DESIGN A PROPER FACILITY AND HAVE IT BUILT OFF-WORLD IN SIX WEEKS. IT'S IMPOSSIBLE.
COME ON NOW, MACK. I THOUGHT YOU WERE THE BEST...?

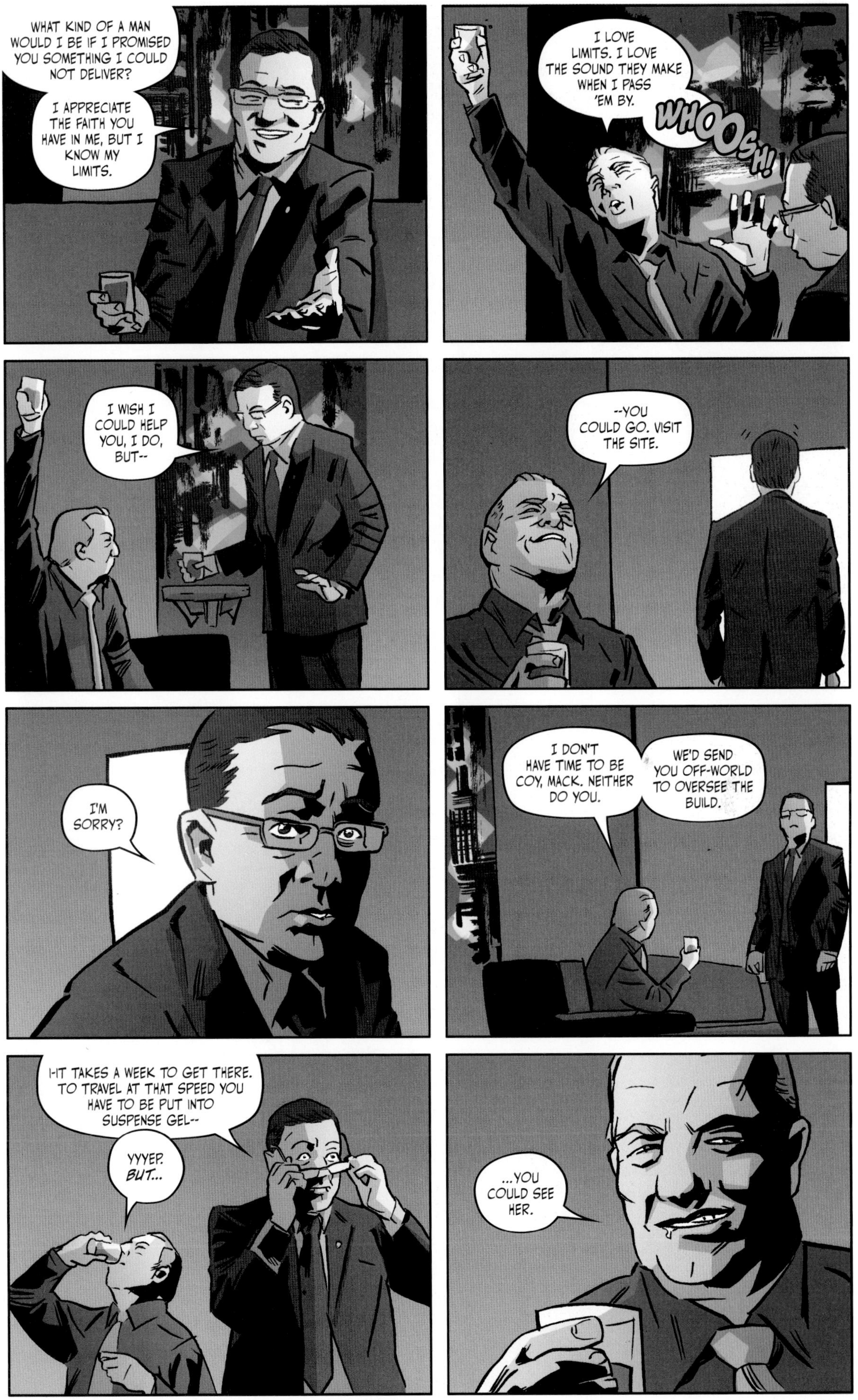
WHAT KIND OF A MAN WOULD I BE IF I PROMISED YOU SOMETHING I COULD NOT DELIVER?
I APPRECIATE THE FAITH YOU HAVE IN ME, BUT I KNOW MY LIMITS.
I LOVE LIMITS. I LOVE THE SOUND THEY MAKE WHEN I PASS 'EM BY.
WHOOSH!
I WISH I COULD HELP YOU, I DO, BUT--
--YOU COULD GO. VISIT THE SITE.
I'M SORRY?
I DON'T HAVE TIME TO BE COY, MACK. NEITHER DO YOU.
WE'D SEND YOU OFF-WORLD TO OVERSEE THE BUILD.
I-IT TAKES A WEEK TO GET THERE. TO TRAVEL AT THAT SPEED YOU HAVE TO BE PUT INTO SUSPENSE GEL--
YYYEP. BUT...
...YOU COULD SEE HER.

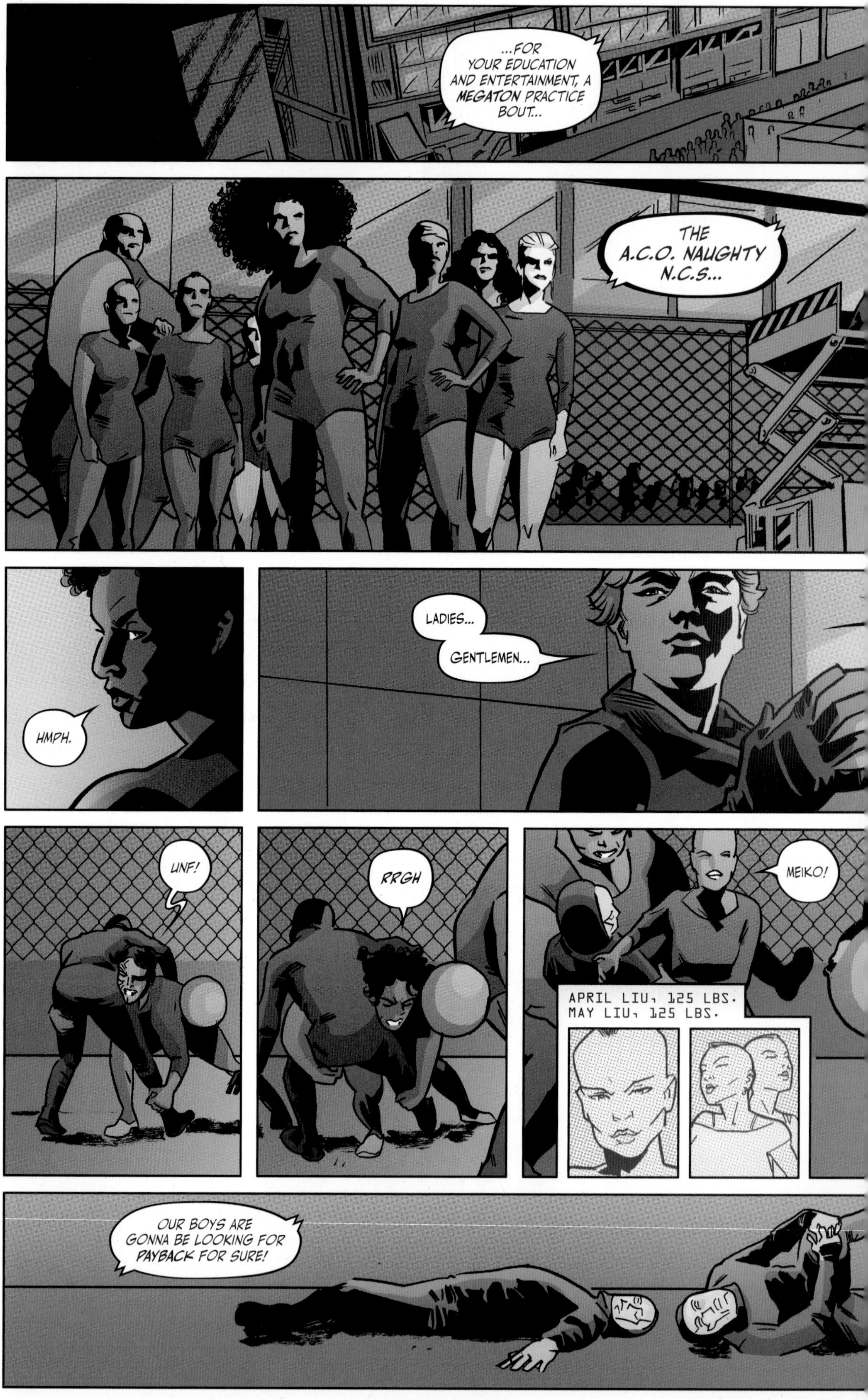
...FOR YOUR EDUCATION AND ENTERTAINMENT, A MEGATON PRACTICE BOUT...
THE A.C.O. NAUGHTY N.C.S...
HMPH.
LADIES...
GENTLEMEN...
UNF!
RRGH
MEIKO!
APRIL LIU, 125 LBS.
MAY LIU, 125 LBS.
OUR BOYS ARE GONNA BE LOOKING FOR PAYBACK FOR SURE!

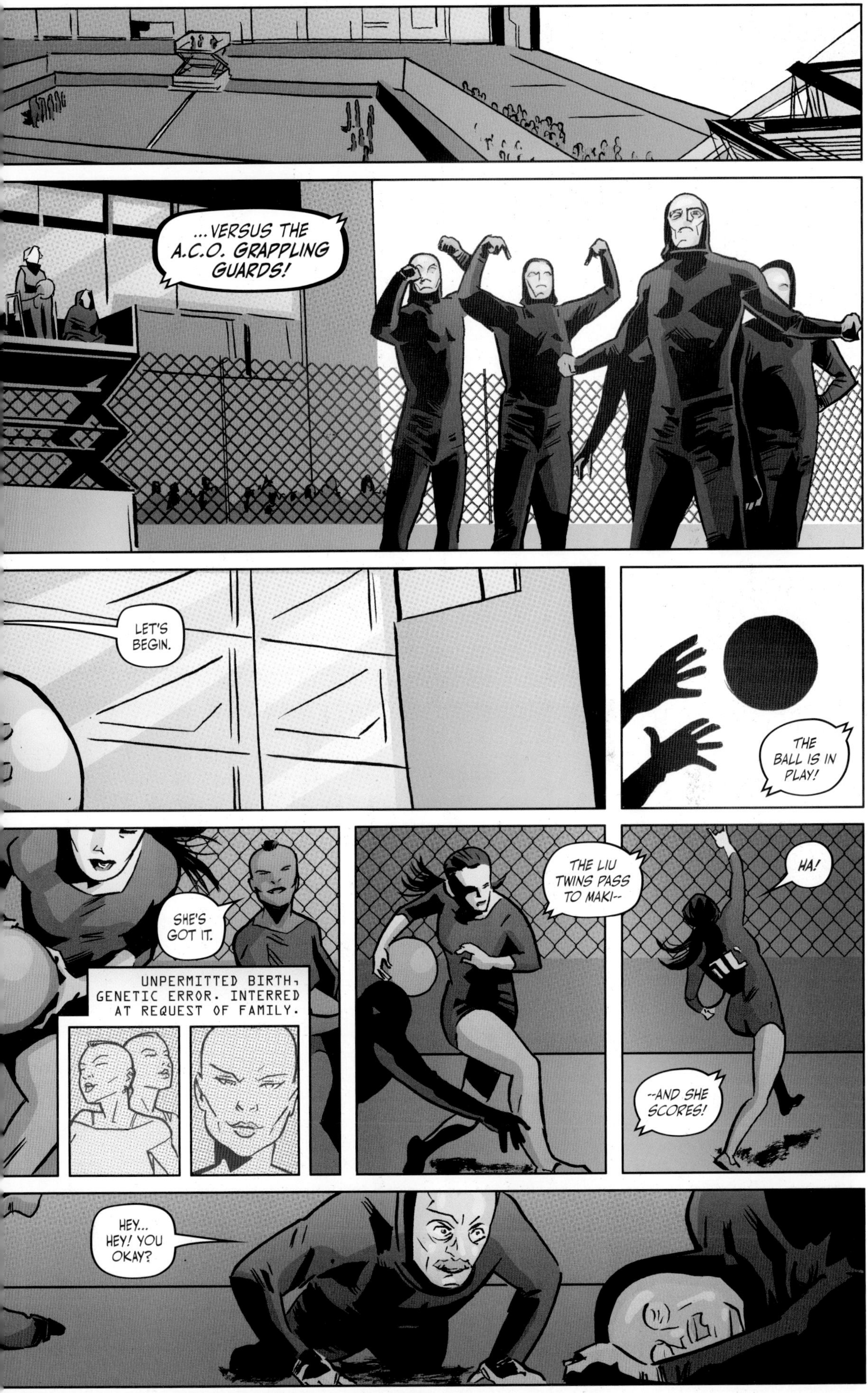
...VERSUS THE A.C.O. GRAPPLING GUARDS!
LET'S BEGIN.
THE BALL IS IN PLAY!
SHE'S GOT IT.
UNPERMITTED BIRTH, GENETIC ERROR. INTERRED AT REQUEST OF FAMILY.
THE LIU TWINS PASS TO MAKI--
HA!
--AND SHE SCORES!
HEY... HEY! YOU OKAY?

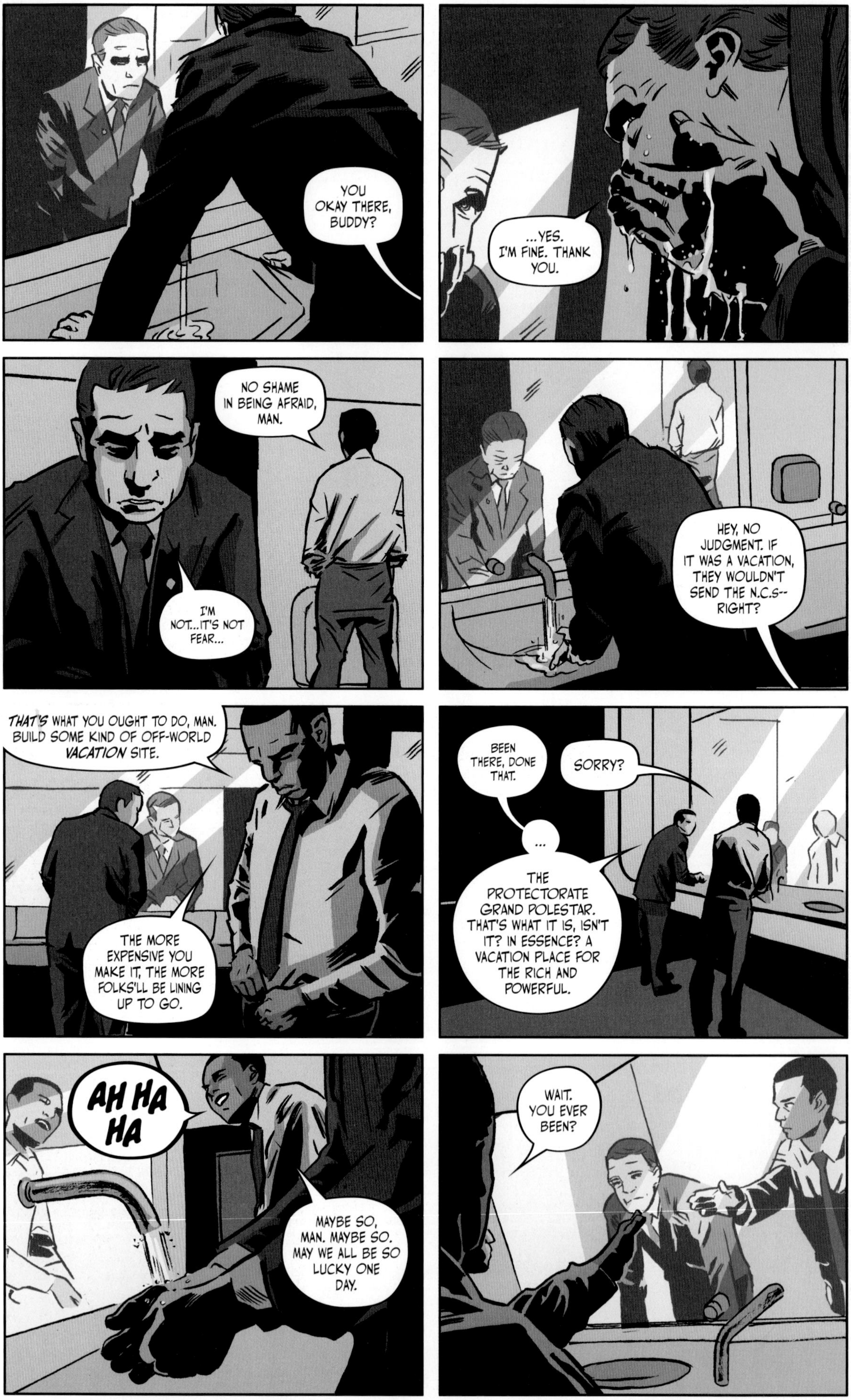
YOU OKAY THERE, BUDDY?
...YES. I'M FINE. THANK YOU.
NO SHAME IN BEING AFRAID, MAN.
I'M NOT...IT'S NOT FEAR...
HEY, NO JUDGMENT. IF IT WAS A VACATION, THEY WOULDN'T SEND THE N.C.s-- RIGHT?
THAT'S WHAT YOU OUGHT TO DO, MAN. BUILD SOME KIND OF OFF-WORLD *VACATION* SITE.
THE MORE EXPENSIVE YOU MAKE IT, THE MORE FOLKS'LL BE LINING UP TO GO.
BEEN THERE, DONE THAT.
SORRY?
...
THE PROTECTORATE GRAND POLESTAR. THAT'S WHAT IT IS, ISN'T IT? IN ESSENCE? A VACATION PLACE FOR THE RICH AND POWERFUL.
AH HA HA
MAYBE SO, MAN. MAYBE SO. MAY WE ALL BE SO LUCKY ONE DAY.
WAIT. YOU EVER BEEN?

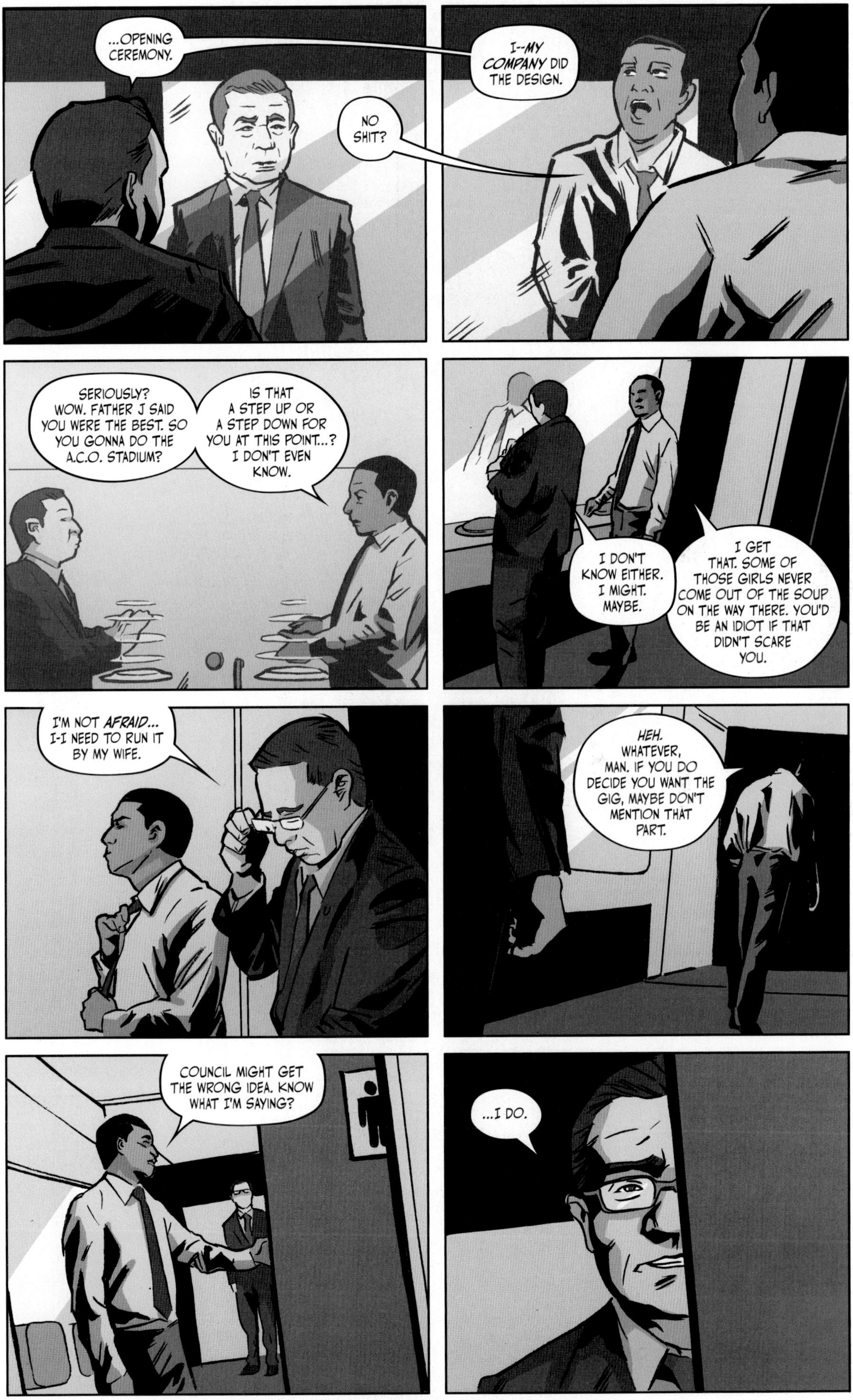
...OPENING CEREMONY.
I--MY COMPANY DID THE DESIGN.
NO SHIT?
SERIOUSLY? WOW. FATHER J SAID YOU WERE THE BEST. SO YOU GONNA DO THE A.C.O. STADIUM?
IS THAT A STEP UP OR A STEP DOWN FOR YOU AT THIS POINT...? I DON'T EVEN KNOW.
I DON'T KNOW EITHER. I MIGHT. MAYBE.
I GET THAT. SOME OF THOSE GIRLS NEVER COME OUT OF THE SOUP ON THE WAY THERE. YOU'D BE AN IDIOT IF THAT DIDN'T SCARE YOU.
I'M NOT AFRAID... I-I NEED TO RUN IT BY MY WIFE.
HEH. WHATEVER, MAN. IF YOU DO DECIDE YOU WANT THE GIG, MAYBE DON'T MENTION THAT PART.
COUNCIL MIGHT GET THE WRONG IDEA. KNOW WHAT I'M SAYING?
...I DO.

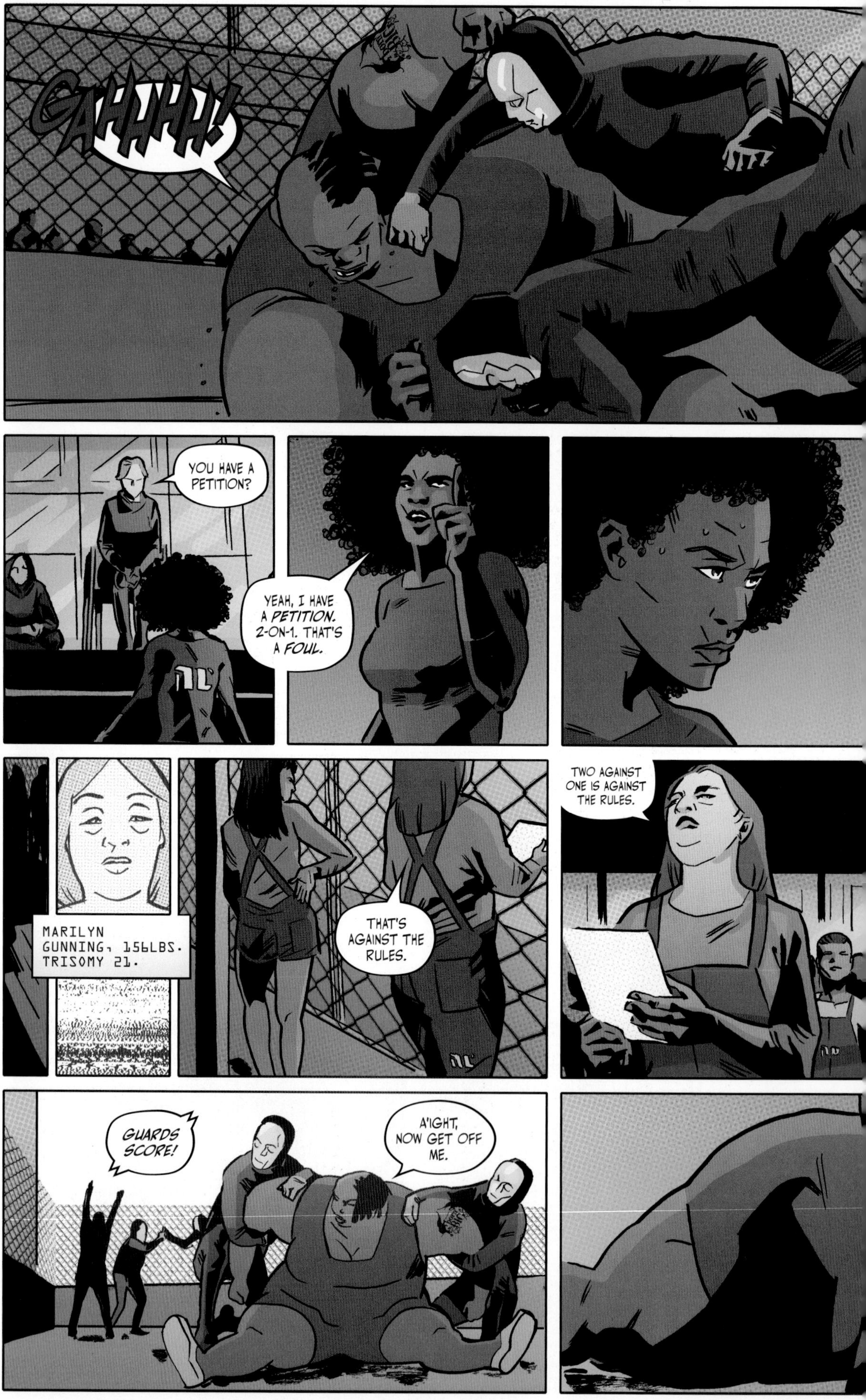
GAHHHH!
YOU HAVE A PETITION?
YEAH, I HAVE A *PETITION.* 2-ON-1. THAT'S A *FOUL.*
MARILYN GUNNING, 156LBS. TRISOMY 21.
THAT'S AGAINST THE RULES.
TWO AGAINST ONE IS AGAINST THE RULES.
GUARDS SCORE!
A'IGHT, NOW GET OFF ME.

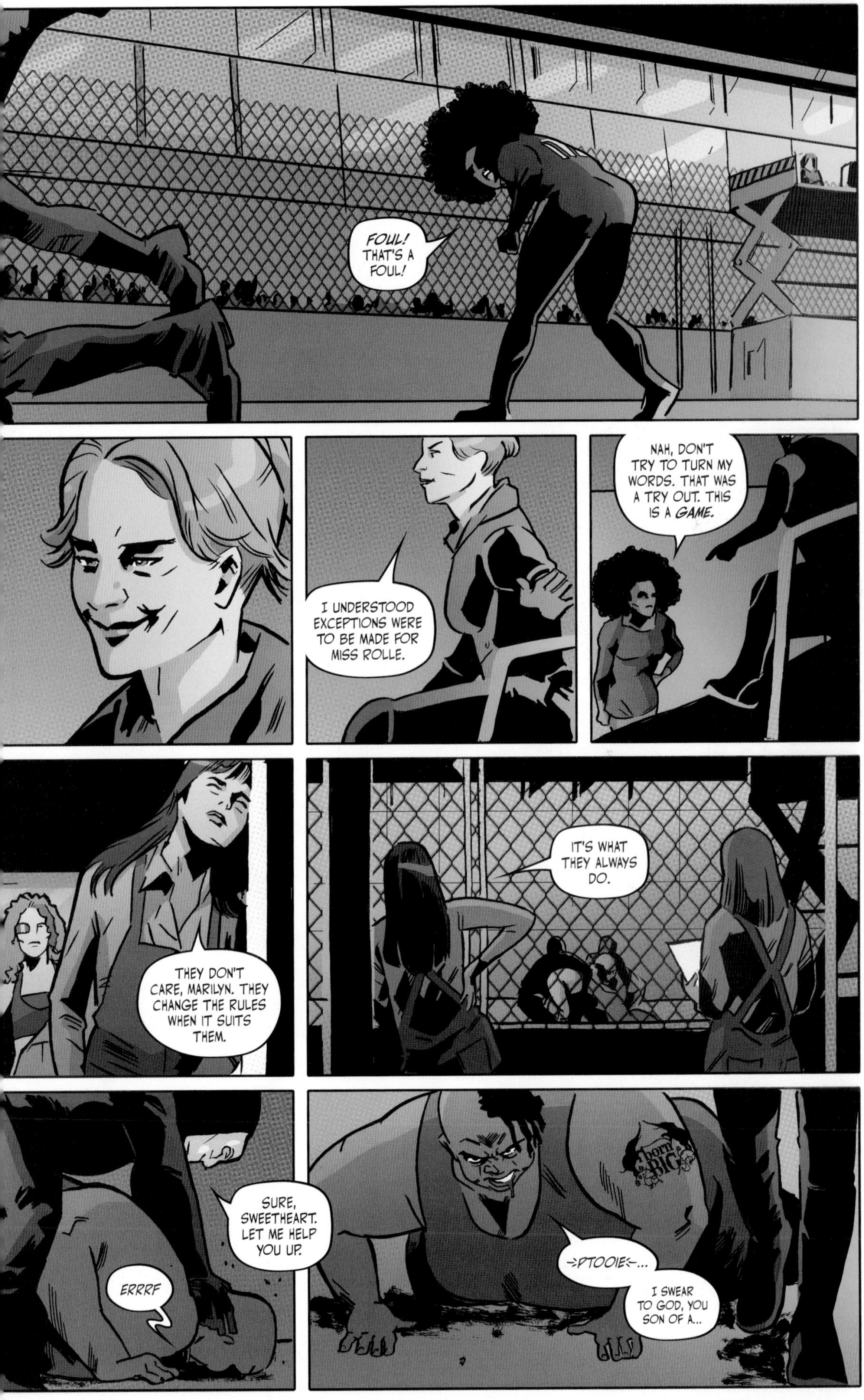
FOUL! THAT'S A FOUL!
I UNDERSTOOD EXCEPTIONS WERE TO BE MADE FOR MISS ROLLE.
NAH, DON'T TRY TO TURN MY WORDS. THAT WAS A TRY OUT. THIS IS A *GAME.*
THEY DON'T CARE, MARILYN. THEY CHANGE THE RULES WHEN IT SUITS THEM.
IT'S WHAT THEY ALWAYS DO.
SURE, SWEETHEART. LET ME HELP YOU UP.
ERRRF
born BIG
⇒PTOOIE⇐...
I SWEAR TO GOD, YOU SON OF A...

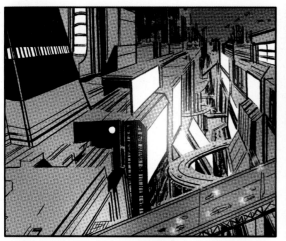

MAKI
ENGINEERING

...

MAKOTO,
I AM *BEGGING*
YOU...DO NOT
DO THIS.

YUMI...
I *HAVE*
TO.

MAKOTO,
NO! THAT'S A *LIE*.
I WON'T *LET* YOU.
I WON'T LET YOU PUT
EVERYTHING WE'VE
BUILT AT RIS--

YOU OKAY
BACK THERE, MR.
MAKI?

...
CAN WE
TAKE THE BRIDGE
TONIGHT, DAVE?

YESSIR.

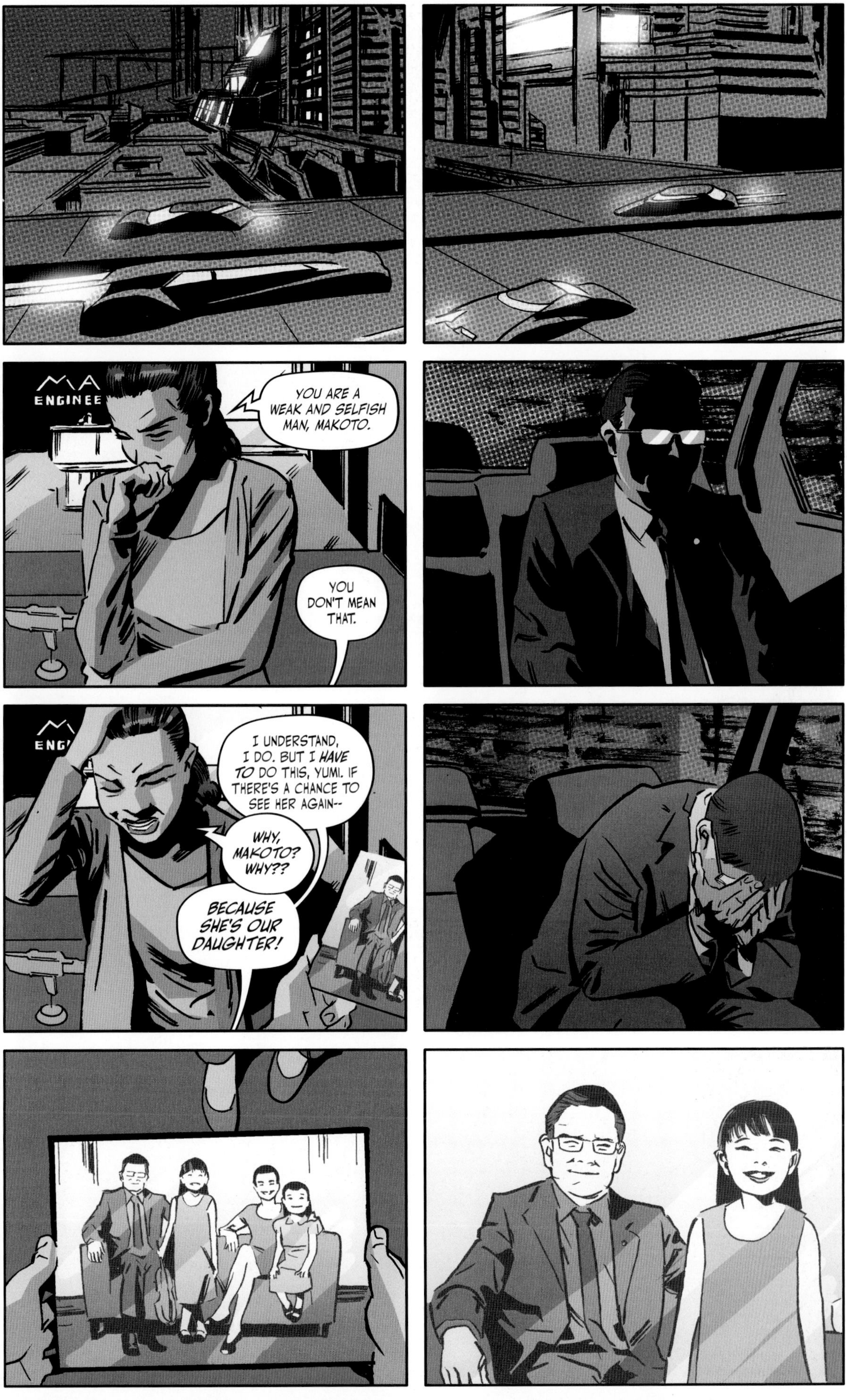
YOU ARE A WEAK AND SELFISH MAN, MAKOTO.
YOU DON'T MEAN THAT.
I UNDERSTAND, I DO. BUT I *HAVE TO* DO THIS, YUMI. IF THERE'S A CHANCE TO SEE HER AGAIN--
WHY, MAKOTO? WHY??
BECAUSE SHE'S OUR DAUGHTER!

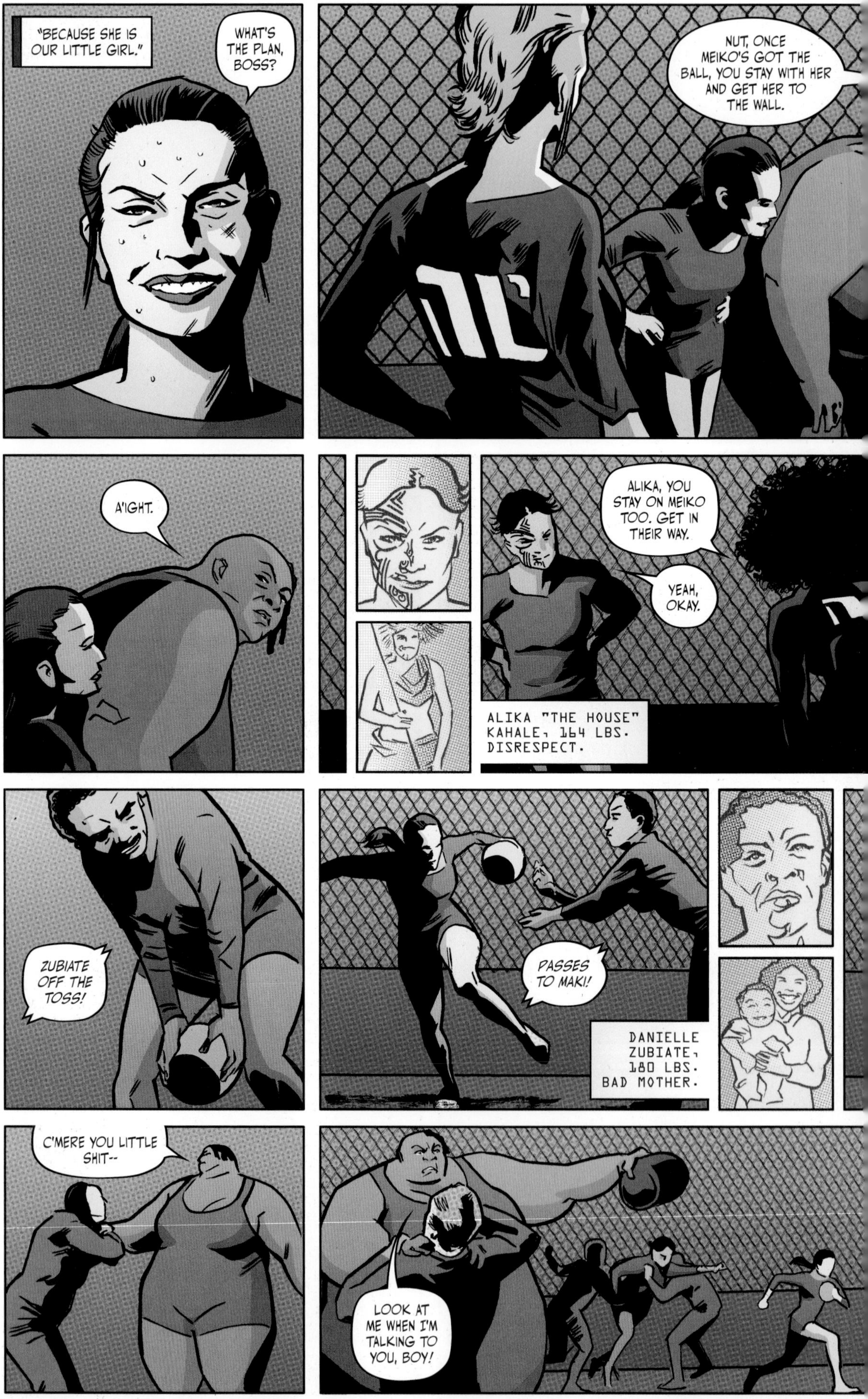
"BECAUSE SHE IS OUR LITTLE GIRL."
WHAT'S THE PLAN, BOSS?
NUT, ONCE MEIKO'S GOT THE BALL, YOU STAY WITH HER AND GET HER TO THE WALL.
A'IGHT.
ALIKA, YOU STAY ON MEIKO TOO. GET IN THEIR WAY.
YEAH, OKAY.
ALIKA "THE HOUSE" KAHALE, 164 LBS. DISRESPECT.
ZUBIATE OFF THE TOSS!
PASSES TO MAKI!
DANIELLE ZUBIATE, 180 LBS. BAD MOTHER.
C'MERE YOU LITTLE SHIT--
LOOK AT ME WHEN I'M TALKING TO YOU, BOY!

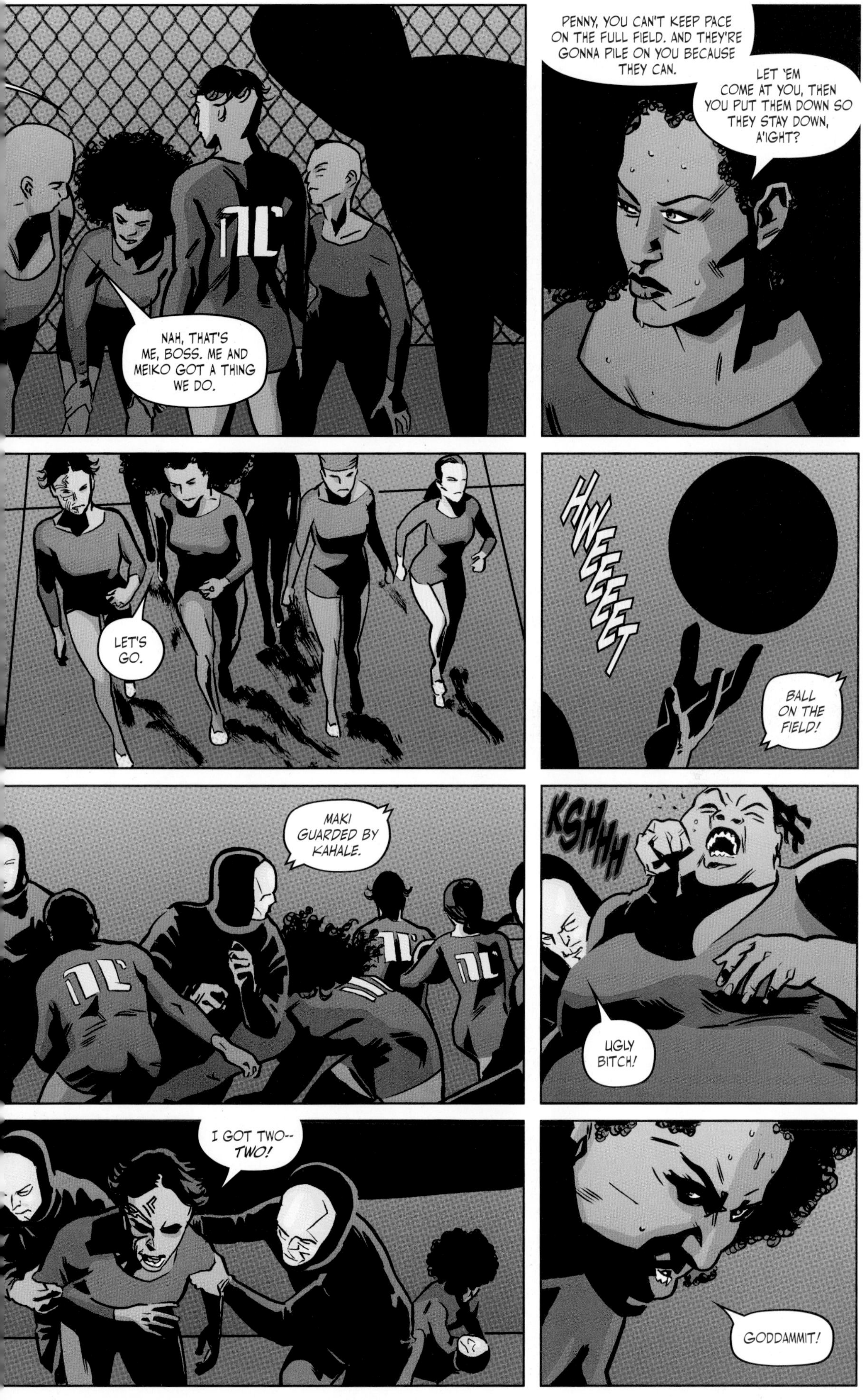
NAH, THAT'S ME, BOSS. ME AND MEIKO GOT A THING WE DO.
PENNY, YOU CAN'T KEEP PACE ON THE FULL FIELD. AND THEY'RE GONNA PILE ON YOU BECAUSE THEY CAN.
LET 'EM COME AT YOU, THEN YOU PUT THEM DOWN SO THEY STAY DOWN, A'IGHT?
LET'S GO.
HWEEEET
BALL ON THE FIELD!
MAKI GUARDED BY KAHALE.
KSHHH
UGLY BITCH!
I GOT TWO-- TWO!
GODDAMMIT!

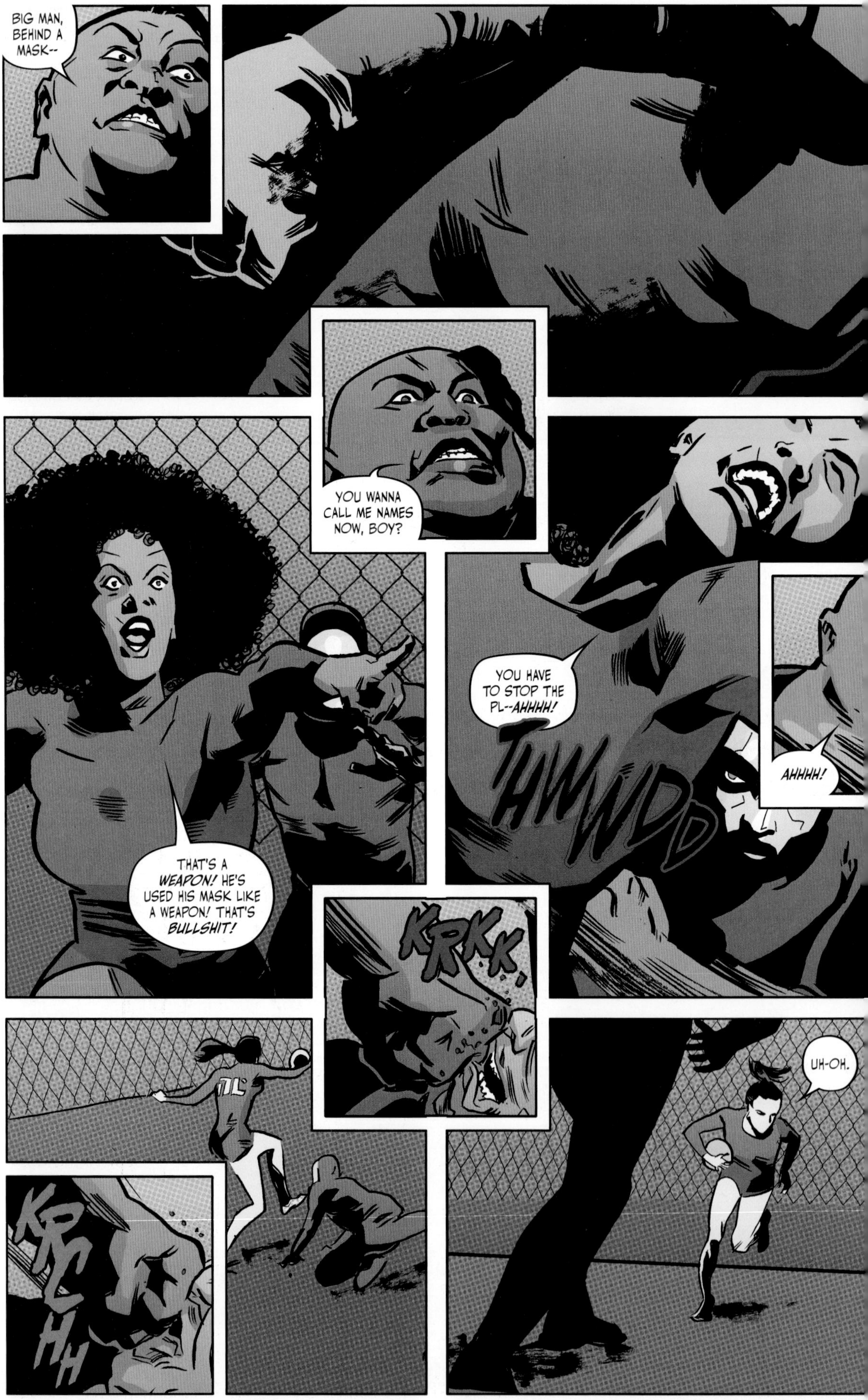
BIG MAN, BEHIND A MASK--
YOU WANNA CALL ME NAMES NOW, BOY?
THAT'S A WEAPON! HE'S USED HIS MASK LIKE A WEAPON! THAT'S BULLSHIT!
YOU HAVE TO STOP THE PL--AHHHH!
THWWDD
AHHHH!
KRKK
UH-OH.
KRCHH

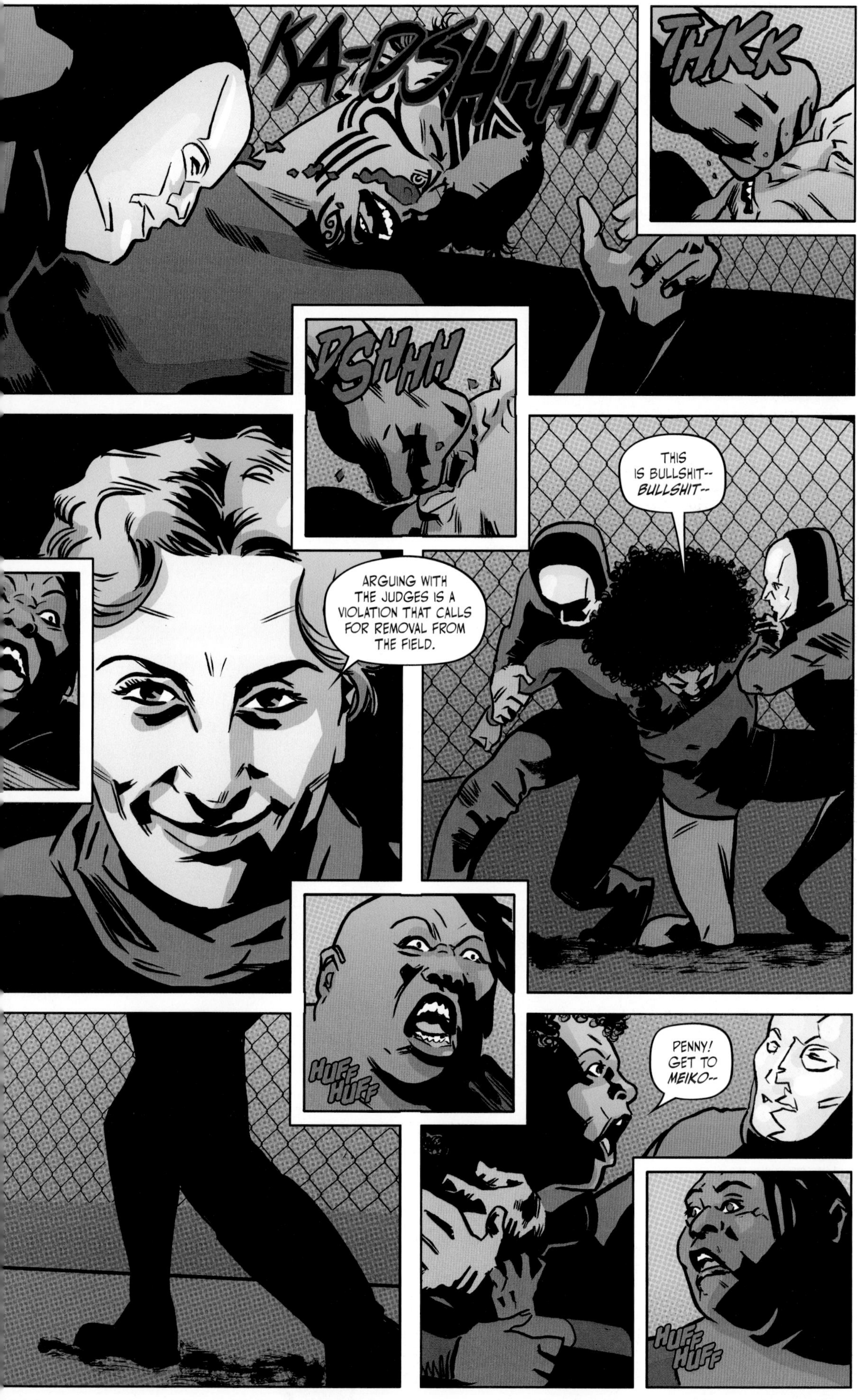
KA-DSHHHHH
THKK
DSHHH
THIS IS BULLSHIT-- BULLSHIT--
ARGUING WITH THE JUDGES IS A VIOLATION THAT CALLS FOR REMOVAL FROM THE FIELD.
HUFF HUFF
PENNY! GET TO MEIKO--
HUFF HUFF

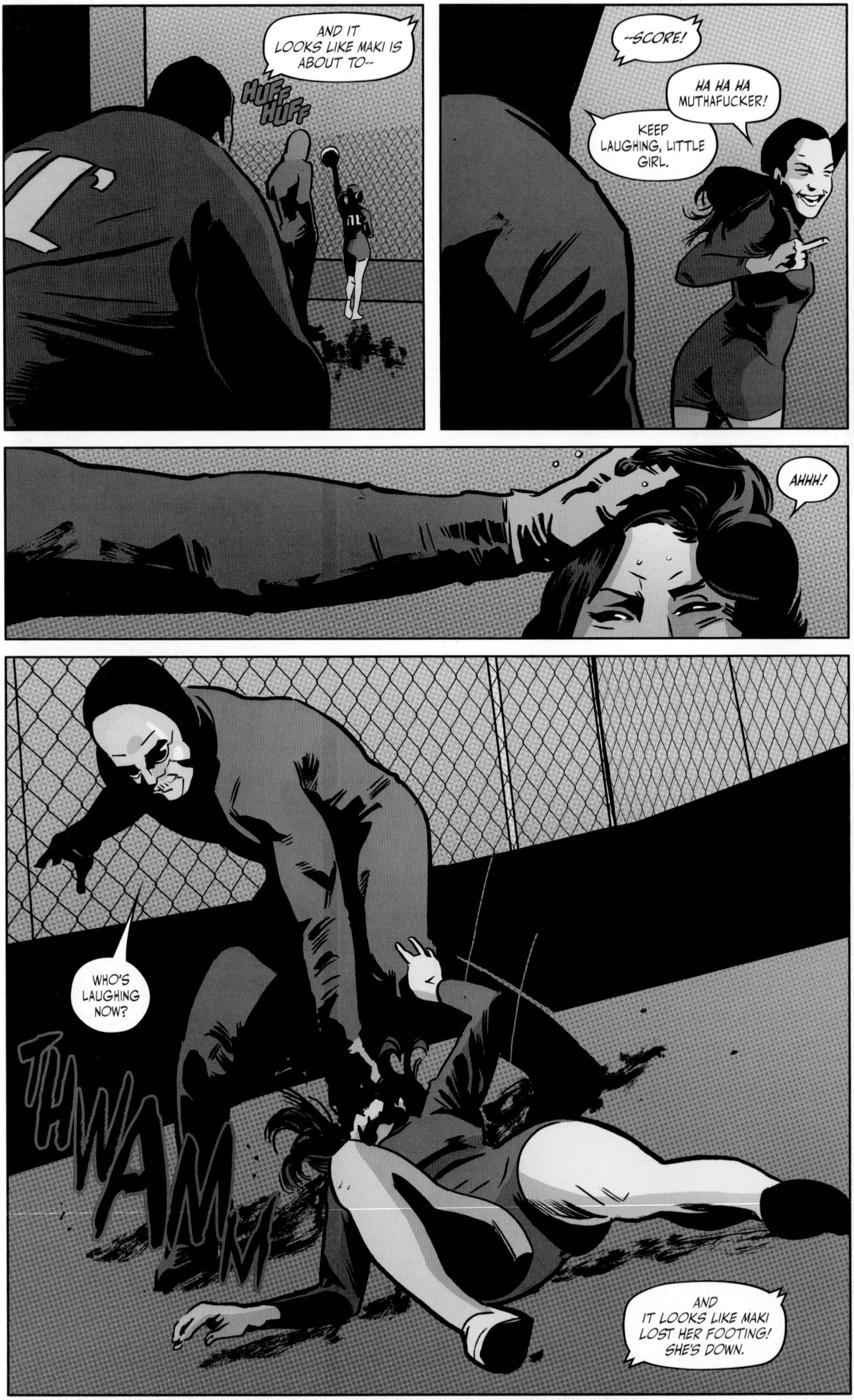
AND IT LOOKS LIKE MAKI IS ABOUT TO--
HUFF HUFF
--SCORE!
HA HA HA MUTHAFUCKER!
KEEP LAUGHING, LITTLE GIRL.
AHHH!
WHO'S LAUGHING NOW?
THWAMM
AND IT LOOKS LIKE MAKI LOST HER FOOTING! SHE'S DOWN.

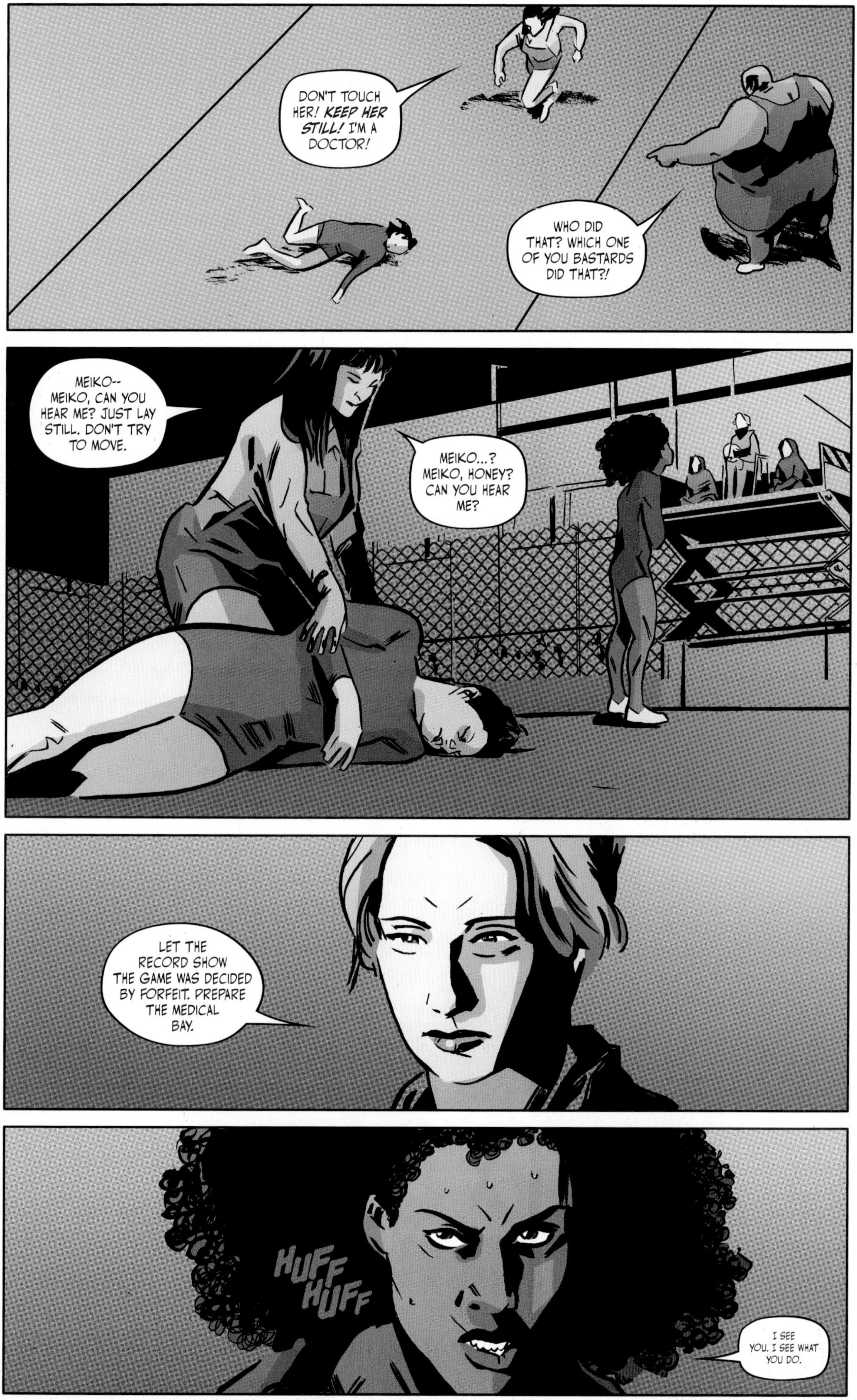
DON'T TOUCH HER! ***KEEP HER STILL!*** I'M A DOCTOR!
WHO DID THAT? WHICH ONE OF YOU BASTARDS DID THAT?!
MEIKO-- MEIKO, CAN YOU HEAR ME? JUST LAY STILL. DON'T TRY TO MOVE.
MEIKO...? MEIKO, HONEY? CAN YOU HEAR ME?
LET THE RECORD SHOW THE GAME WAS DECIDED BY FORFEIT. PREPARE THE MEDICAL BAY.
HUFF HUFF
I SEE YOU. I SEE WHAT YOU DO.

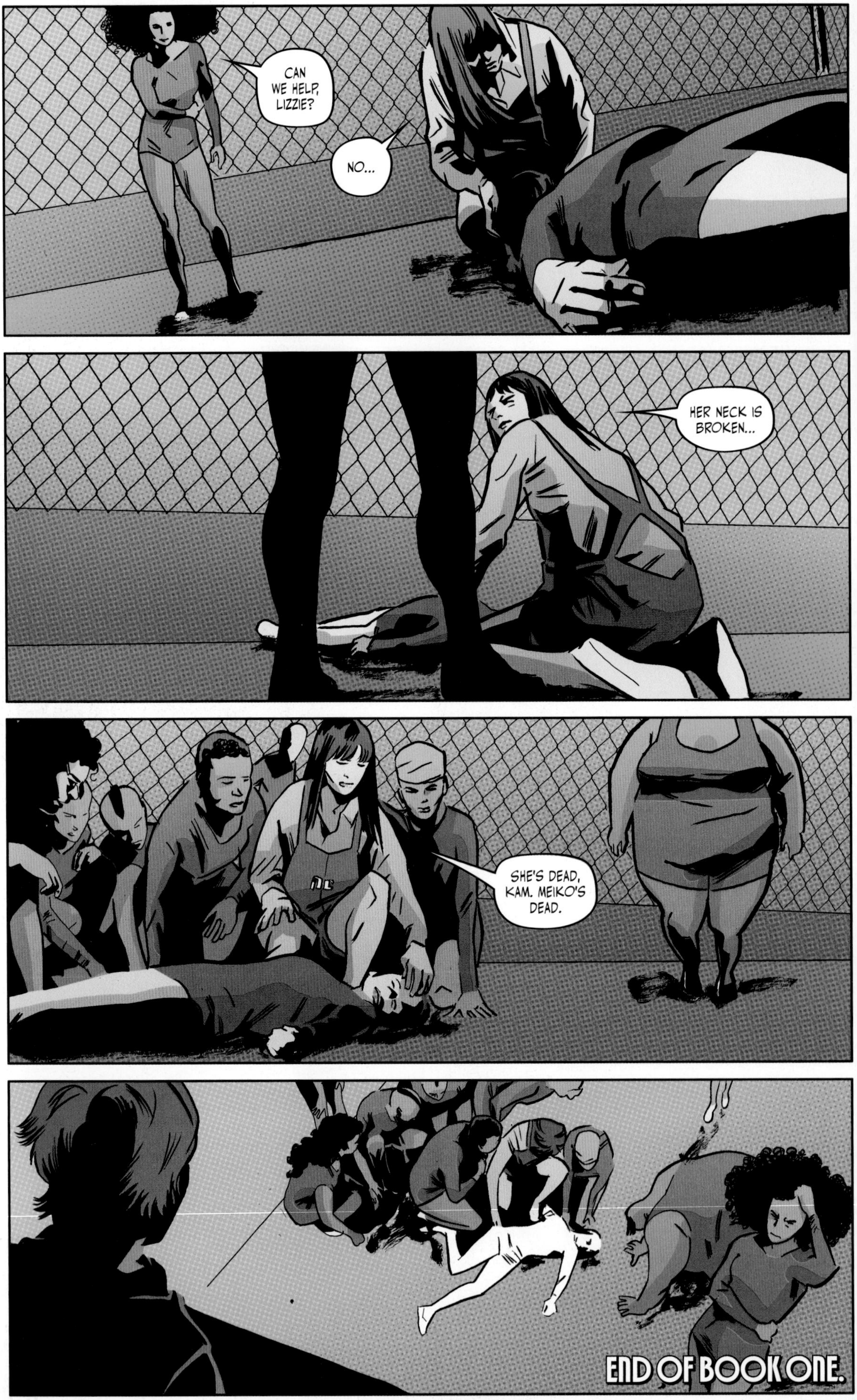
CAN WE HELP, LIZZIE?
NO...
HER NECK IS BROKEN...
SHE'S DEAD, KAM. MEIKO'S DEAD.
END OF BOOK ONE.

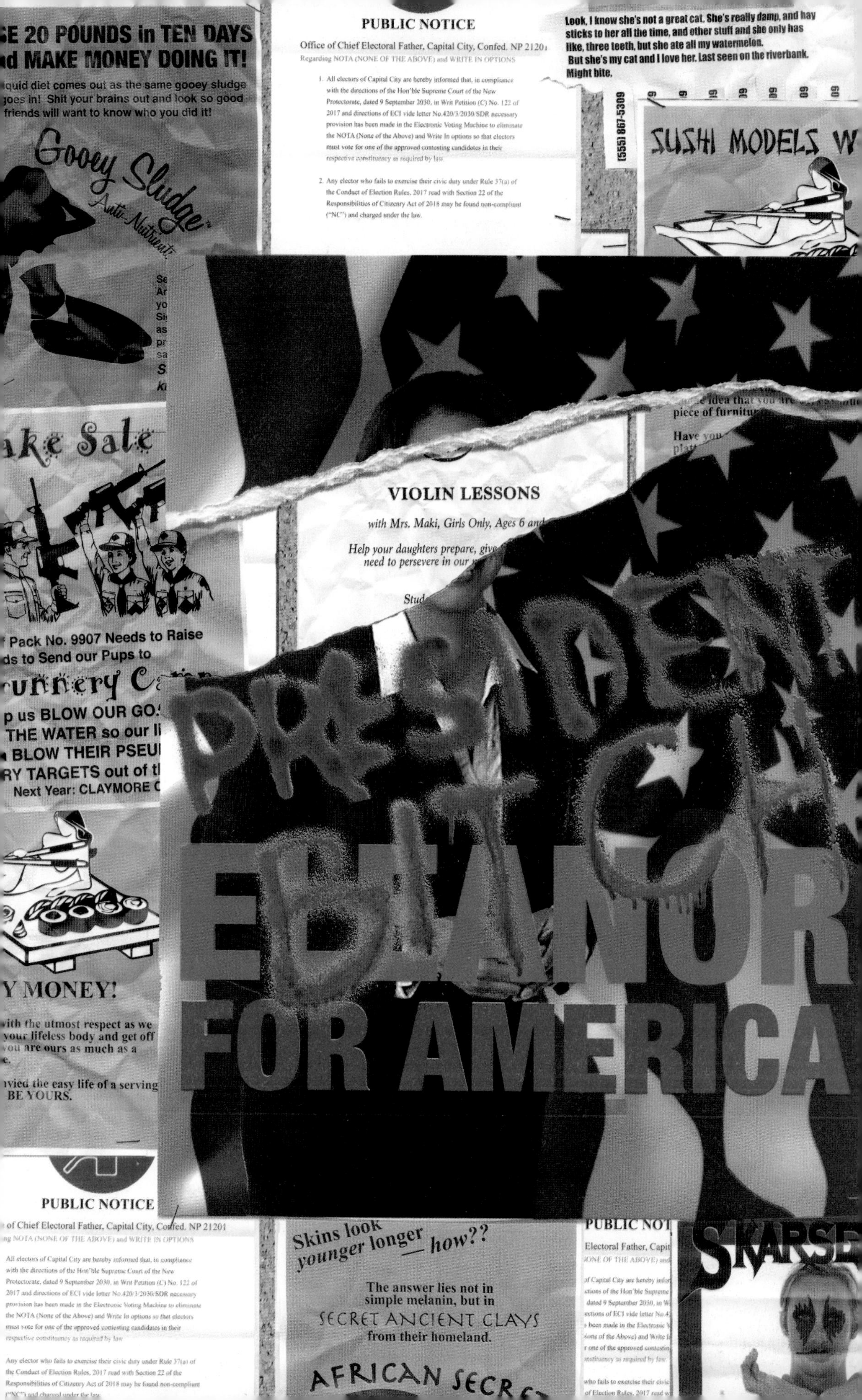

SE 20 POUNDS in TEN DAYS
nd MAKE MONEY DOING IT!
iquid diet comes out as the same gooey sludge
goes in! Shit your brains out and look so good
friends will want to know who you did it!
Gooey Sludge™
Anti-Nutrient
PUBLIC NOTICE
Office of Chief Electoral Father, Capital City, Confed. NP 21201
Regarding NOTA (NONE OF THE ABOVE) and WRITE IN OPTIONS
1. All electors of Capital City are hereby informed that, in compliance with the directions of the Hon'ble Supreme Court of the New Protectorate, dated 9 September 2030, in Writ Petition (C) No. 122 of 2017 and directions of ECI vide letter No.420/3/2030/SDR necessary provision has been made in the Electronic Voting Machine to eliminate the NOTA (None of the Above) and Write In options so that electors must vote for one of the approved contesting candidates in their respective constituency as required by law.
2. Any elector who fails to exercise their civic duty under Rule 37(a) of the Conduct of Election Rules, 2017 read with Section 22 of the Responsibilities of Citizenry Act of 2018 may be found non-compliant ("NC") and charged under the law.
Look, I know she's not a great cat. She's really damp, and hay sticks to her all the time, and other stuff and she only has like, three teeth, but she ate all my watermelon.
But she's my cat and I love her. Last seen on the riverbank.
Might bite.
(555) 867-5309
SUSHI MODELS W
ake Sale
Pack No. 9907 Needs to Raise
ds to Send our Pups to
unnery Ca
p us BLOW OUR GO
THE WATER so our li
BLOW THEIR PSEU
RY TARGETS out of th
Next Year: CLAYMORE C
Y MONEY!
ith the utmost respect as we
your lifeless body and get off
ou are ours as much as a
vied the easy life of a serving
BE YOURS.
idea that you are
piece of furnitu
Have you
VIOLIN LESSONS
with Mrs. Maki, Girls Only, Ages 6 and
Help your daughters prepare, give
need to persevere in our
Stud
PRESIDENT
BITCH
ELEANOR
FOR AMERICA
PUBLIC NOTICE
of Chief Electoral Father, Capital City, Confed. NP 21201
ng NOTA (NONE OF THE ABOVE) and WRITE IN OPTIONS
All electors of Capital City are hereby informed that, in compliance with the directions of the Hon'ble Supreme Court of the New Protectorate, dated 9 September 2030, in Writ Petition (C) No. 122 of 2017 and directions of ECI vide letter No.420/3/2030/SDR necessary provision has been made in the Electronic Voting Machine to eliminate the NOTA (None of the Above) and Write In options so that electors must vote for one of the approved contesting candidates in their respective constituency as required by law.
Any elector who fails to exercise their civic duty under Rule 37(a) of the Conduct of Election Rules, 2017 read with Section 22 of the Responsibilities of Citizenry Act of 2018 may be found non-compliant ("NC") and charged under the law.
Skins look younger longer — how??
The answer lies not in simple melanin, but in
SECRET ANCIENT CLAYS
from their homeland.
AFRICAN SECR
PUBLIC NOT
SKARSE

BITCH PLANET
DISCUSSION GUIDE

● Who is your favorite prisoner, and why? Is she also the one you identify with the most?

● Does the science fiction setting influence your reading of the story? If yes, how?

● How does non-compliance as displayed within the context of *Bitch Planet* work as an allegory for women today? How do characters in *Bitch Planet* use the term "non-compliant"? What does it mean for real women today? What does it mean to you?

● This book builds a culture around itself through the retro art, stylized promotions, essays, the sale of back page garbage, and an active online community. How does this affect the way you read and think about the book?

● Discuss the female characters in *Bitch Planet* who are not prisoners, such as Operative Whitney, Dawn Collins, the Model actors, and the patrons of Penny Rolle's bakery.

● Kamau Kogo doesn't want to accept any compromise with the system that's oppressing her. How much would you get involved in the system to fight against it "from the inside"? Do you think that there's a clear-cut line where dealing with reality as it is becomes subservient cooperation?

● Kam states that she does not want to be a part of any "movement." Do you think that "movements" are fundamental in a fight against oppression, particularly oppressive systems like prisons that rely on stasis as a form of punishment? How structured should they be? How much should they be open to different political positions, or to different tactics to address the same issue?

● Intersectional feminism is the view that women experience oppression in varying configurations and in varying degrees of intensity. Cultural patterns of oppression are not only interrelated, but are bound together and influenced by the intersectional systems of society. Examples of this include race, gender, class, ability, and ethnicity[1]. An example of this would be that black women have higher incarceration rates for the same crimes white women commit. In *Bitch Planet*, Marion expected that, since her experience of being female didn't intersect with someone like Kam or Penny, this difference would protect her or offer her special consideration. Can you think of other instances, either in pop culture, in the media or in your own life, where you can point out the ways that different women's experiences don't always intersect?

---

1. Crenshaw, Kimberlé (1989). "Demarginalizing the Intersection of Race and Sex: A Black Feminist Critique of Antidiscrimination Doctrine. Feminist Theory and Antiracist Politics" (PDF). University of Chicago Legal Forum 1989: 139–67.

DEDICATIONS

TO THE HERETICS OF TODAY
— VALENTINE

…AND YESTERDAY AND TOMORROW
— KELLY SUE

TO ALL THE TALENTED WOMEN I KNOW
THAT AREN'T KNOWN
— CRIS

TO MY MOM, WHO TOLD ME TO LOOK HARDER
— CLAYTON

KELLY SUE DECONNICK - @KELLYSUE
VALENTINE DE LANDRO - @VAL_DELANDRO
ROBERT WILSON IV - @ROBERTWILSONIV
CRIS PETER - @CRISPETER
CLAYTON COWLES - @CLAYTONCOWLES
RIAN HUGHES - @RIANHUGHES
LAURENN MCCUBBIN - @LAURENNMCC
LAUREN SANKOVITCH - @PANCAKELADY
Hashtag for the book: #BitchPlanet
Bitch Planet tumblr: www.bitchpla.net

KELLY SUE DECONNICK got her start in the comics industry adapting Japanese and Korean comics into English. Five years and more than ten thousand pages of adaptation later, she transitioned to American comics with 30 DAYS OF NIGHT: EBEN AND STELLA, for Steve Niles and IDW. Work for Image, Boom, Oni, Humanoids, Dark Horse, DC, Vertigo and Marvel soon followed. Today, DeConnick is best known for surprise hits like Carol Danvers rebranding as Captain Marvel and the Eisner-nominated mythological western, PRETTY DEADLY; the latter was co-created with her friend and long-time collaborator, artist Emma Rios. DeConnick's most recent venture, the sci-fi kidney-punch called BITCH PLANET, co-created with Valentine De Landro, launched to rave reviews in December 2014. DeConnick lives in Portland, Oregon with her husband Matt Fraction and their two children.

VALENTINE DE LANDRO has successfully broken into the comics industry on several different occasions. After art assistant work at Dark Horse Comics (via Toronto-based studio Bright Anvil), the fine folks at Marvel gave him issues of MARVEL AGE SPIDER-MAN, MARVEL KNIGHTS: 4, and X-FACTOR to pencil. Developing and co-creating BITCH PLANET with Kelly Sue DeConnick has changed the entire course of his career. He's heard the reviews are rave, but doesn't read any of them. He's sincerely happy about positive reviews though. De Landro lives east of Toronto, Ontario with his wife Maya and their two children.

IMAGE COMICS, INC.

ROBERT KIRKMAN - CHIEF OPERATING OFFICER
ERIK LARSEN - CHIEF FINANCIAL OFFICER
TODD MCFARLANE - PRESIDENT
MARC SILVESTRI - CHIEF EXECUTIVE OFFICER
JIM VALENTINO - VICE-PRESIDENT
ERIC STEPHENSON - PUBLISHER
CORY MURPHY - DIRECTOR OF SALES
JEREMY SULLIVAN - DIRECTOR OF DIGITAL SALES
KAT SALAZAR - DIRECTOR OF PR AND MARKETING
EMILY MILLER - DIRECTOR OF OPERATIONS
BRANWYN BIGGLESTONE - SENIOR ACCOUNTS MANAGER
SARAH MELLO - ACCOUNTS MANAGER
DREW GILL - ART DIRECTOR
JONATHAN CHAN - PRODUCTION MANAGER
MEREDITH WALLACE - PRINT MANAGER
RANDY OKAMURA - MARKETING PRODUCTION DESIGNER
DAVID BROTHERS - BRANDING MANAGER
ALLY POWER - CONTENT MANAGER
ADDISON DUKE - PRODUCTION ARTIST
VINCENT KUKUA - PRODUCTION ARTIST
SASHA HEAD - PRODUCTION ARTIST
TRICIA RAMOS - PRODUCTION ARTIST
EMILIO BAUTISTA - DIGITAL SALES ASSOCIATE
CHLOE RAMOS-PETERSON - ADMINISTRATIVE ASSISTANT

WWW.IMAGECOMICS.COM

BITCH PLANET, BOOK ONE: EXTRAORDINARY MACHINE

First Printing. October 2015.
Published by Image Comics, Inc.
Office of publication: 2001 Center Street, 6th Floor, Berkeley, CA 94704.
Copyright ©2015 Milkfed Criminal Masterminds, Inc.
All rights reserved.
Originally published in single magazine form as BITCH PLANET #1-5.

PRINTED IN THE U.S.A.
For information regarding the CPSIA on this printed material call: 203-595-3636 and provide reference # RICH – 624835
For international rights, contact: foreignlicensing@imagecomics.com.
ISBN: 978-1-63215-366-1
ISBN DCBS EXCLUSIVE: 978-1-63215-617-4